I HEART NEW YORK

Lindsey Kelk has been writing since she was six, when she read all the books in her room and decided the only course of action was to write a new one. *The Adventures of Tellina the Superhero Teddy Bear*, was tragically never published. Twenty-two years later, she works as a children's book editor in London so that no one else has to resort to such drastic action. When she isn't writing, reading or watching more TV than is healthy, Lindsey likes to wear shoes, shop for shoes and judge the shoes of others.

For more about Lindsey and her next novels, *I Heart Hollywood* and *I Heart Paris*, published in 2010, please go to www.iheartnewyork.co.uk

If you heart this book then you'll love:

I Heart Hollywood
I Heart Paris

LINDSEY KELK

I Heart New York

HARPER

Harper
An imprint of HarperCollins*Publishers*
77–85 Fulham Palace Road,
Hammersmith, London W6 8JB

www.harpercollins.co.uk

A Paperback Original 2009
This production 2012

A catalogue record for this book is available from the British Library

ISBN: 978-0-00-792950-4

Set in Melior by Palimpsest Book Production Limited, Grangemouth, Stirlingshire

Printed and bound in Great Britain by Clays Ltd, St Ives plc

MIX
Paper from responsible sources
FSC® C007454

FSC is a non-profit international organisation established to promote the responsible management of the world's forests. Products carrying the FSC label are independently certified to assure consumers that they come from forests that are managed to meet the social, economic and ecological needs of present and future generations.

Find out more about HarperCollins and the environment at
www.harpercollins.co.uk/green

To the people that taught me everything I need to know: Nana, Granddad, Janice, Phillip and Bobby

And to the people that taught me everything else: James, Della, Catherine, Beth, Mark and Louise

Seventeen shades of thank you to everyone that made this book happen, especially Lynne Drew, Claire Bord and Victoria Hughes-Williams, I heart the second floor. Thank you to Katie Fulford for not putting my manuscript in the bin and telling me she'd read it in the first place. Thank you to Ayshea for putting your foot through that glass door and sending me to New York for the very first time. Thank you to everyone in the children's team (past and present) for putting up with me for so long and keeping quiet from here on in. Thank you to Beth and Janet for putting up with me every time I need to 'research'. And thank you to the dollar for being so weak for the last eighteen months. And thank you to Marc Jacobs for your never-ending parade of pretty. I owe you everything.

CHAPTER ONE

The aisle looks really, really long.

And my tiara feels so tight.

Can you put weight on around your head? Have I got muffin top on my scalp? And my shoes really hurt. No matter how beautiful or how expensive they might be, the balls of my feet feel as if they've been up and down a cheese grater and then dipped in TCP.

I saw Mark standing at the end of the aisle, looking relaxed and happy. Well, I suppose he doesn't have to walk down it in four-inch Christian Louboutins and a fishtail floor-length gown. You can't even see the bloody shoes, Angela, I chide myself. Not even the tip of the toe.

And now my hands feel sweaty. Do I have sweat patches? I tried to sneak a peak under my arms without dislodging anything important from my bouquet.

'Angela? Are you all right?' Louisa frowned at me, a picture of perfection, calm as anything, immaculate make-up and not teetering a touch. And her heels are higher than mine.

'Uh-huh,' I replied, as eloquent as ever. Thank God it's her wedding and not mine. And please God, while

I'm at it, could you not let Mark focus on what a shoddy bridesmaid I'm turning out to be, just in case it puts him off setting our date. Seriously though, sweat patches would show horribly, the dress is a light coffee colour, specially selected to make me look sick as a dog.

I stumbled down the aisle behind Louisa, with a small smile for my mum and dad, looking appropriately happy whilst acknowledging the solemnity of the occasion. I really hope that's how I look, anyway. There is a good chance I look as if I am wondering whether or not I've left my hair straighteners on. Shit! What if I have left my hair straighteners on?

I'm always struck by how short wedding ceremonies are. The months of engagement, hours of planning, a whole weekend for the hen do even, and the lifelong deal was done inside twenty minutes and a couple of hymns. Even the photos took longer than the actual service.

'I can't believe I'm married!' Louisa breathed. We'd got to the not-at-all cheesy bride and head bridesmaid smiling by a fountain section. Oh dear. The poses came naturally, we'd been practising them with each other since we were old enough to hang pillowcases off the back of our heads, after all. 'Angela, can you believe it?'

'Of course I can,' I said, squeezing her closely to me, ignoring the photographer's direction. 'You and Tim have been practically married since you were fourteen.'

We switched positions and paused to smile.

Click, flash.

'It's just unreal, you know?' She flicked a soft blonde curl over her shoulder and patted a stray light brown hair back into my chignon. 'It's really absolutely happened.'

Click, flash.

'Well, get ready,' I said through a pearly smile. 'It'll be me and Mark next and you'll be the one in the bridesmaid dress.'

'Have you talked any more about setting a date?' Louisa asked, fussing with the puddle train behind her. Was I supposed to be doing that?

'Not really,' I shook my head. 'I mean, we talked about it all the time when you two finally set a date, but since Mark got promoted we've hardly had time to blink. You know how it is.'

Louisa waved the photographer away for a moment. 'Mmm. I just mean, do you think you'll definitely get married? To Mark, I mean?'

Click, flash – not a good one.

I had to hold my hands to my eyes to get a proper look at Louisa. The August sun lit her from behind, obscuring her face and highlighting a halo of wispy blonde curls.

'Of course,' I said. 'We're engaged aren't we?'

She sighed and shook her head. 'Yeah, I just worry about you sweetness. With the wedding and stuff I feel like we haven't really talked about you and Mark in ages.'

'There's nothing new to tell you. You probably see him more than I do. At least you get your tennis time every single week.'

'I tried to get you to take up doubles,' she muttered, messing with her hem again. 'I just want you to be as happy as I am right now. Oh, that's so patronizing, sorry. You know what I mean babe, just, be happy.'

'I am happy,' I reassured her, taking her hand and closing in on the dress for a scaffolded hug. 'I am really happy.'

Just after the speeches had finished but a little bit

before the dancing began, I finally managed to escape to the loo.

The reception was being held in a converted barn, that only had two ladies' cubicles, neither of which were big enough to turn around in, so I had escaped up to our room. I looked around at my scattered belongings. I carried my life in my massive, battered handbag – laptop, iPod, phone, a couple of knackered old books. Bits of make-up and scraps of clothes were strewn all over the room, contrasting with Mark's carefully organized suitcase. A place for everything and everything in its place, even in a hotel.

I was happy, I thought to myself, flopping down on the bed and idly flicking the pages of one of my books with my toes. I had a fun job that was flexible, I had Louisa, the best friend in the world, and I'd lost twenty pounds for this wedding, which had put me comfortably in the size twelve bridesmaid dress. I could even convince myself (if no one else) that a ten might have been a better fit. I wasn't horrible to look at, long, light brown hair, greeny-blue eyes and since I dropped the extra weight, I'd discovered a pair of fairly impressive cheekbones. And I had Mark. Who wouldn't love a good-looking, up-and-coming banker boyfriend? He should think himself lucky, I tried to convince myself. Yes, he's got all his own hair, no hereditary diseases, a city banker salary, car and a mortgage, but I'd been attending horribly humiliating weight loss classes for the last six months (it wasn't the weigh-ins that broke you, they were fine, it was the team leader who moonlighted as a dog trainer), I could cook and I cleaned the bathroom every Sunday without being asked. So no, sainthood didn't beckon, but I wasn't an awful girlfriend and we'd been together for ever, since we were sixteen. Ten years. But Louisa's words bothered me a little bit. Was I happy? Maybe more content than bouncing-off-the-sofa-like-Tom-Cruise-ecstatic, but that's still happy isn't it?

I looked at my engagement ring. Classic solitaire. Not huge or flashy trashy, but not magnifying glass necessitating tiny. Mark had bought it with his first paycheque and presented it to me on a holiday to Seville, post-pony and trap ride and pre-lovely sex back at our hotel room. It had seemed horribly romantic at the time, but now it just seemed a horribly long time ago. Shouldn't he be pushing me for a date? Just a little?

'Don't be silly,' I said out loud to my confused reflection. Louisa was probably just getting in front of herself, she was married now after all, I just hadn't expected her smug-married neuroses to kick in before she'd even got out of the church. There was nothing wrong with me and Mark. Ten years of nothing wrong, why would I worry? I tried to slip my beautiful, beautiful heels back on but my left foot seemed to have gained ten of my twenty lost pounds. After five fruitless minutes of searching the suite for my standby flats, I accepted that my shoe bag hadn't made it out of the car. Which meant I would have to brave the drunken uncles, the dancing children high on wedding cake (I had seen balloons too – they were armed) and go to the car park.

CHAPTER TWO

Tiptoeing barefoot, Louboutins in hand, I searched for the car. Over in a dark corner, hidden beneath beautiful weeping willows was Mark's Range Rover. When he had bought it six months before, Louisa had taken it as a direct sign that he was ready for kids. I saw it as a direct sign that he was not ever going to let me drive it on my own. So far, I'd been the one proven right. Scrambling around in my handbag for the spare keys, I noticed that the reading light was on in the back. I smiled to myself, knowing Mark would be so happy that I had come out and saved his battery. Pressing the button to turn off the alarm, instead of the reassuring double pip, I was greeted by a loud siren and flashing indicators. Which was when I realized someone was inside the car.

Shit, our car was being stolen and here I was, hobbling barefoot over gravel with a pair of £400 shoes in one hand and wearing a floor length gown. And I'd just set the alarm off. Brilliant. The car thieves were definitely going to kill me. If I was murdered at Louisa's wedding, she would be furious. All her anniversaries would be ruined. Would she still go on her honeymoon? Maybe I could use my heels as a weapon. Well, maybe not, I didn't want to stain them. But the soles were already red . . .

I was all ready to turn and hightail it out of the headlines when I remembered my shoes. They could take Mark's car but, damn it, they weren't taking my fallback flats. Two-year-old Topshop maybe but they were the comfiest damn shoes I'd ever owned. I pulled open the back door to confront the thief before I bottled it. And then, in a startling moment of clarity, I realized there wasn't a man trying to steal the car or my shoes, but two people, very much having sex on the back seat.

And one of them was Mark.

'Angela,' he stuttered, his red sweaty face staring out at me, indentations from my Hello Kitty seatbelt protectors on his left cheek. He wouldn't let me put them in the front. It took me another moment to register the naked woman underneath him. She looked at me, frozen underneath Mark, with smudged mascara and a red chin from Mark's omnipresent five o'clock shadow. I didn't recognize her at all, blonde, pretty, looked fairly skinny from what I could see of her bony shoulders, and she had a lovely tan. A peacock blue silk dress scrunched up on the parcel shelf suggested she had been at the wedding reception, and the beautiful pair of silver Gina sandals clamped around my boyfriend's waist told me I really should have spotted her earlier. I did love a nicely turned shoe.

'I came to get my flats,' I said, numb, not moving.

I stumbled backwards as Mark pulled himself out of the car on his belly and dropped to the floor in front of me, his boxer shorts working themselves further back down his legs as his sweaty skin peeled away from the leather.

'Angela,' Mark stood up, he pulled his pants up high, and wriggled into his shirt. I looked past him into the car. The girl had managed to get her dress on and was rubbing under her eyes to try to get rid of the mascara. Good luck, I thought, if it's as good a quality as your shoes you won't get that off by rubbing. Shoes still looked great though. Bitch.

'Angela,' he tried again snapping me out of my shoe-induced haze. 'I – what are you doing out here?'

I looked back at him. 'Shoes,' I said, waving my sandals at him and gesturing towards the car. 'You didn't bring my flats in.'

He stared at me wildly, glancing from me to my high heels and then back at the car. Slowly, as though I were a startled animal that might bolt, he took a step back towards the backseat and reached under the passenger seat for a small cloth shoe bag. He held it out to me, afraid to touch me, afraid to make contact. 'Thanks.' I took the bag.

Mark stood, bathed in the backseat light, red, sweaty, trousers off, socks and shoes on with a little wet patch growing on the front of his boxers to add insult to injury.

'What the fuck are you doing?' I asked. Incredibly eloquently.

'Angela,' Mark shuffled forward half an inch.

'And who, the fuck, is she?' I asked, pointing to the girl with my left Louboutin, still in my hand. The girl looked away, trapped in the back of the car.

'Angela,' he stuttered, retreating from the perfectly pointed toe aimed at his temple.

'No, I'm Angela. I can see how you might be confused though,' I said, feeling my eyes starting to well up. My boyfriend was having sex in the back of our car, our beautiful future children's car, at our best friends' wedding. I was not going to cry in front of him while he pissed away ten years together on a cheap shag in a car park.

'Angela, this is Katie. I, erm, I—' he looked back again and met her eyes briefly and I swear I saw a hint of a goofy smile cross his goddamned face. It was the most painful moment of the whole thing. 'We, well, we've been playing tennis together, and, well—'

'This is what you think playing tennis is? Shit, does Louisa know you've been "playing tennis" with Tim?' I wanted to hit him, I wanted to hit her, and just as I was about to toss a coin to see who was getting it first, I realized. 'You haven't been playing tennis with Tim,' I said.

'No.' He shook his head.

'And you haven't been working late.' It was all making a horrible sort of sense.

'No.' He sighed, his shoulders dropping with acceptance.

'Does Tim know?' I asked.

'Yes.' I didn't even look up.

'And Louisa knows?' I gripped my heels tightly and was vaguely aware of a buckle cutting into the flesh of my palm.

'I think so.' He nodded. 'I mean, well, we do play tennis sometimes. Doubles. I – I'm not sure though.'

Was I happy? Louisa had wanted to know if I knew.

'You've all been playing doubles together?' I gulped, trying not to be sick.

He looked at me, eyebrows raised, breath caught in his throat. 'Angela, don't,' he put a hand out towards my forearm.

'Don't you dare!' I said, feeling the bile rise in my throat and pulling my arm away. 'Don't you dare touch me.' Heel raised high above my head, I saw for a second how easy it would be. He was frozen and she was trapped in the back seat and Louboutins are beautifully made, I'm fairly sure they would do two skulls without breaking.

But, instead of seeing two bloody corpses, all I could see was Tim and Louisa laughing hysterically in their tennis whites after a game of doubles with Mark and Katie. While I sat at home, tapping away on my laptop, not eating and waiting for my cheating, lying, scumbag boyfriend.

Potential murder weapon in hand, I turned on my heel and started back across the car park. Mark was still pitifully calling my name as I charged through the French doors and across the dance floor, cutting a swathe through the tiny bridesmaids dancing to the poptastic disco. Tim and Louisa were standing by the dance floor cradling champagne, waiting for the DJ to announce their first dance, when Louisa saw me.

'Angela,' she said as I ploughed to a stop in front of them. Right away, I knew she knew.

'Why didn't you tell me?' I shouted. All concern for ruining her wedding was long gone. I had been completely betrayed by the people I trusted most in the world.

'Angela, I – why don't we —' Tim reached out and placed his hand on my forearm. Before I knew what I was doing, I snatched my arm away and cracked his knuckles with my shoe.

'Will you stop saying my name like it's a bloody tranquillizer!' I paused, gritting my teeth. 'I have just caught Mark shagging your tennis buddy in the back of our car.'

If I didn't have everyone's attention before I broke the groom's knuckles, I did now.

‘Oh, Angela,’ Louisa sobbed. ‘I tried to tell you, I just, I thought you must already know. You know, somehow, deep down.’

‘At what point did you think that? When I told you I was perfectly happy and was still sure I was marrying Mark? When I didn’t tell you my boyfriend was a cheating shit? Or when you first started playing *doubles* with him and that slag?’

Louisa burst into tears and turned to run out of the room, but her exit through the French doors was blocked by Mark. Still in his stained boxers, socks, and half buttoned-up shirt, he stood frozen under the gaze of three hundred wedding guests, most of whom had just about worked out what was happening. Finally remembering to breathe, I took a moment to observe the scene. Tim looked at me with pale terror as he clutched his bloody hand, Louisa was standing bawling in the middle of the dance floor, surrounded by crying children, and Mark, clutching at the doorframe as though it was all that was holding him up, stared at me in disbelief. I looked backwards towards the guests and saw my mum emerge from the crowd. She looked everyone up and down, paused, pursed her lips and walked right up to me. Loosening my white knuckles, she prised my Louboutins out of my left hand, then gripped it tightly in her own.

‘Come on,’ she said quietly, placing a hand on the small of my back and guiding me across the room. I couldn’t see anything but the floor in front of my feet, or hear any of the murmurings around me. All I knew was my mum’s hand and the gravel still stuck to my bare feet.

It must have been about five in the morning when I woke up. The room was so big and quiet and I could hear the bones of my bridesmaid dress scrunching into my ribs. I turned over and realized that lying next to me in the big beautiful bed wasn't my fiancé, my Mark, but my mother. Her perfect wedding outfit was carefully folded over the back of a chair and I hesitated for a moment before looking down at what she was wearing instead. It's a bit weird to see your mum wearing an old Blondie T-shirt and a pair of your boyfriend's boxers. Ex-boyfriend. I sat up slowly and tried not to catch sight of myself in the mirror until I'd locked myself in the bathroom. My hair was a bird's nest of slept-in chignon, my make-up smeared with sleep, tears and pillow creases and the parts of my dress that hadn't already been torn or muddied, were twisted and creased up beyond all recognition.

Stripping myself of everything, earrings, necklace, engagement ring, I stepped into the giant shower and just let the water run. How had this happened? Destroying my best friend's wedding aside, how had I not noticed that my boyfriend was cheating on me and had been doing so for so long and so openly that my friends all knew? It wasn't just a quick shag, it was clearly serious. What would I do? Where would I go? As the shower stall steamed up and I lathered, rinsed and repeated, I tried to be rational. Keep a clear head in any situation. Mum always said it was one of our strengths.

I'd have to go home and get my stuff. Home. I supposed it wasn't even my home any more. He'd probably move her in tomorrow. 'Katie,' said a little pixie-ish voice in my head. 'Not "her", it's Katie.'

'This shower feels amazing,' I said out loud, pushing that voice out of my head as the hot, hot water streamed down from three different jets. It was as if none of it was real. If only I could live in a hotel. Not having to go back to that shit heap and rummage through my stuff like I was the one that had done something wrong. Jesus, the splitting of the CDs. I just couldn't face it. A couple of renegade tears started to seep out of my eyes. If only I could stay in this hotel for ever and pretend none of it had happened.

Why not stay in a hotel?

Not this hotel, clearly. I had a strange feeling I wasn't going to be terribly welcome at breakfast, but another hotel. Somewhere impersonal and wonderful where the staff's only concern would be keeping me happy rather than whether or not I was going to ruin another gala event. I had a little bit of money, we'd been saving for my non-existent wedding for years, and it seemed fairly appropriate to tax Mark his share of the cash for shitting on me. My work was freelance, I had my passport, credit cards, driver's license (no burglar was stealing my identity while I was away at a wedding for almost a week!) enough clothes, my favourite shoes, what else would I need? I definitely had enough stuff not to need to go home for a while. Screw the CDs even, I had my iPod. There was really no reason not to go, and God knows, I am the queen of talking myself out of anything even vaguely confrontational.

I forced myself out of the shower and into the bathroom. For a second my gaze rested on Mark's wash bag, next to my engagement ring. A lovely leather piece I'd bought him last Christmas. He's bound to want to come back for that, I thought as I slipped on my earrings, my necklace, it's full of all his fancy shaving stuff his mum buys him for his birthday. For a moment I thought about filling it with shaving foam, but froze with a flashback as I picked up the can. Him, hunched over that cow, all sweaty and confused. Maybe I should throw it out of the window. Then I remembered him smiling at her. Smiling at her, in front of me, in those scummy boxer shorts.

And so I sat on the loo and pissed in the bag. It was the most disgusting thing I'd ever done, and I was so so proud. Once it was nicely ruined, I dropped in my engagement ring, zipped up the bag and left the bathroom.

'Mum,' I whispered, sitting beside her on the bed. 'Mum, I'm off.'

She opened her eyes and looked a bit confused as she remembered everything, and then she looked at me as though she was going to commit me to the same home where she had stashed my nan.

'What do you mean?' she asked, sitting up, looking even more confused at the sight of her nightwear. 'You don't have to go anywhere because of that shit.'

It was the first time I'd heard her call Mark anything other than 'darling boy' or 'that lovely Mark', and I was quite touched.

'I know,' I nodded towards my packed travel bag. 'But with the wedding and everything, I think I'd better get off early. Thing is, I thought I might nip off for a few days to sort myself out.'

'Oh no,' she said, taking my hand. 'You're just coming home with me and your father, he's going to come and collect us later. You've done nothing wrong, you know. Well . . .'

'I know, Mum,' I said. 'But I think it would do me good to get away. I've booked a taxi to the airport.'

She looked at me slightly oddly. 'Really?' she asked. 'You're really going somewhere on a plane?'

'Yes,' I said, standing up, clutching my bag.

'Where are you going?' she asked, looking at the clock. 'Wouldn't you rather just come home with me and your dad?'

'Hmm,' I pecked her on the cheek. 'I think I'm actually going to go with my first idea.'

Mum shook her head. 'But where is better than home at a time like this?'

CHAPTER THREE

The plane landed at JFK without a hitch and, while the homeland security guard didn't seem that interested in my break-up (business or pleasure didn't seem to cover why I was there), he did let me into the country. Good start. Once I stepped out into the sunshine, everything began to feel real. The cabs were yellow, they were on the wrong side of the road, and my taxi driver even swore a blue streak tossing my bag into the boot of his car. Man alive, it was warm. If women glow, men perspire, and horses sweat, right at that moment, I was one sweaty bloody horse.

'Where to?' the driver asked.

'Erm, a hotel?' I asked, plugging in my seatbelt as we took off. 'I need a hotel.'

'You fuckin' serious?' he asked, swerving onto the highway before I could even reply. 'Which fuckin' hotel? There are fuckin' millions of hotels.'

'Oh, yeah, I – well – I—' before I could finish my sentence, I started to tear up. 'I don't know anywhere. I just sort of got here.'

'Well, guess what lady?' the driver yelled back at me, 'I'm a fuckin' taxi driver, not tourist information.

You want me to fuckin' drop you here in the middle of Queens or you want to give me the name of a hotel?'

In response, I burst into tears. Witty comeback, thy name is Angela.

'Jesus fuckin' Christ. I'm dropping you off at the first fuckin' hotel we pass,' he muttered, turning the radio all the way up.

Twenty minutes of talk radio later, I was hanging out of the window like a dog in a bandana, and I had *just* about stopped crying when I spotted it.

The New York City skyline. Manhattan. The Empire State Building. The beautiful, beautiful Chrysler Building. The Woolworth Building with its big old churchy steeple. And I fell in love. It hit me so hard that I stopped crying, stopped thinking, stopped breathing. I felt as if I'd been winded. Winding the cab window all the way down, I breathed in the skyscrapers, the giant billboards, the industrial riverside stretches and the sweaty, steamy air. I was in New York. Not at home in London, not at Louisa's wedding, and nowhere near my filthy, cheating fiancé. And so, for the want of something else to do, as we disappeared down into the midtown tunnel, I burst into tears again.

The first hotel we passed turned out to be the last hotel the cabbie had dropped off at, and it was beautiful. The Union was set just off Union Square Park, with a lobby dimly lit to the point of a power cut, and filled with the overpowering scent of Diptyque candles that smelled like fresh washing on the line. Overstuffed sofas and ancient leather armchairs filled the space, and the reception was picked out in fairylights. Suddenly finding myself in such perfect surroundings, I was very aware of the state of my hair, my dehydrated skin and my rumpled clothes. I really, really did look like complete crap, but this place couldn't be further from a two-bedroomed terrace in south west London. It was just what I needed.

'Welcome to The Union,' said the incredibly beautiful woman behind the counter. 'My name is Jennifer, how can we help you today?'

'Hi,' I said, pulling my handbag high up on my shoulder and kicking my travel bag towards the reception desk. 'I was wondering if you had a room available?'

She smiled serenely and began clicking away on a keyboard. As she tapped, her glossy spiral curls bounced away behind her. 'OK, we are a little busy but . . . I have a junior suite at $800 a night?' She looked up. My expression apparently suggested that was a little bit out of my price range. 'Or I have a single at $350. But it only sleeps one.'

'Oh, OK,' I fished around in my battered old bag for a credit card and tried not to work out the cost of the room in real money, 'it's just me. Well, I just found out my boyfriend was cheating on me and we broke up and I had to leave home and I thought, well, where's better to get away to than New York? And,' I paused and looked up. She was still smiling at me, but with a healthy dose of terror in her eyes. 'Sorry, I'm sorry. A single would be fine.'

'And how long would you be staying with us?' she asked, tapping away again. I guessed she was alerting everyone to the fact that there was a desperate woman checking in. My photo was probably being distributed to the whole staff with a 'do not engage in conversation' note.

'Sorry?' I hadn't thought that far ahead.

'When will you be going home?' she said slowly.

'I – I don't have a home,' I said, equally slowly. 'So,

I don't know.' I was dangerously close to tears and really didn't want to let them go in the reception of the swankiest hotel I'd ever stepped in. But, wow, I really didn't have a home.

'Well, I kinda just wanted to know when you would be checking out, but the room is free for the next week, shall I put you in for seven nights and see where we go from there?' she suggested. I nodded and handed over my credit card. Jennifer exchanged it for a sexy black room pass key, emblazoned with a silver U. 'Room 1126 on floor eleven, take the elevator and then turn left. It's at the end of the corridor.'

I nodded numbly and took the key, tripping over my own bag as I turned.

'Do you need anything at all, Miss Clark?' Jennifer asked. I turned and tried to smile, shaking my head.

'Head check?' I could only make jokes for so long before I evaporated.

'Just phone down if you want anything at all,' I heard her call. Hopefully, she wouldn't send up a therapist, I had always been warned that Americans didn't always get sarcasm.

If the room was a single, Mark's house was a mansion. A huge, white bed dominated the tastefully painted cream bedroom, topped off by a dramatic brown leather headboard. Past the bed, a floor to ceiling window with beautiful views of Union Square Park below. A walk-in wardrobe was tucked away to my left, and to my right was the bathroom. I dropped my travel bag and opened the door. It was beautiful. White tiled walls, black slate floor. The toilet and sink were tucked neatly away against the wall, while the rest of the room was completely taken over by a glass encased bath and shower. Two chrome showerheads jutted out from opposite walls, and a glass shelf held small but perfectly formed designer toiletries. A chrome shelf by the sink groaned under the weight of fluffy towels, and a thick waffle robe hung behind the bathroom door.

I backed back into the bedroom and looked out at the window, but paused before I got there. This was just what I'd been looking for, but between being completely exhausted and suddenly incredibly hungry, I just couldn't bring myself to look outside and see a strange city. Instead, I headed back into the bathroom, via the well-stocked mini bar, and ran a bath, using the whole bottle of bubbles. Stripping off my clothes, I stepped into the bath, wishing that my brain would stop ticking over for just a second. Using the edge of the bath as a makeshift bar, I mixed a $15 vodka and coke in the toothbrush glass and poured half a packet of $8 peanut butter M&Ms into my mouth. It was less than twenty-four hours since I was in that shower back in the UK, thinking how badly I needed to get away, and here I was. Away.

I lay back and sighed deeply, letting the ends of my hair soak through. Gradually the sigh turned into a whimper, and the whimper became a sob. I was allowed to cry, wasn't I? I'd been cheated on by my fiancé, deceived by my best friend, and humiliated in front of all my friends and family. Reaching for the M&Ms, I managed to polish them off in one go, washing them down with a large swig of my drink. What was I thinking, coming all the way to New York on my own? I wasn't being brave, I was being stupid. There was no one here to help me, to talk to me, to watch *Pretty Woman*, *Dirty Dancing* and *Breakfast at Tiffany's* with me. I should towel off, call my mum and get a plane home. This wasn't impulsive and exciting, it was immature and cowardly. Just a really, really elaborate version of hiding in my room and getting wasted. I'd made my point, and more or less paid a grand for a bath and a bag of sweets, now it was time to face reality.

Pulling myself out of the bath, I slipped on the robe and padded across the carpet, leaving miserable-looking footprints behind me. I rummaged around in my bag for my phone, half hoping it was old and crappy enough not to work in America. Bugger, five whole bars of reception. I stared at the screen. Three messages. Hmm. Did I really want to do this with only one vodka in me? Forcing myself to stand up, I walked over to the window. If I was just going to turn around and go home, I wanted at least to get my money's worth out of the view. It really was beautiful, the sun was shining, people were wandering through the park, dashing to the subway, ducking into shops, carrying bags and bags and bags.

How weird would it be if I went home and it was as if nothing had happened? If I'd been confused somehow and it wasn't what I thought. Or Mark had realized what an idiot he was and did everything he could to win me back. And in years to come, we'd be able to smile ruefully, maybe even laugh, at Mark's mad moment and the time I ran away to New York for fourteen hours.

'Angela, it's your mum, just calling to say I got the hotel to refund the cost of my room since I stayed with you, so that will go back on your credit card.' Bless my mother for always thinking of the practical things in life. 'I spoke to Louisa and she was very apologetic – very, oh Annette, I don't know what to do – well, that young lady should know better, and I spoke to Mark as well. The less said about that right now the better, I think. Anyway, call me when you can and give me your flight details for coming back. Dad'll come and get you and I've made up your room. Call me when you get a chance, I hope you're having . . .' cue slightly awkward pause while my mother looks for the right word. 'I hope you're safe. Love you dear.'

'Angela, it's Louisa, please call me back? It's Sunday morning and I know you must be really angry and everything but, well, I'm sorry. And I didn't know what to do and, oh God, I can't do this over the phone. I'm such a shit friend.' Yes, you are, I thought. She sounded gutted, but I really couldn't have cared less. 'I spoke to your mum, it was horrible, she hasn't been that mad with me since I brought you home drunk from that sixth form party at Tim's house . . . Oh and Tim's hand is broken, but he'll be OK in a couple of weeks. It's not a serious fracture. Erm, call me?'

I decided she could stew for a while longer.

'Hi, it's me,' he started. I pressed my hand against the window and watched the people below. 'I had to call and say something.' Even from way up on the eleventh floor I could see people emerging from Starbucks with huge vats of coffee. Coffee would be great right now. Coffee or Sambuca. 'I'm so sorry for what happened, it was incredibly stupid of me and heartless and, well, just awful.' There were so many shops around the square. I would definitely feel better if I could go shopping. 'I should have told you what was happening.' Even though the aircon was high in the room, I could see how hard the sun was beating down on all the gorgeous people in their tiny shorts and cute T-shirts. 'Katie and I, well, I should have told you, it's sort of serious.' So many people were bustling around. 'I think we need to have a really sensible chat about the mortgage and everything, I mean, you can't just vanish, Angela.' And I could see squirrels darting around in the trees. 'Your mum said something about you being in New York? I don't know, well, can you call me? I know I fucked up, but you have to call me, you can't just hide. I'm not going back to the house, I'll stay with, well, I won't go back to the house until we've spoken.' I spotted a subway station peeping out from the trees. Wow, the subway. 'We have to talk about what's going to happen. I do love you Angela, but, well, I'm just not in love with you any more. Anyway, call me.'

I rested my forehead against the glass and hung up. So much for him doing anything he could to get me back. Just because this was all a big shock to me, didn't mean it was a shock to him, more like a relief. Shit. What the hell was I going to do now? I couldn't stay with my mum for the rest of my life and I couldn't rely on my friends any more. I couldn't even throw myself into my work, I was freelance, and it was a really slow time for me. I breathed in deeply and stepped back from the window, keeping the tips of my fingers on the glass as I dialled Mark's number.

'Hello?' His voice.

'It's me,' I said, pressing my fingers harder against the window, against the skyline. 'I'm sending Mum over for my stuff, she'll pack it up.' I traced the tops of the opposite buildings and carried on breathing. 'I won't be coming back to the house, so do whatever, just, I'm not coming back.'

'You're at your mum's?' he said hesitantly.

'I can't talk to you,' I said, looking down on the park and breathing deeply and slowly. 'And I'm not at my mum's, I'm in New York and I don't know when I'm coming back, so go and do whatever you want to do with whoever you want to do it with, and don't ever, ever call me again.'

I hung up and leaned my entire weight against the window. So, I'd chosen New York, now I needed it to support me in that decision. And to celebrate, I dashed to the bathroom and threw up the vodka and Coke, followed by the peanut M&Ms. Nice.

'Hi, Miss Clark?' The door opened, leaving me just enough time to pull my robe tightly around me and push myself up from my comfy fetal position around the toilet bowl. The girl from reception pushed through the door with a trolley. 'It's Jennifer, the concierge? Is it OK for me to come in?'

'Yes,' I called, checking nothing was flashing in the mirror and staggering across the room to let her in. 'Of course.'

'I wasn't sure that you would have all your essentials,' she presented the trolley with a flourish. It was stacked with piles of giant cookies, boxes of cereal, a kettle of steaming water, hot milk, cold milk, pancakes, toast and a big box of beauty products. 'And, you know, you mentioned a break-up and no one should be on their own after a break-up. This is our complimentary "All Men Are Shits" break-up service.' She picked up a cookie, snapped it in half and grinned.

'God, thank you, and it's Angela, please,' I said, feeling incredibly English. I took the half cookie she offered and stood awkwardly, taking it in. 'This is wonderful, thank you, I was starving.'

'Well, we're a whatever, whenever hotel, and I'm a whatever, whenever kind of a person,' she said, hopping on to the bed. 'Say if you want me to go though, I'm totally overstepping my concierge boundaries. I just thought, if I'd come to New York after a break-up with one tiny travel bag and no hotel booked, what would I want? So I hit the supplies room, dug out some pyjamas,' she pulled out a pair of white cotton button-up PJs from the bottom of the trolley, 'slippers, socks, cleansing stuff, sewing kits – I don't know, everyone seems to need a sewing kit – and all the food I thought I would want if I was post-break-up. And tea, because, you know, you're English.'

I didn't know whether to laugh or cry, but I was more than happy for this girl to keep talking until I made a decision. 'Thank you again, I suppose I do need pyjamas, I hadn't thought about it really. About anything, actually.'

She mixed a hot chocolate for both of us and broke up another cookie. 'They're the first thing I need when I break-up with someone, I just take to my bed for like, a week or something, and then I eat until I'm over him. So, that's why all the food. I'm guessing it was a bad break-up if it sent you all the way across the Atlantic, huh?'

I took the pyjamas and instinctively made towards the bathroom, but I had a feeling this girl wasn't going to mind me putting them on in front of her. She had already flicked on the TV and was nodding to a music video. I slipped the bottoms on under my robe and quickly dropped it to slide on the top. They felt great, like the coolest, softest sheets I'd ever slept in.

'Too bad to talk to a stranger about?' she asked. 'It's OK, I am the hotel's resident shrink.' She patted the bed and I flopped down, like the pyjamas, it felt completely luxurious and inviting.

'Well, I haven't talked to anyone so far,' I sighed sipping the hot chocolate. 'I literally just found out my boyfriend is cheating on me so I decided to take a holiday to sort my head out.'

'Seriously? What a douche. How did you find out?' Jennifer asked, moving on from the cookies to a bowl of Lucky Charms.

'I caught them having sex in the back of his car at our best friends' wedding. Our friends all knew. Just me the moron that hadn't noticed.' I paused to accept a bowl of cereal. So much sugar in one bowl. Amazing. 'We always said we would just walk away if either one of us cheated, so . . . I think I'm single.'

'Ouch,' she said, crossing her legs under her and shifting a couple of pillows. 'That sucks. But you've got friends in New York?'

'Nope.' I munched on mini marshmallow pieces and watched the milk turn green. Eww and yum. 'I sort of got on the first available flight at Heathrow that met my criteria of English-speaking, full of shops and really fucking far away from Mark.'

'You picked good. New York is like Mecca for people that have had horrible break-ups, trust me, I'm president, treasury and social secretary of the local broken heart society. But not many people just get up and leave the country though honey, you're real brave.'

'Not really,' I confessed. 'I couldn't go back home and I just really can't bear the idea of talking to my friends now and finding out they've all known for months. And well, when you break the groom's hand and make the bride cry all before the first dance at their wedding when you are the maid of honour, you think about leaving the country.'

'Wow,' she said, staring at me. 'You're my new personal hero.'

She looked so genuine, I burst into tears. Seriously, I'm not a crier, but this had been a tough twenty-four hours.

'God, that's so sad,' I mumbled through the tears. 'I'm almost twenty-seven, I've been cheated on, I'm homeless, my friends are all arseholes and I'm alone in a city with one tiny travel bag, a pair of £400 shoes that double as a weapon, and half a Toblerone. That's not my definition of a hero.'

'Nope, I think you're a hero. You confronted a life changing situation head on, you challenged people who were negative influences on your life even though they were cornerstones in your social system and you came to the best city in the world to rediscover yourself. And, you're not alone now, you've got me whether you like it or not,' she said, smiling broadly and scraping her mass of dark brown curls back into a loosely contained ponytail. 'Jenny Lopez, New York's number one free psychiatrist. Make the most of me before I cost you a billion bucks an hour. And don't laugh at my name. And can I see those shoes?'

'I won't make fun,' I said, wondering how I could drink the milk out of my bowl without her seeing. Proof that E numbers are addictive. 'And thank you, for all this and for listening and well, talking. And yes, the shoes are by the bed.'

'Oh, never thank me for talking,' she laughed, hopping up off the bed and picking up a shoe. 'Wow, Hyde Park Louboutins, nice. Well, I've got to get back to the desk and I would guess that you need to sleep, the jet lag must be kicking in about now.'

I nodded, she was strangely insightful. When I tried to stand up to see her out, my legs were like lead.

'Don't get up,' she said, opening the door. 'Just enjoy the food, watch some shitty TV and get ready for tomorrow.'

'What's tomorrow?' I asked, cracking into the pancakes. I was so hungry and everything was so good.

Jenny grinned from the doorway. 'Lots of things. It's my day off, it's the day I'm taking you out so you don't spend a second longer than necessary alone watching cable, and it's the first day of your New York adventure. Be up and in reception by nine-thirty.'

And she was gone.

I sat on the bed, slightly shell-shocked. Opposite the bed was a large mirror, six feet high, leaning against the wall. I could hardly believe it was me staring back out. Me in New York. Me, single. Me with a friend, (albeit a pity friend) taking me on a tour of the city in twelve hours. The jet lag was starting to make me feel as though I'd drunk a lot more vodka than I really had and all the food on the trolley was starting to blur out of focus. Pushing backwards and kicking the covers down around me, I collapsed into the feather bed. Happily, the remote control surfed to the top of the quilt and found its way into my hand. I flicked and flicked until I found something familiar. Ahhh, *Friends*. Perfect. The insanity of the last twenty-four hours flitted around in the back of my mind as I tried to relax. The sun had started to set outside, casting long shadows across my room.

Aren't you feeling lonely? You should go home and confront things, the dark room whispered. I had always hated how things seemed ever so slightly worse, ever so slightly more insane at night. I defiantly stuck my hand out and fumbled around on the trolley for another cookie, the final act of exertion that pushed me over the edge. I collapsed into a dreamless, jet lag induced sleep before I even got it to my mouth.

CHAPTER FOUR

The next morning, I woke up just as suddenly as I'd fallen asleep. Having more or less passed out, I hadn't drawn the curtains and August's sweaty sunlight streamed through my window, demanding I get up immediately. In one hand was a half melted cookie and in the other, the remote control. *Friends* was still playing on the TV. I was more or less sure that it was a different episode . . . According to the clock on the nightstand, it was Monday, eight a.m. and my first full day in New York. I rolled out of bed, trying not to look in the mirror, and took a glance out of the window. Union Square was already buzzing. The subway station was swarming with people and a sprawling market had sprung up and taken over. I was just about to hop in the shower, as a knock at the door shook me out of my wow-I'm-really-in-New-York-and-let's-not-think-about-why trance.

'Room service,' a polite, cool voice accompanied the knock and without thinking, I opened the door to easily one of the best looking men I'd ever, ever seen. He was over six feet tall, thick black hair, parted in the middle and falling to his collar, deep doe brown eyes and baby soft olive skin that contrasted sharply with his crisp white collarless shirt. 'Miss Clark?'

I think I made some sort of noise but it wasn't really an acknowledgement, so I followed it up with a nod. I knew my face was covered in pillow creases, I still had melted chocolate chip cookie on my right hand and I really, really wanted to be wearing my bra. Which was at least ten feet away from where it needed to be, strewn on the floor by the corner of the bed.

'Jenny asked me to make sure I brought up everything she would want for breakfast, so that's pretty much everything on our menu. I'm Joe,' he pushed a fresh, steaming trolley into the room and quickly swapped it for the ravaged mess Jenny had left last night. 'She also asked me to give you a note, it's just there. Enjoy your breakfast.' He flashed the most amazing smile and strolled out of the room. How was he a hotel waiter? I wondered, lifting lids and taking big sniffs of everything on the trolley. Omelette, not a fan, bacon and eggs, maybe a little early, pancakes, always time for pancakes, and on the bottom shelf, an array of cereals, pastries, hot chocolate, milk and my because-you're-English tea. I was so thankful.

Post-shower, post-breakfast, post-another episode of *Friends*, I opened Jenny's note.

Hey,
Hope you found something you enjoyed, like I said, I'm an eater.

I'll be in reception at 9.30 a.m. sharp, don't bail on me or I'll cut off the room service. Today is the first day of your recovery program with Dr Jenny, I hope you're ready for it!

Jenny x

p.s. hope you enjoyed Joe too, I bet your ex didn't

bring you pancakes in the morning looking like that . . .

I laughed out loud, but it sounded so strange. I realized I hadn't heard myself laugh for a good couple of days. Better than crying. But laughter and hot waiters aside, it was time to face facts. And more terrifyingly, it was time to look in the mirror.

The lighting in The Union had been designed to be as flattering as possible but even low wattage bulbs, soft focus mirrors and twelve hours' sleep couldn't repair the damage a break-up could do to your skin. I rummaged around for my make-up bag and emptied the contents out on the bathroom counter. Not a lot to work with. I flicked on some mascara and dabbed gloss onto my lips. Not a lot happening there. And my hair was the same tragic story. I'd been growing it for what seemed like for ever to achieve Louisa's dream bridesmaids' chignon, but now it just looked limp and pathetic. I managed a ponytail and hoped for the best. My wardrobe choices were even more limited. Jeans, T-shirt or bridesmaid dress. And I really hoped Jenny would be taking me somewhere I could grab some new underwear, because I was seriously lacking. When I'd decided to take on my great adventure, I figured I had everything I could need. In reality, I had two T-shirts, three pairs of knickers and a bra. And the Louboutins. Sigh. Beautiful. I grabbed my handbag and bit the bullet. It was 9.25, time to meet Jenny in reception.

Jenny was easy enough to spot. The reception was just as dark and cool as it had been last night, but Jenny glowed in a corner, leaning against the concierge desk in a flirty lemon sundress and delicate gold flip-flops. I felt like her grandmother. And I hadn't noticed how impossibly long her legs were last night. Maybe this wasn't a great person to befriend mid-break-up . . . Before I could bolt for the door, she saw me and beckoned me over.

'See!' she said to the girl behind the counter. Another glowing goddess, this one decked out in the concierge uniform of black collarless shirt and trousers. 'She's real! She's a total hero!'

'Wow,' the girl breathed, staring at me. I felt like a museum exhibit from a 1997 *Eastenders* set. A ponytail? I thought I could get away with wet hair in a ponytail? 'You're like, a total inspiration. You rock. I'm Vanessa.'

I smiled awkwardly. I rocked?

'Hi,' I said to them both, trying not to think about whether or not I had muffin top. 'I wasn't sure what we were doing so I wasn't sure what to wear.' According to the mirror behind Vanessa, I *did* have muffin top.

'You're dressed fine,' Jenny said waving away my concerns and taking my arm. I waved goodbye to Vanessa, but instead of heading to the door, we were moving towards the lift. 'Today is phase one of your transformation.'

'Transformation?' I asked. We slipped into the lift and Jenny pressed a button labelled Rapture Spa. Did I look *that* bad?

'Sure,' she said. 'Rule one after a major break-up, you must submit yourself to complete and utter pampering. Welcome to Rapture.'

The lift doors opened on a large airy space, the complete opposite of the hotel reception. It was flooded with light and smelt of citrus and vanilla. Dozens of serene looking beauticians wandered around in pale blue tunics laughing and joking, carrying salon sized bottles of shampoo, massage oils and bundles of towels. Motown played on the PA system, low but loud enough to sing along to. One of the girls spotted us and waved us over. She was tiny with jet black hair pulled back in a severe bun, emphasizing ridiculously sharp cheekbones and beautiful lips Angelina Jolie would need Restylene to achieve.

'Hi!' She and Jenny kissed briefly on each cheek and then the girl pulled back and looked at me. 'This has got to be her, right?'

Jenny nodded. 'Angela Clark, meet Gina Fox, our hottest beautician. She's going to make you over from head to toe. Sound good?'

Without giving me time to respond, Gina took my hand and walked me through the spa, past reception and back towards a large locker room area. 'Jenny told us about your break-up honey, you're amazing.' She gestured towards one of the pale blue robes and I guessed I was supposed to get undressed. 'But when you break-up with someone, you got to make some changes. You heard the saying "Wash that man right outta your hair"? Well, I'm going to cut him out of yours.'

Jenny was picking at a plate of brownies on the bar by the doorway. 'I think a cute little bob, something classic,' she mumbled through a mouthful of pecans.

Gina spun me around and considered my hair from every angle. 'Great cheekbones, a bob would look good. A few highlights, maybe . . .'

'Oh, I don't think I'm a highlights kind of a girl,' I stuttered, starting to panic. Highlights sounded very white jeans and glittery vest top, not very me.

Gina looked at me sharply and then back at Jenny. 'Is she going to give me trouble?' she asked.

Jenny shook her head quickly. 'Uh-uh, just go easy

on the girl, Gina. She's been through some stuff.' She bagged another brownie.

I sat down in a shampoo chair and let Gina snap a 'before' picture on a Rapture branded camera. As she lathered me up, I mentally congratulated myself on washing it already this morning, it really had been a big skanky mess.

'So, honey,' Gina said, 'tell us about yourself.'

'Well,' The hairwashing chair had an amazing in-built back massager that was pummeling me into soggy submission, 'I'm a writer, sort of, I write the books of children's films and TV shows and stuff.'

'Really? That sounds fun,' Gina said moving on to work the shampoo through. Ouch, a touch too harsh. 'Anything we'd know?'

'Maybe,' I muttered, giving in as Gina began to knead my scalp. 'I've worked on pretty much any kids' film that's been out in the last five years, big green ogres, radioactive spiders, talking turtles.'

'Fun!' She nodded, pushing her knuckles into my temples.

Oooohhhh.

'At first it is, but you know, after a while a job's a job.'

'So, what do you want to do?' Jenny piped up from the next shampooing chair. 'If you could do anything, what would it be?'

'I don't know,' I purred, giving in to the wonderful conditioning massage. 'I guess I'd be a proper writer, you know, write my own stuff. I just never had time for it before.'

'You've got time for it now,' Jenny said. It sounded as if she was back on the brownies. All I knew about this woman so far was that she was the nicest kind of bully and she ate more than anyone I knew, even though her waist was about the circumference of my left thigh. 'You're not on deadline now, right?'

'No,' I admitted. 'I don't have anything at the moment.'

'So, stay, write,' she said while Gina wrapped my head in a towel and guided me over to the styling station. 'You're in New York, it's like, the best place on earth to be a writer. There are a million books inspired by Manhattan.'

Gina snorted. 'Name one Jenny Lopez, and I will give you a hundred dollars, right now.'

'Yeah, so technically, I'm not a reader,' Jenny made bunny ear quotations in the air. 'But I have to immerse myself in my subject. I read a lot of self-help books.'

'If you mean you buy a lot of self-help books and leave them littered around our apartment, then yes, I guess you do,' Gina said.

'So, you live together?' I asked, trying to diffuse the daggers Jenny was glaring at Gina. Must be a fun old time in that house.

'We do until Gina leaves me on Wednesday,' Jenny pretended to sob. 'I can't believe you're ditching me just to be manager of a salon.'

Gina started to comb my hair straight down and flip the parting, centre, left, right, back to centre. 'Yeah, sure, just some salon. Not manager of the first international outpost of Rapture in Paris. You'll live, Jenny,' she said, looking at me in the mirror. When she relaxed she actually looked as if she could be fun and not just some impeccably groomed beauty terrorist. 'So, Angie, what else do you like? Music, theatre, self-help books?'

'Whatever,' Jenny interrupted. 'I think it's interesting that you answered the question "tell us about yourself" with information about your job. You think you spend too much time working and not enough working on other areas of your life?'

'You think, Dr Phil?' said Gina, saving me from having to come up with a response. 'You are so full of shit sometimes. But seriously, apart from your writing, what else are you into? Music? Fashion? Dog shows?'

'I do love music,' I offered, glad to be back in safe territory. 'I love live music, gigs and festivals and stuff. And I've always had a soft spot for an indie boy. You know, skinny tie, leather jacket, Converse, the whole bit.'

Jenny and Gina were smiling and nodding. 'Oh yeah, we've both been there,' Jenny said, her eyes misting over slightly. 'You just need to go down town and shout out some obscure band name. Cute British girl like you? They'll come running.'

Gina laughed. 'Yeah, you can totally work that accent. But I'm so too old for that now,' she said. 'I'm more into hanging around Wall Street on a Friday evening. I need to meet someone who can take me back to a Park Avenue apartment via Tiffany's, not a loft in Brooklyn via the free clinic. Oh, I miss my twenties.'

'Well, I'm twenty-seven in October,' I said while Gina started to chop away at my hair with her tiny scissors. 'Doesn't that make me too old for skinny indie kids?'

'Nah, you got a good coupla years in you,' Gina said. 'But wouldn't you like someone to take care of you? Some big, strong guy? Worked-out six-pack, black Amex, well dressed. Someone to totally spoil you?'

'I don't know, I suppose that wouldn't be a bad thing. My – ex – was a city boy but he wasn't exactly what you'd call worked out. And he was totally tight,' I said slowly. 'I've never even really looked at boys like that. I didn't think I was a proper grown-up I suppose. Isn't that tragic?'

'Well, you've got to stop calling them "boys" for a start, Angie,' Jenny chipped in. 'You want a man. Maybe even a couple of men.'

'Maybe that wouldn't be so bad. Someone who actually weighs more than me . . . Oh God, no, I'm too old for all that dating nonsense. I can't imagine actually doing it. God, I'm going to have to start dating at twenty-six.' I couldn't quite believe it.

Jenny shook her head. 'I wish my next birthday was twenty-seven. I'm thirty next July.' She dropped her head onto the arm of my chair. 'Can you believe it? I can't turn thirty without achieving any of my life's ambitions.'

'But your life's ambitions are to meet Oprah, get a job with Oprah, make friends with all of Oprah's friends then slowly usurp Oprah in the hearts of the nation,' Gina said. There was a lot of hair on my shoulders and a whole lot more on the floor. 'So far, you've read Oprah's books, bought Oprah's magazines, watched Oprah's show and pissed off all your friends by talking constantly about Oprah.'

'Yes, but they are all important steps on becoming the next heart of the nation. And obviously, a billionaire.' Jenny looked resolute. 'What are your life's ambitions, honey?'

I thought hard for a moment.

'I don't think I have any,' I said. 'Maybe I would like to have an original book published or have a column in a magazine or something. I don't know, that stuff isn't easy.'

'But you can absolutely do it,' Jenny said, pulling a pad and pen out of her handbag. 'You just have to get organized. Let's make a list. God, I love this!'

Gina pulled strands of my hair down to my chin to check the lengths. 'Jesus, you've created a monster.

Never give that girl a project.' She tapped Jenny's pad with her scissors. 'Now no talking, I'm about to blow this baby out.'

Twenty minutes later I had a beautiful, chin-length swishy bob with a sweeping fringe, cutting across my right cheekbone. It looked grown-up but cute, stylish but not try hard. I doubted it would look this great ever again.

'Now,' Gina said scooping out a thumbnail of waxy looking product. 'We have options, depending on what you decide to do with your life. What you're looking at now is Park Avenue Princess. You could walk into any of the publishers right now and demand a book deal – super sophisticated.' Jenny was nodding enthusiastically.

'But now . . .' Gina rubbed the wax into the palms of her hands and then attacked my hair, pushing it over the front of my head and raking her fingers through every section. When she flicked it all back, the smooth bob had given way to a choppy, layered, messed up look. Something I had tried to achieve in the past and just ended up looking as though I'd slept with wet hair. 'Now you are ready to go and rock the Lower East Side with the rest of the hipsters. You like?'

'Thank you,' I muttered, so so happy. 'I didn't even know my hair could look this good.' I couldn't stop touching it, just tiny pinches at the ends in case too much contact made it poof . . . disappear.

'I don't want to see you with a hair out of place from now on.' Gina stared me down and for a moment I thanked the managers of Rapture Paris.

'OK, Angie honey, grab your bag. I'm taking that cute do of yours out on the town.' Jenny forced down a final half brownie and pulled me out of the chair.

'Where are we going?' I asked, letting Gina comb out some of the volume, returning to somewhere in between the sleek bob and the crazy chop. 'Because I'm not really dressed for –'

Jenny took my hand and gave me a look you might give an elderly relative who thinks it's still 1947. 'Sweetness, that's exactly why we're going where we're going.'

CHAPTER FIVE

Bloomingdale's.

I'd heard of it, I'd seen the little brown bags but I hadn't ever really thought about going there. In the cab, Jenny had briefed me on what we were looking for. She'd started my new life plan during my blow dry and the first thing we needed was to get properly kitted out for a stay in New York City. It just so happened to tie-in to Jenny's number two rule on how to handle a major break-up. Buy yourself a new *everything*.

Now, I had shopped. Tackled TopShop Oxford Circus on a Friday evening, been elbow deep in the Selfridges' sale, found diamond buys on Portobello Market, but this was a completely different beast. After a quick appraisal of my existing make-up (not enough) and a short description of my make-up bag (sheer revulsion) and confirmation that my credit limit wasn't really an issue as long as we weren't being silly, Jenny decided we would start on the ground floor, in cosmetics. She hit the MAC counter with all the determination of a cross-Channel swimmer. Within seconds I was sitting in another stylist's chair being stripped of the basic make-up I'd slapped on that morning by Razor.

Razor was the most charming man with a mohawk I'd ever had the pleasure to meet. His make-up was amazing, and quite frankly, what he could do with eyeliner put me to shame.

'So we need a proper base to even out the red skin tone, you're very pale, doll, and then we'll work with a blush – maybe an apricot for day and something pinker for night-time? Then we'll do a bit of a workshop on your eyes. Since you're fairly new to this, we'll leave lips for another day and just hook you up with a few neutrals. Maybe a classic red if you're feeling brave,' he said amid a flurry of sponges, brushes, tubes and tubs.

'We can do lips today,' I said meekly, feeling bad for being so pale and letting Razor down. 'I know I'm not wearing a lot today but I do like make-up, I do wear it quite a lot.'

Razor and Jenny exchanged a doubtful glance. 'Take hold of this eyeliner brush for me, sweetness,' Razor suggested, holding it out like a golden sceptre. I took it from him and looked at it quizzically.

'This is for eyeliner? I suppose I only really use pencils,' I said thoughtfully, tilting my head because I was too afraid to move the brush. Not a problem, because Razor snatched it out of my hand before I could even try to apply it to my face.

'Yeah, I think we'll just start with the basics,' he said sweetly, patting my shoulder. I think it was supposed to be comforting but really, it wasn't. Nonetheless, within thirty minutes, I had a face to match my new do. My skin glowed, my eyes were smoky and wide and my lips, as promised, neutral and easy to touch up. Jenny was busy playing with some fluro green eyeshadow when Razor announced I was done with a dramatic, ta-da. He looked as if his pedigree puppy had won first prize at Crufts.

'Wow,' Jenny said, not really smiling but taking in my makeover with complete seriousness. 'Razor, this is amazing. And Angie! You look gorgeous!'

And even if it was just for that moment, I really felt it. I couldn't remember the last time I'd actually bought new make-up.

'I'll take all of it,' I said hurriedly before I had time to think about it. Razor was carefully talking me through every bottle, every brush, every palette and tossing in 'how to' sheets so I could at least attempt it at home, but I was too excited and pressed my plastic into his hand. Soon, I was $250 down and a medium brown bag of MAC up. And it felt good.

As we strolled through the hall, Jenny stopped at various counters, picking out 'essentials' I couldn't be without. Soon we both had very full bags and enough make-up to do the faces of every guest in The Union.

'I need perfume,' I said as we passed by the Chanel counter. 'I've been wearing the same perfume for the last ten years. Mar – my ex used to buy it for me every Christmas,' I explained, 'and I don't ever want to smell it again.'

Jenny hugged me, wrapping her arms and brown paper bags all the way around my neck. 'You're getting it now,' she said steering me towards Chanel. 'Angela Clark, by the end of today, I'll have made a New Yorker out of you. It's got to be No. 5 and then some lunch.'

By the time I'd put away a chicken club sandwich and Diet Coke and Jenny had packed in a burger, fries and yet another chocolate brownie, I'd discovered that she was a true New Yorker born and bred, she had moved to the city after college to follow her dream of becoming the next Oprah. After a summer off in California, she had taken a job as a waitress in a big tourist hotel restaurant back in NYC to 'study her medium' (I think she meant people) but was accidentally so good that she was soon headhunted to move on to the reception desk. When The Union had opened the previous spring, she'd applied for a concierge position to improve her contacts. The boutique hotel apparently attracted a lot of young celebrities, generally blonde, tanned and emaciated or butch, gorgeous and gay. She now considered herself the best connected amateur psychologist in New York, a position that afforded her entrance to the best clubs and restaurants and the personal mobile phone numbers of several Hollywood starlets, and, more importantly, their agents.

'So how come you're not plastered all over the TV yet?' I asked, dipping a spoon into her brownie. It was delicious.

'Haven't had my break yet,' she shrugged. 'The average agent doesn't have the power to get a nobody like me a chat show. You have to be Tyra Banks to walk into something like that.'

She was so pretty, so lovely and so bloody determined, it seemed crazy that she wasn't on the front cover of every magazine in the country. 'You'll get there,' I smiled, pushing the last spoonful of brownie over to her. 'I've never met anyone like you before, honestly. You've done an amazing job of sorting me out. I would be sitting on the sofa in three-day-old pyjamas, eating ice cream and crying at Living TV if I were at home.'

'Well, you're going to take more than one day, a haircut and some make-up, but we'll get there,' she grinned, scooping up dessert. 'God, you haven't even been to Soho yet. I've got a whole plan for you, doll. Do you think you could let this interfering yank take you through Angela Clark version two?'

'I don't have anything better to do,' I laughed. It was so weird to be taken in hand by someone I had met twenty-four hours ago, and, for some reason, it made perfect sense. I already felt as if I'd known Jenny all my life and being with her in New York made London and Mark feel a very long way away and a very long time ago.

After lunch we moved on to the very important job of creating my new wardrobe. A quick run around the fourth floor and three armloads of clothes later, I was ordered into a changing room while Jenny and two assistants appeared intermittently with racks and racks of clothes. Soon I was clad in beautiful 7 for All Mankind skinny jeans that made even my short legs look sexy (according to Jenny) and a flared pair of J Brands that I could dress down with my Converse and an old T-shirt, or dress up with my Louboutins (according to Jenny). One of the helpful and definitely on commission assistants declared that, despite my legs being a little on the short side, they were a good shape and as such, should be on display. Excitingly, I found out I was just a size 8 in America, reason enough to hang around a couple of weeks at least. She had brought in a whole rail of bum-skimmingly short dresses before we both accepted that I would never be able to walk more than ten yards down the road without pulling them down. After that, we added a couple of inches to the length and I relented on a cute blue French Connection jersey dress, a gorgeous Marc by Marc Jacobs printed smock and several stunning bits from Ella Moss and Splendid – T-shirt dresses so soft they felt like clouds! I had no idea. Primark was over for me in that instant. Several C&C California T-shirts and a couple of pairs of shorts and easy to wear skirts later, we moved on to evening wear.

'So, for dates . . . I'm thinking something flirty but fun? Classic though. And easy to wear. You can't be sexy if you don't feel good.' Jenny sent the assistants scurrying across the shop floor with another flick of her wrist. I stood in my pants, peeping round the corner of the slatted wooden door waiting for the next rack of clothes. And in no time they arrived. Vera Wang Lavender. Tory Burch. Nanette Lepore. DVF. 3.1. phillip lim. Paul & Joe Sister. More Marc Jacobs. This was *so* much fun.

'What are you wearing right now?' Jenny asked loudly through the door.

'Nothing?' I replied, slipping out of a gorgeous Marc by Marc Jacobs printed silk halter dress. 'Underwear?'

'I have a horrible feeling I ought to take a look at that too.'

Jenny's level of horror raised to orange alert when she saw my M&S heart print boy shorts and mismatched bra. Then she went a funny pink colour when I admitted that I didn't exactly know what bra size I was.

'It's just not OK,' she said, shaking her head and snatching up several styles and sizes. 'Do you want your rack around your knees at forty?' I was pushed back into my new natural habitat of the changing room, armed with balconettes, backless, strapless, plunge, soft, full cup and half cup bras.

Before my credit card company could know what had happened, I was up another floor buying flip-flops, flats and full-on heels to match all my outfits. Despite Jenny's insistence that gladiator sandals were the shoe of the season, I couldn't help but feel as if they were more my great aunt Agatha than me and eventually, she let it go. But the ballet pumps, the Havaianas and two pairs of wedges were coming with us.

We headed back down through the store, laden with bags – big, medium and little – I had spent more than a month's income in only four hours but I was too happy at the teeny tiny numbers on the labels (a SIX on one of them!) to feel any buyer's remorse, (even if it was just a ten in translation). Riding back down to the ground floor, I adopted the official lift position as Jenny fannied around in her handbag. Clutch purchases, do not make eye contact with fellow lift riders, stare straight ahead. But instead of seeing myself in the mirrored doors, I saw someone completely different. Not different like Louisa's wedding day (just me with more make-up and elaborate hair) but glossy different. My hair swished as I turned my head slightly, Razor's make-up had given me huge Bambi eyes and just-bitten lips, and the thrill of spending more than an entire month's mortgage payment on clothes and slap had given me a giddy flush that I just couldn't get from any blusher. But I knew I had several different versions of the stuff in my bag to give it a good go back at the hotel.

'Come on, we're so gonna struggle to get a cab at this time,' Jenny muttered as the doors slid open, taking my lovely new reflection with them. 'Were you checking yourself out?'

'Yes?'

'Good girl,' Jenny said catching hold of my arm and dragging me out of my New Favourite Place in the Whole World.

So what if I was now officially broke. Why else did I have an emergency credit card? And I was stylishly broke at least. Plus I was too busy staring up and down

Lexington Avenue really to think about it. Everywhere was too busy, too hot and too noisy but it was amazing to me. Looking right, I swam in the endless downtown view afforded by the New York grid system, channels framed by skyscrapers rising high into the sky. To the left, dozens of honking, screeching cabs and searing sunshine contributed to the glowing heat haze rising up and distorting the air. I thought it was beautiful.

'How far do you think you can walk before you pass out?' Jenny asked, nudging me out of my daydream.

'Maybe fifteen minutes?' I wasn't sure if it was really a question or a challenge. I really, really didn't feel like walking.

'Then we should do as much of this on foot as we can.' She nodded to the crossing and threw herself into the traffic. 'Come on, Angie!'

We marched across the road and then down the block, across another road, straight over Park Avenue and ever onwards, crossing Madison. Dragging my precious bags behind me, my fifteen minutes of walking time were quickly wasting away.

'I just wanted to make it to Fifth,' Jenny yelled, holding out her arm, as we crossed for the last time. 'Let's get a cab.'

If it was humanly possible, the cab ride through Manhattan was even more exciting than the ride into the city. We cruised down Fifth Avenue, whizzing for five blocks then crashing to a stop at a red light, with my bags, my head and my stomach crashing into the partition between us and the driver more than once. Every time we stopped it was outside another landmark. St Patrick's Cathedral rose up amongst all the shops, so totally out of place, like putting a Brownie hut next to Harvey Nicks, but here in New York, it just seemed to make perfect sense. I couldn't help but think, as we passed the lions roaring out in front of the huge public library, that if all libraries had giant lions outside, people might read more. Or at least rock up to have their picture taken on their backs.

'Hey, do you see the Empire State Building?' Jenny pointed out of my window to an inconspicuous looking building by the side of us. I couldn't see anything but a huge queue of people, even when I pressed my head right up against the window of the cab and recoiling only when I saw the nasty, greasy marks left by a previous passenger.

'Oh bugger, I really wanted to see that,' I said, leaning in slightly and trying not to think about any other stains that might be around.

'Pretty sure it'll still be there tomorrow,' Jenny said as I leaned into the back window, watching the tower go on and on into the sky as we moved further away. Until we came to a sudden halt again and I smashed my chin against the back seat. 'We're coming up to the Flatiron in a moment, that's way cooler.'

She wasn't wrong, the Flatiron building was incredible, all triangular and pointy but everything we passed was cool. Gorgeous, organized, New Yorky and cool. So incredibly different to London and, if this cab driver didn't start taking corners with a less cavalier attitude, the last place I would ever see. Fifteen minutes later, we reached the tip of the island and pulled up outside the South Ferry Terminal.

'We're going on a ferry?' I asked. Jenny had been enigmatically and uncharacteristically silent on the journey downtown and I'd been too busy taking in the city and counting the Starbucks to worry about it.

'You're so not ready for Staten Island,' she laughed, passing the driver a twenty and hopping out, taking several of my bags with her. I crawled out with my other bags and trailed behind her. 'But you're totally ready to see this.'

We marched along the pavement and down into a busy park, I was so consumed with checking out the various sculptures and lines of people chatting, laughing, eating ice cream, I was almost at the fence before I saw it. When I did, I stopped dead. There it was. The clearest, truest symbol of New York, of America, standing proud and keeping guard across the bay. The Statue of Liberty.

Jenny turned around to look for me, holding her hand over her eyes. 'Pretty great, huh?'

I nodded, without anything to say and walked slowly towards her. We dropped our bags and leaned over the railings. It was beautiful, my very own movie moment.

'I was thinking where we should go when you were trying on clothes,' Jenny said softly. 'And I figured where better than the first place thousands of people first experienced New York. Cheesy maybe, but who better to officially welcome you to the city than Lady Liberty.'

'It's so weird,' I said, still staring out across the river. 'I've seen it a thousand times on TV and stuff but to actually see it, there, real. Wow.'

'Yeah,' Jenny agreed. 'I remember the first time I saw her, it was the first thing I did when I moved to the city. We never, ever came down here as kids, my mom hates it. But she's here to look after everyone. New York is made up of millions of different people, Angie, and they all come here looking for something, just like you.'

'Please, you're giving me too much credit. I wasn't looking for something,' I said, looking across at what I guessed to be Ellis Island. 'I was running away.'

'No, you're not giving yourself enough,' Jenny said,

turning to me. 'Yeah, so maybe not everyone puts an ocean between themselves and their ex but you've got a lot to work through. And that's not psychobabble, that's genuine life experience talking. When my ex left me, I fell apart and I mean it. Fell. Apart. And I had no excuse to be so incredibly pathetic, it was all totally my fault and I had the most amazing friends to look after me. If you didn't feel like your support system was strong enough, then getting yourself out of the situation was the best thing to do. And New York is a great place to do that. It's a city of new beginnings. People go to LA to "find themselves", they come to New York to become someone new.'

'I suppose,' I said, thinking about everything that had happened. Was it weird that Mark hadn't even crossed my mind since the Chanel counter? 'It all just seems so strange and unreal. I feel like I ought to be, I don't know, feeling more.'

'So you're still in shock,' Jenny said, turning back towards the bay. 'There are worse places to be in shock than in Bloomingdale's. Seriously though, you've suffered a huge personal trauma, a break-up is the closest thing to a bereavement, you know.'

'I do feel kind of like that,' I admitted. I really didn't want to dwell on it in such a public place. I was English after all, we're not public criers. 'One minute I'm like, it's over, I'm not even going to think about any of it and then the next, I just can't believe what's happened. I think I'm doing the right thing by being here at the moment though.'

Before Jenny could back me up or shoot me down, a loud ringing interrupted us. My phone. I pulled it out of my bag, ready to remind my mum how expensive international calls were on a mobile when I saw who it was.

Mark.

I looked at the flashing screen for a split second and wondered what he could possibly be ringing for after our last conversation. Had he changed his mind? Was he feeling awful? Was Tim's hand so badly damaged he was having it amputated?

Ring ring. Answer me. Answer me.

Without another thought, I threw my phone, as hard as I could over the railings and into the water. And it felt really, really good.

'Sorry,' I said, inhaling deeply. Had I really just done that?

'This city is a good place to deal with trauma, honey, we've been through a lot ourselves and we've come out of it just fine.' Jenny pulled a pack of tissues out of her handbag and passed them over as a precautionary measure, completely ignoring the phone missile I'd just launched.

'God, I know,' I said quickly, taking the tissues. 'I suppose when you think what everyone has been through here, what they survived, it puts a break-up into perspective.'

'True, but that's not what I meant, sweetie,' Jenny said. 'I meant that you've come to the right place to pull yourself through something that's difficult and hard and tears your insides out. Whatever that something is, is different for everyone. For me, Century 21 reopening five months after 9/11 was my epiphany. I knew I'd be brave enough to get through anything if they could open their doors and sell me designer shoes at a seventy per cent discount.' She took my hand. 'Now I've got to get to my evening shift. And you must be completely wiped. Want to head back to the hotel?'

I took one last look out at the statue. Wowsers. I was in New York.

And I was so incredibly tired.

'Yes please.'

We gathered up all of our bags and flagged down yet another cab. Hmm, a new friend, a new wardrobe and a new city. Compared to Saturday, this hadn't been a bad day.

CHAPTER SIX

After a nap, a shower and several false starts at international dialling from the hotel room phone I finally did what I had to do.

'Annette Clark speaking.'

'Mum, it's me.'

'Oh, Angela, thank goodness. I've been trying to get hold of you all day,' she breathed out in an overly dramatic gesture. This was going to be quick and easy, then.

'Well, my phone doesn't work over here.' We generally found it easier to rely on white lies, a much healthier mother/daughter relationship, than telling the truth, and I wasn't ready to have my mental state questioned. Again. 'I just wanted to let you know I'm safe and I've got somewhere to stay and I'll give you another call when I know what I'm doing.'

'Somewhere to stay?' she repeated.

'Yes, with a friend,' I said, keen to get off the phone before the conversation turned to a subject I just didn't want to deal with. 'Now, can you do me a favour and pick up my stuff from the house? He knows—'

'Angela, slow down,' Mum said. I could see her,

cradling the phone between her shoulder and ear, rubbing her cheeks with her palms, just like she always did when she was confused. 'What do you mean "a friend"? You don't know anyone in America. Please just come home. Dad has sorted out your room and everyone feels just awful, you know, but no one blames you for what happened at the wedding.'

'No one blames me!' I said, my voice getting a tiny bit higher than it needed to be. 'No one blames me . . . Right, well, yes, I've made a friend. No, I didn't know I could make a friend in a day but then until Saturday, I didn't realize the friends I've had all my life could lie to me so well, so maybe it's time to take a chance on new people.'

'Angela, don't start, that's not what I meant,' she sighed. 'I just want to know you're all right. Sod the rest of them.'

'Yes, I'm fine,' I said, catching a glimpse of my new hairdo and beautiful, albeit slightly melted, make-up in the mirror. Damn, I looked pretty bloody good. 'I really am. Look, I'm staying at a – with my friend Jenny and she's really nice. I'm going to be here for a while I think, but I'll call you if I need anything and you can call me on this number for the next couple of days, just 1471 it. Love you.'

'Love you too, sweetheart,' she said, sounding slightly mollified. 'Dad and I will go and get your things from your house. Don't worry, just come home soon.'

Five minutes after my mother had hung up, I realized I was still gripping the receiver so tightly my knuckles had turned white. Just hearing her mention Mark, the wedding, everything back home had put me in a foul mood. Not a good move when I had to spend the night in by myself. I walked over to the window, looking for somewhere to hide out, people watch and basically listen in on other people's conversations. A huge, familiar beacon of normality stared back at me.

Starbucks.

Perfect. And there was even an HSBC next door.

Multinational corporations be praised.

I emptied two of the Big Brown Bags onto the bed and found a pair of tiny shorts and some colourful T-shirts. Peeling off my sweaty jeans and old graying T-shirt, I swapped outfits and slipped into my new Havaianas. My handbag looked too formal, too structured and altogether too much like it came from Next to wear with the outfit, so I slipped my room key and cash card into my back pocket and hoped for the best. Sporting a big black pleather handbag with flip-flops and hot pants did seem a bit silly.

Jenny wasn't on the desk when I passed through reception so I escaped without questioning and, even though it was past seven, the air outside was still balmy and dense. I visited the bank first, struggling for a second with having to put my card in and take it back out again before the buttons would work. Just before I could withdraw some cash, the related accounts link danced in the corner of my eye. The joint account. I pressed the button, just to check. It was looking really, really healthy. Mark and I had always had an agreement that I put in a certain amount each month to cover the mortgage and bills and then he paid them all. From the looks of this, he'd been covering a lot more than half the bills for some time and never mentioned it. For a brief moment, I felt a pang, maybe he wasn't all bad, he did look after me after all.

And then a devil appeared on my shoulder with a quick reminder of his sweaty, pathetic face. Before I even knew what I'd done, I moved half the cash from the joint account over to my personal account. He was hardly going to miss it, he earned a fortune, and by rights, half of it was allegedly mine. And more importantly, it covered my shopping spree. Result.

Breathing fast and heavy, I withdrew a couple of hundred dollars, not knowing what I'd be doing for the next few days, and dashed into Starbucks with my ill-gotten gains.

'What can I get you?' asked the cute assistant. Under normal circumstances, I'd have been flustered and blushing, he was absolutely my crush type. Tall, skinny, floppy brown hair and had the look of a man that new his way around a Stratocaster. The complete opposite of Mark, to be specific. But I was too confused by the coffee menu to take in his messy prettiness.

'Er, I just want, a, erm,' this wasn't me projecting my most confident and beautiful self, as recommended by Jenny, 'a large coffee?'

'A regular coffee?' he asked. 'Like, a Venti Americano?'

'Very possibly? And a muffin, blueberry muffin.'

'Five thirty-five,' he said, flipping the fringe across his eyes. Now the coffee issue was out of the way, I had a chance to check out just how good-looking he was. And he really was. 'I'll bring them over.'

I scooted over to a table for one by the window and tried to relax. Looking at the bank account had actually been even worse than talking to my mum. I felt as if I'd actually taken money out of his wallet. I rested my head on my forearms and breathed deeply. Sod it, he could consider that his Dickhead Tax.

'Venti Americano and a blueberry muffin.' Starbucks boy deposited my drink and snack on the table in front of me with a flourish.

'Thanks,' I said, suddenly as hungry as Jenny, looking at the giant, berry-studded muffin.

'So, are you on vacation?' he asked.

I wasn't really used to getting into conversations with strangers, let alone fit male ones. Working from home limited my access to the outside world and the people in my local Costa were not chatty. I don't think they liked me using their place of work as a makeshift office.

'Sort of, I suppose.' I didn't really want to get into the reasons behind my visit to the city with a hot barista. 'I'm staying here for a while. With a friend.'

'Cool,' he nodded. 'So you're from England right? I really want to go to London. The music scene there is so cool right now.'

'I am,' I nodded back, sipping my bucket of coffee, wishing I'd asked for a decaf and trying to think of something cool to say. 'It's really – cool.'

'Yeah, totally,' he agreed. 'If you're around next month, you should check out my band. We're playing at the Cake Shop in a couple of weeks.' He pulled a napkin from under my plate and took a pen out of his pocket. 'Give me a call and I'll put you on the guest list. I'm Johnny.'

I took the napkin, turning bright red and not from the sunburn I'd picked up in Battery Park. 'Thank you,' I said, tucking it into my pocket and looking hard at my coffee.

'And, if you're not doing anything at the weekend, you could give me a call or something. We could, like, go to a show or something,' he said, flicking his fringe back the other way. 'Or you know, if you just want some coffee, I'm usually here.'

I gulped my coffee and broke off the edge of the muffin as Johnny sauntered back behind his counter. Had I just been asked out by a cute boy? Since I'd been engaged, I'd assumed (or hoped) I was giving off an 'I'm taken' vibe that put off all reasonable men. There had been the odd sleaze who would have a crack at the end of the night, or the dodgy friend whose best mate had already got off with someone, but I really couldn't remember the last time an actual honest to God, good-looking man had even attempted to have a go.

'But you're not engaged any more, you're single,' whispered the increasingly irritating devil on my shoulder, who apparently had not done enough damage in the bank. I drained my coffee quickly and nibbled the other edge of my muffin, my appetite gone. Johnny was serving another customer as I left. He gave me a quick wave, I nodded and smiled back shyly.

Outside it was starting to cool a little at last. I crossed over the road into Union Square Park and sat down on the first bench I passed. For a split second, I couldn't feel my cash card in my pocket. I fished around the oddly deep back pocket of the implausibly short shorts until I gripped the card, my room key and the roll of cash I'd just withdrawn. People were still streaming out of the subway, looking harassed, hot and tired, while a younger, cooler crowd surged down the steps. I wondered where they were all going when a short, suit-wearing middle-aged man sat down on the bench next to me.

'Hi,' he said, sitting at the far end of the bench.

'Hello,' I replied, grasping the roll of cash in my hand. He didn't look like a mugger but I couldn't be sure, I was in a strange city after all.

'So, I don't usually do this kind of thing, but how much for a blow job?' he asked quietly, talking to my knees.

'Sorry?'

'A, ah, a blow job. I have a hundred bucks or so,' Sweat was beading on his top lip but I didn't think it was from the heat. 'I've had a hell of a day.'

'I – I'm not a, not a prostitute,' I spluttered, unable to move.

'Oh,' he stood up quickly, shuffling backwards but still staring at my legs. 'I'm sorry, I just thought, because the cash and – and . . . I'm sorry.'

Before I could get up, he had shuffled away, out of the park and down the street. I stared after him. Did I look like a prostitute? Quickly, I shoved everything back in my pockets and ran back across the road and into the safety of the dimly lit hotel lobby.

'Hey,' called Jenny from the concierge desk. 'Where have you been? I called up to see what you wanted for dinner.'

I stopped dead in the middle of the busy lobby and turned to face her. 'These shorts are going back.'

It took an emergency cup of tea and full packet of Chips Ahoy! cookies on the floor behind the concierge desk, before Jenny could get any sort of sense out of me. Naturally, she managed to find the positive in my being mistaken for a hooker who gives blowjobs in public parks.

'A hundred dollars is way above average, I'm sure,' she said, topping up my tea with hot water. I'd already had to demand a mug, no matter how against cute English stereotype, I didn't want to have to get into the 'we don't top it up with hot water, we make more tea' conversation when I was having absolutely the wrong kind of Julia Roberts/*Pretty Woman* moment. 'And more importantly, Starbucks Johnny totally hit on you! You hit one out of the park on your first try, honey!'

'Do you know him?' I sniffed, necking the weak, milkless excuse for tea. 'He was quite cute.'

'Know him?' Jenny whistled. 'Half the girls working in this hotel would like to know him a whole lot better. He's the reason we all have caffeine addiction. Ask Van next time she's on the desk. She's got a four machiatos a day habit because of that boy.'

'It was just so weird, I don't think I handled it that well. I don't think I've even got his number still.'

'He gave you his number?' she shrieked, scalding me with more unnecessary hot water. 'Jesus, Angie! What do you need me for? You're already picking up grade A guys on your second day in the city. I don't think anyone here got his number.'

And admittedly, that did make me feel quite good. 'It's only because I'm English or something, he doesn't think I'll call. And I won't anyway, will I?'

Jenny looked at me for a second and then sat down.'Why not?'

'Because I haven't called anyone in, well actually ever. I've literally just had a monumental break-up, I don't need to start dating right away.'

'You know what? A couple of dates might be the best thing for you. This is kind of a vacation, right? So let's find you a vacation fling, a holiday romance.'

'I don't know, I mean, isn't dating really hard?' I pulled my top down over my knees. 'I've only ever, well, you know, *been* with Mark. I don't know if I can do "dating", like proper going out and dating.'

'Seriously? And don't stretch that,' Jenny asked, pulling my top back off my knees like my mum. 'If that's the case honey, we definitely have to get you a couple of dates. You need to realize how much fun it is! A couple of non-pressure, well behaved gentleman-type dates. Just some fun. Nothing big.'

'Are you sure?' I certainly wasn't.

'Totally,' she said, easing up off the floor and pulling me up with her. 'Now, you go upstairs, call down when you know what you want to eat and read this over dinner.' She handed me a notebook with my name written across the front in big lettering, decorated with glittery star stickers and a huge 'I Heart NY' postcard.

'What's this?' I asked. Wasn't I a little too old for star stickers?

'It's for you to write in,' Jenny explained, opening the notebook to the first page. 'You said that you didn't really know what your ambitions were earlier, now I want you to work some out. And make sure you include getting laid. Now upstairs, dinner, ambitions and then sleep.'

She shooed me away and turned to a hotel guest waiting patiently in front of the counter with a megawatt smile. 'How can I help you, Mr Roberts?' I heard her purr as I slipped into the lift, my nose already in the notebook.

Name: Easy, Angela Clark.

Age: Twenty-six and six months. More of a wince with that one.

Ambition: To be a published writer.

Next to published writer, I added, 'To be happy'.

And next to that, 'Get laid'.

CHAPTER SEVEN

The next morning, I woke up feeling I had to meet my new life head on. So what if I'd never done anything impulsive before today? I was now a born again New Yorker and a New New Yorker needed a New Handbag. I'd put together a simple outfit, short shorts, a beautifully cut white shirt and cute little lemon ballet slippers. My make-up and hair might not have been up to Razor/Gina standards but I still looked better than I had in, well, since the last time I'd actually bothered to look in a mirror.

Jenny had been insistent that I travel everywhere by subway until I knew the system as well as the London Underground. I hadn't had the heart to tell her that even after nearly seven years in London, I could still pretty much only find my way from Waterloo to TopShop Oxford Circus without looking at the map. Cautiously, I slipped down the subway steps, scoping out a Metrocard machine and feeding in my cash. So far, so London. Twenty-four dollars for a one week pass? Not so London. I knew TFL had been ripping me off . . .

According to my notes, I was supposed to take the

6 train to Spring Street – easy. But looking at the map, I was sure it would have been quicker to walk. Immediately I was confused, why didn't the lines just have names? What was with the colours, the letters and the numbers? And how did I know what stopped where? Jenny's notes expressly forbade asking anyone for directions or getting a guidebook out. Halfway around Bloomingdale's the day before, she had grabbed my *Rough Guide* out of my handbag and ceremoniously dropped it in a rubbish bin.

The subway was hot in the sticky August heat, but the platforms were much bigger than the Underground. When the train arrived, it was huge inside compared to the cramped little District line. At first I couldn't work out why the carriage looked so familiar and then I remembered, *Ghost. This is my train!* Louisa and I must have watched that film a thousand times as teenagers. But Louisa's not here, I reminded myself. She's probably playing mixed doubles with her husband, your ex and his mistress. The fact that I knew she was probably on her honeymoon in Grenada did nothing to dispel the ugly fantasy I'd created for myself. Before I could slink off the train and back into the hotel, the doors closed and we pulled off. I dropped backwards onto the hard metal bench and studiously avoided eye contact with the other travellers while sneakily trying to get a good look at them.

It would be such a New York cliché to call the subway a melting pot but it really was. Businessmen in suits clung to the straps, tourist shoppers from Fifth Avenue clutched their Saks and Tiffany's bags nervously, while a group of Hispanic girls with truly gravity defying hair backcombed each other beside me. In between them, older travellers rode the train with their eyes closed. Before I knew it, we were at my stop. I dashed through the open doors and headed up the steps, trying not to look around with too much confusion. As I exited on to Spring Street, the super strong sun caught me off guard and I almost toppled backwards into a girl, so cool looking I felt sure that she must be famous. Or at least sleeping with someone famous.

'Sorry,' I gave her my best 'what a tit' grin.

The girl gave me an uncomfortable stare and moved on. Watching her lithe limbs saunter on down the street as if she owned it, I wondered how much I would have to offer her for a blowjob. If I was commanding a hundred dollars, she could be into five figures.

Jenny had told me I'd love Soho and she was right. It was so different to the strict, structured grid system of midtown. I loved being able to see for what seemed like for ever, up and across Manhattan, but this was like stepping into a film set. Even though I'd never been here, the streets seemed so familiar. Either I'd found my spiritual home or I'd watched too much TV. I wandered down the street, towards what I hoped was Broadway, peering in windows, watching the people and intermittently looking down at my shameful old handbag. Before I could decide what to do with it, I found Broadway. And another Bloomingdale's. Hurrah.

I fought my way through the cosmetics counters, trying to strike a balance between peeping at the magical make-up on the counters without attracting the attention of the vulture-like assistants. Dashing past the Bliss counter, I bounded onto the escalator, sailing up and away to credit card safety. For the moment at least. The bags were helpfully right where I stumbled off the escalator, but the number of bags crammed into this small space was completely overwhelming. Stalking around the counters and shelves,

I evaded the gaze of the assistants for as long as I could before I braved a young brunette with approximately three hairs out of place. A relative slattern by Soho standards.

'Hi, can I help you find something?' she asked.

'I'm looking for a bag,' I nodded, trying not to sound like someone who really didn't do this often, but at the same time not wanting to get fleeced out of my of entire wedding savings for a handbag. 'Something I can use for everyday really, for carrying my laptop, my wallet, phone, stuff like that.'

'OK.' She began rocketing around the department, pulling out various bags of various sizes, all extraordinarily expensive, I was sure. 'You'll probably want leather if it's for everyday. It's the most durable material and it wears well. And you want room for your laptop . . .' she paused, biting her full bottom lip and glancing around the shelves before pulling some more bags out from hidden drawers behind her counter. 'Any favourite designers?'

'Marc Jacobs?' I offered, thinking back to yesterday's induction into the fashion floor. It seemed to be the right answer because she smiled and finished off the collection of luxury leather in front of her with the most beautiful, beautiful bag I had ever laid eyes on. I reached out to stroke its buttery softness, the dark brown of the leather looked like milk chocolate and the subtle gold detailing winked at me.

'*Buy me,*' it whispered tantalizingly. '*I complete you.*'

The sales girl was making noises about updated classic satchel design, Italian leather and brass fixings but I was already working out how much I could ram in there and still wedge my arm through the strap.

'How much?' I asked, picking it up delicately. It was heart-stoppingly beautiful. Was it wrong that I felt more passion for this bag than I had felt in my and Mark's bedroom for the last three years?

'It's $895.00,' she said, sensing the commission. I figured she could smell a sale like a horse smells fear. 'Plus tax.'

My shoddy internal exchange rate brought that out at more or less £500. I'd never ever spent more than thirty quid on a bag. But I needed it. I thought back to when Louisa and I went shopping for bridesmaid shoes in Harvey Nicks and reasoned with myself. If she could spend £400 on my shoes for one day (albeit guilt shoes, I realized now) I could *invest* £500 in a bag I would use for the rest of my life. I'd just use it all the time. For every occasion. Every single day.

'Anything else?' the girl piped up.

I smiled feverishly back at her. 'I need a clutch.'

A thousand dollars down and two amazing handbags up, I sloped down Bloomingdale's steps into the searing summer heat. I figured at £500 I had to get my money out of this bad boy by using it absolutely immediately, rolling my Next pleather wonder into as small a scrunchy ball and dropping it into my Big Brown Bag. Compared to midtown yesterday, Broadway was relatively quiet. A few tourists wandered around in combat shorts and red shoulders with digital cameras constantly clicking, while the beautiful and hip with no perceivable employment, swanned in and out of the shops, weaving around Mercer, Spring and Prince Streets, weighing down their skinny forearms with massive stiff paper bags. It took staring at these girls for less than a minute before I realized how starving I was. Luckily, this was New York City and Starbucks was never more than two minutes away. One quick muffin, I promised myself as I stumbled gratefully back into multinational air-conditioning, and then I'll head back to the hotel.

My promises were short-lived. If the people watching outside Bloomingdale's had been good, standing in the ten minute queue at Starbucks was like watching a David Attenborough documentary. I'd never seen such a mix of people. More skinny women ordering non-fat caffeine shots, businessmen holding meetings over blueberry scones, cute muso types intensely discussing the newest guitar band (and not even ordering coffee – rebels.) But the most popular customers were the men and women studiously ignoring the rest of the patrons and desperately tapping away on laptops, intermittently stopping to check their WiFi connections, sigh loudly and sip their huge drinks.

'You can never get a fuckin' seat in this fuckin' place,' breathed the man behind me. 'Fuckin' bloggers.'

I turned and smiled politely even though I didn't know what he was talking about, assuming he was addressing me. He stared back at me as if I were mentally ill.

'Bloggers?' I enquired, suddenly feeling very English as he stared me down.

'What?' he snapped. Apparently, he was not talking to me.

'Sorry,' I mumbled, turning away, looking for a rock to crawl under.

'You said something about bloggers, I thought you meant . . .' and I let myself trail off with an intense stare into the pastry cabinet.

'Oh,' he said, still not exactly what you'd call friendly. 'Just thinking out loud. You can never sit down in a Starbucks for all these cocksucking bloggers posting their whiny diatribes about how shitty their lives are. No one cares, people! Go find some real friends to talk to!'

At this point he was really shouting at the laptop brigade and I was really, really wishing I hadn't encouraged the conversation.

'Next?'

Saved by the coffee order.

I ordered my muffin and Americano to go and immediately hailed a cab. I'd taken the subway once today and my Marc Jacobs satchel really didn't feel like slumming it.

'The Union hotel, on Union Square,' I said, settling back as we turned off Broadway. I watched carefully for street signs, trying to ignore further credit card destroying shopping opportunities. Down East Houston and then up the Bowery, or was it Fourth Avenue? I was confused but happy confused.

'You on vacation?' the cabbie yelled through the grid.

'Yes,' I called back, happily taking in the sights. 'I am on vacation.'

'Girl like you on your own?' he asked. 'Don't get many girls on their own. Mainly get the packs of three or four doing the *Sex and the City* thing. Can't tell you how many times I've been down to Magnolia Bakery.'

Oh. Cupcakes! 'I haven't been there yet.'

'Yeah, I don't get it,' he laughed. 'They sit in the back of the cab complaining about not being able to get into some dumb dress they can't afford and then they go eat cupcakes. I just don't get it.'

The cab ride was so short, I hardly had time to find my wallet inside my beautiful new bag when we pulled up outside the hotel. And it was only six dollars! This was the best city and clearly, clearly offset the insanity of my purchases.

The thing I loved best about my hotel room was that no matter how messy I left it, how many towels I'd used and how many of the mini Rapture toiletries I'd used up in the shower, it was always blissfully restored to pristine condition when I returned. I gently placed my Marc Jacobs bag on the side table and pulled my laptop out of the desk. Setting up a selection of soft drinks and snacks on the tiny table I'd dragged across the room, I grabbed a pillow from the bed and perched the computer onto my knee. The hotel had supplied me with a UK power adaptor without me even asking. Wow. I couldn't remember the last time Mark had so much as intuitively supplied me with a cup of tea. I also spotted a note from Jenny, reminding me tonight was Gina's leaving party and that I was to meet her in reception at nine.

Within fifteen minutes of settling into my chair and not typing a single word, my laptop had gone to sleep and so had I. I was back to dreaming my New York life, instead of living my New York dream. For the last six months or so, while Mark had been putting in extra hours at the office and at the tennis club (and in Katie as it turned out) I'd thought about joining gyms, taking yoga classes, even teaching creative writing classes, but I hadn't actually acted on any of them. Maybe, if I tried, I could genuinely see the positives in what had happened. I had already made a friend in Jenny, even if I didn't really know her that well. I'd got a new do, a new wardrobe and I was now in possession of the most beautiful handbag I'd ever seen in almost twenty-seven years of life. Who needed what I'd left behind?

While all these thoughts ran through my head, I started typing. For the want of a plot or a storyline, I started writing every single thing that had happened to me in the last week. It seemed like a good place to start, documenting everything for fear of a single second of it escaping. It all came out, the wedding ceremony, the dinner, the toasts, finding Mark in the car with his pants down, bashing Tim's hand, and my bolt to New York. Before I knew what had happened, it was almost eight, I'd been typing for more than three hours and in just over one, I had to meet Jenny, Gina and Vanessa.

CHAPTER EIGHT

Dead on the dot of nine, fuelled by a hastily necked vodka from the mini bar, I stepped out of the lift and into the lobby.

'Jesus, Angela Clark,' Jenny said as I skulked into the bar. I'd never in my life been one of those girls who can look in a mirror and think, yeah, I look good. Even at Louisa's wedding, after an hour and a half at the mercy of a hairdresser and make-up artist, I hadn't looked good – I'd looked like a bridesmaid, but things were changing. If I didn't look at least OK tonight, I knew I never would. It had taken me twenty minutes and three attempts at Razor's smoky eye make-up tips, but I was more or less there (and he'd promised it would only look better the more smudged it got). My hair was elegantly messy and I'd gone for a simple black v-neck dress I'd bought that afternoon, with my Louboutins, new clutch and bare legs. I'd never felt so great but so nervous in all my life.

'Hey,' I held my hand out in a small wave.

'Remind me again why I'm giving you shopping advice?' Jenny kissed me on both cheeks and presented me to the girls. 'Gina and Vanessa, you know, this is

Erin.' They all raised a hand and I ordered a vodka and cranberry hoping it would come soon. 'I've told the girls all about you but I didn't tell them you were a complete glamazon,' Jenny said, checking me out from every angle. 'You did me proud, doll!'

'I didn't really know what I should wear so I just went for black. And I didn't have to make too many choices about going out shoes,' I held out a foot for inspection to approving hums and nods.

'Well, you did good, honey,' Gina said, sipping her cocktail. 'You'll be just fine.'

At least I'd got the level of dressing up right. Gina looked ridiculously sexy in high, high heels and a knee-length, skin-tight silk dress in a rich purple. Jenny was putting her namesake to shame in a plunging cream dress that cut way past her cleavage and the other two girls had really taken the 'short is the new black' mantra I'd seen in fashion magazines to heart. Individually they looked super sexy but as a pack, they looked unreal. If I were a man, I'd have been terrified.

Not at all strangely, for five scantily-clad women, we found cabs right away and were climbing out at the Soho Grand in minutes. From the outside, nothing really looked that grand but the ordinary façade belied an amazing interior. Like The Union, it was dimly lit but decked out with chandeliers and amazing wrought iron-work. The Grand Bar was lined with chrome stools that were occupied by equally beautiful people befitting the decor. Jenny had reserved a section of the lounge, which was already spilling over with people I recognized from the hotel and people I didn't. Everyone was all about the hugs, kisses and 'you rock' affirmations, but I wasn't drunk enough not to feel self-conscious.

'Hey, you really do look great,' Jenny whispered in my ear as we were ushered through into our own private slice of opulence. 'And you'll be just fine. Just talk to people, you're practically a local celebrity and shit, you look so hot!' A reassuring squeeze on the shoulder and she was gone.

No matter how great I was told I looked and how fabulous my surroundings, I still felt like a fish out of water. The first two drinks were wearing off and all of a sudden, I was just Angela Clark in a room full of strangers wearing a really short dress. For the want of something to do, I went to the bar. If I was holding a drink, at least I'd have something to do with my hands. Even though it wasn't even ten, the bar was busy with hotel guests and after-work drinkers but I managed to slip onto a stool as a sweaty man in a suit vacated, and checked out the cocktail menu. From here, Gina's group looked as if it could be any A-lister's after party. I didn't think anyone at home would believe me if I told them that the gorgeous, groomed minxes in the VIP area were hotel workers and hairdressers. They looked like movie stars to me and no matter how many makeovers I had, it had still only been three days since I was just Angela Clark, nobody. Maybe I wasn't ready to become Angela Clark, somebody, just yet.

'Waiting for someone?' asked a voice at my side.

If this man was going to offer me money for sex, I would have had to consider it. Please ask me how much for a blow job, I prayed. He was tall, broad shouldered and very handsome. I instantly imagined him to be called Chip or Brad and to ride very fast, manly motorcycles on the weekends.

'I'm actually with some friends,' I said, pointing over at the group who were getting louder by the second. 'I was just taking a break. Getting a drink.'

'Me too,' he said smoothly. His eyes were a light blue and even in the dim, sultry lighting, I could see them twinkling as he nodded towards a group of guys sitting around one of the low coffee tables opposite the bar. 'I needed two minutes out of the zoo. Don't you hate it when you go for a drink after work and then just talk about work?'

I laughed, not really sure why. It wasn't even vaguely funny. 'I don't think I've ever had after work drinks,' I said, thanking every god I could think of as the stool next to me freed up and he sat down. 'I'm a freelancer so I work from home most of the time.'

'What'll it be?' the bartender interrupted. I looked down at the menu, flustered. Not a Sex on the Beach or a Woo Woo to be seen.

'We'll have two Perfect Tens,' the guy ordered. 'Sorry, you like them?'

'This is my first time here, I'll have to try it.' It took me a moment to realize he'd just bought me a drink. 'I mean, thank you.' I was desperately trying not to blush and completely blanked. He ran his hand through his light brown hair, which moved just enough to make my heart melt but was still short enough to make it through a game of squash unscathed. Probably.

'So you're a freelance what?' he asked as the bartender presented us with a pair of huge, citrussy-looking drinks.

'Oh, writer,' I said, taking a sip. Whatever alcohol was in this was well hidden behind a whole lot of pineapple juice. It was the perfect summertime drink. 'I write children's books.' It didn't seem worth going into any more detail at this point. That and the fact that I was struggling to put my thoughts into a workable sentence. He was so ridiculously hot!

'That's great,' he said, pulling the straw out of his drink and sipping straight from the glass. Manly. 'It must be fulfilling to do something so creative.'

'Uh-huh,' I nodded, realizing too late that I was making really short work of this drink and not really wanting to go into why I wasn't creatively sated by writing about toys that go on magic journeys when they shake their musical bells. 'And what do you do?'

'I work on Wall Street,' he said, almost an admission. 'It's not exactly creative, huh?' Even sitting down and wearing a suit I could see how worked out his upper body was. As unaccustomed as I was to talking to a hot man in a hot bar, I could feel my confidence having a crack at coming back up again, like the little engine that could. If that little engine was fuelled by vodka.

'But it must be challenging?' I said, trying to slide my empty glass back onto the bar without him noticing. No such luck. 'I can't imagine how much responsibility that must be.'

'Well, yeah,' he agreed, signalling to the bartender to refill my glass. I reached for my purse and he held out his hand. 'It is challenging and thankfully, it's well paid, so I can afford to buy children's book writers drinks.'

'You buy a lot of children's book writers drinks?' I asked, attempting to flirt. I was rusty but good God, I was going to have a go.

'Just you and JK Rowling, if I ever meet her,' he joked. Pulling out his wallet, he passed the bartender what looked suspiciously like a hundred dollar bill, simultaneously impressing and terrifying me. 'So I gotta ask, do two drinks get me your name?' he asked, passing me a refreshed glass.

'Angela,' I obliged, sipping slowly. 'Angela Clark. And does accepting them get me yours?'

'Tyler Moore,' he said, replacing the wallet and removing something else. A tiny silver business card case. 'So, Angela, are you on vacation in New York or are we lucky enough to add you to our swelling ranks of writers?'

'You're lucky enough to have me for a while,' I said, trying not to stare at his chest. Reaching in and out for the wallet had revealed a thin white shirt that in turn hinted at a very hard, very toned six-pack. 'I'm staying for the time being, but I'm not sure how long for.'

'I hope it's long enough for me to take you out,' he said, opening the business card holder and passing me one of the cards. I took it and slipped it straight into my bag. I didn't want to lose it. 'Where are you staying?'

'The Union,' I spotted the men on the sofa standing up and throwing bills on the table. 'On Union Square?'

'I love that hotel. There's this great noodle place across the square too, haven't been there in ages,' he said, swapping the business card holder for a Black-Berry. How many pockets did he have in there? His jacket was like the Tardis. 'Well now you've got me hungry, how about dinner on Thursday? Could I get your number?'

'Oh, I don't have a phone yet,' I winced as he stepped down from the stool. 'But Thursday would be great, really. Would it be OK if I called you?'

'You got my numbers, I'd love to hear from you,' he said and held out a hand, which I shook gladly. Soft hands, firm grip and possibly manicured but I wasn't complaining. The way I figured it, he was a karmic gift from the universe. 'Bye Angela Clark.'

And with that I was in love.

I stared after him as he vanished down the wrought-iron staircase with his friends and sipped my drink. Oh, his rear view was every bit as good as the front.

'Could I get another Perfect Ten?' I asked as the

bartender passed my way. He nodded and miraculously, another appeared from nowhere.

I left a twenty on the bar and hopped off the stool. Turned out I wasn't that steady on my heels and I wobbled over to Gina's reserved area.

'Hey, girl!' Jenny waved me over from a low bench by the window. 'I was worried about you until I saw you talking to tall, rich and handsome over by the bar. Johnny yesterday, hot banker tonight, seriously, why do you need my help again?'

I flopped onto the bench and sighed. 'But they're both because of you,' I said, throwing an arm around her. 'It's the hair and the make-up and stuff. Not me. Jesus, I couldn't even get my own boyfriend to have sex with me, let alone seduce strangers.'

'Seriously?' she asked, sipping on what looked like a Cosmopolitan. Hmm, I thought, apparently not a cliché. One of those next for me. 'But why wouldn't he want to throw you down and ravish you?'

'Because he was ravishing someone else,' I laughed loudly. 'And he never saw me looking like this. I wore nothing but hoodies and baggy jeans. We had sex about once a month on principal. And it had been shit for about, God, do you know I can't actually remember the last time it was good.'

'That's really sad,' sighed Jenny. I dropped my head onto her shoulder and nodded. 'He has absolutely no excuse for cheating but if things were that bad, you should have been out of there a long time ago.'

'And you know what's really sad?' I whispered loudly with dramatic hand gestures. 'He is the only man I've ever done it with.' I nodded to myself and finished my drink. It was definitely time for another. 'Yeah, maybe I should do it with Tyler, that man at the bar. He asked me out for dinner.'

'And you're gonna go, right?' she asked, taking my empty glass. 'You should totally go.'

'I said I'd let him know about Thursday,' I noticed I was slurring a little bit. The two drinks I'd necked at The Union must have been really kicking in. 'He was really, really good-looking.'

'Well, don't make it too easy for him,' she said, patting my hand. The room was starting to spin a little, it was so hot. I really wanted another drink. 'But you should definitely go out on Thursday and if it goes well, I say you do whatever you gotta do. You so need to get back on the horse, Angie.'

'Yeah, ride that horse,' I sighed, looking for a server. How long did it take for a waitress to make her way around here? 'What about you? You're bloody gorgeous? What about you and horse riding?'

Jenny laughed out loud. 'How many drinks did you have over there?' she asked. 'I've ridden far too many horses, kissed too many frogs. When I turned twenty-nine I decided I wasn't going to keep dating useless guys just for the sake of dating, so I'm holding out for a good guy.'

'That's great,' I said, squeezing her hand hard. 'That's really, really great. You know what? I feel a bit sick.'

The room started to spin a little bit faster and I started to feel a little bit hotter. Jenny helped me up and somehow we made it outside to the little yard on the side of the hotel.

'How many drinks did you have?' Jenny asked, returning from the bar with a tall glass of water. It was the most wonderful thing I'd ever drunk.

'Just two at the hotel and three pineapple things here,' I said, breathing deeply. 'But I have only had breakfast.'

'You really will fit in here if you carry on like that,'

Jenny said. 'Drink that water and we'll stop on the way to Planet Rose for food.'

'Planet Rose?' I asked, trying to stand up, starting to feel a bit drunk again rather than a bit sick. Standing up still felt a long way away.

'Karaoke,' Jenny said, looking back towards the garden entrance where Gina and the rest of the gang were starting to bring their party out on to the pavement. 'Will you be OK? Do you want me to take you back to the hotel?'

'Nope,' I said, flinging myself to my feet. Man, these heels were high. 'I might not be able to hold my drink or my man, but what I can hold, is a tune. Point me in the right direction and give me a bloody mic.' I was wobbling a bit but at least I was upright.

'Okaaay,' said Jenny, looking at me nervously. 'Sure you're gonna be OK?'

'I'll be fine,' I slurred, 'let's just get to karaoke. Seriously, I have Singstar, it will be fine.'

'I kinda meant are you sure you're not gonna puke,' Jenny said as I marched off after the girls. 'But apparently you're good.'

We walked until I sobered up and hit a completely different part of town. The shops and hotels of Soho gave way to dark loud bar after dark loud bar, punctuated by little random-looking shops.

'Welcome to the East Village,' Jenny gestured around. The glossy girls looked a little out of place alongside the hipsters and goths that spilled out of the bars and smoked on the pavement, but they really didn't look as if they cared. A couple more blocks away, we piled into a slightly slutty looking bar, all red walls and zebra skin booths with *Black Velvet* belting out of the stereo, with more than thirty of Gina's friends, colleagues, well-wishers and good-looking people picked up along the way. And it seemed that out of all of them, I was the only one half-cut. It was only once I'd been pushed all the way down the narrow bar, I realized they weren't playing *Black Velvet*. Someone was singing *Black Velvet*. Someone really bloody good. This wasn't Singstar territory.

I'll just take it easy, I told myself as I slid onto a bench and tried to look casually through the song list. I won't drink, I'll just sit here and be calm. These people are my potential friends. I don't want them to think I'm some loser lush who got dumped and came to New York to drink herself to death.

'Hey, English,' Gina stood in front of me with an enormous, lurid margarita. 'This is yours. I put me and you down for some Spice Girls. Make you feel at home.'

'Oh, thanks.' One more drink couldn't hurt, could it?

CHAPTER NINE

The next morning, or early afternoon, came all too quickly, given that I couldn't remember anything after my rousing rendition of 'Wannabe'. Glancing around the room (which would have been much easier if it would have just stopped spinning) I saw my dress, my shoes and my handbag all littered across the floor, so at least there didn't appear to be too much collateral damage. As I tried to roll over, the bed covers turned into a straitjacket and alcohol induced kitten-like weakness or not, I had to get them off. Kicking madly, I pushed all the sheets off until I was laid, in my underwear, diagonally across the bare bed.

And that was when I heard the shower.

Nowhere in the room was there evidence of another person. I hurled myself off the edge of the bed, fighting back the urge to throw up, and pulled on the first thing I found, yesterday's white shirt, but the shower stopped. I froze, squatting in the open shirt, hanging onto the edge of the covers. The lock on the bathroom door clunked out of place. Unkindly, the full-length mirror showed me exactly what the person in the shower would be seeing in a couple of seconds and it wasn't pretty. Elegantly messy bob was a bird's nest and Razor had lied. There was definitely a cut-off point when smudging my eye make-up did not just make it look better. And the idea of a woman in a black bra, black pants and white shirt over the top might *sound* sexy, but trust me, right then, it was not. I desperately, desperately tried to think back – who could it be? It wasn't the banker guy, he hadn't even been at karaoke, it could be Gina's friend, Ray, who had performed a show-stopping duet of 'You're the One That I Want' with me, but no, he was definitely gay. What about the short bellhop who had completely wowed us with 'Don't Stop Me Now'. Nope, gay again. Shit, it couldn't be Joe. Not the impossibly gorgeous waiter, Joe. Please no. Please no. Please – too late, the bathroom door opened.

'Afternoon, sleepyhead,' the voice sang happily. 'Now, I had a great time and I think you're a great girl but, well, I have to get going.'

Thank God, it was Jenny.

She stood in front of me, all smiles, fluffy towels and wet hair, laughing her back off.

'You didn't know who I was did you?' she managed to squeeze in between chuckles. 'Shit, Angie, you are the worst drinker I've ever seen. And not to be funny but you're not looking your best either. You might want to work on that before you ride that horse.'

I stood and stared for a moment, waiting for it all to come back to me. Nope. The only thing that was coming back was . . . sushi. I'd eaten sushi. And now, it really was coming back to me. I pushed past Jenny and headed straight for the toilet. Thankfully, this time she didn't just laugh and proved herself to be not just a great life coach but a great hair-holder-backer and glasses of water provider. Once she'd stripped me down and helped me into the shower, I began to feel slightly more human. This was definitely a crash course in friendship.

'Feeling better?' Jenny was back in last night's dress and had pulled her hair into a high ponytail. At least she sounded sympathetic even if she looked as though she might crease herself laughing at any second. 'I guess you learned not to mix your drinks. Those Perfect Tens you were drinking in the Grand so do not mix well with margaritas.'

'I thought they were non-alcoholic,' I said, slathering my face in moisturizer and slipping into a waffle robe. It felt as if dozens of little clouds had attached themselves to my body to carry me back to bed. 'I guess not.'

'Not so much,' Jenny said. 'Listen, I have to get back to the apartment to see Gina off, but meet me in reception at seven – sound OK?'

I nodded. 'Will you tell her I'm sorry I can't be there and about last night and stuff?'

'You don't need to apologize,' Jenny said as she slipped into her stilettos as if they were slippers. A skill I needed to learn. 'Seriously, we had a great night. And I was glad for the excuse to leave when you passed out. It was way past my bedtime.'

'I passed out?' I couldn't believe it. Even during the annual Drink the Bar Dry event at uni, even after five jugs of sangria on holiday, even after eight shots of Sambuca on Louisa's hen night, I had never passed out from drinking. Thrown up, yes, lost some shoes, OK, yes, but never passed out.

'It's OK, Angie,' Jenny said vanishing through the door. 'Consider that a baptism of fire. We're going out again tonight, if you want to come. Just for dinner? Oh and Erin said she would meet you for lunch if you were feeling human. She's so the perfect girl to give you dating advice before your hot date.'

After Jenny had gone and I had puked a few more times, I steeled myself to leave the hotel. It was another beautiful day in Union Square Park. The sun shone just as it had on Sunday. In three short days, the sheen of 'new', of 'other', had worn away leaving something even more exciting to me. It looked familiar. It looked like home. I had walked through that gate, I had used that subway station, I had run full pelt away from that bench. I picked up my (still beautiful) Marc Jacobs bag, swiped on some MAC Lipglass, a wipe of mascara and a bucket load of blusher. Even with one of the worst hangovers I'd ever had, I still looked a million times better than I had pre-makeover. Jenny Lopez was a saint.

Manatus was a sweet looking restaurant, nestled at the top of Bleecker Street in Greenwich Village in between a twenty-four-hour pharmacy and a designer lingerie store. I loved New York. I'd grabbed a cab outside the hotel, against Jenny's express orders to take the subway, but I really didn't like my chances of staying vomit-free on the train, so instead I motored along with my head out of the window. Luckily, I recognized Erin from the window. Petite, long blonde hair tied up in a ponytail, really pretty. No wonder she was Jenny's dating guru, I just couldn't believe she wasn't taken already.

'Hey!' she stood up and welcomed me with a kiss on the cheek as I manoeuvred myself through the tables and prams. 'I was worried you might not recognize me.'

'You don't forget someone you've shared a duet of "Baby, One More Time" with that easily,' I said, quickly sitting and taking a long sip of iced water. 'It's all starting to come back to me now. Tragically, all of it.' I shook my head shamefully.

'It was fun,' Erin said, waving over a waitress for a menu. 'And we were relieved to see you were human. Since Sunday, all I've heard from Jenny is how incredible you are and, not to sound like a total bitch, when you walked into the bar, looking like a model, I kind of found it difficult to feel sorry for you. I mean, who looks that amazing and needs man help?'

'Oh, I, well, me? And I think it's just help in general I need.' I wasn't sure whether to thank her for the compliment or apologize. 'And no one is mistaking me for a model. Really.'

'Well, the hair, the dress, and wow, the shoes,' she said. Luckily her eyes were shining brightly and I knew I'd found another genuine person. 'But when you get drunk, you get drunk, huh? Now what are you having?'

The waiter hovered at our side, waiting patiently.

'Toast,' I said, not even having looked at the menu. I had a feeling Erin didn't waste a lot of time with things as trivial as menus.

'And I'll take the granola with a fresh fruit cup,' she said, handing the menus back to the waiter. 'Anyhoo, Jenny tells me that hot thing you were talking to at the bar in the Grand has asked you out. Did you call him yet?'

'Shit, no,' I said, scrabbling for my wallet. There was his card. Safe and not vomited on. 'I've been in no fit state.'

'OK, call him now,' Erin said, signalling for more coffee. 'Seriously, call him.'

She passed me her phone but I just stared at the numbers. 'What do I say?'

'Hi, it's Angela Clark, we met at the Grand last night,'

she said breezily. 'I just wondered if you still wanted to meet up for dinner tomorrow? How's that?'

'Better than what I had,' I muttered, dialling before I could think about it.

'Tyler Moore,' he answered on the first ring.

'Hi, uh, it's Angela, Angela, erm, Clark?' I stumbled over my own name. Sexy.

'Hello, Angela Clark,' he replied. I couldn't tell if he recognized me or not. 'I was wondering if you'd call.'

He did remember me!

'Of course,' I said, trying to emulate Erin's breezy approach. She made a rolling motion with her hands, I needed to get on with it. 'I just wondered if you still wanted to meet up for dinner?'

'Yeah, tomorrow right,' he said. It sounded as though he was leaning forwards, flexing those muscles. Oh, dear. 'How about the Mercer Kitchen at eight?'

'That sounds great,' I said. I'd done it! I'd got a date! 'Shall I meet you there?'

'Perfect, that'll give me time to go home and change,' he said. 'See you in the bar at eight, Angela Clark.' And he was gone.

'So, you're going?' Erin asked, tapping her feet under the table.

I nodded and bit my lip. 'We're meeting at the Mercer Kitchen at eight. Is that good?'

'That's really good,' she approved as our food arrived. 'Mercer Kitchen is a great first date. Low lighting, great food, cool people and lots of potential for after date drinking. That's a good pick.'

I nibbled on a piece of dry toast. Maybe this wouldn't be as terrifying as I had thought. 'What's the dress code, is it posh?' I asked, worrying slightly. I couldn't afford to go shopping again.

'Mmm, lots of after work suits and trendy girls but

nothing too try-hard,' she said shrugging. 'You'll be just fine in a cute dress or jeans and a cool shirt. He'll probably just be in his suit.'

'He said he was going home to change,' I said, gingerly nibbling at my toast.

I could keep it down. I could keep it down.

'Really? Hope he doesn't show up dressed like Fabio or something,' Erin laughed. Seeing the fear in my eyes, she stopped with a little cough. 'Sure he won't. Now, New York dating basics?'

'Definitely,' I nodded. 'Dating basics in general. I don't know how much Jenny told you . . .'

'More or less everything,' Erin said. 'And what she didn't know, you filled in last night. I'm guessing I know more about your sex life than your ex.'

I blanched and swapped the toast for the tea again. The waitress had topped it up with hot water making it weak as wee but I drank it anyway. 'Sorry.'

'No need, I have to have all the facts before I take on a pupil,' she said. As Erin reached out for the honey I noticed her fingers were completely decked out in diamonds – solitaires, eternity rings, trilogy rings, every finger except her ring finger. 'And believe me when I tell you I know *everything*. You were really quite graphic.'

'Oh, God,' I rubbed my forehead trying to remember exactly what I'd told her. Maybe I hadn't remembered everything. 'Go on then.'

Over the next hour and several cups of coffee for her and weak, weak tea for me, Erin, my answer to Dr Laura crossed with a head cheerleader, briefed me on the dating dos and don'ts of New York City. A beginner's guide to The Rules. Do let him pay if he offers, don't forget to bring your credit card in case he doesn't. Do ask him questions about himself but don't ask about exes. You can talk about jobs but don't push financial questions, you don't want to come across money hungry. If he asks you about your relationship history, give him the facts but not the details. Should the date go really well, you can accept a second date then and there, but since the date was on a Thursday, I was, under no circumstances, to accept a date for Friday or Saturday night. Saturday daytime maybe, Sunday, fine. It all seemed a little bit unnecessary.

'You just don't want to reveal anything that would put him off. And I mean anything at all,' she said with incredible seriousness, ticking off her points on her diamond laden fingers. 'Don't be too funny, guys like funny but they don't want to marry a comedian, right? The guy is supposed to be the funny one. Don't overeat, if he orders for you, all the better. Don't drink too much, at best he'll think you're an easy lush. At worst he'll bail altogether.'

'You mean it's worse to have a man ditch me than sleep with me and then never call again?'

'Oh honey, this is New York,' Erin shook her head. 'Getting him as far as the bedroom is half the battle – fingers crossed you've got *some* skills there, and then there's a chance he'll take you out for a second spin. It's hard, but if you're a really great lay, you can change a first impression. Sometimes.'

'Okaaaaaay,' I felt myself colour up. 'I'm not sure I have that many "skills" so I'd just better not drink too much.'

'Hmm. Well these are just the dinner rules, there's a whole heap of other rules for when you start sleeping with him. But basically, don't screw on the first date. Ever.'

'Not a problem, I'm sure. So since it seems I know absolutely nothing about dating or men, tell me everything else I need to know.'

Listening to Erin's instructions, helpful, well-intentioned and requested as they were, was a little bit like being given driving instructions, so I'd more or less lost her by the third turn. Now, rather than being a bit worried about my date with Tyler, I was scared shitless. While she was clarifying how far I was allowed to 'go' if I wanted to see Tyler again I was too busy trying not to get caught looking at the man in the corner of the restaurant. He was hiding behind his battered Murakami novel, emerging only to fiddle with his iPod and order more coffee. Something about his messy black hair and vivid green eyes was vaguely familiar, but I wrote it off as him just being really, really hot.

'So as long as you play by The Rules, you'll be fine,' Erin carried right on, not even noticing that she had completely lost my attention. 'And it's not like you're wanting this guy to marry you right now is it, you just want some fun, yeah?'

'Um, yes, nothing serious,' I said, trying to push away the idea of myself and Tyler in Tiffany's, Tyler on one knee, me crying and everyone clapping. 'Erin, can I ask you a question?'

'Of course,' she said. 'What kind of teacher would I be if I wasn't open to criticism?'

'Oh, nothing like that,' I said quickly. 'I was just wondering, well, I was just wondering why you aren't married? I know it's not the law to be married, but you're just a complete dating encyclopedia and you're so perfect looking and you're so nice and . . .'

'I was married,' she said simply, holding out her right hand. 'I was married when I was twenty-one to the sweetest guy you ever met.' She presented one of the rock-like solitaires for inspection. 'But by the time I turned twenty-three, he had grown up into a complete shit. Cheating on me with everything that moved.'

'I'm sorry,' I said, not really knowing where to put myself. 'I guess it's definitely better to be single than in a bad marriage.'

'Mmm, well, I'm not done yet,' she sighed, looking at her rings. 'And then I was engaged to a hotel owner. That's this one,' she held out a beautiful sapphire and diamond eternity band, 'but it was a total rebound relationship, you know, so I called it off a month before the big day. And when I was twenty-nine, I married Joel, my hairdresser.' The diamond trilogy ring.

'Oh,' I said quietly. She clearly *was* the person to go to for advice on how to get a man down the aisle, just not how to avoid repeat trips.

'But we both knew it wouldn't work, so I took off,' she said thinly, tipping her head to one side. 'I won't do it again.'

'Wow,' I didn't really know what else to say. All of a sudden I had a little less faith in The Rules.

'Don't get me wrong, I love to date and I hope I'll meet someone to maybe have kids with, but I don't think I'll get married again. It's not a problem, I've got a great career and fantastic friends. I think it just took me too long to realize I don't need a man to validate me.'

'I think that's so cool,' I said. 'I feel really silly now though.'

'No way,' Erin laughed. 'I really hope my friends do find nice guys to marry and settle down with, I just don't worry about it as much as some other people. I've got a successful PR company, two healthy divorce settlements and I go on great dates all the time, it's just, I'm thirty-seven and I'm just not prepared to settle any more.'

'Firstly, you are never thirty-seven,' I gaped. I had her down as Jenny's younger friend and Jenny was no candidate for Botox. 'And secondly, do you think I'm being silly, going on this date? Should I just take time to be me?'

'Do you want to go on the date?' she asked.

I thought about it for all of a split second. 'Yes, I do.'

'Then you should go, have fun,' she said, fishing a beautiful Chanel wallet out of her handbag. 'Just don't let it be everything to you. Jenny said you're a writer, right?'

'I want to be,' I shrugged. 'All I'm writing right now is a sort of, well, a diary.'

'But your diary right now must be fascinating!' she said, flicking through business cards. 'I represent *The Look* magazine and they're always looking for bloggers to post on their site. It's not much but it could get a mention in the magazine and who knows who might see it. Want me to set up a meeting?'

'God, yes!' I said, already picturing myself in Starbucks, tapping away, annoying people with my dramatic sighs. 'If anyone was interested I'd love to write for them.'

'Well, let me talk to some people when I'm there later,' Erin said, tossing a couple of bills on the table and waving away my protest. 'And I'll let you know how it goes tonight. You're coming for dinner tonight, aren't you?'

'Only if you promise not to let me drink any of those awful margaritas,' I grimaced. Just thinking about them made me look around for the ladies' loo.

With two quick kisses and a 'call me' Erin was gone. None of the waiters seemed to mind that we'd been sitting for well over an hour without ordering anything but tea and coffee top-ups, but I asked for a hot chocolate anyway. Pulling out my notebook and hotel room pen, I started to scribble my thoughts. God, imagine writing an online diary for *The Look* magazine! Maybe it wasn't as internationally well known as *Elle* or as respected as *Vogue*, but it was definitely up there. Note to self, buy some magazines. I found my iPod in the bottom of my bag and scrolled through for some inspirational music. Hmm, shouty rock girls, floppy fringed indie boys or Britney. After my girl power lecture from Erin, didn't it have to be shouty rock girls?

A page into my scribblings, I saw the hot chocolate being placed in front of me. I nodded a thanks, too lost in my rant about how hard dating rules were to understand when I realized whoever had delivered the hot chocolate had sat down opposite me. I looked up slowly to see the cute guy from the corner of the restaurant smiling at me, resting his chin in his palm, elbows firmly on the table.

'Hi,' he mouthed.

I paused my iPod and stared.

'Don't you just wish you could go up to people and say, hey, let me take a look at your iPod?' he said, reaching out and taking mine from the table. The earbuds popped out onto my notebook. 'That way, you would know whether or not to ask that person out right away. Say, they were listening to . . . angsty lesbians,' he looked up at me. He had a sexy pale skin, dark eyes thing happening, as if he was pretty much nocturnal. 'Most men would be scared off. But some other men would go back to the artists page and look for some other, more encouraging signs, like . . . hmmm, Justin Timberlake?'

'It's a good song,' I defended weakly. Even I didn't believe me.

'Well, the ladies love Justin,' he said and carried on scrolling. 'And at least it cancels out the lesbian thing.'

'I'm not a lesbian!' Too quick to my own defence.

He looked up again and laughed. 'Great.' He pulled his chair a little closer to the table. 'Oh, this just gets better. Bon Jovi?'

'It's "Living on a Prayer", it's a classic?' I protested weakly, dropping my head to my hands. 'Why aren't you looking at the cool stuff? I like cool stuff too . . .'

'Like what?' he asked, looking back at the iPod. 'And don't say all kinds of music. I hate when people say they like all kinds of music. That just means you don't love any. Well, you've got the new Stills album, I hear they're good.'

'I've seen them live!' I said quickly. 'I saw them in London. They were quite good. I actually prefer the first album though.'

'Always good to get honest feedback,' he held his hand out. 'Alex Reid.'

I took his hand and bit my lip. 'You're in Stills, aren't you?'

'I am.'

'And you saw Justin Timberlake on my iPod.'

'And Bon Jovi.'

This was not how I had imagined meeting the ridiculously sexy lead singer of a super cool New York band. In most of my rock star fantasies, (which were wide and varied), I was usually looking dishevelled and sexy, wearing fishnets, heeled boots and a lot of black eyeliner at some swank after party at an edgy East London bar. Instead I was wearing a pink T-shirt and baggy jeans with bright orange flip-flops, had a crunchy, damp ponytail and hoped, just hoped, that my mascara hadn't completely melted away under my eyes just yet.

'But I do have your album,' I said, trying to buy some cool points. 'And, like, I don't know, The Arctic Monkeys?'

'Very 2006,' he said, handing me back my iPod and settling into his chair. He was still smiling and it was very off-putting. 'But you do have some cool stuff and you did come and see my band.'

'I do and I did,' I confirmed. Please ask me out. Please ask me out. I couldn't be further away from not needing a man to 'validate' me. I needed the good-looking man to ask me out. Fuck you Mark Davis, the hot rock star asked me out. Bwah ha ha.

'And if you bought both albums and a ticket to the gig,' he sighed and ran a hand through his messy, floppy black hair, letting it drop back down over his eyes.

Oh.

'With the weak dollar, I figure you have spent, what, twenty pounds on the band?'

'And I bought a T-shirt,' I said seriously. 'That was twenty on its own.'

'As long as it was from inside,' he said, shaking his head. 'Those sons of bitches outside selling my T-shirts for ten bucks? Don't they know all the money comes from the T-shirts?'

I laughed nervously waiting for him to join in. He did, thank God.

'So, I know you have an . . . "eclectic" taste in music,' Alex started, 'and I owe you about, what, sixty, nearly eighty bucks? But I still don't know your name.'

'I suppose since I know yours,' I said, hoping I was coming across funny and flirty and not nervous and starstruck. The more I thought about it, the more I remembered how good his band really was. 'Angela Clark.'

'And are you on vacation, Angela Clark?' he asked, helping himself to my hot chocolate. I was about to complain but figured I could afford to lose one hot chocolate in the pursuit of a rock star. Well, lead singer of a slightly obscure indie band I'd seen once in Islington. Much closer to rock star than the banker at HSBC who I'd been going out with for ten years.

'Sort of,' I said, not wanting to get into it any more than I had to. 'I'm staying with a friend for a while.'

'Well, if you're not planning to stay in and listen to Justin, would you like to go to a party with me tonight?'

He asked me out. He had asked me out.

And I couldn't go.

'I would really like to,' I said, desperately trying to work out my excuse. 'But I already have plans tonight.'

'Should have guessed,' he said, picking up my pen and opening my notebook to a blank page. 'So here's my number, I've got tickets to the best show on Saturday night and I would love for you to go with me. What do you think?'

'I would love to,' I agreed, watching all of Erin's advice flying out of the window and down the road to tell her what a bad student I was. Accepting a Saturday night date on a Wednesday, shocking.

'Good, I kind of thought you might blow me off.' He stood up and stretched. Skinny jeans, but not too skinny, obligatory faded band T-shirt, just short enough to reveal his flat stomach when he stretched, accessorized by a thin trail of black hair tracing a path from his belly button to his waistband. And of course, sunglasses. He dropped his book into a leather satchel so battered, I was afraid to let my Marc Jacobs catch sight of such appalling abuse. 'If your friend hadn't left when she did, I was going to give up. Who listens to all that bullshit?'

'What bullshit?' I asked, distracted by his oddly muscly biceps. I guessed from playing guitar. Again, oh.

'Yeah, seriously,' he said as he walked away. 'Don't

listen to her, dating rules are bullshit. Engaged three times and not married? Not the best person for advice.'

I felt my mouth drop open. He had heard all of it? 'But how could you hear? You had your iPod on?'

'So you had noticed me.'

So bloody cocky.

'Anyway, Max Brenner's at Union Square on Saturday – about seven? It's kinda touristy but it's the best hot chocolate in town. No offence to this place.' He gave the waitress a puppy dog smile on the way out. I watched her visibly wilt as he strode past the window without a second look.

And with that, I was in love.

Again.

CHAPTER TEN

Vanessa was on the concierge desk as I blew into the lobby, the overpowering whiff of the scented candles already feeling like home.

'Hey, Vanessa. Is Jenny around?'

She nodded. 'Sure, she's in the back. We have this band staying and they've decided she's their favourite concierge in the whole of for ever. You want to go bust her out of hiding?' Vanessa buzzed me through the seamless, invisible door and into the employee lounge where I saw Jenny's high ponytail peeping over the top of a squishy sofa.

'You'll never ever guess what,' I yelled across the room. 'I've only bloody found myself a rock star . . . Jenny?'

Rounding the sofa I stopped short. Jenny was red, blotchy and her mascara had run all down her pretty face.

'You're crying,' I said, stating the bloody obvious.

'Hey, that's great,' she sniffed, rubbing her face on the arm of her black shirt. 'Tell me all about it.'

'No, you tell me,' I said, sitting beside her. 'What's wrong?'

'Oh, it's stupid.' She tried to smile but just succeeded in letting some more tears slip out. 'I saw Jeff. My ex.'

'Oh,' I said, not really knowing what else to say.

'Well, what happened? Did he say anything?'

'Nothing good,'

'What a shit!' I shook my head and sat down beside her.

'Uh-uh,' Jenny shook her head sadly. 'I'm the shit. I cheated on him.'

'Really?' Jenny wasn't a cheater, she was such a nice, considerate person who cared horribly about other people. It wasn't possible. 'You did?'

'Yeah, I was really, really stupid,' she sighed, rubbing her forehead. 'And he just came by to accidentally let it slip that he's seeing someone else.'

'But, I mean, you broke up with him for someone else?' I tried to make sense of it in my head without sounding judgemental but it was hard. Turned out I was pretty judgemental.

'No, I got really drunk, slept with Joe from the hotel and then I told my boyfriend because I felt so guilty,' Jenny said numbly. 'So he called me a whore, kicked me out and I moved in with Gina. I never wanted to break-up, I just made a mistake and there was no way to take it back.'

'Oh.'

'I know what you must be thinking,' she said quietly.

'Honestly, I don't know what I'm thinking,' I said, squeezing her hand. 'But I can only go on what *I* know about you, which is that you're lovely.'

'Oh, God!' Jenny burst out crying loudly. 'I miss him so much.' She dropped slowly sideways into my lap. Not knowing what else to do, I gently combed my fingers through her ponytail and stayed silent until she stopped sobbing. It was a long five minutes before Jenny let out a big sniff and pulled herself up. She smiled and squeezed my hands in hers.

'I know you must be thinking I'm a complete slut, but honestly, it wasn't like that,' she said earnestly. 'It's not something I do. Sometimes people just make mistakes. I wish I could make Jeff see that I would do anything to get him back. Anything.'

'If it's meant to be, he'll realize eventually,' I offered, but I didn't know if it was true.

'Yeah,' Jenny nodded. 'What do you say we go get gussied up and celebrate your rock star? I could use a drink.'

I smiled and took her hand. 'Sounds like a plan.'

The celebratory night on the town I'd anticipated quickly dissolved into a strained silent meal at a neighbourhood restaurant near Jenny's apartment. Between Jenny's frequent teary trips to the bathroom, punctuated by several dirty Martinis and torrents of filth aimed at the band staying at The Union who had decided that Jenny was in fact not a concierge but their own personal plaything, my delayed hangover and the details of Erin's failed pitch for a new cosmetics client, the night was a complete nightmare. Three Cosmos later and tongues were loosening, even if things weren't exactly picking up.

'If someone cheated on you, would you take them back?' Jenny asked, drawing the burned orange peel across the surface of her drink. 'And I don't mean, like, had a relationship, I mean a one off.'

I pursed my lips and sat back. I really didn't want to get into a 'once a cheater, always a cheater' conversation.

'I don't know,' Erin said, sipping her drink. 'If I cared

about him, then no. But if I would be prepared to cheat on him, then yes.'

'I took a boyfriend back when he cheated,' Vanessa said. 'And he cheated again and again. I think once they know they can get away with it, they'll cheat on you as long as you'll let them. I know it's a cliché but it's true.'

'Hmm,' Jenny looked at me sideways. 'What do you think, Angela? If your ex turned up right now with a bunch of roses and an apology, what would you do?'

'I don't know,' I said, staring hard at my glass. 'I suppose I'd just send him right back where he came from.'

'No, you wouldn't,' Jenny shook her head and downed her drink. 'You'd take him back in a heartbeat. You know it.'

'Wow,' I bit my lip. 'Where did the anti-Oprah come from?'

'Jesus,' Erin said, putting the cocktail menu down and standing up. 'Welcome to the dark side, Angela. Meet Drunk Jenny.'

I looked at my new friend, her head resting on the edge of the bar, her shoulders drooped.

'Deep depression, check. Determined to bring everyone else down, check. Won't quit until she's offended everyone she's ever met, even when she's a new friend and she's celebrating getting a great job, check,' she shrugged on her coat. 'I'm not hanging around for this sweetheart. She'll be fine tomorrow'

Erin kissed me and Vanessa on the cheek and slapped Jenny on the backside on her way out. 'Buck up doll or that one night stand is going to cost you more than just a boyfriend.'

'This is so the opposite of fun,' Vanessa sighed, finishing up her drink and making to leave. 'I'm sorry,

Angela, I can't do this again. Some friends of mine are going down to Bungalow, why don't you come? There's no point when she's like this.'

'No, I'll stick it out,' I shook my head, not sure what sticking it out would mean, 'but thanks.'

'You sure? Lots of hot guys and my friend can totally get us in?' Vanessa gave me half a second to change my mind and then she was gone, waving as she went.

I looked back at Jenny.

'I'm so pathetic,' she mumbled into her folded arms. 'You should leave me here.'

'I should, but I guess I won't,' I said. I had some tolerance for self-pity but not enough. 'Does this happen often?'

'Only if I think about him,' she replied, still face down.

'And do you think about him often?' My turn to finish my drink and put on my coat.

'All the time,' same muffled whine.

'Have you thought about putting your own advice into practice at all?' Pulling her up off her stool was harder than it should have been given she weighed as much as a flea.

'Thought about it,' she said, allowing me to slide her jacket onto her shoulders. 'Never managed it. I don't deserve to be over him.'

'Look,' I said, staring her hard in the eyes. 'You did something wrong and you might never get back with your ex, but if I've learned one thing from the last week, it's that there's running away, wallowing and, hopefully, a happy medium called getting on with life. And you're going to have to get on with life, otherwise, you have no authority as my life coach and then where will I be?'

'I suppose you do need me,' she sniffed. 'I just can't work out *how* to get over him.'

'Have you tried running halfway around the world? It works wonders.' I grimaced as we shuffled out of the bar. 'And I've got to say, right now, running away looks a lot better than your moping.'

'But don't you lie awake at night, wishing he was with you?' she said, tipping her head back and leaning into me.

'Actually, no,' I said, the fresh evening air hitting me as we staggered down the steps outside. 'We had really different sleep patterns anyway so we didn't often go to bed together. I can't recommend being dog tired at the end of every day enough as a break-up recovery system.'

'You so know what I mean,' she slurred, throwing herself into the road without even looking for the walk sign. 'Don't you want him with you? You know, *with* you? Just to feel the weight of him on top of you?'

'Oh.' I walked a little further in silence. 'Well, I sort of haven't felt that for a while anyway. We didn't have the best sex life ever. I suppose if I think about it that way, I've been on my own for a long time . . .'

As I thought about how long I had been on my own, I realized I really was on my own. Jenny wasn't beside me. Looking back, I spotted her hanging in the doorway of a diner, shouting at someone.

'Turn it up!' I heard her yell as I scurried back down the street. 'Turn the goddamned song UP!'

'Get lost!' The guy behind the counter turned away as I grabbed for Jenny's arm. 'Control your friend, lady,' he muttered at me.

'Hey, Jenny,' I pulled her gently away from the door, 'come on, let's get you home.'

'This song was on all the time when we were dating,' she said, allowing me to move her down the street and towards her doorway. 'I hated it.'

'Jenny, listen to me,' I said, fumbling in Jenny's handbag for her keys while she slumped against the doorframe. 'You've got to snap out of this. Would Oprah behave like this after too many cocktails?'

'Fuck Oprah,' she said, falling through the door and up the stairs to the second-floor apartment.

'God, this is serious,' I said to myself. It didn't take me long to realize that firstly, this is what happens when you spend a lot of time with someone you don't know and secondly, my time in New York was not going to be all hot boys and fabulous shopping.

Bugger.

As I watched Jenny throw herself into a sobbing heap on the sofa, I wondered if this was how I was supposed to be feeling about Mark when in reality, I just felt empty when I thought of him. 'Let's get you into bed,' I said. 'Hopefully, tomorrow, you'll have stopped putting yourself through this, whatever it is. Try and get some sleep.' I felt awful, but I just didn't know what to do and she seemed pretty happy wallowing.

'Hey, Angie, I'm really sorry,' she said as we staggered through the dark apartment towards what I assumed was her bedroom. 'Why don't you stay here tonight? I've got to be back at the hotel in the morning anyway and I don't want you to have to get back on your own.'

'Well, it is late and I am lazy . . .' I pushed Jenny across the giant squishy mattress and dropped down beside her. 'Only on the condition that you promise not to spoon me.'

'I won't spoon if you won't sing.'

'Shut up, Lopez.'

'Night, English.'

* * *

Eventually, after rolling over seven times, the summer sunshine streaming through Jenny's windows forced me to roll out of bed.

'What, I don't even get a kiss?' Jenny mumbled from under the covers.

'Not until you've brushed your teeth.' I stretched and took a look around. Jenny's room was a mess. Aside from piles of self-help books peeking out from underneath half a dozen half empty coffee cups, every surface in the room was taken up by shoes. There were shoes in boxes, shoes spilling out of the wardrobe, even shoes on display in the bookcase – half sling-backs, half self-help books. The walls were lined with hundreds of photos in clip frames. Several were dedicated to Jenny and a good-looking blond guy who I guessed was Jeff. No wonder she didn't have a new boyfriend, the walls of her room were like a shrine to her ex.

'So, I was thinking,' Jenny started, holding her arm across her eyes to block out the sunlight.

'Really? I didn't see an awful lot of evidence of that last night.'

'Shut up before I change my mind.' She sat up, looked down at last night's clothes and shook her head at herself. 'Like I said, I was thinking. So, Gina left yesterday and won't be back for at least three months, if she comes back at all, and I can't afford to maintain what you can see is a very expensive shoe habit unless I find a new roommate. I figure you can't afford to stay at The Union for ever, and I don't think you want to go home yet. You want to be my roomie?'

'Wow, Jenny, really?' Moving in to an apartment would be huge. It would mean I was staying. 'I don't know . . .'

'But you've already proved that you can get me home

safely when I'm wasted. Would you want me wandering around alone on your conscience?' Jenny said. 'And I'm really sorry about the whole freak out thing last night. Promise that won't happen again. I so need to get over Jeff.'

'Have you thought about taking some of his pictures down?' I suggested. They really did make a gorgeous couple. Jenny's big dark eyes and wild curly hair contrasting against Jeff's close blond crop and crinkly blue Robert Redford eyes. 'I hear that helps.'

'Yeah, not gonna happen just yet,' she shook her head. 'Unless I had a new roomie to take pictures of? So, you in?'

'If you take the pictures down,' I nodded and held out my hand.

'Well, OK,' she sighed, 'but only because I already gave your room away at The Union from tomorrow, so if you don't move in here you're pretty much screwed.'

CHAPTER ELEVEN

The pain of moving out of The Union was cushioned slightly by the fact that Jenny's apartment was practically a two-bed mini version of the hotel. Every single thing that wasn't screwed down had been 'borrowed' by Jenny and Gina.

'Welcome home!' Jenny said, waving her arms around the place. The whole apartment worked out to be the size of my room at The Union, but it was nice. Hardwood floors, creamy walls, a kitchenette in the living room and a hallway that led off to three doors.

'OK, so this is the bathroom, only one person will actually fit in, so you take a quick look,' Jenny opened the door closest to the living room. I peeped in, toilet, basin, shower cubicle, Rapture towels, robes and product everywhere. 'And here's your room. You're lucky, Gina was the one with the view.'

Jenny opened the door on my new room. It was perfect. A huge double bed took up most of the floor space, leaving a tiny desk-cum-dressing table nestled in next to a hanging rail for clothes. Gina had more or less stripped the room bare, but the bed was made (Union bedding, I noticed) and a little TV was perched on the desk. I placed my bags carefully on the bed and manoeuvred past it to the window. We were seven floors up on Lexington Avenue, just by 39th Street and when I craned my neck, I could see the Chrysler Building, pushing up into the early evening sky. So beautiful. Below, people wandered around, the hustle and bustle of their working day left behind as they meandered, enjoying their lunch hour in the sunshine.

Inside I was grilling Jenny on the sexual preferences of my favourite celebrities who had stayed at her hotel.

'Vince Vaughn?'

'Straight.'

'Owen Wilson?'

'Super straight.'

'That really cute boy off that TV show I like?'

'Flaming.'

'Does flaming mean straight?'

'Nu-uh.'

'Oh.'

'So, what do you think?' Jenny asked, leaning against my doorframe. 'Not bad, huh? Gina's cousin sublet to us, we got so lucky.'

'Jenny, it's gorgeous,' I said. 'I can't believe how lovely. You only ever hear horror stories about New York apartments on TV.'

'Yeah, well, I won't deny that you might see a roach before you leave,' Jenny admitted. 'But they're few and far between. It's a good building. But now,' she held out a hand and pulled me up off the bed as the buzzer went. 'We celebrate!'

Since Jenny's idea of a celebration was an afternoon of pepperoni pizza and some beers sitting on her living-room floor watching *America's Next Top Model*, I knew we were going to get along just fine. We ate, we bitched and she filled me in on her New York apartment history, rat-infested flatshare on the Lower East Side before it got trendy, studio in a Harlem building that was converted into luxury apartments, a one-bed in Chelsea with her ex, and then this place with Gina. Not too bad, she assured me.

'I've only ever lived with Mark, how tragic is that?' I said, chewing a slice thoughtfully. 'Apart from at college but even then, we were together all the time. God, that's so pathetic.' I felt the gloom settling around me.

'You know I think you're amazing, right?' Jenny started, flipping the tops off two more beers and passing one my way. 'And that coming here to work out what you want out of life is great. Really great.'

'I feel like there's a but coming,' I said, taking a precautionary swig.

'Well, not exactly, but I think the best way to get over your Mark, is to talk about it,' Jenny said cautiously. 'Not just push it away. Otherwise it pops up when you're not expecting it and makes you feel crappy.'

'I suppose,' I mumbled through my pizza. That was exactly what I'd been trying not to do. My Mark issues were happily between me and my computer at that exact moment in time. 'But whenever I think about him, no matter how great I feel, I just come crashing down. I was going to ask you about that actually. I'm normally a very stable person.'

'Stable, or just not feeling one thing or the other? Sometimes we get so used to not really feeling anything, just going with the flow, that we forget how it feels to be really happy or really sad. And if Mark is the only guy you've ever gone out with, I'm guessing heartbreak is a new one to you too.'

'I don't think I'm heartbroken,' I shook my head. 'He

was cheating on me, I'm best off out of it. Besides, I think you're right. We hadn't really been happy together for the longest time, I'd just shut myself off to it and convinced myself it was normal. I'm probably just still jetlagged if anything.'

I reached out for more pizza and looked up at Jenny. She was staring at me intently with the same sympathetic look she'd given me the morning I threw up.

'Angela, you're totally brave and a genuine hero,' she began, 'but it's OK to be upset about this. You put all your trust and ten years of your life into that relationship, even if they weren't all great, and he cheated on you, no one gets over something like that in three days.'

'I'm OK,' I said. Here came those crashing lows again. 'I've never had a break-up to get over before. Maybe I'm just really really good at it?'

'I'm just saying, it's OK not to be OK,' Jenny scooted across the floor. 'You might even feel better if you let yourself get upset. Might even out some of those crazy emotions.'

'I just think, I would never have cheated on him,' I said slowly. 'Even if I'd met someone else, I would never have cheated on him.'

The tears started to come, slowly at first.

'I know, honey,' Jenny said, taking the beer out of my hand. 'You're a good person and you're right, you are better off out of the relationship.'

'But why did he do it?' I wailed. 'Why did he cheat on me? And why doesn't he love me any more?'

I turned to Jenny's shoulder and saturated her T-shirt.

That was what I'd been avoiding. The hair, the make-up, the clothes, they didn't cover up the real me, the me that Mark had spent ten years with and then decided to trade in for a cheap tennis playing tart.

'People fall out of love, Angie,' Jenny said, her voice thick with a few of her own tears. 'It's happened to all of us, it's just going to be a bit of a shock to the system because, well, most people go through it before they get to twenty-seven. You'll be OK though, look at what you've already achieved.'

'Twenty-six!' I bawled, grabbing the beer back and gesticulating wildly with the bottle. It made a brilliant prop. 'And what exactly have I achieved? Mark had known me for ten years and he couldn't love me. Anyone I meet is going to sit down, talk to me for ten minutes and come to the same conclusions he did, new hair or not.'

'That's not true,' Jenny said. 'Did that guy the other night only ask you out because of your hair?'

'He probably thinks I'm a prostitute like the one in the park. Or at least a piss-head English girl on holiday who will be an easy shag.'

'And what did you think about him?' Jenny snatched my beer back again, trying to avoid spillage.

'I thought he was lovely.'

Jenny gave me the look.

'And really hot. And probably quite rich.'

'And you didn't think about hooking up with him?' she asked, raising an eyebrow.

'Yes,' I said. 'I suppose I did. And you told me to!'

'There you go,' she said. 'Maybe he was just thinking, I'd like to get this girl into bed, but you were thinking the same thing! You weren't thinking about marrying him, you just wanted to get laid. That is allowed, you know.'

I was thinking about marrying him a bit, I thought to myself. Probably best not to share that right now.

'But I, I wouldn't know how to just "get laid",' I

panicked, realizing she was right. 'Me and Mark were just awful in the bedroom, I just thought it wasn't the most important thing. What am I supposed to do now I've got to do it with other people?'

'Hey, you don't know that you were awful,' Jenny pointed at me, turning serious. 'A workman is only as good as his tools and, sorry, but if he was getting it from someone else, how were you supposed to keep it going? And FYI, it's totally that important.'

I thought about it for a second. It made sense. Mark hadn't even really tried to get me into bed for months, and even though I knew why, that didn't make me feel better about having to get into bed with anyone else.

'But what if he fell out of love with me because I was so bad in bed?' I went through a mental replay of our last few half-arsed fumblings.

'Then maybe, *maybe*, a little more experience will help, *if* that was a contributing factor,' Jenny said. 'And after ten years together, if that's why he cheated then he's even lower scum than I have him down for right now. The bottom line is, you might never know why he did what he did but you do need to own up to the fact that you're single now and make that work for you.'

'How?' I sighed. And how could the pizza be all gone already? 'I've never had to be single before.'

'You'd never been to New York before but you're making that work,' Jenny said, standing up and vanishing into the freezer. She stood up, displaying a tub of Ben & Jerry's. Truly she had all the answers. 'And you'll make this work. If you have to sit in the apartment and cry for a month, I'll come home with ice cream every day. If you want to go fuck every man on Wall Street, I'll come home every night with condoms. And earplugs. But you will find a way to deal with it.'

I gratefully took a spoon and plunged into the ice cream. 'Thank you,' I whispered and promptly burst into tears.

'Hey,' Jenny rested my head on her shoulder. 'Just so you know, they were pretty extreme examples. I'm going to go roommate from hell on your ass if you really do start bringing every guy in New York home.'

'I don't think I'd be a very good slut. Look at the state of me, I'm supposed to be going on my first date in ten years in, what, three hours? And I'm sat here full of pizza and beer, sobbing on your shoulder about being crap in bed.'

'Shit girl!' Jenny pulled the beer out of my hand again. This was getting annoying. 'You're going to go on the best date anyone ever had, and do not worry. Gina might not be here but I'm kinda an amazing stylist myself. Give me an hour and you will look the absolute shit.'

'Just clean and without pizza sauce around my mouth would be good right now,' I muttered catching sight of myself in the mirror.

The wealth of taxies running past our block had thinned out by the time I emerged onto Lexington looking if not *the* shit then not quite as shit as I had looked an hour or so ago, so I started walking. I couldn't believe I was going on a date. With a beautiful man. In a beautiful pink, silk Marc by Marc Jacobs halter dress. With a smug little smile on my face that was growing every second. And I couldn't believe I'd agreed to meet Alex on Saturday night. Was it really tacky to accept a date with someone when you had another date already lined up? And I'd completely forgotten all of Erin's advice, I hadn't been on a date since Mark had taken me to see *Speed 2* (and I'm not sure that counted as a date, Mark actually watched every second of the film from start to finish), and here I was strutting down the street in New York on my way to dinner with a gorgeous, rich banker. But instead of visualizing myself and Tyler sharing a joke and a bottle of red, all I could see was Mark and that slag laughing theatrically together, holding hands and reading home décor magazines. I fumbled around in my (divine) handbag until I found the crappy old mobile phone Jenny had loaned me and dialled Erin's number.

'Erin White.'

'Hi, Erin? It's Angela Clark?'

'Hey, I was just gonna call Jenny, I have some amazing news,' Erin's cheerful voice was just what I needed to distract me.

'I could use some good news, I'm just on my way to meet Tyler,' I said, keeping an eye and an arm out for a passing cab.

'Oh, awesome. Remember, be interested, ask lots of questions, don't talk too much about your past or exes and don't be too keen. You want to keep him on his toes.'

'That was your good news?' I waved down a lit cab. He swerved dramatically towards me and stopped inches from my Louboutins. Shoe-icide, a fate worse than death. 'Mercer Kitchen? Uh, Mercer Street?'

'No! I am such a retard,' Erin laughed down the crackly line, ignoring my directions to the driver. 'I was at *The Look* today. They want to meet you. Tomorrow.'

'Oh my God, seriously?' I couldn't believe it. 'The editor of *The Look* wants to see me?'

'The online editor, Mary Stein. Can you be there at ten?'

'Yes!' I squealed. 'This is amazing! Thank you so much, Erin.'

'No worries, just be honest. Mary can be a tough cookie but she's cool. Now more importantly, back to your date.'

'I'm a bit worried to be honest,' I peered out of the windows as we took a hard right. Eventually I spotted a sign for West Houston. 'But I'm almost there. Wish me luck.'

'You don't need luck, just stick to The Rules. Bye hon.'

It took a couple of seconds for me to realize which building was the Mercer Kitchen after my cab unceremoniously tossed me out on the middle of Mercer Street, because of the non-existent 'traffic'. After watching a few beautiful people head into a nameless glass door that opened to release delicious smells, loungey music and lots of laughter, I bit the bullet and opened the door for myself. The place was small but crowded with lots of happy looking people. I hoped the relaxed atmosphere would be contagious or at least available in a glass for a reasonable fee. Sitting at the bar, wearing another beautifully cut suit, white shirt and no tie was Tyler. He looked completely at ease, even though he was alone amongst half a dozen cliquey clusters of people, giggling, hugging, touching and kissing. Narrowly avoiding falling down the large staircase in the middle of the room, I sidled around to the bar and raised a hand in hello. Tyler hopped off his stool to welcome me with a kiss on the cheek. He smelt divine, fresh and clean but masculine and delicious.

'Hi,' he said, making eye contact with the barman, pointing at his drink and then holding up two fingers. Ultra smooth. 'I had a last minute panic that you wouldn't know where you were going.'

'I checked with a friend,' I said, settling on the next stool. 'I don't know what the rules are on being late or early or whatever so I just thought, you know, be different, be on time.' I looked at the clock on the wall. 'Or maybe I'm a little bit late. Sorry.'

'It's fine,' he said. 'I was actually a little late. Work overran, I didn't even have time to go home, so really, don't worry about it.'

'You don't live nearby?' I asked, trying to stick to approved topics. 'I mean, near your work?'

'No,' he shook his head making his hair swish. Really, it was just like a men's L'Oréal ad. He was *so* worth it. 'I live uptown, work downtown. Sometimes it's a pain, but I couldn't live downtown again. You still at The Union?'

'No actually, I moved today,' I said. This was going OK, I was having a conversation! 'I'm in Murray Hill at my friend's apartment, 39th and Lexington?'

'Great, I'm on Park, a little further up.' The waiter presented Tyler with our drinks and a bill face down, which he answered with a black Amex. Wow, I'd only ever read about them. 'Hope you don't mind me ordering your drink, they do great cocktails here.'

I took the cocktail graciously and sipped it. Man alive, it was like straight vodka mixed with a drop of Ribena. Maybe I should go slow.

'I think our table should be ready now,' he said, picking up both drinks and standing. I didn't remember him being so tall . . . 'Ready?'

The hostess smiled warmly and guided us to a table in the back corner of the restaurant where we could see absolutely everyone. And absolutely everyone looked as if they were enjoying their food.

'God, I could eat a horse,' I said, taking a menu from

the waitress and hungrily scanning. 'Oooh, have you ever had the burger?'

'I do love a girl that eats,' Tyler laughed, nodding to the waitress and accepting his menu. 'I know everyone says it, but there really is nothing worse than bringing a girl out for dinner and then watching her push a lettuce leaf around her plate.'

I smiled tensely. Was that good or bad? Did he just call me a fatty?

'Honestly,' he went on without looking away from the menu. 'I dated this French model for a while and I swear I never saw her consume more than a Diet Coke.'

And was it usual for a man to start a first date talking about ex-girlfriends? And had he called me a fatty?

'Well, I do eat,' I said, not really knowing where to go. 'What do you recommend?'

'It's all good,' he said, putting his menu down and fixing me with his clear eyes. 'The fish is always great, burgers *are* good. And I like the chicken, but I think, yeah, I'm having the lamb tonight.'

'You come here a lot?' I asked, starting to get the feeling I was not Tyler's one special girl.

'I like to,' he said. 'It's quiet, great food, and always a bunch of interesting people hanging out.'

Oh, he meant me. Sweet. 'In that case I'll have the chicken.'

As he started the small talk rolling, what did I do for a living, what did he do for a living, how long had I been in the city, what sights had I seen, I ran a quick comparison on Tyler and Alex. Alex was sexy and cocky and had the whole I'm-in-a-band thing going on, whereas Tyler was good-looking in a clean-cut, I take care of myself, let me take care of you, sort of a way.

'Oh, well, I'm kind of a venture capitalist,' he said,

after he had ordered for us both. 'But unless you've written some kids' books about banking, I won't even try to explain. Not to be patronizing but it's impossibly dull. And I don't want to put you off already.'

'That's OK,' I said, brushing my hair behind my ears and ripping apart my warm bread roll as soon as it was put on my side plate. 'I'm not a numbers person. I only really do words. And words for children at that.'

'That saves us a really boring fifteen minutes,' he said, pushing the olive oil towards me for dipping. 'What is more exciting, is what you're doing in New York? How do you know your friend?'

'Oh, slightly longer story.' I swallowed my bread in preparation. 'Without going into a lot of off-putting detail, I broke up with . . . someone, so I decided to take a holiday and I'd never been to New York. I met my friend, the girl I'm staying with, in my hotel. She was looking for a roommate, I was looking for a room and so, here I am.'

'Wow,' Tyler looked bemused. 'You just upped and came to New York? Must have been a bad break-up.'

'I'm not supposed to tell you about it,' I said. 'My friend said no specifics about exes until the fourth date.'

Tyler laughed, nodding. 'I do love The Rules. You can't even tell me if I ask?'

'You might not want to know.' I paused, trying to weigh up Erin's sacred advice over Tyler's warm smile and crinkly eyes. Our first course appeared over his shoulder. Maybe if I told him while he was distracted by lamb. I would have to tell him eventually, anyway, wouldn't I? It would surely come out before the black Amex funded wedding . . .

'Go for it,' he said, making room for his plate. 'I'm asking.'

'OK, but don't you dare walk out before you've eaten.'

I didn't want to pick up my fork until I'd got the whole story out. Even the short version. 'I found my boyfriend having sex with this girl he'd been seeing in the back of our car at our best friends' wedding, screamed at the bride and made her cry, broke the groom's hand with my shoe and more or less ruined the wedding. Then I ran away to New York. How does that grab you?'

'And I thought a children's writer would be shy and retiring,' he whistled. 'Now it's getting interesting.'

'I suppose before Saturday, I could have been called shy and retiring,' I said, cutting into the chicken. 'But seeing your boyfriend's boxer shorts around his ankles while you're in a grand's worth of bridesmaid dress will really give you a kick up the arse.'

'Wait a minute,' Tyler put down his knife and fork. 'You're talking about this Saturday? Saturday five days ago?'

I nodded thoughtfully. 'It seems such a long time ago to me now, but I think that's why I'm not supposed to tell you. Are you freaking out?'

'Maybe I'll get around to that later. At the moment I'm still trying to work out why you came to New York when you didn't know anyone,' he said. Knife and fork still down. 'Jesus, all I did on Saturday was go for a run and get a haircut.'

Uh-oh.

'I accept that it was possibly an extreme reaction. I don't know, I just always wanted to go to New York, my boyfriend, my ex, never wanted to visit America, he hates to fly, so I thought this would be the perfect time to just get away,' I said, going in for the mashed potato. If this was the only meal we were ever going to have I was going to eat it all. The mashed potato was amazing. 'How do they get the potatoes so creamy without them going runny with the gravy? Wow.'

'I can't imagine ever doing anything like that,' Tyler said. He reached for his fork, good sign. 'The furthest I've gone when I've been pissed off after a break-up is the China Town Ice Cream Factory.'

'Well, they were extreme circumstances,' I said observing him closely. Had I blown it? He picked up his knife. Phew.

'So this would be your first date since you broke up?' The knife hovered.

'Yes,' I admitted, my eyes glued to the indecisive cutlery. 'I just, I, well, honestly? I wasn't really planning on going on dates or anything, but you seemed, you know, nice and normal so I just thought, why not?'

'Well, I'm glad you did,' he said. Knife back on the plate. 'Your ex's loss is Manhattan's gain.'

'Not all of Manhattan,' I shook my head, 'my roommate has laid down some fairly strict ground rules about that. The truth is, I haven't really ever dated so I've got a lot to learn, I suppose.'

'I think there's a whole lot more I could learn from you,' Tyler gave me a small smile and sliced up his lamb. 'Want to try?'

And before I knew it, there I was eating food from his fork, just like in the movies.

A flourless Valrhona chocolate cake, two cappuccinos and a moonlit stroll through Soho later and the date was over. And I was sort of gutted.

'I had a great time tonight,' Tyler said, holding his arm out for a cab. 'Best date with a children's writer who broke a guy's hand with a stiletto I ever had.'

'Can I ask you something?' I asked, clutching Tyler's free hand. Even holding hands felt weird, Mark and I hadn't been a hand holding couple. He nodded as a cab pulled over to the kerb. 'Do you date a lot? I'm not going all *Fatal Attraction* on you, I just haven't really spoken to many men since I got here so I don't really know how this works.'

He held the door open for me to climb in and then slipped in beside me before he answered. '39th and Lex?' he said to the driver, then turned to me. 'I guess, honestly, I date kind of a lot. I haven't had a serious girlfriend in about two years and it's not for the lack of looking.'

'OK,' I said, staring straight ahead. He was being honest, that was good. Wasn't it?

'But I don't date a lot of people at once,' he went on. 'And you usually know after one or two dates if it's going somewhere.'

'Really?' I asked, turning towards him. He was even handsome in cab-lit profile. 'It usually takes me ages to make my mind up about, well, anything.'

'It sounds to me like you've been making some pretty snap decisions lately,' he said, brushing my hair behind my ear. 'And I for one am really glad about that.'

'Maybe that's another part of the new me,' I said, not really knowing where to look any more. 'But then again, I'm a Libran, indecisive, I suppose that will come out in the end . . .'

Before I could waffle on any more, he cut me off with a soft, gentle kiss. I closed my eyes and let him kiss me in the back of the cab, his right hand firmly holding my cheek, sliding back around my neck and into my hair. I could feel his left hand pressing against my thigh. For my first kiss with another man in ten years, it felt pretty good.

'So can I see you again?' Tyler asked as he broke away.

'Mmm,' I nodded, trying to control my breathing, I'd forgotten how delicious kisses could be. 'I would really like that.'

'How about Sunday evening?' He still hadn't moved his hand and my whole back was tingling. 'Something fun, maybe the movies?'

'Sounds great,' I mumbled. Please kiss me again.

'Fantastic. I'll call you.' He combed his fingers through the hair at the nape of my neck making me shiver all over.

'Or I'll call you? I mean, you can call me or I'll call you or whatever,' I'd more or less forgotten the date let alone The Rules.

'I'll call you, I promise,' he said. And then he came back in for a second kiss, complete with tongues and a little bit of touching up. I did think he might have brushed my boob by accident, but I kind of hoped it was accidentally on purpose. The cab pulled up outside the apartment well before I was ready to stop but I knew, despite Jenny's advice, I should just go in alone. One more kiss (closed mouths, but firm pressure) and I let myself out of the cab. My first date had been a success, at least as far as I was concerned.

'So, how'd it go?' Jenny was at the door before I'd even managed to work my key into the lock. She stood in front of me in pyjamas, hair in a towel turban, face mask on and feet in Bliss Softening Socks. 'Oh my God, look at you, you kissed him!'

I felt myself blush from head to toe.

'Oh my God, you did!' she shrieked, jumping up and down. 'Give me two secs.'

I let myself in and collapsed onto the sofa. It was such a strange feeling! A couple of moments later, Jenny reappeared minus the towel and with a peachy fresh complexion, softening socks still very much in evidence.

'So, tell me everything,' she said, bringing over a packet of Oreos and two cans of Diet Coke. 'All the gory details. Did he pay? Was he amazing? Are you seeing him again?'

'Um, yes, yes, lovely, and yes, Sunday!' I said, staring ahead, slightly dazed still. 'It was really nice, we just talked for ages and ate and then wandered through Soho for a little bit and then got a cab. And he asked me to go to the cinema on Sunday night, he's going to call me.'

'Wow,' Jenny said, curling up and splitting her cookie in half to lick out the centre. 'Sounds like the perfect first date. I'm so jealous.'

'It was really nice,' I admitted. 'It still feels weird though. I just feel all, I don't know, light and fluffy and like I want to scrunch myself all up into a ball and then explode or something.'

'Well, let me see,' Jenny went back in for the Oreos, not even bothering to split and lick, 'you just went on a date with a hot Wall Street banker who arranged another date with you on the spot *and* you've got a date with a hot guy in a band who picked you up at brunch. I'd say not only are you dating but you are dating pretty well. You're born to this honey!'

I sipped my Coke and shook my head. 'I'm not going to say it doesn't feel nice because it does. And I was a bit freaked out about kissing Tyler, but it was lovely actually. Really good.' I took another sip and then a deep breath. 'And when I was talking to Alex, I swear, I felt better than I had with Mark in, well, in for ever. I don't know, it's probably just a big rebound reaction thing.'

'Maybe it is,' Jenny shrugged, 'but there's nothing

wrong with that. No one's proposing, dating doesn't have to be totally serious. Unless Tyler turns out to be a millionaire.'

'He had a black Amex,' I said, grabbing her arm.

'Get the ring!' she screeched. 'Get the ring!'

CHAPTER TWELVE

Thankfully by morning, the city had the decency to cool down half a degree so I decided to walk to *The Look*. I grasped Erin's directions in one sweaty palm, crossed Park and then made my way up and across to Times Square. The streets slowly became busier and busier, until I was really just being pulled along by the swarm. Even in the high heat of summer, it was heaving. I stared around, taking in the giant billboards, the garish restaurant signs, the rolling news tickers and tried to spot my destination without getting taken out by a Japanese tourist and his huge camera bag. I felt tiny. Everything looked as though the real world had been scanned, had the contrast turned right up and then enlarged by 500 per cent. It made Piccadilly Circus look positively anaemic. After I had crossed the same road about five times, I spotted a steady stream of very thin, very beautiful women dressed head to toe in black, heading into a narrow black glass doorway back where I had come from. The small tasteful sign next to the door? Spencer Media. Ah. Of course.

The building was tucked away in a corner off Broadway, a beautiful art deco building that stretched high into the Manhattan skyline, past the animated billboards and brightly lit ads. As I rode higher and higher in the lift, I passed my weight from foot to foot. Erin had said (*my* editor!) was called Mary Stein, but I had no idea what she was expecting. I'd printed out my last few diary entries and printed off the Amazon records of some of my books in lieu of a portfolio. Hopefully she wouldn't just laugh me out of the office.

Mary's secretary ushered me into her office after a quick silent appraisal. Apparently I passed and was offered a coffee before being left alone. The office was bright and light, with stunning views of the city. I stood staring out of the window and promised myself I'd go to the Empire State Building as soon as I'd finished.

'Angela Clark?'

It was Mary. She hardly looked like a magazine editor, let alone a super cool web editor. Mary was easily in her fifties, no taller than five feet, had a short grey bob and just looked really, really nice.

'Yes.' I stretched my hand out for a firm and welcoming shake. 'You must be Mary.'

She gestured to a seat in front of her desk and then sat herself down. 'Erin tells me you're a writer?'

Straight to business. 'Yes,' I nodded eagerly, bringing out my sales sheets. 'I don't have my portfolio with me right now, but I have some sheets showing the books I've written. They're mostly children's movie tie-in books but I can turn my hand to anything, really.'

'Hmm.' Mary flicked through the pages and then pushed them back at me. Maybe she wasn't going to be so nice. 'I need a blogger. You'll have looked at what we have on the website already so where do you think your blog will fit in?'

She fixed me with a serious gaze. I hadn't looked at the website. Eeep. But praise be for the hateful man in Starbucks, I did know what a blogger was.

'Well, I'm going through a pretty one-of-a-kind situation right now,' I started.

'One-of-a-kind has no appeal to my readers,' she said, already looking away at her flat screen monitor and wheeling her mouse.

'Well, one-of-a-kind in a way, but in another way, it's something every girl has gone through,' I blagged. 'I've split up with my boyfriend of ten years and now I'm dating for the first time.'

'Go on,' she said, still looking away, but the wheeling had stopped.

'Well, I found out he was cheating on me at my friend's wedding, made a bit of a scene and then sort of ran away to New York,' I explained quickly. 'And now I'm dating. Two men. A banker and this guy in a band.' I had to admit, I thought it sounded pretty bloody interesting. Probably even more so if you weren't having to go through it yourself.

'Do you have some sample copy?' she asked, her full attention back with me. 'You're what, Bridget Jones in New York?'

I handed over the print-outs of my diary. 'I'm really not Bridget Jones,' I said. 'I'm not all about dating, I think it's more about finding my feet and finding out who I am again.'

'Hmm,' she said, scanning the copy with pursed lips and a frown. 'You're certainly not Bridget Jones, but there is something here. And it is about dating.'

'OK,' I shrugged. I would write about being a one-armed gypsy horse rider if she would give me a writing job. 'It can be about dating.'

'Tell me more about the break-up. Is it funny? It

sounds funny,' she slapped the pages of diary I'd given her.

OK, suck it up, I told myself. She's going to make you a proper writer. So I went through every detail of the break-up, trying to make it sound funny rather than bursting into tears. Mary stared at me emotionless and silent until I was finished.

'Great. It is funny and I suppose you can write,' she said, 'OK, you write two to three hundred words a day and email it to me. The pay wouldn't be great but it's only on the website. If we go ahead, I'll need a picture of you so find one, but it's fine to keep everyone else anonymous.'

'Oh.' I didn't know what to say. This wasn't the glorious big break moment I'd always envisioned. There was no champagne for one. 'Oh, I just thought, I don't have a work visa. Is that going to be a problem?'

'Are you kidding me?' Mary looked really, really pissed off. 'I can't pay you as staff if you don't have a visa. You may as well just go.'

'But I only just got here on Sunday.' I stood up, desperately trying to get this back. 'And, and, you don't have to pay me! I'll work for free!'

'Free?' She raised an eyebrow. 'Really?'

I nodded, half in, half out of my seat. 'Anything Mary, please, I'll write the funniest dating column you've ever read. Honestly.'

'I guess I can't let you work for free . . . I could pay you as a freelance contributor,' she mused, looking back at the diary. 'And you say you only got here Sunday? So this happened *this* week?'

I nodded again.

'Bring me your first three days' diary, along with a 1000-word establishing piece and a photo on Monday and we'll talk about everything else then.'

The meeting was over. I don't know if Mary had a silent buzzer or made invisible semaphore signals but her secretary appeared at the door and gestured for me to leave. I never did get that coffee.

I couldn't believe what was happening. I was going to be a writer. Actually writing for an actual magazine. OK, website of a magazine, but still. Clearly getting on that plane on Sunday was the best thing I'd ever, ever done. Jenny was working a double shift and Erin was out of town for the weekend but I needed to find some way of celebrating my job, my New York minute. Surely there was only one way? I set off down Broadway, proud, confident and on my way to the Empire State Building to share my success with the city.

Which would have been great if the city hadn't been twenty-five degrees above average for August, full of overheated tourists, a whole load of children on their school holidays all with one very clear brief, to barge past me and, whenever possible, knock my (delicious) Marc Jacobs bag off my shoulder. Which was already tingling and a delightful shade of pink. By the time I'd staggered all the way down to 34th Street in the searing sunshine, I must have been suffering mild sunstroke as I attempted to pass Macy's. Before I knew what was happening, I'd been sucked through the doors and was drinking a refreshing iced tea, using a comfortable and clean bathroom and spending $250 on the Benetfit cosmetics counter. An hour later, I wandered back out onto the pavement and around the corner, the queue for the Empire State Building was insanely long. The sun was beating down on me and my new purchases, threatening to melt my new make-up, and I was so close to home. My new writer's pride had been replaced with buyer's remorse, and before I knew what I was doing, my legs were carrying me across to Lexington, back to the apartment, back to my laptop and back to bed.

Waking up on Saturday morning, I couldn't believe it was a week since I'd woken up in my own bed. So much had happened in such a short space of time and yet, as soon as I remembered my date with Alex was later that evening, time seemed to start going backwards. It was Jenny's first twenty-four hours off duty in over a week, meaning she would pretty much be asleep for fourteen hours. She'd made some half-hearted offers to take me out when she got in from work, but the girl was dead on her stylishly shod feet, so I'd let her off. I went out to get breakfast, washed up, cleaned the kitchen, scoured the bathroom and took all my clothes to the dry cleaners. It seemed insane to me that practically no one in the entire city did their own washing, but Jenny assured me only the hyper rich had a laundry room, and taking your washing out was perfectly normal. I managed to contain a mild panic attack over what to do when you wanted to wear something the very next day when it was dirty after Jenny had presented me with a bottle of hand-washing liquid for emergencies. And I had pretended not to notice her kicking several half-empty bottles of Febreze under the sink. So they had that here too . . .

For the want of something to do with myself, I was showered, blow-dried and dressed in a cute Ella Moss stripy mini dress by five-thirty, giving me a whole hour and a half to apply my make-up, reapply my make-up, add some more make-up, and then completely shit myself about going on a date with someone in a band. Boosted by a quick home-mixed margarita and a kiss – both from a very sleepy Jenny, I grabbed my bag and braced myself. My heart beat sped up as I shut the door behind me and stepped out to hail a cab. I checked my phone a grand total of eight times in the cab, just in case. Nothing from Alex to cancel, nothing to confirm, but there was a sweet voice message from Tyler saying what a great night he'd had and that he would pick me up outside my building at six-thirty on Sunday.

Max Brenner's was tucked away on Broadway, just opposite the Virgin Megastore. At least, I can see The Union from here in case things don't go well, I told myself as I pushed myself out of the cab, The doors to Max Brenner's opened to reveal a huge *Charlie and the Chocolate Factory* style chocolate lab. Absolutely not what I had expected. Absolutely not the place for the amount of eyeliner I was wearing. And the first place in all of New York that was incredibly brightly lit. Shit. Sitting right in the middle of the whispering mothers and staring fathers, was Alex. I couldn't imagine a more incongruous scene. His black hair looked as though it hadn't seen a brush or a comb, well, ever, the creases in his green T-shirt had creases, and compared to 'weekend dad' and 'let's get chocolate shakes for dessert! mom' he looked as if he might start shooting up any second. Out of place, maybe, a complete scruff, definitely, and hot? Absolutely. He broke into a slow smile and a wave as he recognized me, my heart apparently the only muscle in my body able to move. If my pulse had been racing when I left the apartment, it was positively making a break for freedom now.

'Hey,' he said as I slid into the booth, finally forcing my feet to move one in front of the other. 'You made it.'

'I did,' I said, checking the clock. Late again. 'Sorry, I couldn't remember exactly where this was.'

'Cool,' he was still smiling. I started to worry that he was stoned.

'I wouldn't have thought this was your sort of place,' I said, glancing around at the churning vats of chocolate. 'It's not that rock and roll, is it?'

'No,' he said, taking his turn to glance around. 'But addiction is pretty rock and roll, and I might not broadcast it, but I have a real problem with hot chocolate. Seriously, you won't believe this stuff until you've tried it.'

I picked up the menu and looked through all the treats, hot chocolate, milk, dark, white, with chilli, with nutmeg, with cinnamon, chocolate ice cream, chocolate pizza – all this chocolate and a really hot man from a band? There was such a good chance I was in heaven, I wondered if I'd been run over on the way there.

'Wow,' I said, looking back up at him. If he carried on staring at me with that little smile, I was going to run out of things to say really soon. 'So you're a chocoholic?'

'Guilty as charged,' he nodded, raising a weird shaped mug with no handle. 'I blame it on the band. You feel like you've got to be in rehab for something sooner or later, or you're just not committed to the music.'

'I can imagine,' I said, starting to panic. What were we going to talk about? I hadn't prepared anything at all. This was such a bad idea.

'Everyone's got their dirty little secrets,' he said, swirling the thick chocolaty soup in the bottom of his mug. 'You want to confess to yours?'

'I'm a bit tame,' I admitted, feeling a blush creep up

over my face. 'Since I got to New York, it's been Ring Dings. At home, I'm a Cadbury's Creme Egg girl. Sometimes, I'll eat three. All at once.'

'Wow, that is close to the edge,' he laughed, waving over the waitress and ordering two regular hot chocolates. Was I not going to be allowed to order anything for myself while I was in this city? 'Although I'm not sure you should be telling me that. Wouldn't it be against your friend's rules?'

'I believe you are referring to "The Rules", and I don't know. Would that come under "Don't tell him anything that would scare him away" or "Don't overeat"?'

'Possibly "Do not reveal any sort of personality of any kind for fear of him not having one of his own".'

I nodded, biting my lip to stop myself from smiling too much. Maybe I just wasn't ever going to be able to play by Erin's rules.

'So, how long have you been in New York?' he asked, propping himself up on the table with his elbows.

'Just a week,' I said. As much as I wanted to think of something to talk to Alex about, I really didn't think I could go through it all again. 'I'm staying with my friend in Murray Hill.'

'And you're "sort of" on vacation?' he sat back as the drinks arrived at our table. Oh no, now I had to navigate through a hot chocolate moustache *and* an awkward conversation with a very sexy, cool man. It was the cool that was throwing me, I knew it. Tyler was super sexy, but it never felt that if I said the wrong thing, he would go home to some downtown loft and sit laughing at me with members of The Strokes. Maybe I was putting too much thought into this.

'Well, apart from the sort of vacation, I'm doing this online writing thing for *The Look* magazine,' I said, so proud of myself for finding a reason to be there that didn't involve breaking someone's hand. 'So I'm here for a couple of months or so.'

'That's cool,' he said. 'I love New York, but I don't know how you can leave London. It's such a great city.'

'Are you kidding?' I asked, making a brave go at drinking and talking at the same time. 'New York is so amazing. It makes me feel like . . . like I'm really living, you know? It makes me want to do new things and just discover every inch of it. See everything there is to see.'

'And London doesn't?' he asked, brushing his hair back off his forehead. I sipped my hot chocolate. Definitely in heaven.

'When I was young, we lived about an hour away from London by train and all I wanted to do, was be in the city,' I explained, trying not to be distracted by his eyes. They were so green. 'And then when I got there, it was like, wow, London! But after a while, it starts to drain you. Everything is such hard work, everything is so expensive, the Tube costs about five times as much as the subway, and when I get home, I just feel like I need a shower right away. I don't know, there are things I love about London and there are things I can take or leave.'

'You'll get to feeling that way about New York eventually.'

'Can't imagine it,' I said, smiling my first easy, genuine smile. 'God, I feel like I'm cheating on London. I do love it, I just needed a break I think, I'm just tired of London.'

'When a man is tired of London, he is tired of life,' Alex quoted.

I stared back at him, smiling. 'I've got an English degree, I know my Samuel Johnson. But how do you?'

'Well, I might be American but,' he leaned over and whispered, 'I read. Don't tell anyone.'

'I give you my Brownie Guide promise,' I saluted. This was getting easier, but he was still much much cooler than I would ever be. 'Have you always lived in New York then?'

He nodded. 'My family is from upstate but I always wanted to come to the city, same as you, I guess. It just gets under your skin. I went to college in Brooklyn and never left.'

'You live in Brooklyn?' I asked, going back in for more hot chocolate. Honestly, if he stood up and walked out right now I'd still be grateful for introducing me to this place. Willy Wonkaville or not, the hot chocolate was amazing. 'I always imagined it as being a million miles away.'

'Well, to some people, three stops on the L is a million miles away.' Alex reached over to wipe away some stray melted marshmallow from my top lip. I noticed immediately how calloused the tips of his fingers were, my lips tingled under his touch. 'It's only ten minutes from Union Square, but people get this whole "Manhattan is New York" thing going on. It's not true, Brooklyn is amazing. I love living there and I could never get such a great apartment over here.'

'I'll have to trek over there and have a look.' I bit my bottom lip to stop the buzz. 'It hadn't really occurred to me to go.'

'Did you just invite yourself over to my place?' he asked, eyebrows creased, smile vanishing. 'Seriously? How forward are you?'

'No, I, I meant Brooklyn,' I faltered, squeezing my mug tightly. 'I meant, trek over to Brooklyn and look at, stuff.' Stuff. Nice one, Angela. I may as well have told him I'd carried a watermelon.

'Because you're welcome any time,' he teased. 'I just hope your friend would approve.'

Mean, mean man.

And I really liked it.

'I don't think I have to get permission to go into another part of town,' I said, refusing to smile at him even though I wanted to. There were a lot of things I wanted to do at that moment in time, but I was hardly about to do them in this place.

'Well, she had some pretty strict rules about that date you were going on.' He slid out of the booth and held out his hand to help me up. We were leaving the hot chocolate already? 'How did that go by the way? Not that great obviously, because you're here.'

'It was fine, thanks for asking,' I said. Discussing my Tyler date with Alex would be too weird. And things were already weird enough.

'You seeing him again?' he asked, leaving a twenty-dollar bill on the table with the bill. How much was hot chocolate? Maybe I wouldn't come back here with Jenny tomorrow.

'I think this is definitely against The Rules.'

I really didn't know what to say. Was it normal to ask about other dates while you were *on* a date? But what if it wasn't a date. Maybe he had asked me out as a friend.

Shit!

Was this a friend date?

'Hmm,' he was still smiling, his eyes twinkling as we walked out onto the sweaty sidewalk. I mean pavement. God, it was starting to happen already, 'I didn't think it would get past one date.'

'And why not?' I asked. I wasn't refusing to look at him this time, I just couldn't. I was so embarrassed.

'You knew you were going out with me tonight,' he

said, stopping and standing close to me. 'And I couldn't stop thinking about it so I figured you would be feeling the same.' He leaned in and kissed me softly on the lips. It was chocolaty and gentle and electric. I wasn't going to need to bolt to The Union for refuge after all, but at this rate, I was going to need to get a room. I hoped Jenny or Van would give me a good rate. Did they run any rooms by the hour?

'The gig isn't that far, you want to walk?' he asked, pulling away and taking my hand in his. At least I knew it was definitely a date.

'Walking's good,' I managed, replaying the kiss in my head. I couldn't help but compare it to Tyler's. His kisses had been firm and insistent, yet tender at the same time. Alex's kiss was so gentle and soft, but absolutely full of confidence. And it made me want so many more.

We wandered down Broadway, talking about our families, our friends, what we wanted to achieve. I managed to turn my blog at *The Look* into a six-book deal and a film, while Alex talked about creating scores for movies, acting and a passion for architecture, but he hardly mentioned the band.

'That's a pretty full agenda,' I said, loving the feeling of holding hands. 'How are you going to manage all that and put a new album out?'

'Good question,' he replied. 'Who knows if there will be another album? I'm sort of putting the whole thing on hold at the moment. We're just a little wiped out and I don't know if I can carry the whole thing right now. We've been together for like, eight years when you add in all the time before we were signed. Gets to a point where you just want to do something else.'

'I know what you mean,' I said, trying not to sound

like a disappointed fan. 'Must be hard making a group decision about something that big.'

'It is,' he agreed, 'but once one person's heart is out of it, it's really all over. We're still playing live around town, but I just don't feel we want it like we did before. These things come to an end, like anything else. There's nothing worse than staying when there's nothing to stay for.'

I walked on, nodding and thinking. It made sense. And not just about his band.

'Did I say something wrong?' he asked after our third block of silence.

'Not at all.' Rules or no rules, I really didn't want to broach the Mark subject with him. 'I was just thinking about how right you are. And how sometimes you just have to bite the bullet and make a change.'

'Exactly,' he gave my hand a squeeze and stopped in front of a queue of people decked out in skinny jeans, faded T-shirts and bored expressions. Looked like the queue for a gig to me. 'Shall we?'

'Hey, man,' the gangly bouncer on the door nodded to Alex and waved us through and down some stairs into a cramped bar. I glanced around, trying to look like I belonged, while Alex talked to the girl behind the ticket counter. Across the room, a group of girls were craning their necks to get a better look and not exactly whispering about their intentions towards him. I suddenly felt defensive, how dare they say that about my date right in front of me? But somewhere, not too well hidden, I felt the tiniest bit smug. Here was this super hot man who could have had any girl in that line and he was here with me.

'Hey,' Alex called, holding the door to the main floor open. 'You want a drink?'

I took one last look at the girls and then turned my

back. 'I'll get them,' I nodded. 'What are you having?'

'Beer?'

I took the official bar position, forearms resting on the counter, ten dollar bill in hand and slightly impatient look on my face as I tried to make eye contact with one of the bartenders. Behind the bar was a dirty old mirror, hidden behind the rows and rows of bottles. For a moment I didn't recognize the girl standing beside Alex, all messy hair, sexy heavy eye make-up that would have looked a little bit slutty if she wasn't working the whole look, and then I realized that slutty-looking girl was me. I didn't know if it was the close proximity of a genuine bonafide rocker or Jenny's fine prep work but I looked actually OK. Or maybe it was just because I was having fun. I was officially dating and having fun. Wowsers.

A gig is a gig is a gig, I realized as we passed through to the back of the bar, up onto the (thankfully) dim, smoky main floor, New York or London. Sticky floor, crammed bar with overpriced warm beer in plastic cups, small cliques of hipsters in too tight jeans, CBGBs T-shirts, and their tiny girlfriends in equally skinny jeans. As intimidated as I felt by all the unspoken attention Alex was receiving, I felt kind of at home. This could just as easily be any small venue in London as the Bowery Ballroom in New York.

'You go to a lot of gigs at home?' Alex asked, yelling into my ear as the first support act began thrashing at their guitars and brutally assaulting their drum kit.

I nodded and leaned in to his ear, my nose poking through his lovely floppy hair. 'Yeah, I used to go a lot more, but my friends aren't really that into the same kind of music as me.'

I didn't tell him that in reality, none of my friends was into the same kind of music as me, and that Mark had been my only gig buddy for the last ten years.

When we first moved to London, we'd gone out at least once every week, but in the last two years, he'd started complaining that the gigs went on too late, that he couldn't sit down, that the beer was expensive and flat, and more than once in the last few months I'd sat at the back, alone after a short text to say he was working late. But that didn't feel like something Alex needed to know right away. I wanted this to be fun.

'Yeah,' he said, sipping his beer without a word of complaint. 'Sometimes I think it's just so much easier to go places on your own. The movies I've missed because I didn't have a date.'

I couldn't imagine him not having a date for a second. Almost every girl in the place had checked him out on their way in and I was starting to prickle with their not so silent appraisals of me, as his date.

'So apart from listening to Justin, what did you do today?' he grinned, steering me to the side of the stage to a quiet corner and a better view. 'This writing gig sounds really cool.'

'Apart from listen to Justin? God, that takes up so much of my time,' I said trying not to listen to the people whispering around us, not so subtly. 'But yeah, the writing thing is really cool, I hope. It's just an online diary, a blog, but, oh, I don't want to jinx it. I've never really had anything published as myself before, so it's a big thing to me even though it's probably not really.'

'Sounds like a good break though,' he said and raised his glass. 'You going to write about our date?'

'I suppose I'll have to,' I said, not having really thought about it. 'Purely in the interests of journalistic integrity, of course. Totally anonymous though. I will protect your innocence.'

He leaned in towards me again, pushing me back against the wall, and kissed me hard. As his lips pressed down on mine, any concerns about protecting his innocence dissipated, my body caught between the sticky, cold wall and Alex's taut frame. It was all I could do not to drop my beer.

'If you're going to write about me, you should know,' he breathed as we pulled apart, 'I take bad reviews very personally.'

'Shouldn't be a problem,' I chirped, not really knowing where to put myself. Feeling his warm, chocolaty breath so close to my ear was making me shiver and I closed my eyes to commit the kiss properly to memory. Stumbling backwards into the wall, his soft lips, the way his body felt pressed against the thin material of my dress. Before I could completely relive it, I felt Alex close behind me again, his arm draped around my waist, hand resting on my hip. I let myself lean against him, dropping my head backwards onto his chest. It felt so nice, so easy.

We stood in comfortable silence until Alex had to excuse himself to the bathroom and bar, just before the main act. I watched him wander off downstairs, letting myself check him out shamelessly, with a huge smile on my face. It was weird, I was having so much fun, but Alex made me so nervous, as in major butterflies. Tyler didn't make me nervous at all, everything he said and did was designed to make me comfortable. I sort of understood him, bank job, smart suits and all, but I'd felt more awkward about getting dressed up and being in a smart restaurant. It was everything I could do not to spill gravy down my dress. And cream. And coffee.

'You're here with Alex?' In front of me was a petite, pretty girl, head to toe in skintight black with a Debbie Harry platinum bob.

'Erm, yes?' I replied. She didn't look as if she'd come over to make friends.

'You should know, he's a complete asshole,' she said casually. 'He's screwed just about every girl in here. Maybe even some of the guys.'

'Oh, well, we've only just met,' I said, not really sure what to do with the information she was just throwing away and not really wanting to get into a conversation with her. 'I wasn't really planning that far ahead.'

'Yeah, whatever.' She looked me up and down and sipped her drink. 'I'm just telling you what everyone here already knows.' I spotted Alex looking over from the bar and he didn't look happy. 'So, you know, if I were you, I'd be careful if you do "plan that far ahead". Whatever.' She turned on her heel and vanished into the crowd.

'Hey,' Alex said, returning with my drink and a dark expression. 'Did she just say something to you?'

'Er, yes,' I said. What should I tell him? Why would she say that? But right at that moment, I didn't want to believe a word.

'Oh.' He looked into the crowd for the blonde girl. 'Do you know her?'

'No, but, well, seemed like she knew you,' I replied. She had completely vanished.

'I used to date one of her friends for ever ago, is all,' he said, resuming his position behind me. 'Wasn't a great break-up.'

'I can more or less see any bad break-up and raise you,' I said, skimming the subject. 'Don't worry about it.' Bitter friend of the ex, made perfect sense. I just wished I could believe Louisa was making up bitchy lies about Mark, but she was probably swapping cupcake recipes with 'Katie' by now. Alex replied with a gentle kiss on my neck and I let myself relax into him and the music as the main band took to the stage.

* * *

'They were so good,' I said as we emptied out onto the street at midnight. I loved the post-good-gig-buzz. 'Just, wow, really good!'

Alex laughed and took my hand. 'You want to go get a drink or something?'

I looked at my watch and pulled a face. It was already after twelve and even though I was having a great time, a tiny part of my mind kept reminding me that I was seeing Tyler on Sunday evening and I really didn't want to show up looking like complete crap. But the look on Alex's face and the way he was squeezing my hand made it a really difficult decision. Well, the look on his face, the hand-holding, and the four beers I'd already had on nothing but Ring Dings for dinner. Any more to drink and I didn't know if I'd be able to make my best judgements.

'I should really think about getting back,' I said, not really believing the words coming out of my mouth. 'I told my roommate I'd be back and . . .' He gave me the same puppy dog look I'd seen him work on the waitress at Manatus.

'Just one drink?' I said, allowing myself to be pulled down the street.

Really, just one.

Three drinks later, we were nestled in a tiny dive bar with a fantastic jukebox and cold, fizzy beer. We talked about music, about gigs we'd been to, about gigs we'd missed, argued about our favourite albums and dreamed up our ideal festival line up, him headlining, of course. Soon three drinks turned into four, and just after twelve turned into almost two before I remembered I was supposed to be home by now. I was drunk enough to have to watch my step on the way to the toilet, but sober enough to recognize that I was well on my way to wasted. Thank God for weak American lager. Checking the gig damage to my make-up in the mirror, I figured I still looked OK and managed not to apply any more make-up (so I couldn't have been as drunk as I thought), but slicked on several layers of lip balm. Alex's kisses were getting more aggressive with each swoop and I was starting to feel a little bit tender. And more than a little bit turned on. I traced my lips with the tip of my index finger, this was so strange. Tyler's kisses had been firm and gentle, whereas Alex wasn't backwards about coming forwards. The old me would have freaked out at any kind of public display of affection, but the new me seemed to be pretty OK with it. And with dating two men. And with hanging around in nasty toilets for more than the necessary amount of time. Ew. I really had to get home, my head was starting to teeter between 'go home with him' and 'go home and vomit' and in those cases, there was only ever going to be one winner.

Heading back out to the bar, I saw Alex talking to a couple of girls, laughing easily and giving them the same soft smiles and intense eyes that had made me feel like the only girl in New York. It was definitely time to go. 'I should probably make a move,' I said loudly. The girls looked at each other, smiled gleefully at Alex and dropped onto my empty seat, one on top of the other.

'Sure, let's go,' Alex said, standing up and putting his arm around my shoulders. I smiled a tiny smile to myself, head down, and let Alex guide me out of the bar, leaving the girls sulking in my seat.

'Murray Hill?' he asked, as we jumped into an empty yellow taxi before one of the other dozens of couples with their arms in the air could take it.

'39th and Lexington,' I said to the driver, sitting back against the cracked seats. Alex didn't give me a chance to wonder if he would make a move, wait for a sign or even for the cab to pull into traffic before he stretched his long, lean body right across the backseat and took my face in both of his hands. As the taxi bolted through the late-night streets of New York City, I was thrown into a half-sitting, half-lying position on the back seat. Even though the night wasn't cold, there was a chill that was completely dispelled by the warmth of Alex's body as he pushed himself against me. I could feel his hand travel down my side and on to bare flesh at the top of my thigh where my dress had ridden up, and although I knew things were moving altogether too fast, I didn't want to stop him. Before I had to make a really difficult decision, the taxi pulled to a juddering halt, throwing us both into the foot well. I giggled nervously, straddling him and trying to work out how to get up, off and out without giving everything away.

'Do you want to come in?'

The words were out of my mouth before I even thought about them. So this is what women are talking about when we complain that men let their penises make all their decisions for them.

'I *really* want to come in,' he said, helping me push myself back into a sitting position, 'but I'm not going to.'

I looked at him, surprised. Not that I thought I was such a prize catch who would never get blown out, but that I just really felt that was where this was going. And when we were kissing, I'd felt something else that biologically suggested that he thought the same.

'If I come in now,' he whispered, leaning across and opening my door, 'what's left to guess?'

I smiled shyly. I could hardly pass for coy, but I hadn't expected him to be such a romantic.

'Can you wait a sec while I see the lady to the door?'

he asked the cabbie, who grunted something along the lines of an agreement.

Alex pushed my hair behind my ear, holding my gaze just a moment more than he needed to. 'I had a really good time, Angela,' he said, giving me one of his gentlest kisses. 'Will you call me?'

I nodded, having completely lost the ability to speak, and watched him get back in the cab. Malicious bleached blonde aside, I thought the evening had gone fairly well.

CHAPTER THIRTEEN

I was on my third Starbucks venti wet latte on Sunday morning before I was prepared to accept that writing a blog wasn't going to be as easy as I'd hoped. I stared at the blank white screen waiting for inspiration. I knew Mary wanted the intro and three diary pieces and I knew it would make sense to do Thursday, Friday and Saturday. Mary had been quite insistent on the dating theme, and that would cover my first dates with Tyler and Alex. But I didn't know how to talk about the dates without a) sounding like a total tart, and b) sounding like I was gossiping about two different guys with the whole city. Wasn't that rude? Should I blog about Tyler and Alex without their permission? Was I genuinely sitting in Starbucks in New York all hopped up on caffeine asking myself ridiculous questions? I necked the dregs of my coffee and started typing. Instead of worrying about what other people would think, I tried to think about what I would want to read. So I started out writing about something easy. Something I loved.

My lovely, lovely Marc Jacobs handbag.

The Adventures of Angela: How a handbag healed a broken heart

I gave it a loving look and a gentle pat, nothing potentially damaging though, obviously. I still couldn't quite believe I'd spent half a mortgage payment on a bag. On some bits of leather and metal, stitched together to hold my stuff. Stitched together by angels . . . Why had I never bought something so fabulous before? Probably because I didn't think I deserved it. Probably like I didn't think I deserved to be dating gorgeous guys like Tyler and Alex. Probably like I thought I didn't think I deserved the blogging job. Probably like I didn't need another coffee. Oh, wait, that I didn't need, but it was what I had. Like the bag. Sod it. I started typing and went for it. All the details. It was almost fun, the Angela in my diary was living such a great life and without any of the pesky concerns that plagued the real Angela. Once I'd finished, I went through and deleted anything that would upset my mother. Then I put it back in. No more coffee for me.

With the diary pieces in place, I went back to the introduction. I had to front my break-up while I was on a roll, Mary was expecting it, but even as highly caffeinated as I was, this was much trickier than writing about dating. All my life I'd been someone's something, Annette's daughter, Louisa's friend, Mark's girlfriend, but who was I now? I had run away from being Mark's ex, the bridesmaid who ruined the wedding, the girl who lived with her mum. For the last week, with Jenny, Erin, Vanessa, I'd been the slightly crazy girl with the bad/heroic break-up. With Tyler I'd been the quirky English girl who liked to break men's hands, and with Alex, I'd managed to barter my way down to just a slightly quirky English girl. With any luck, I'd be able to have someone describe me as 'just some girl I met, I think she's British' by the end of the month.

I decided there was only one thing to do. Be completely and brutally honest. I opened up the diary I'd written back in The Union and re-read it. It was all there, finding Mark in the car park, yelling at Louisa, bashing Tim with my shoe, right through to pissing in Mark's toiletry bag. This was the version for Mary. Maybe not the weeing in the toiletry bag. I apple-X-ed the incident, but still sat there with a little smile, imagining the look on his face the next time he went to use his badger hair shaving brush. Yes Mark, it does smell a bit funny.

Despite Jenny's insistence that it was absolutely fine to date two men at once (and blog about it), it still felt a bit weird going out with Tyler less than twenty-four hours after seeing Alex. I'd even wondered what the protocol would be on suggesting Jenny dated him instead, he was just her type, but when I opened the apartment door and saw him standing there, head to toe in black Armani, I reconsidered.

'Hi,' I said, accepting his kiss on the cheek and feeling distinctly underdressed in a little Splendid T-shirt dress and Havaianas. 'Erm, you did say cinema, didn't you?'

'I did,' he said, nodding towards a cab across the street with its engine running. 'But then I thought, you've only been in the city for a week, and I'd really be doing New York a disservice if I took you to a multiplex to see some Cameron Diaz movie, so I had a rethink. I hope you don't mind?'

'Not at all,' I said, getting into the waiting yellow car. 'I just, am I dressed OK?'

Seriously. Black Armani suit, white shirt open at the neck, and there was not even a hair out of place.

'You're dressed just fine,' he said, sliding his arm around my shoulder. 'You'll love it, I promise.'

I shrugged and smiled. So far, so good. A little surprise like a change of venue couldn't hurt.

A few tense horn-honking minutes later, we pulled up outside a theatre.

'It's kind of like going to the movies,' Tyler said, opening the door and letting me out. It was nothing like going to the movies. It was absolutely like going to a Broadway show. I was so excited. 'I managed to score some tickets to *Wicked* from a guy at work. It's supposed to be really good, have you seen it?'

I shook my head. 'That's amazing! I wanted to see this in London but never made it. Musicals are my guilty pleasure.'

'Well, you said you liked music,' he said, leading me through the lobby like a pro. It was an interesting interpretation of my liking music but I wasn't complaining. What a thoughtful, nice man. And with his arm around my waist, guiding me into my third-row seat, I was reminded that the nice man attended the gym very regularly. 'So, have you broken any hands since I last saw you?'

I shook my head, starting to regret having told him any details of my break-up. The Rules were rules for a reason, I understood that now. 'Nope, I did get a job though,' I offered, filling him in. This time, I did hold back a little on the detail. I just didn't feel as if he'd necessarily be ecstatic about being the star of an online search for love.

'Well, that's great!' he said, kissing me quickly and unexpectedly. 'This is a celebration then. You should have told me.'

'It's nothing huge,' I said, blushing. He thought I should have told him. Ahh. 'Just an online thing, it won't go in the magazine at all.'

'Don't talk it down,' he admonished, taking my hand

in his as the lights flashed twice. 'You said you wanted to be a proper writer and now you are.' He looked across at me. 'You're a real inspiration, you know? One week in the city and see what you've achieved. I really hope some of this luck is going to rub off on me.' He really did know just what to say to make me feel amazing. The orchestra struck up as he leaned across the velvet-covered armrest and kissed me deeply.

'I suppose that might help the luck rub off quicker,' I said, pressing my lips together after the endless kiss.

'I'm prepared to keep trying until it does,' Tyler whispered while the actors took the stage.

I sank back in my seat and grinned in the dark. At least I was going to have something to write about in my diary tonight.

The rest of the evening was so special. I was completely carried away with the romance of the show, squeezing Tyler's hand, resting my head on his shoulder, burying my face in his jacket during the sad bits. Afterwards, we wandered down to a tiny candlelit restaurant around the corner. In no time at all, I'd turned into a purring kitten, all coquettish giggles and bicep stroking. God, if Mark had known musicals had this effect on me, he might have taken me to more.

'You really are remarkable,' Tyler said, spoonfeeding me ice cream. Usually that kind of couplish behaviour made me want to vom, but with Tyler, it just seemed sweet and loving. 'I can't believe you've managed all this in a week. I guess I'm just not a risk taker like you.'

'It's so weird being described by someone else,' I said, offering a spoonful of cheesecake in return for the ice cream. 'The one risky thing I've ever done is come to New York, but that is working out fairly well.

Maybe I ought to look into this risk taking thing more.'

'I think that sounds like a wonderful idea,' Tyler said. 'I've always had my life so mapped out. Ivy league college, good job with a great bank, next is supposed to be wife and kids, move to Connecticut, retire to Florida.'

'Sounds like fun,' I said, shaking my head. 'I think I had something like that planned, and then I found my boyfriend with his pants around his ankles. I don't recommend it.'

'If I were to find my boyfriend with his shorts around his ankles, something would have gone wildly wrong with my plan.' His eyes crinkled lightly as he shook his head and laughed. Oh, he looks nice when he laughs, I thought, musing over his good points. Sweet, funny, great prospects, makes me feel like royalty, and quite frankly, not bad to look at, and there were rock hard abs under that suit.

'If you *were* going to go wildly off plan,' I had to find a chink in the perfection somewhere, 'what would you do?'

'I don't know,' he said, leaning back in his chair. 'If I were being totally selfish? Do anything I want?'

'Anything you want,' I confirmed.

'I'd take a year off and follow the Yankees. Every game,' he said, smiling to himself. 'Can you imagine?'

'Not really,' I frowned. Not the romantic answer I'd been hoping for.

'Or, I would rent an island, like the one the Virgin guy has,' he suggested.

'Necker Island?' More like it.

'Yeah,' he nodded. 'I'd rent Necker island and just hide away for a few months. Just the sun and the sand and some great wines and whiskeys. And a satellite TV for Yankees' games. And a WiFi connection so you could keep writing, of course.'

'I'm there?' I asked, playing with my napkin.

'It's my fantasy, right?' he said, reaching out for my hand across the table. 'So I get to take whoever I want.'

Silently blushing from head to toe, I tried to meet his gaze, but I had instantly become a Complete Girl and couldn't even look at him.

'The food here is really great, but the coffee is awful,' he whispered just loud enough for the waiter to hear as he walked by. He sniffed loudly and carried on walking. 'And I have a suspicion we're not that welcome any more,' he laughed. 'I, however, have great coffee. You want to come back for a while?'

I looked over at the waiter who was already running up our bill. It really did look as if he might spit in our coffees. At best.

'I'm only ten minutes from here,' Tyler said, pulling out his wallet and placing the fabled black Amex on the bill the second it arrived without even looking. I really had wanted to pay tonight, but in a way, I really did love the fact that he wouldn't let me. 'And it's really good coffee. I have a Gaggia.'

Whatever a Gaggia might have been, it swung the deal. It was just coffee after all, there was no way Tyler was going to be less of a gentleman than Alex. We ducked out into a cab and drove slowly around the park. Somewhere I still hadn't visited, it looked so beautiful lit up at night.

'You want to walk the last couple of blocks?' Tyler asked, reading my mind. I nodded eagerly and jumped out onto the pavement, leaning against the wall and looking out across the lake. It was like a scene from a movie. My movie.

'Sometimes you forget how lucky you are to live with all this on your doorstep,' he sighed, taking off his jacket and resting it on my shoulders. It was lightly scented with his aftershave and still warm. 'It's amazing to see it through someone else's eyes.'

I turned to say something, but was cut off by his kiss. His arms encircled my waist and without breaking away, he lifted me up and placed me on the wall, as if I were made of air, as if I weighed nothing. Pressing against him, I let the kiss grow deeper and deeper until my hands were lost in his thick hair and my legs were carelessly knotted around his. I had completely forgotten I was in the middle of a busy street, I was so entirely given over to this kiss, this moment. Suddenly, I felt all of my frustrations bubble up to the surface, every night I'd laid in bed alone waiting for Mark to come home, every hopeful smile I'd had rejected, every touch that had gone unacknowledged, even Alex's refusal to come upstairs with me the night before, however honorable his reasons, it all burst out in that one kiss.

'My apartment is just around the corner,' Tyler pushed me away gently. His eyes burned and I knew I just had to. I wanted him so badly. The absolute certainty that I was in for a thoroughly good seeing to burned in my chest as we moved in silence, somewhere between a quick walk and a slow run. It was only a couple of minutes to his Park Avenue apartment, but it felt like a million miles. Falling through the door, I tore at Tyler's beautiful suit and kicked away my flip-flops as we rolled down the hallway. I knew that I should step back, work out what I was doing. But I didn't care. I didn't care if it was revenge sex, a sexorcism, or just something I needed with someone I wanted. All I knew was that the doorknob pushing into my lower back needed to be turned if it led to the bedroom. And it did. Tyler pulled me in, flicking on the low bedside light as we crashed on to his huge bed. This wasn't the time to work out my motives, I told myself, feeling so small and delicate as Tyler lay on top of me, his hands frisking my curves firmly, his lips still pressing against mine. This was time to let my body make some decisions for me. And if all my body's decisions felt this good, I would be consulting it far more regularly from now on.

Morning declared itself with a chirping alarm clock. I had absolutely no idea what time it was, but it felt early. Really early. Stretching my arms out, I marvelled at how wide the bed felt, how soft my sheets were. How bright the sun was through the giant picture window . . . hang on a minute.

'Morning,' Tyler appeared in the doorway, fully dressed in a suit and tie as I clutched the covers tightly around my chin. Quick visual check, yes, I was naked. He sat down on the edge of the bed and placed two steaming cups of coffee on the side table. 'Since we never got to it last night,' he said, bending down and offering a long, slow kiss.

I still wasn't quite sure what to say.

'Sorry, it's so early,' he carried on regardless, picking up his coffee and sipping thoughtfully. 'Monday's are a bitch, I have to be in before all the meetings start, otherwise I don't stand a chance. I'm usually tied to my BlackBerry all Sunday night and, as you know, I had better things to do last night.'

I smiled weakly and fumbled for my coffee. 'Mm-hm,' I nodded and sipped slowly. The longer this took, the less likely it would be that I might have to make conversation. Damn, I thought, sipping again, he really does make fantastic coffee.

'Anyway, I'm gonna get gone.' He smoothed my hair and came in for another kiss. 'Just let yourself out whenever, OK? The door locks itself, so don't worry about alarms or anything. Call me later?'

I nodded and accepted one more kiss before he stood up to leave. I set my coffee down and buried my face in the pillow, not seeing Tyler pause in the doorway.

'I just wanted to say,' he called across the room, 'good luck for your meeting.'

Thank God he hadn't said anything about how amazing it had been. I just couldn't cope. 'Thanks,' I managed without sitting up.

'And I actually just wanted to say, last night was really,' I'd spoken to soon, 'really amazing.'

Ooh, so close.

CHAPTER FOURTEEN

'So, before you tell me anything else, without even thinking,' she commanded, unloading the Starbucks bags and newspapers I'd bought to camouflage my Walk of Shame. 'How was the sex?'

'It was amazing,' I said. 'Honestly, I know my sex life has been pretty shitty for a while, but he was incredible. He's strong and big and he goes to the gym and we did it three times and I, God, I don't know.'

'OK, you've answered my next three questions,' she said, sinking her teeth into a doughnut. 'So you're seeing him again when?'

'Oh shut up!' I grabbed a doughnut of my own and shook my head. 'He had to leave early.'

'That's OK, as long as he calls like, today or tomorrow,' Jenny said, staring me down. 'But I don't think that's bothering you. You know he's going to call, right? So what's up? Why aren't you bouncing off the ceiling?'

'OK, don't get mad but because I was sort of thinking on the way back . . . I've only ever been with Mark,' I said, plopping onto a stool and pulling my hair back into a messy ponytail. 'I know you're going to punch me, but even though it was amazing at the time, this morning I felt, well, like I had cheated on him. I know, I know,' I held out my hand to cut her off, 'I know it doesn't make sense, he didn't even wait to break-up with me before he started sleeping with someone else, but I can't help the way it feels.'

'True, you can't,' Jenny nodded. 'But you're not going to let this stop you seeing him? If anything honey, you ought to be throwing another couple of guys into the mix.'

'I don't know. What if I don't stop feeling weird? And what about Alex? Twenty-four hours ago or so, I'd invited him up here, and now I've slept with Tyler? I've only just got my head around going on dates with two men let alone sleeping with them both.'

'This one's easy,' Jenny said, slapping my hands away from my hair when I tried to retie my ponytail again. 'Do you want to see Alex again?'

I nodded.

'And do you want to see and potentially sleep with Tyler again?'

I nodded.

'Then fine. You don't have to choose until you're ready.' She picked up her coffee and two more of the doughnuts. 'And by the way, three times in one night, Park Avenue apartment *and* a black Amex? You sure as hell are seeing him again or you're giving me his number.' She leaned over the bar and kissed me on the cheek. 'Go get ready for your meeting with Mary, I'm going to bed.'

Knowing I had a meeting meant that I didn't have enough time to go over and over what had happened in my head, but I did manage a quick self-analysis while applying mascara (Razor would have been so proud). Looking myself in the eyes, I tried to smile at the new girl looking back. It wasn't the clothes or the hair or even the faint tan I'd acquired in the past week, although all of that was new, I just couldn't remember the last time I'd looked in a mirror before I came to New York. Not caught sight of myself as I walked by, not sorted out my dodgy parting, but really looked myself in the eye. At best I managed a quick sideways glance on my way out of the shower to see how my Weight Watchers torment was coming along, never a happy moment. And now, there was this strange girl staring back at me. A girl who dates two guys at once, writes for the website of a fashion glossy, who lives in New York. Meep.

On the way out of the door, I picked up my mobile and looked at the phone book – Jenny, Erin, *The Look*, Tyler, and first in the list? Alex. I'd promised I'd call and I really really wanted to, but it felt so weird, ringing a man I wanted to sleep with when I'd just slept with someone else. No matter how many times Jenny told me it wasn't a big deal, that New York dating came with different rules (The Rules again!) it just felt wrong to me. And to be honest, no matter how far I was putting feminism back, I wanted any man that wanted to sleep with me, to want to sleep only with me. There, it was out there. I was practically a Puritan.

The safest time to get Alex's answering machine would be early, I reasoned, that sexy deathly pallor didn't come from early morning jogs along the river. Convincing myself he wouldn't answer, I sucked it up and dialled. And he answered on the first ring.

'Y'ello?' He sounded sleepy and cute.

'Hi, Alex?' I panicked, not having anything prepared except a random babbled statement about calling him back later.

'Yeah?' So far so he-didn't-recognize-my-voice.

'It's Angela,' I said, cursing myself for calling. 'Angela Clark?'

'Oh, hi.' He yawned loudly. This plan had not gone well. 'I wondered when you were going to call.'

'I said I would,' I defended myself. It had only been a day. Should I have called by now? Erin had said three days. Bloody Erin. 'So, you know, Saturday was really fun, thanks.'

'Uh-huh,' he replied. 'Sorry, I just woke up, I'm not really a morning person.'

'Oh, me neither,' I said, rushing towards Times Square. 'But I have a meeting, so I thought I'd call and . . . sorry. I should have called later.'

'No, it's fine,' he said with another deep yawn. I wondered how he looked first thing. I imagined his hair all stuck over on one side, pillow creases in his cheek. 'Listen, you want to do something Wednesday? You want to go to MoMA?'

'Sounds great,' I said, relieved that I would have two days to sort my head out and wondering what a MoMA was.

'Cool, meet you outside the main entrance at three?'

'Perfect, see you then.' Instead of looking for the Spencer Media building, I found myself guessing what he slept in. Maybe he was wandering around his apartment naked. Not the right chain of thought. Bad Angela.

'Good, Angela,' Mary said, pacing around her office clutching my diaries. 'It's actually good. It's pacy, it's funny – funny-ish – and I'm thinking I'm a reader and I'm kind of interested in these men you're dating. You're still seeing both of them?'

'Yes,' I said, watching her anxiously and looking out

for the coffee I was offered on my way in. 'I am, but I feeling a bit weird about it. I don't know, maybe I should just be seeing one of them. Or just slowing it down a little, but with one of them. Or both of them. Or something.'

'I don't think so,' Mary said, finally settling behind her desk. 'If you want this blog, you keep dating. We need to give them nicknames so that they don't sue – I'm calling them Wall Street and Brooklyn – they are your story, until something or someone else, comes along.'

'I suppose,' I said slowly. I really should have re-read the pieces post-caffeine-high, but I wanted this so badly. 'I'm seeing Alex on Wednesday but I haven't made plans with Tyler yet.'

'Make them.' Mary buzzed in her secretary and handed me a business card. 'You'll email me your column every day by four, keep it detailed on locations, light on the gory details. We want the readers interested in where you're going on your dates, which guy you're going to pick, not getting off on your sex life.'

'OK,' I nodded eagerly, 'I can do that.'

'So you'll email your piece to me every day by four. I have a meeting with the editorial and marketing team on Thursday, and if your pieces keep coming in at this standard, I'll be putting them to the team then.'

'Thanks,' I replied, completely shell-shocked. 'I won't let you down, Mary.'

'No, you'd better not,' she said, turning back to her computer. 'Be here at four on Friday for a catch-up and we'll talk about posting *The Adventures of Angela*.'

'*The Adventures of Angela*?' I backed out of the office, smiling with an awkward half wave. 'See you Friday. Thanks Mary.'

* * *

I emerged, blinking, into the sunlight, not really knowing what had just happened, but pretty sure the meeting had gone well. Pausing outside the terrifyingly neon behemoth that was ToysЯus, it took me a whole minute to work out what the vibrating against my hip was, before I realized that I'd stuck my mobile in my pocket after calling Alex. It had been over a week since I'd received a text message and I'd almost forgotten they existed. Who knew that could happen?

Hi lunch meeting cancelled, have res at Tao. Shame to waste it. Abuse my corporate account with me at 1.00?

It was Tyler.

I had sworn that I would eventually make it to the Empire State Building today, but I had something else to think about other than my tourist agenda now.

My column.

Mary had told me to make plans with Tyler hadn't she? She was practically forcing me to accept his offer. And I had even heard of Tao, it was supposed to be amazing. With my career and stomach in mind I accepted, by text, whilst trying to keep last night's marathon firmly out of mind. It wasn't easy though. As I drifted around midtown, killing time, my mind kept wantonly wandering over the details. His soft hands, his hard body, the warmth of his kisses and how, for those blissful few hours, I didn't have to be anyone at all, I was just part of the act. No disastrous life back in England, no double-dating concerns in New York, nothing but me and Tyler. Such a welcome relief and very welcome release. A little tiny part of me was also pretty pleased that I'd remembered at least some of what I was doing. It really was just like riding a bike, I smiled to myself. Ooh, I should put that in the column. Or maybe not – no porno details.

By one, I'd managed to spend $500 accidentally on underwear in Saks on Fifth Avenue, egged on by the newly awakened sex goddess in me. Nothing overly saucy, just really beautiful matching bras and 'briefs'. Couldn't say knickers in New York, and I couldn't bring myself to say panties without giggling like a child. I arrived at Tao ten minutes early (get me!) and was directed over to Tyler's table, where he was tapping away at his BlackBerry. Would I ever beat a man to a date? Maybe lateness was one of my new things, I mused, feeling a post-coital nervousness well up in my chest as we kissed hello. Nothing salacious, a warm, firm kiss square on the lips.

'Hi,' he said, pulling my chair out for me. 'Been shopping?' he nodded towards my giant bags, and it suddenly occurred to me how it must look. I practically devour him in the street, then turn up for lunch the next day with bags and bags of underwear.

Wow, what a slut.

'They're gifts,' I said.

Wow, what a liar.

'Oh, OK. Gifts.' He smiled. 'How did your meeting go? Are you editor-in-chief yet?'

Grateful that he had changed the subject to something I could talk about without having to imagine him hot, sweaty and naked, I stopped hiding behind my menu and shook my head.

'It went well,' I said, 'she liked the pieces that I'd written and she's asked me to send her 500 words a day, then go in for another meeting on Friday. It's not a done deal by a long stretch though. Not a big deal. Really.'

It was a big deal.

'Are you kidding?' he said, putting his menu down. 'That's fantastic! We're officially celebrating.'

I smiled.

I liked celebrating.

I liked Tyler.

Soon, I was two glasses into a bottle of Laurent Perrier at one in the afternoon, and several wild gesticulations into my future career plans. 'I mean eventually,' I waved my arms around, almost knocking the bottle out of the waiter's hand. 'I'd really like to write. Just write, whether it's magazines or books, whatever. Not necessarily deep and meaningful, but just something that someone can enjoy. Something that they can sit down with for an hour to enjoy, and escape from, I don't know, whatever it is they need to escape from.'

Tyler nodded, sipping his water. He wasn't drinking, he had meetings all afternoon and the more tipsy I got, the more startlingly sober he seemed. From the occasional glass of wine with dinner I'd gone to drunk most nights of the week and in the middle of a Monday afternoon startlingly quickly. So far today I'd found out I was a writer, a wanton sex goddess, and apparently a bit of a lush.

'Once we're done here, I think we should go do something to really commemorate this occasion,' he said, 'in case you don't remember lunch.'

I looked down at my plate. Still full. My glass. Completely empty.

Tyler picked up the bill and before I knew it, we were leaving the beautiful, opulent restaurant and moving out into town.

'Where are we going?' I asked, letting Tyler take my hand and guide me through the busy streets. Midtown was absolutely crazy.

'Just somewhere,' he smiled, pulling me up short in

front of a large Fifth Avenue store. Oh Lord it was Tiffany. 'To get something special to commemorate a special occasion.'

He kissed me squarely on the lips reminding me how I was thinking about suggesting we slow it down a bit. But not outside Tiffany, that would just be rude. Tyler pulled me through the doors and straight through to the lifts at the back of the shop. I desperately tried to sober up and absorb every second. A beautiful man with no known credit card limit had brought me to Tiffany's. This was something to remember. Everything sparkled and glinted at me as we rushed past, diamonds and rubies and sapphires and every other precious gem you could ever imagine, all sparkling in the carefully designed lighting. The lift doors slid together and the diamonds winked goodbye as we began to move upwards. The lift teased me relentlessly, opening on floor after floor of gorgeous jewellery, trinkets and treasures, while we remained inside. I began to think he'd just brought me here to use the toilets, which considering what I'd drunk, wouldn't have been a bad plan. Eventually, the doors opened on gifts and we strolled out. Tyler seemed to know exactly where he was going, silently smiling and drawing me across the floor. If I hadn't been so desperate for a) the toilet and b) something wrapped in a little blue box, I would have said he was being irritatingly smug. Plus I couldn't help but wonder how he knew his way around such a maze-like jewellery store quite so well.

'Here,' he said, stopping in front of a display case. Inside were dozens of sterling silver objects, business card holders, letter openers, keyring upon keyring upon keyring and, I finally worked out what he was pointing at, beautiful silver pens. 'Which one do you like?'

I was so lost for words and overwhelmed by the

need to pee, I didn't know what to say. I couldn't remember a time anyone had done something so thoughtful. Even Mark's proposal hadn't been so well considered and he'd (allegedly) been planning it for months. 'Will you marry me?' doesn't have the same ring to it when you've just been arguing the toss with a Sevillian pony and trap driver over five Euros.

'Honestly, you shouldn't,' I murmured, clutching at his arm and feeling very feminine all of a sudden. Maybe they put something in the air conditioning to make you more susceptible to romantic gestures, I thought to myself.

'But I want to,' he said, pointing the sale girls towards a delicate silver ballpoint pen. 'And I'm going to.' The girl nodded and took the pen away.

I looked away, smiling happily. And slightly tipsily. I could really get used to this kind of treatment quite quickly, but before I did, I really really had to talk to him about slowing things down. It wasn't fair to accept expensive gifts and lavish dinners when I was still feeling guilty about having slept with him. But I didn't want to offend him.

'I just need to nip to the ladies' room,' I whispered as the sales girl appeared with my beautifully wrapped parcel. Oh, the white ribbon against the stiff eggshell cardboard bag. It made my heart leap right into my mouth.

Tyler nodded and took the gift bag. 'I'll wait outside, I have a couple of calls to make.'

The bathroom was every bit as beautiful as I had expected, but I was so desperate, I would have taken a hole in the ground. Oh the relief. Washing my hands, I took a moment to think about the Tyler situation. I didn't know if it was the pheromones I was convinced Tiffany were pumping into their store or possibly the champagne that was still raging around my system, but it struck me that I was taking the Tyler/Alex thing altogether too seriously. Jenny was right, we were just having fun, Tyler had bought me a pen, not an engagement ring, and Alex and I had only been on one date! There was no need to say anything to Tyler right now except thank you very much. I would have to be crazy to knock back a generous, thoughtful (rich, hot) man like him for no reason. Besides, he had seemed very comfortable in Tiffany's, maybe he bought a lot of gifts for his friends. It would be rude of me to make a big deal out of it. After all, it was just a pen. My mind made up to ask Tyler out for dinner for Thursday night, I went back downstairs. It would be totally straight forward, I told myself. I would ask him if he would like to go out, and if he were to ask me if I'm seeing anyone else, I'd say yes. We're just dating, just a notch above friends really. Friends with benefits in fact, I'd read all about that and it seemed fine.

Resentfully, I left Tiffany's and looked for Tyler. For some reason, the sun didn't seem to leave him hot, sweaty and lobster red like everyone else, but glinted off his hair and accentuated his tan. He was the Kentucky Derby racehorse to my Blackpool seafront donkey. Eeyore.

'There you are,' he said, handing me the bag and kissing me on the cheek. 'Real sorry but I've got to get back to the office. Something's come up that I have to deal with.'

'Oh, I hate when that happens,' I joked feebly. Now or never, time for me to propose my first ever date. 'Do you want to go to dinner with me on Thursday?' I garbled.

'Sorry?' he asked, sliding a pair of expensive-looking sunglasses out of his jacket pocket.

'Thursday night?' I tried more slowly. 'Would you like to go for dinner with me?'

'Oh, I can't make Thursday,' he said, looking around for a cab. 'What about Wednesday?'

'I can't make Wednesday,' I said, really hoping he wasn't going to ask me why. 'Tomorrow?'

'How about Saturday?' he suggested. 'My week is pretty crazed. We could do a picnic in the park? It might be a little busy but it's always fun.'

Before I could really give a yes or no, he pecked me on the cheek (it was definitely only a peck) and jumped into a taxi slowed by traffic, whilst making the universally acknowledged 'I'll call you' sign. I waved goodbye and watched him pull off, already on his phone.

'I don't think that's a bad sign,' Jenny said through a mouthful of lasagne. I'd demanded we stay in and cook that evening, much to her disgust, but she seemed to be packing away the meal 'we' had made fairly quickly. 'He offered Wednesday, you couldn't make it. Five days isn't really that long between dates, especially when you've only just started seeing each other. Now make with the pen!'

I'd refused to show Jenny the pen until we'd discussed the million different interpretations of Tyler's actions. The invite to lunch – good. He could have asked anyone but he'd invited me. The trip to Tiffany – very good whichever way you looked at it. The picnic suggestion – sweet, definitely a date thing, not a friend thing. The distracted goodbye – probably just concerned about work, I was reading too much into it.

'I just thought maybe, I don't know, he'd want to see me before the weekend,' I shrugged, stretching the mozzarella between my knife and fork. 'After last night and everything.'

'What, you're so hot in bed you thought he couldn't

wait for a second helping?' Jenny smiled, shovelling her pasta.

'Technically it would be his fourth.' I stuck my tongue out and brought the Tiffany bag out from its hiding place. 'And no, I don't think that, I just, I don't know. Maybe it wasn't as great as I thought. I suppose I'm really rusty.'

'You can't be that freaking rusty!' Jenny squealed, ripping the tissue paper out of the bag and holding up a gorgeous white gold lariat chain with a diamond-studded star on one end.

'Where's my pen?' I gasped, staring at the chain, not daring to touch it. 'Did I steal someone else's bag? I wasn't that drunk!'

'The pen's in here too,' Jenny said, emptying the bag out onto the counter with a clatter. I winced, watching the pen crash out of its pouch and onto the work surface. 'There's a note, read the note, read the note!'

I took the slip of paper and started to read.

'OUT LOUD!' Jenny shouted, giving me a drum roll.

'A shooting star for my shooting star. Tyler,' I read. It was so romantic. He must have—

'Stop thinking, start talking!' Jenny yelled, grabbing the note.

'He must have gone and bought it when I was in the bathroom,' I breathed. I had been completely bowled over by the pen, but this? 'I can't believe he did this. I should call him.'

'Text,' Jenny said, still holding the necklace. I felt that if I took it from her it would melt away into thin air. 'You don't want to overdo it, you're not seeing him until Saturday, you should text. Keep it short and flirty, "Thank you, can't wait for you to unwrap your present on Saturday", something like that.'

'Jenny!' I said, still transfixed by the sparkles. 'I can't

say that. It's too much, I should just say thank you or something.'

Jenny pulled a face.

I pulled a face.

Jenny pulled another face, snatched the phone out of my hands and sprinted into the bathroom.

'Jenny, you cow, give me my bloody phone,' I shouted through the door.

Emerging triumphant, Jenny handed me the phone. 'What would you do without me, doll?'

'Tell me you didn't?'

'Now is so not the time to be coy, honey.' Jenny sauntered back through to the living room and dropped onto the sofa, dipping into an open bag of Doritos.

I hardly dared look in my sent messages, but since it was done . . . 'Hey, loved my present, maybe I'll have a surprise for you to unwrap soon, Angela xox'. I shook my head while Jenny giggled, peeping over the back of the sofa.

'Honestly, it's not nearly as slutty as I thought it would be,' I sighed, setting down the phone and shoving Jenny up the sofa.

Full of food and vicarious romance, she eventually fell asleep in front of the TV. Once I was satisfied she was genuinely asleep, I took the pen, the necklace and the note into my room and spread them out on my bed. It was genuinely the sweetest thing anyone had ever done for me. I tried to think back to some of Mark's better moments and was saddened to realize that out of ten years, aside from the half-arsed proposal, I couldn't think of more than a handful. Roses delivered to my lecture on our first valentine's apart, flowers in every room of the house when we moved in together, planting a giant sunflower in the garden of our flat every year on our anniversary. It didn't take me long to recognize a theme, and even less time to realize we hadn't even planted a sunflower for the last three years. Mark was probably too busy planting something else. After fifteen minutes of shamelessly ogling Tyler's gifts, I wrapped them carefully in their tissue and placed them back into the bag. And then I slipped between the sheets with the same level of care and allowed myself fifteen more minutes' shameless recollection of some of Tyler's other gifts.

CHAPTER FIFTEEN

Officially one day into my blog, it was a bit early for writer's block. I had so much to go on, yesterday's lunch with Tyler, making the second date with Alex, finding the necklace, everything, but I didn't know where to start. Eventually I gave up typing 'The quick brown fox jumped over the lazy dog' and got dressed. I was happier with my make-up, I could even do my eyes without Razor's crib sheets. I hadn't stuck the mascara wand in my eye for two days and I hadn't gone out with stripes of blusher down my cheeks for three. Not to mention the fact that I had put on cropped leggings and a Twenty-Eight Twelve T-shirt dress without even thinking about whether or not you could see my arse. The four walls of the apartment weren't offering me inspiration, so I picked up my (gorgeous) bag, slid my laptop inside and made for the great outdoors.

Murray Hill was the perfect place from which to start an aimless wander around Manhattan. At first I thought maybe I'd just pop out and get more coffee, but as I got further and further downtown, I just couldn't seem to stop walking down, down, across, down.

Sunshine slanted through the narrow channels between the streets and swam across the avenues. Everywhere I turned I saw something mundane, everyday and completely exciting. The office of Dr Jeffrey Walker DDS, the Episcopalian church on Fifth, the Korean deli stocked with Wonder Bread, Milk Duds and Vanilla Coke. Eventually I hit Bleecker Street, but instead of carrying on down to Houston and dipping my toe (and credit cards) in Soho, I carried on walking into the Village. The shops got smaller and more quirky, I paused outside pet shops and lost my heart to every puppy I passed. I browsed in record shops until I was frowned out by the intense-looking guys in Iggy and the Stooges shirts behind the ridiculously high counters. I wandered around Duane Reade drugstores wondering how anyone could need to self-medicate so incredibly heavily. And eventually I found my inspiration.

A Marc by Marc Jacobs standalone store.

My handbag was drawn to the mothership from across the road. I wandered up and down the clothes, stroking them lovingly and wondering how they got so many models to work in their shop. I managed to put a beautiful silk shirtdress back on the rack before my bag pulled me directly to the accessories, practically purring at the matching wallets. Before I knew what I was doing, my old Accessorize purse was emptying itself out on to the counter, prostrating itself in front of what it clearly recognized as its superiors.

Opposite the store was a small playground, full of children and ridiculously chic nannies and cool boho mothers clutching coffees and cupcakes from the Magnolia Bakery. I plopped down on one of the benches and set my laptop up on one of the concrete chessboards. I'd got cupcakes too, but I was determined to save them for girls' night back at the flat with Vanessa and Jenny. Or maybe I'd just have one. By God it was delicious. I'd never eaten a cake that was more icing than actual sponge before and it turned out that writing the blog on a sugar high was as easy as writing it when I was completely caffeinated. I tapped away merrily, bag tucked on my lap, icing all over my face and eyes completely wired. *The Adventures of Angela: Gifting at Tiffany's*

There, that was as good a headline as any . . .

By the time I'd cabbed it home, emailed the blog to Mary and eaten another cupcake (shamefully, I'd gone back for more after eating two to get me through the blog), it was three-fifty. Jenny and Vanessa were coming home together to watch *America's Next Top Model*, but not for another few hours, so I happily installed myself on the sofa with a giant box of cookies and the TV for company, only getting up to answer the phone to Jenny's mother and take a long, unnecessarily detailed message about her father's trip to his prostate doctor but not to worry, he was fine. Speaking to Jenny's slightly manic mother made me think about mine. Not that there was anything even vaguely manic about her, she was more than chemically balanced, but she did like to go into detail on her doctor's appointments. I'd left her a voicemail with my new number, but even if she didn't need to talk to me, I sort of felt that I wouldn't mind speaking to her. Just to let her know I was OK. Just get it out of the way. Just tell her I'm fine, that I'm working and that I'll call her again in a week or so. If I need to.

Or that she can ring me.

Next month or something.

Long pause.

Clicking.

Ringing.

'Hello?'

My arm shot out and I stared at the phone in front of me.

That wasn't my mother.

That was Mark.

I scrabbled for the off button and hung up, switched off and threw the phone at the sofa. What the hell was he doing at my mother's?

I sat on the end of the sofa, rocking lightly, unable to take my eyes off the phone in case it started ringing. I didn't want to think about this, I told myself, I couldn't think about this. I could just about stand thinking about him in the past, us in the past, but I didn't want to have to think about him now, and I definitely didn't want to think about him in my mother's house.

I threw myself back onto the sofa, turned up the TV and finished the rest of my cupcake, staring at the screen and refusing to think about anything but *Super Sweet Sixteens*, *Cribs* and whether or not I might have a shot at love with *Tila Tequila* until Vanessa and Jenny came cackling through the door.

Even with the music from my iPod drowning out any thoughts of Mark overnight, I really didn't sleep well, and the next morning, it showed. Even the Touche Éclat didn't shift the dark shadows I'd picked up overnight. Great, some literal baggage to go with the emotional stuff. Looking like crap or not, I was excited about going to MoMA (since Jenny had sighed and explained it was an art gallery). One of my favourite weekend treats, when Mark had to 'work', was to lose myself in the Tate Modern for hours.

Taking in the galleries, checking out new exhibitions, sometimes just sitting outside or in the turbine hall, people watching for hours. I was even more excited when I saw Alex hovering outside the entrance. He looked just as cute as last time with added Brownie points for apparently having thought about combing his hair.

'Hey,' he gave me his trademark slow smile as I approached. Without an ounce of concern for public opinion, he scooped me up into a long, lazy kiss. It was delicious.

'So what you been up to?' he asked, swinging my hand as we rode the escalators up to the galleries. 'Anything I should know about?'

'I had my meeting at *The Look*,' I said, glossing over my Tyler incidents. I filed them safely under things he did not need to know about *right now*, which meant I wasn't lying, just not oversharing. 'I've got another meeting on Friday and then hopefully it'll go online. The editor said she really liked my stuff.'

'Really? That's amazing. I'm sure it's going to be really great.'

'Yeah, hopefully,' I said, squeezing back. 'What about you, have you reached any life-changing decisions?'

He shook his head, pulling me around to the next escalator. 'Nope. Band rehearsal tomorrow though and we have a gig on Friday. There might not be many more, you want to come?'

'I'd love to,' I said, terrified at the idea of being a groupie and thrilled at the idea of, well, being a groupie. 'Where is it?'

'Music Hall of Williamsburg,' Another escalator. 'You should bring your roommate, it'll be fun.'

'Sounds good,' I replied. Another escalator. 'I don't think she's doing anything.' I had no idea what she was doing, but as far as I was concerned, she was now coming to Alex's gig. 'Are we actually going to get off the escalators or is this some sort of new performance art I should know about?' I asked as we finally stepped onto solid ground.

'There's something I really want to show you.' Alex walked around the corner, to a painting hanging just inside the corridor, more or less on its own. 'This is my favourite picture in the entire world,' he said, standing a respectful distance back from the painting.

It was small, showing the back of a girl staring at a wooden farmhouse in the near distance. Even from behind, I felt as though I could see she was crying, unable to escape her situation. Unable to tear herself away, even though she wanted to. Needed to. There was nowhere else for her to go.

'*Christina's World*, Andrew Wyeth,' I read out quietly. The fifth floor was almost empty and the silence was eerie. I clutched at Alex's hand, still gazing at the painting. I wanted look away but I couldn't. Before I knew what was happening, tears were streaming down my cheeks.

'It's . . .' I started, not knowing where to go. I dropped Alex's hand and took a half-step closer. 'It's just . . .'

'I know,' he said, putting his hands on my shoulders. 'When I feel trapped or confused or I just forget myself I come here and remind myself. I'm sorry, I thought you would like it. The woman in the painting is paralysed and crawling back to the house but I don't know. Always seems to me like she's wanting to get away from the house rather than back to it.'

'Maybe she doesn't know what she wants,' I said, staring through the girl into the farmhouse. 'Running to, running from, same difference.'

We stood looking at the picture together for what

felt like for ever. Eventually, and only when I'd committed every inch of it to memory, we walked away in silence and wandered around the rest of the gallery.

It took me a while to loosen up, but Alex was the perfect art buddy. He knew so much about the place I was sure he must actually live in the basement and the museum happily swallowed up our afternoon without even a whisper of a ticking clock. We saw everything there was to see, Monet, Pollock, Picasso, Gaugin, Van Gogh. It was like the whole New York experience encapsulated in one space. By the time I realized how long we'd been aimlessly ambling, I was dying of thirst.

'Want to get a drink?' I asked, pulling Alex out of his reverie in front of a collection of design classics.

'Shit, what time is it?' he asked, himself rather than me. 'We have to go or we're going to miss it!'

'Where are we going?' I asked, allowing myself to be dragged mercilessly down Sixth Avenue, trying not to run into meandering tourists or the weaving and dodging commuters. 'Seriously, I really need a drink, just, can we just stop for a second?'

'Let's get in a cab,' he said, not even listening to me. 'It'll probably be quicker in a cab.' He flagged a taxi down and threw me in as it pulled to a stop.

But the traffic was moving almost as slowly as the people on the street and as we inched along, Alex was getting more and more frustrated.

West 50th, 49th, 48th . . .

'Alex,' I said, not too politely. 'Will you tell me where we're bloody going?'

'Bloody? How cute is that?' he said, smiling for the first time since we left the museum. 'Sorry, I wanted to surprise you, but we have to get there before sunset.'

'It's only seven-thirty,' I said, looking at my watch.

And it was still broad daylight outside. 'Why are we rushing?'

'Because we have to queue,' he said, sticking his head out of the window to check the traffic.

45th, 44th, 43rd . . .

'Queue for what?' I was trying not to be incredibly irritating but I had a mouth like Ghandi's flip-flop. 'Please can we just stop and get a drink?'

'It's a surprise,' he said, squeezing my leg and still looking out of the window as though he could will the traffic to move more quickly. 'Trust me, I'll get you a dozen drinks once we're there.'

37th, 36th, 35th, 34th . . .

'Thanks, man,' Alex tossed some cash at the driver. 'Just let us out here.' He pulled me out onto the street and checked his watch. 'Perfect. Now, you wanted a drink?'

I nodded. This wasn't quite the princess treatment I'd been getting used to from Tyler. Alex pointed at a cart on the corner, selling pretzels and, thank God, freezing cold cans of Pepsi. I wrestled a dollar out of my jeans pocket, too busy trying to get my sugary caffeine fix to realize where we were.

'You want to go inside now?' Alex asked, a bemused look on his face while he watched me neck the entire can in less than a minute. I had to admit, it was more to prove a point than anything else, drinking fizzy stuff that quickly just makes me feel sick. I didn't care how cute he looked, standing grinning at me with his arms folded, while I guzzled my Pepsi.

'Inside where?' I asked, draining the can and giving a dramatic, satisfied sigh.

Alex shook his head and pointed upwards. 'Honestly, you try and do something romantic . . .'

I craned my neck up and stared into the skyline.

We were at the foot of the tallest building I'd ever seen.

It was the Empire State Building.

I grabbed onto Alex's arm to stop myself falling over. 'We're going up there?' I asked, breaking into a huge grin.

'We are,' he nodded. 'If you still want to. I know you said you wanted to, but I didn't know if you'd managed it yet.'

'No,' I shook my head and steadied myself for another look up into the cloudless sky, 'I still haven't been. And it's all I've wanted to do.'

'You said.' He smiled and let me stand staring, even though we were clearly in everyone's way. I didn't care, it was amazing. I'd only been in New York for a week and a half and I'd already become oblivious to anything that wasn't directly in front of me. The city was the opposite of an iceberg. What you saw on the surface, what was right in your face every day, that was only a third of it, the rest was up in the sky.

'And we have to be up there for sunset,' Alex said, finally pulling me away from the street corner and towards the entrance.

We queued slowly, moving up and down the lines with hundreds of tourists. It was weird, I really didn't consider myself to be one. Not while I could feel Alex squeezing my hand every time I went silent to stare out of the windows. And queuing is hardly a chore when you have a super hot man kissing your neck and telling you how gorgeous you are for half an hour. By the time we got up to the top, I was pretty much desperate for some air and had forgotten what I was there for entirely. Alex pulled me straight through the racks and racks of wonderfully crappy souvenirs in the gift shop and out to the south side of the observation deck.

I stopped in the doorway for a second, readying myself to take it all in. And it was genuinely, heart-stoppingly beautiful.

Once I had my breath back and had been pushed and pummelled by half a dozen high-school kids, I spotted Alex. He had squeezed himself into a prime position to watch the sunset spread itself across the skyline, and without words, he pulled me in and moved behind me to rest his chin on my shoulder. I shivered and snuggled backwards into him. I wasn't dressed for the altitude, but before I could so much as break into a goosebump, Alex was slipping off his beat-up leather jacket and slipping it on my shoulders, wrapping his arms around me. The city sighed beneath us, preparing itself for the shift from day to night. Lights began to ripple off then on from the southern tip of the island upwards, as people made their journeys from work to home. I worked my fingers into the metal bars and felt my entire body give. It made the views from Mary's office, from my room at The Union, look like something from a View-Master toy. It made this whole New York adventure real.

'Isn't it great?' I asked Alex. 'How can anything be so confusing and shitty when this is so beautiful?'

'Pretty much everything up here is beautiful,' Alex whispered, nuzzling my hair. 'It looks unreal when it snows or when there's a storm. Just like a painting. Pretty cold though.'

'I was going to say, I can imagine,' I said, eyes fixed on the Statue of Liberty, which was blinking at us in the distance. 'But I really can't.'

'Well, we'll just have to come and see it next time it snows,' he replied.

I nodded happily, still searching the horizon for confirmation that everything was going to be OK. And then I realized what he'd said. 'But, I won't be here when it snows,' I said, tensing up. 'I'll have to go home when my visa waiver thingy expires.'

'You never know where you're going to be,' Alex said, brushing my hair aside and kissing my neck to melt away the tension. 'Six months ago, did you know you would be here, now?'

'I didn't know I'd be here six week ago,' I said, leaning into him again. 'I don't know where I'll be six weeks from now.'

'Does it matter right now?' he asked, his warm lips tracing a path down to my collarbone. 'Here with me, home in London, surfing in Honolulu?'

This time, my whole body tensed and I shook my hair back into the path of his kisses.

'Can I ask you something?' he said, gently turning me around to face him. I looked past him, avoiding his eyes, but nodded. 'Why did you cry when you saw the painting?'

'It's an emotional painting.' I offered, not even believing it myself.

'It is, it's a heartbreaking painting, but I've never seen anyone have that reaction to it before and I'm there all the time,' he said. I flickered my eyes across his face. He looked genuinely concerned. 'You can talk to me about stuff, you know? I don't want to think you can't because of all those dumb rules your friend was telling you.'

'It's not about that.' I shook my head, refusing to cry. This was supposed to be fun, this was what I'd dreamed of. 'It's other stuff, home stuff. The fact that I don't have a home, stuff.'

'Want to elaborate?' he asked, placing what was

supposed to be a comforting hand on my shoulder. I shrugged him off and turned back to the city. Here it comes, I thought, here's the big messy break-up story. 'I'm a pretty good listener for a guy.'

'OK, I'm just going to tell you all of it and then, when you've finished laughing, you can be on your way,' I said, leaning my head on my hands and taking a deep breath.

Alex leaned against the railings by my side. Staring straight ahead, not pausing for breath, I told him all of it. It didn't sound funny to me this time, it didn't sound brave, it just sounded sad. I was sure this should get easier, I thought to myself, not harder. When I had finished speaking, I finally found the strength to look at him. He wasn't laughing, he wasn't even smiling, he was just looking at me.

'So you think you're the only person who has a big scary break-up story?' he asked, eyebrows raised. 'It's OK to have a past you know, even if it's a recent past. Seriously, so many people put so much faith in those dumbass rules. I hate that you thought you couldn't tell me that.'

I looked back at him, trying to work out what to say next. 'No, it wasn't that, I, well, I think I could have told you. If I'd wanted to. But I don't want to be that person any more. I don't think I liked her very much and I didn't want to be that person with you. Now, when I'm here,' with you, I didn't say, but I wanted to, 'when I'm here, I like the person I am.'

'I like her too,' Alex said, stroking my cheek and wiping away stray tears I hadn't even felt escape. 'And I do know how you feel. You're not the only one that has had shitty things happen to them and then reacted, you know.'

'I left the bloody country,' I said, furiously rubbing

the tears away myself. Why wouldn't they stop? 'The more I think about it, the more pathetic it was. I can't believe I would do that.'

'Maybe you wouldn't if it happened today,' he suggested. 'Maybe you wouldn't have if it had happened a day earlier. Who knows? And while we're sharing, I have your "I'm pathetic" break-up story beat hands down.'

'I don't believe it,' I said, trying a weak smile. 'What's more tragic than running away?'

'I really don't think you want to know,' Alex smiled.

'Out with it, Reid.'

'OK, since we're sharing, but you'd better know this breaks every one of your friend's rules.'

'You don't have to tell me if you don't want to,' I said hurriedly. I had a feeling I really didn't want to hear his story after all.

'You caught your boyfriend cheating, right?' he asked. I nodded. 'I caught my girlfriend cheating too. With my best friend. In my bed.'

'That's horrible,' I said. He looked so sad. 'No one can blame you for taking that badly, surely?'

'Apparently it had been going on for months,' he continued, taking his turn to stare out over the rooftops. 'On and off, they said. Needless to say, I didn't take it well.'

'Well, what happened?' I wondered what he could possibly have done that made him feel so bad. 'Did you hit him?'

'Yes but that he had coming,' he said simply. 'The dumb thing is, what they did to me wasn't half as bad as what I did to myself.' He let out a long sigh. 'And I just want to preface this with this is what I *was* doing, this isn't what I'm doing now.'

I nodded cautiously. 'You don't have to tell me anything you don't want to,' I said again, really wishing he would listen, praying he wasn't going to tell me something that would reveal him to be anything other than super perfect.

'They didn't stay together once I found out, she kept telling me it was a mistake, that she wanted to come back, that we could work it out, but I couldn't accept it. I was, whatever, heartbroken I guess, but I had this wounded male pride thing going on too, you know? So, instead of meeting her to talk like I said I would, I went out with the guys, I picked up this girl and for a couple of hours, I didn't have to think about what they had done to me.'

'That's not that bad,' I said, trying not to be jealous. This wasn't about me. I wondered what she looked like? 'Just a rebound thing, right?'

'You're going to have to let me finish, it gets a little shittier.' He tried a smile but it didn't really work. 'After that first night, it just got easier and easier to go out, pick up a girl each night and just forget about everything. I kind of convinced myself I was making up for lost time, but at a pretty speedy rate.'

'Oh?' I couldn't really think of specific words to put together into a sentence. And he didn't want to come upstairs with me? This is not about you! a little voice reminded me. 'But to make her jealous?'

'Yeah, except somewhere along the line, I stopped being devastated and just turned into a total dick. And I know it's a cliché, but it didn't make me happy.' He paused to bite at an already gnawed-down fingernail. 'In the morning, I hadn't changed anything. I was still the guy who had been cheated on, only now I was just as much of a shit.'

'But why keep . . . well, why do it if it didn't make you happy?' I asked. My imagination was being stretched to its limit today.

'I didn't know what else to do,' he said. 'And then I kind of figured I'd finally come up against someone who made me want to stop. I met you.'

'Oh.' I let go of his hand. This was all so confusing. 'But when I asked you upstairs, you said no?' It was also getting more and more difficult not to take this all to heart.

'I know,' he said, snatching my hand back. 'It's just, when we started talking it was different. Usually, when a girl knows you're in a band they start acting differently and it stops being honest, it's just about hooking up with the guy in the band, which I get sounds totally pretentious but it's true. But you, you knew and it didn't phase you at all. I was just me, I didn't have to be the guy in the band.'

'I didn't say I would go out with you because you're in a band,' I lied a little bit. It didn't feel like the time to get into my groupie fantasies.

'And that's the reason I didn't come upstairs with you,' Alex said urgently. 'If I had it would have been just the same, another night, another girl. I had a really great time with you. For the first time in a year, I wanted to see someone again. I'm kind of having to learn how to date again, to be with someone for more than just, you know, sex.'

I didn't know what to think. Part of me was saying he had been hurt the same way I had, he'd just handled it differently. But another, really loud part of me was telling me he was trouble, did I really think it was a good idea to keep seeing someone who had slept his way around most of downtown Manhattan? I didn't know what to trust.

'So that girl at the gig, she was telling the truth?' I said, piecing things together.

'I don't know exactly what she said, but probably,'

he said. 'Jesus, I shouldn't have told you any of this. I just thought, while we were laying our cards on the table, I wanted you to know I'm not perfect. I really like you, I really like the way I feel when I'm with you and I want to see you again, however long you're going to be in New York.'

'I like you too,' I said slowly. 'But it's all a bit much at once to be honest.'

Alex nodded and looked down. I hated this, I didn't want to feel this way. And I hated the thought that he might be feeling this way too. Not knowing what else to do, I reached my arms up around his neck and slid in front of him, brushing his floppy fringe out of his eyes. He looked at me, surprised.

'You're not going?' he asked, leaning in close.

'Every single little part of me is saying I should,' I said, not sure I was making the right decision. 'But I'm trying new things, right?'

I closed my eyes and let myself go. We kissed for a long time, but it wasn't hot and heavy. It was soft and warm and searching. Two people looking for something in each other, something we'd lost and didn't really know how to find.

'Can we start again?' Alex asked, holding me tightly to him. For the first time since I got to New York, I was actually cold. 'Can we just pretend none of this happened?'

I nodded. 'Sounds good.'

We stood and looked out over the city. The sun was long gone from the sky and a blanket of reassuring darkness had been tucked over New York, with the newly lit Empire State Building and the Chrysler Building acting like giant nightlights, keeping everyone safe. It looked so completely different, this magical island out there on its own, defiantly sparkling away.

We walked around the deck, Alex pointing out his favourite landmarks, me making comedy comparisons with Blackpool, which were sort of lost him. The way I figured it, if a city could change so completely just because the sun had set, maybe I could learn to manage a few changes of my own.

CHAPTER SIXTEEN

'No way,' Jenny said. 'And you're seriously still going to see him again?'

'Yes,' I said, as we strode down the street towards the cinema on Thursday afternoon. It was the first time we'd seen each other since Alex's Empire State confessional and I needed to empty my head completely. Plus it was ninety-eight degrees and our apartment was sadly lacking air con. 'Honestly, it's fine. It's all out there now and we're just going to start again, no baggage, no secrets, no rules. Just nice and easy simple dating.'

'It'll never happen,' Jenny declared. 'I'm really sorry honey but you know too much about each other, you're both *completely* co-dependent and there's just altogether too much riding on it. Stick with Tyler. In fact, let's find another guy to replace Alex right now.'

'I'm not *not* sticking with Tyler,' I protested, 'but I'm not going to stop seeing Alex either. I really like him, Jenny, and I know you would too.'

'I just think you're making it really hard for yourself,' she said, linking arms with me as we crossed the street. 'This was supposed to be a fun and easy intro, easing you back into the dating game. All of a sudden you're juggling a rich sex god and a poor sexaholic. I don't really see what Alex has going for him.'

'He's cute, clever, funny, we like *all* the same stuff,' I listed, 'when his fringe drops into his eyes, I have to sit on my hands to stop myself from brushing it away, and when he smiles, I melt. I just melt.'

'And what about Tyler?' she asked, smiling. 'He didn't make you melt three times on Sunday night?'

'OK,' I said, blushing. 'Tyler is gorgeous, he's sweet, he's clever, and he treats me like an absolute princess, but, I don't know, I don't connect to him in the same way.'

'I think you have connected,' Jenny nodded vehemently. 'You connected all the way to Tiffany's. I'd take that kind of connection over some floppy-haired man ho, doll.'

'Stop it,' I laughed. 'I do like Tyler and when I'm with him, I really like him. It's just when I'm not, when I'm on my own, my thoughts always end up on Alex.'

'I still think you're making this really hard,' she said, squeezing my hand. 'But whatever works for you, sweetie. This Alex guy just sounds so much like trouble.'

'Well, you can judge for yourself. Are you working tomorrow evening?'

Jenny shook her head. 'Nope, I have a very important date with TiVo and *America's Next Top Model*. We've had the cast of some new teen movie in all week and they've been working me like a dog. For seventeen-year-old boys, they have some freaky requests . . .'

'And I expect to hear every last detail about every last one.' I loved Jenny's sneaky celebrity stories. 'But you are coming to Brooklyn to Alex's gig with me.'

'Firstly honey, I'm absolutely not going to Brooklyn

on my one night off in for ever,' she said, striking off her points on her fingers. 'Secondly, my skinny indie boy days are as far behind me as my skinny jeans days, and thirdly, I'm not going to play chaperone to you two. It's not healthy.'

I smiled sweetly, waiting a moment.

'Brooklyn? Really?'

'I'll even take the subway and I'll buy all your drinks,' I promised. 'I really want you to meet Alex.'

'Jesus, I'd better dig out my Chucks,' she sighed. 'You're totally buying the candy tonight as well.'

'Never a problem,' I said staring at the Milk Duds, Raisanettes, Sour Worms, and wondering which of the bags and bags of new sweets to try. America the Brave.

Before I could get excited about introducing Alex to Jenny, I had my Friday morning meeting with Mary to get worked up about. I took it as a good sign when her assistant greeted me with a smile and, I nearly fainted, a coffee.

'Angela,' Mary was sort of smiling, her wire-rimmed glasses propped up on the top of her insanely shiny grey bob. I had to remember to ask what shampoo she used. 'Tell me why you want to write for me.'

'Because I love to write,' I said, a little thrown by her idea of a hello.

'And?' Mary turned her back to me and looked out of the window.

'Because, I,' I wasn't sure what she wanted me to say. 'I have something to say?'

'And what is that exactly?' Mary asked, turning to face me. Literally, she leaned right into my chair.

'I'm not sure yet.' Honest, if not my best answer ever.

'Neither am I. The thing is, everyone in the team meeting loved your writing. I like your writing,' Mary said, sitting down behind her desk. 'It's funny, it makes me like you and want to read about you, but I don't know where it's going.'

'Oh,' I deflated in front of her. 'Where do you want it to go?'

'I need it to go somewhere,' Mary said, picking up a pencil and flicking it on the table. 'Let's look at what we like.'

She pulled all the columns I had sent over out of a drawer. My witty little, self-effacing dating diaries were covered in scratchy red pen, questions marks and illegible notes, which I was sure more or less amounted to 'pile of steaming poo'.

'I like seeing New York through your eyes,' she started, pulling a piece from the bottom of the pile. 'I like how you talk about what you're doing, where you're going in the city, but I need more. *Look* readers love to read about New York, and it's great to get it from a fresh pair of eyes, but the whole blog can't depend on it. Lots of readers already live here, and they need more than travel writing.'

'OK.' I nodded, taking out a pad and pencil and scribbling notes. They were scribbles too, it had been so long since I'd had to put pen to paper. 'I can definitely work on that.'

'And the dates, I'm kind of confused,' Mary stopped tapping and stared at me intently. 'On paper, there isn't that much of a contest, is there?'

'There isn't?' I asked. I had hoped that my blogs hadn't made it entirely obvious who I was most interested in. I'd even elaborated a little bit to try and stir up some contention amongst my potential 'readers'.

'Let me think.' Mary began to read from one of my entries. '*Wall Street really made me feel like a princess last night. From the way he always opens the door and pulls out my chair to the way he holds my hand and acts as though I'm the entire only person in the world when we're together, I just can't get enough of this treatment. It's a whole new world.*'

'Really?' I said. I was so surprised.

'You know how many of my readers are looking for a Wall Street banker to make them feel like a princess? This is gold to us.' Mary slapped the piece of paper down on the desk. 'Downtown guy, he's a plot twist at the moment honey, a distraction, but everyone knows his kind is never going to get you anywhere.'

'I guess,' I smiled. At least I'd managed not to make it obvious how much I really liked Alex.

'Word of advice, and this is as a woman, not an editor,' Mary leaned back and shook her head. 'You just got out of a long relationship that ended badly. You need to be spoiled, wooed and screwed six ways from Sunday. If you want the blog to work, you have to keep dating. From what you've told me so far, this Alex guy is going to screw you, but not in the right way. Date around for a while, keep the blog fun, but Angela, they don't call them *investment* bankers for nothing.'

'I suppose it does all make sense on paper,' I acknowledged. Tyler really did have everything going for him, great in bed, generous, hot, and most importantly, he might have told me he had dated around a lot, but he hadn't slept with every girl that had ever made eye contact with him for the last year.

'Life is rarely as simple as it looks on paper,' Mary smiled again. Two in one meeting, yes! 'So here's the deal. *The Adventures of Angela* are go. I'm going to put the intro piece online when we refresh the site tonight, and then we'll start publishing the blog every day from Monday. You keep sending in entries every day by four and I keep a few days back in the bank. We meet again in a fortnight to sense check everything.'

'Really?'

'Really.'

I wanted to jump up and down and hug her, but despite her dating advice, Mary didn't strike me as the hugging kind. She struck me as the 'What the hell are you doing?' kind, so I figured I'd save that for Jenny.

'Any plans for the weekend?' Mary asked as I stood up to leave after we'd discussed the wonderful issue of my expenses. Basically, she was going to pay for everything and give me $75 for each piece. She was paying me actual money to write. Ha! 'Apart from clicking on your own link a thousand times?'

'Oh, I wouldn't do that,' I blushed. I'd have repetitive strain in my index finger by Monday if it would help me keep this job. 'But yep, I'm going to Alex's gig tonight with my friend, and tomorrow I'm going to Central Park with Tyler, for a picnic.'

'Picnic in the park?' Mary raised an eyebrow. 'Keep this up and we're going to have to change this to a bridal blog.'

'Oh no,' I half laughed. 'It's not like that, really, it's not.'

'It's dinner, theatre and Tiffany's,' Mary said bluntly. 'Is he good in bed?'

'You said not to put that in the blog,' I blanched.

'I did. Now I'm asking you a question.' She stared me down. Definitely not a hugger.

'Erm, yes?' I said.

'Have fun at the gig tonight, but work that picnic like it's paying your rent.' She almost cracked a record third smile. 'Angela, he's a keeper.'

* * *

'Angie, he's hot!' Jenny squeezed my hand as we walked into the club to find Alex already on stage. By the time Jenny had decided on a hipster-friendly outfit that didn't clash with her 'I can't believe I'm almost thirty' freak out, approved my black Splendid smock dress and Keds, briefed me on how I was under orders to get down and dirty with Alex tonight, *and* necked three dozen beers in a bar by the subway, it was after ten when we made it into the gig.

However, tardy she might be, wrong she was not. He looked amazing up there.

'What is it about guys in bands?' Jenny asked, grabbing two beers from the bar and passing me one, eyes fixed on the stage. 'I'd forgotten how much hotter they get just being elevated by three feet, even when they're not hot. I remember when we had The Chili Peppers at The Union. Man, busy week . . .'

'I think it's a passion thing,' I said, mesmerized by Alex's sweaty stage presence. Seeing him up there now, writhing around under the hot lights, I was glad we hadn't talked to him before the show. I just wanted to watch for a while without him knowing. 'It's the whole thing about them being so passionate about something that they had to write a song to express it. It's the same with artists, writers, maybe not bongo players.'

'And because holding a guitar makes you look so damn cool,' Jenny breathed, swaying to the music. 'If he can do that with six strings, imagine what he can do with one of you.'

'That too,' I admitted. It had crossed my mind.

'I wonder if the bassist is seeing anyone,' Jenny nudged me in the ribs and pulled me into the crowd to dance.

It was one of those gigs where the bass is turned up

so high that you can almost feel it retraining your heartbeat in time with its own. There was nothing to do but clap, sing along and move with the music. With Jenny beside me, I didn't need to worry about any of Alex's conquests who might be in the club. I couldn't hand on heart say I hadn't thought about what would happen if the blonde girl from Saturday night appeared again, especially now I knew she was telling the truth, but dancing with Jenny, it all felt far away. The band was on fire, cranking out song after song. I just couldn't marry this amazing show to everything Alex had told me about breaking up the band, to their hearts just not being in it. They were so tight, so electric, and the crowd in the hot sweaty club was just eating up everything they put out there.

I couldn't remember the last time I'd been out dancing, let alone dancing at a gig, just that feeling of being a cog in the machine of this pulsing crowd felt so good. And with a few beers in me and a hot girl to dance with, I was having the best time. For someone who said her best gig days were behind her, Jenny certainly seemed to remember some moves. Within minutes, she had a whole gaggle of guys stalking around her like lions, but she just kept dancing with me regardless. After a few more short, sharp numbers, Alex signed off in a frenzy of feedback, ear-piercing screaming and more manly appreciative hollering. I could see how easy it must have been for him to pick up girls who were, well, easy.

'I want to meet him,' Jenny slurred, holding on to my arm tightly, but still dancing. 'Where did he go? Are we going? I demand to meet him.'

'You will,' I said, half drunk myself, but sobering slightly when I realized one of us had to find a way home later and it clearly wasn't going to be her. 'Alex just said he'd meet us by the bar afterwards. Do you want some water?'

'I'll get the drinks.' She bopped over to the bar, leaving me in a sea of warm, moist bodies, half milling towards the exit, the other half eyeing each other up to see where the night was going to take them. I just hoped Jenny would make it back from the bar in one piece. And without more beers.

'Hey, beautiful.' A pair of arms snaked around my waist and I felt a steamy, wet body pushing up against me. 'Did you see the show?'

'I did,' I said, writhing around to face Alex. His face was flushed, his hair stuck to his forehead, his T-shirt clinging to his body. 'You were great.'

'We were, weren't we?' He gave me a hot sticky kiss, rubbing away any remains of make-up that might have survived the show. 'Man, it was awesome. It was the best show in months.'

'I can't believe you would want to give this up,' I said, scraping his hair back. His eyes were burning so brightly and he looked so vital, so alive.

'Don't want to talk about it,' he smiled, picking me up and spinning me around. 'Now where's this friend of yours?'

'At the bar, I hope.' I looked over into the mass of people surrounding the two harassed-looking barmen. 'And I'm warning you, she's got a thing for your bassist.'

'Well, he's got a thing for guys, so I don't like her chances,' he said, holding me tightly around the waist, making me waddle towards the bar with him still attached.

Luckily, Jenny was at the bar. Unluckily, Jenny had seen something she shouldn't have. She was frozen to a stool, with two beers in front of her and no end of guys milling around her, but she wasn't talking or flirting, she wasn't even drinking. Jenny was staring at someone across the room, standing by the door. Her eyes were on fire and she was biting down on her bottom lip so hard, I felt sure she would draw blood.

'Jenny?' I said, breaking Alex's hold around my waist and holding him back at a safe distance. 'Jenny, are you OK?'

'It's Jeff,' she pointed at a tall, fair-haired man standing across the room. Judging by his easy smile and the way he was laughing and joking with his friends, he clearly hadn't seen Jenny. Or if he had, he must have been one pretty heartless bastard.

'You know Jeff?' Alex stumbled past me, arm stuck out for a handshake. 'Cool. I'm Alex.'

Jenny stared at him. 'You know Jeff?'

'Yeah,' Alex said, arm still out there. 'He just moved into my building, maybe, three months ago or something.'

'Is he single?' Jenny asked.

I stood between them, not really knowing what answer I wanted Alex to give. Jenny seemed to have sobered up dangerously quickly, which could not possibly be a good thing.

'I guess so,' Alex's arm began to drop slightly. He looked across at me, but I didn't even know what sort of expression to give him. 'I've never seen him with a girl anyway. Kind of thought he might be gay,' he mused.

It was the best answer he could have given. Jenny brightened up, but still eyed Jeff warily over my shoulder. Finally she shook Alex's hand as the stocky man in the sound booth in the middle of the room cranked up the stereo.

'I'm Jenny, smile,' she shouted, snapping a photo of the two of us with her phone. 'And if you fuck with

Angie, I'm going to use this photo to hunt you down and kill you.'

Alex stepped back and nodded. 'Sounds fair,' he yelled over the music. It was getting louder by the second.

'I have to go talk to him,' Jenny said, freeing herself from her barstool and passing us the two beers. 'I can't just sit here and not go say something.'

'Jenny,' I stepped in front of her and held her shoulders lightly. 'Are you sure? We could just go somewhere else?' I didn't know if I could take a rerun of last week, and that time, she'd only seen him for five minutes in the hotel.

'It's fine,' she said, gently pushing my arms down. 'I'm in a good place, I'm owning my past and I'm just going to say, hi, how are you doing, yes, I do look hot, and then I'll come back, we can go home, and I'll cry myself to sleep.'

'Sounds like fun,' Alex murmured into my hair.

'Jenny, really, don't do it to yourself,' I tried, but she was already gone. 'I can't look,' I said, turning into Alex's sweaty green T-shirt. 'What's happening?'

'I was sort of hoping we might be,' he raised my chin to kiss me, but I pushed him away.

'What's happening with Jenny and Jeff?' I hissed as quietly as I could.

'Uh, she's talking, he's talking, he's kissing her on the cheek—' Alex commentated.

'He's kissing her?' I squealed, spinning around to see. Jeff was indeed kissing Jenny on the cheek, and it wasn't a quick peck. It was a poorly disguised 'I really want to kiss you but I can't' kiss on the cheek. I watched his lips linger near her face, in her hair, as they whispered to each other, staring earnestly into each other's eyes, squeezing forearms and generally failing to disguise how badly they were still into each other. Looked as though Jeff's 'new girlfriend' was nowhere to be seen.

'So they know each other then?' Alex asked, as we watched Jenny practically wind herself around Jeff. 'And woah, that guy is not gay.'

'Why did you think he was?' I asked, turning away before they made me blush.

'I don't know, he's seems cool, he's got a great design job, great apartment and everything,' Alex shrugged. 'He's never got a girl with him and he's just got a vibe, you know? And the man is well dressed. Always.'

'Well, if in doubt go with a stereotype,' I said, turning back for a quick peek. He certainly wasn't giving off gay vibes at that precise moment in time. 'He's her ex, but she's never got over him.'

'She carries on doing what she's doing now and she's definitely not going to get over him.' Alex chugged his beer then pointed with his bottle. 'Under him, maybe. You had your meeting today, right?' Alex asked, turning his full attention back to me. 'How did it go?'

'Oh my God, I completely forgot!' I clapped a hand to my mouth. 'My blog is being uploaded at midnight!'

'How do you forget something like that? That's fantastic!' Alex scooped me up in a bear hug. For a skinny boy, those muscles were so strong. 'So as of midnight you're a published columnist?'

'As of midnight,' I nodded and looked at my watch 'In ten minutes!'

'You know what I think?' Alex moved closer, his breath tickling my ear. 'I think we should finish up here and then go check out your blog. At my apartment.'

'Oh,' I said, my whole body prickling with anticipation. 'What about Jenny?'

'I was kind of thinking just me and you, but sure, if you're into that,' he grinned, that sneaky wink reappearing. 'Just checking out the blog, scout's honour.'

'You were absolutely never a scout.' I pushed him playfully. 'And I can't just leave Jenny here . . .' but I couldn't actually even see her. She wouldn't have left without me, would she? She was supposed to be my chaperone!

'Hey, Angie!'

She sneaked up behind me, hand in hand with Jeff, her face flushed bright red. Jeff stood behind her, a completely besotted look on his face.

'Hey, man,' Alex nodded to Jeff.

'Hey!' Jeff replied, snapping out of his trance for a split second. 'Great show.'

'Can I just have a quick word?' I took Jenny's arm and pulled her away, towards the doors. 'What are you doing?'

'Oh, Ange,' Jenny mooned, hugging me tightly. How did she still smell so nice? I was fairly sure I stank by now. 'It's so good! He wants to go back to his to talk. He says he wants to talk about 'stuff'. Isn't that so good?'

'It's great,' I said, peeling her arms from around my neck. 'But shouldn't you do it tomorrow, when you're sober? When you're both sober?'

'No, no, no, no!' When Jenny shook her head, her whole body followed. 'This is it, this is fate. We're absolutely meant to be together.'

'OK, so you're just going to go back to his?' I asked. 'What about us going home together?'

'Oh, yeah, well,' she looked back into the bar. 'You know, you're right. Jeff can come back with us!'

The idea of sharing a cab all the way back to the apartment with the two of them dry humping (at best) all over the back seat was even scarier than what would happen if I went back to Alex's. 'Come on then,' I sighed, dragging her back into the bar. 'But you're coming to Alex's for coffee before you roll into Jeff's. You do want to remember this in the morning, don't you?'

'So, back to mine?' Alex asked, putting his arm around my shoulders as Jenny collapsed back into Jeff's arms. I had to admit, they both looked really happy.

'Jenny and Jeff are going to come and see the website with us,' I nodded.

'I think Jenny and Jeff could make some money with a website of their own,' Alex said, pulling me behind him while I chivvied Jenny along. 'Why did they even break-up?'

'Long story,' I said, following him out onto the street. 'And I think we've had enough of those to last us a while as it is.'

Alex and Jeff's building was only five minutes' walk away, but my nerves and Jenny's drunken stumbling-slash-fumbling tripled the journey time. Alex hadn't been kidding when he said Jeff lived in a nice building, what I hadn't worked out was that by default, that meant so did he. For building, read huge converted warehouse, and for apartment, substitute fifth-floor loft with huge windows and views across the river.

'How do you have this?' I asked, drawn to the windows. I was such a lemming these days, too long stuck in a ground-floor maisonette. 'I thought you were a penniless artist?'

'I never said I was penniless,' he said, fiddling with a Macbook and then Googling *The Look* website. Jenny and Jeff finally made it out of the lift and appeared in the doorway, making up for lost time, fast.

'Clearly,' I said. The whole place reeked of Alex. The original artwork from the band's albums hung in frames on the white walls, cracked leather sofas, huge CD collection taking up practically a whole wall, and a tiny kitchenette that looked like the place takeaway cartons came to die. 'It's gorgeous, Alex.'

'Thanks,' he said, looking up from the computer. 'My brother is in real estate so it's really his find. We bought it a few years ago when prices across here were nothing. The page is loading, come see.'

I dropped onto the sofa beside him and peeked out from behind his shoulder as the different elements of the page flashed into life. *The Look* main banner, the navigation bar. And finally, the text box flashed into life.

'Jenny, come and look!' I squealed, clutching Alex's arms and reading. It was surreal! 'I can't believe this.'

'*The Adventures of Angela*: Twenty-six-year-old Angela is the latest recruit to our ever-growing glamorous group of bloggers. Read all about her New York adventures, only at TheLook.com . . .' Alex read out loud.

'Stop it, stop it,' I wailed, proud and embarrassed and scared all at once. 'Seriously, you don't need to read it ever. It's just – really, you don't need to read it. Please?'

'Twenty-six, huh? I'd have said twenty-five tops.' He turned and smiled. 'It sounds great. Now can I read it or not?'

'Not?' I winced as he started anyway.

Jenny prised herself away from Jeff just long enough for the two of them to come and look at the page. 'I'm so proud of you, doll,' she said, hugging me again. I couldn't help but notice the traces of her perfume were now long gone but Jeff's post-gig 'glow' was all over her. 'Don't be embarrassed! This is great!'

'I couldn't have done it without you and Erin,' I said, hugging back. 'I know I shouldn't be embarrassed, it's just so out there. I just keep trying to think about all the things I've written in the diary and then trying not to think that they're going to be on a website for everyone to read.' For Alex and Tyler to read, I added silently.

'Everyone knows not to take these things so seriously,' Jenny said, easing herself back towards the sofa, where Jeff was waiting with open arms and, oh look at that, an erection. 'Everyone totally reads it as fiction.'

'Do you think so?' I asked Alex, nibbling at my little fingernail. I hadn't bitten my nails since Louisa had made me use some horrible-tasting stuff, a month before the wedding.

'Yeah, she's right,' he said, gently brushing his free hand up and down my back. 'Besides, what's it matter what strangers read?'

'Strangers, school teachers, my mum,' I said out loud, but silently repeating Jenny's comment about guitarists while his fingers played up and down my spine. We're taking it slowly, I reminded myself. We're taking it slowly. 'It's not all strangers, is it?'

'I guess not, but anyone who knows you will know what's real and what isn't,' he said, finally turning back to me. 'You want me to print it out?'

'No, that would be too cheesy,' I said, trying to tear my eyes away from the screen. 'Actually, maybe we should. Just in case they take it down again in the morning.'

Alex laughed, pressed print and placed the laptop on the low coffee table in front of us. 'You think they're going to make it back to Jeff's place?' he asked, looking over at Jenny and her 'ex' furiously kissing. It was more or less impossible to work out which denim-clad limb belonged to which person.

'I don't know.' It was like a car crash, I couldn't stop looking, but I knew that I really shouldn't be. 'How far away is it?'

'Across the hall.' Alex stood up and lowered the lights. I wasn't sure if that made things better or worse. 'I really hope they make it, that couch isn't going to take much more.'

He held out his hand, which I gladly took. It was either leave the room now or settle in with some popcorn for the live action porno. Really, people paid a lot of money to see what we were getting for free. Whether we liked it or not.

'I vote we leave them to it,' Alex pulled me gently towards a dark doorway. 'I don't think we're going to be playing late-night Boggle.'

The dark doorway led to his bedroom. A rumpled, but made, futon took centre stage, accessorized by an acoustic guitar, another stereo and an open wardrobe, packed full of faded T-shirts and leather jackets. Weirdly, hiding at the very end, was a suit. I supposed everyone had to have one. The low windowsill was lined with candles and I noted that without exception, they all had fresh wicks, so either Alex went through a lot of candles or they had been laid on for my benefit. I wasn't sure if it was too sweet or too smooth, a potential throwback to his serial shagging days. I lingered in the doorway while he turned on the stereo.

'We might not be able to see them in here, but I don't really want to hear them, either.' He took a matchbook from a tall thin chest of drawers by the bed and started lighting the candles. I was starting to err towards too smooth.

'Yeah,' I replied, my eyes being drawn back to the bed again and again. On what I assumed was Alex's side was a big stack of well-read books, biographies, classics, newer cult stuff. Was he really a reader or were they just more props?

'Angela, I didn't bring you in here to . . .' he trailed off and stood awkwardly by the window. I realized I was clinging on to the doorframe for dear life. 'You can come in, I'm not going to attack you.'

I laughed softly, at myself, and moved over to the bed, perching on the very edge. 'Sorry, I know. I should just go home,' I said, looking at my shoes. They were edged in black crap from the gig. Now all I could think about was whether or not I'd trekked it all round Alex's apartment. 'Jenny's safe and everything.'

'I don't want you to go home,' Alex joined me on the foot of the bed, 'but if you want me to call you a cab, I will. Or you can stay, we can talk a while and I promise I'll keep my hands where you can see them.'

He looked so sweet, so earnest and held out his hands, palm up. How could someone who had crashed up and down the stage, writhing around a guitar and thrashing into his microphone stand so many times I was sure he'd have bruises, become this tender, soft guy in just a couple of hours? Was this all part of the act? There's only one way to find out, I thought, taking one of the hands in mine.

'You're going to have to do most of the talking,' I said, lurching backwards and leaning on an elbow. 'I'm actually shattered.'

'Not a problem,' he smiled, giving my hand a squeeze and then rolling over onto his side. 'I can go all night.'

I burst out laughing. 'Did you really just say that?' I asked, punching him in the shoulder.

'You know what I mean.' He laughed, rubbing his

shoulder with a hurt expression. 'You punch pretty hard for a girl.'

'You've got to be able to defend yourself if you're going to go into cheesy boys' bedrooms and sit through their terrible chat-up lines.' I smiled, relaxing a little bit. 'That was awful.'

'Yeah, whatever,' Alex pulled a face. 'You know what, I really stink. Do you mind if I take a quick shower?'

I shook my head. 'Not at all but don't expect me to be awake when you're done.'

'I won't wake you,' he rolled towards me and kissed me gently, 'unless you want me to.'

Before I could work out what I wanted, he pushed up off the bed and disappeared through the door.

'Not looking, guys,' I heard him call out into the darkness. 'You just keep on desecrating my couch.'

I smiled and dropped backwards. Now all I had to do was work out what I was going to do when Alex came out of the shower, all clean and fresh and wet and . . . I closed my eyes for just a second, the candle-light blurring at the edge of my vision.

'Someone should blow them out . . .' I muttered to the empty room.

By the time I opened my eyes, someone had. I felt a body above me, breathing softly and stroking my hair back off my face, gently bringing me round.

'Alex?' I murmured as soft, hot lips pressed against my bare neck and a damp hand trailed along my collar-bone. My eyes flickered open but it was pitch black in the room, the only light coming from the city, a world away in the window.

'Sorry,' he whispered. 'I know I said I wouldn't wake you, but . . .'

'S'OK,' I said sleepily, shifting slightly, accepting the weight of his body. His damp hair fell against my face as we kissed lazily, our hands entwined above my head. Slowly, I began to wake up, and steadily, the kisses grew stronger and more urgent. I pulled my legs up, accidentally pulling his towel away as we slid up the bed, and felt his soft skin all around me, warm from the shower. In the dark, without visuals, it seemed his skinny boy act was entirely illusory, the muscles in his back moving under his skin as lowered himself onto me. Just as our legs began to wind themselves around each other and my hands lost themselves in his thick black hair, the bedroom door was flung open, spilling light all over the bed.

'Shit, sorry,' Jeff said, purposefully looking away. 'Alex, man, Jenny threw up on your rug. Do you have cleaning stuff anywhere?'

I covered my face with my hands, not knowing whether to laugh or cry. Even if she didn't know it, Jenny had implemented her chaperone role just in time.

'Is she OK?' Alex rolled off the bed, wrapping his towel around his waist as he went. 'Is she in the bathroom?'

I loved that he asked if she was OK before he had even put his boxers on. Which tragically, he did next.

'Not tonight, huh?' He gave me a lopsided smile from the doorway. I shook my head and smiled back. Damn it, Jenny, I thought, why did you have to make me stick to my word? Tiptoeing through the big, stinky mess in the living room, I found Jenny had taken up residency in the bathroom face down in the toilet, kneeling on top of Alex's sweaty T-shirt.

'Oh, Jenny,' I sighed and knelt down beside her, scraping her hair back from her face in an entirely unromantic gesture. 'Are you going to be OK?'

Words were still a way off, but she managed to nod before she started retching again. Once she had calmed down to one dry heave every three minutes, I left to get some water and find the bottom half of her outfit. Apparently things had got fairly far with Jeff before all her beers made a break for freedom, and, as close as we now were, I would have been much happier if she had some pants on. American usage or English.

Back in the living room, Alex and Jeff, both half naked, were scrubbing away at a big watery stain with spray-on cleaners and makeshift cloths. I knew it would be a bad time to laugh out loud, but I couldn't help a bit of a smile.

'You two all right?' I asked, filling up an empty, cleanish-looking glass I found on the kitchen top.

'Uh-huh,' Alex grunted from the floor. He didn't look all right. Jeff looked as if he'd been all right until about ten minutes ago when things had gone horribly wrong. His T-shirt was stained and his trousers, like Jenny's were MIA. I sidled over with my glass and gingerly picked up Jenny's jeans. Giving them a quick once-over, I was satisfied that they had come off pre-puke and took them into the bathroom. Jenny was trying to prop herself up against the shower stall and wash her face, but without much luck.

'Hey you,' I said, giving her the water, which she sipped delicately. 'You feel any better?'

'I am so fucking embarrassed,' she groaned, passing me the glass back and holding her hands under the running cold tap, then pressing them to her face. 'I threw up on Jeff.'

'That's not all you did on Jeff, now is it?' I said, taking a tissue and wiping a tiny bit of sick off her shoulder. 'What's going on there then?'

She gave me a weak, pale smile. 'We're going to try again. He says he missed me.' She rubbed under her eyes, magnifying an attractive panda effect. 'He says there hasn't been anyone else since me.'

'Wow,' I said, passing her the glass back and forcing her to drink more water. 'That's brilliant. I'm really pleased for you.'

'And just think, if we hadn't come to Brooklyn, I might never have bumped into him again,' she sighed, her back, thankfully, to the bathroom mirror. 'And how weird would it have been if you had seen him when you were here and not known it was my Jeff? Too weird. It's all fate.'

'Maybe it is,' I said, sitting on the closed toilet seat and flushing just to make sure. 'There's definitely something at work stopping me and Alex doing any more than getting me really, really worked up.'

'Oh shit, sorry babe,' Jenny tried another weak smile.

'But it's OK,' I told myself, 'it's for the best. We said we were going to go slow and I think it was speeding up a bit too fast. Besides, I have a date with Tyler tomorrow afternoon and I don't think I could go through with it if anything more serious had happened with Alex.'

'See, this doesn't sound like fun. I thought you were just supposed to be having fun,' Jenny groaned. 'Why do they have to make everything so damned tricky?'

'Are you two having some sort of secret meeting in there or can I please pee?' Alex called through the door. Helping Jenny find her balance, I emerged blinking into the now lit up living room.

'I'm so sorry,' I said quietly as Alex passed into the bathroom.

'Harsh lighting, not cool.' Jenny stumbled, holding

her hands over her eyes. I looked from her to Jeff to Alex. It was weird being the only person in a group of four who was dressed.

'We should go,' I said, scanning the room for my bag and passing custody of Jenny over to Jeff, who took her happily. It must have been love if he could smile at her in that state. 'Can we get a taxi from here?'

'Not easily at this time,' Alex yelled from the bathroom, mid-pee. 'It's cool, you can stay here if you want.'

I looked at Jenny, bracing herself against the sofa while Jeff tentatively patted her shoulder, and gratefully nodded in agreement. God knows I didn't feel great about getting in a taxi with vom-stained Jenny, and it was after two. I was completely knackered. Alex reappeared and gave me two T-shirts. 'You two take my room, I'll be on the couch,' he said, kissing me on the cheek and motioning to Jeff that it was time to leave.

'Yeah, of course,' Jeff said, passing Jenny back to me. 'So sorry about the rug, man, I'll get a cleaner in or something. Bye,' he said to Jenny mooning in the doorway. 'I'll call you tomorrow?'

Before Jenny could answer, Alex had shut the door, arms folding, foot tapping.

'Bed then,' I said. Jenny had gone right through the drunken spectrum and crashed somewhere around comatose. I guided her into the bedroom and pulled off her strappy black top, replacing it with Alex's Ramones T-shirt. She crawled up the bed until her head was almost on the pillows and passed out.

'I'm sorry,' I said again to Alex. 'This isn't really how I imagined tonight would go.'

'Another time,' he said, pulling a spare pillow out

from under the couch. 'You know what they say about the best laid plans.'

I just want to get laid, I thought.

'You going to be OK in there with her?'

'I don't know, but I'll shout if she tries anything.'

CHAPTER SEVENTEEN

The next morning, Jenny woke early, still half drunk and craving something sweet. I tried to convince her the best thing for everyone in these circumstances is a bacon sandwich, but she wasn't convinced. In so far as she retched at the suggestion. I tried not to catch sight of myself in the mirror as I slipped out of bed but I accidentally caught a quick glimpse and couldn't tear my eyes away. It wasn't pretty. Post-gig, my hair was greasy and huge, having backcombed itself into a sweaty bouffant during last night's fumblings. My melted make-up had managed to lodge itself into every burgeoning wrinkle and pillow crease, making me look ten years older, and, best of all, I had badger's arse breath. This was not a good look for mine and Alex's first morning-after-the-nothing-before.

'At least you don't look like this,' Jenny grumbled, joining me in an unhappy stare before she retched suddenly and (thankfully) dry heaved over the bed.

'That's true,' I said, half carrying her to the bathroom. 'That is true.'

'Thanks,' she stared daggers at me, curled around the base of the toilet while trying to pull her hair into something resembling a style. There really was no use.

Despite Jenny's best efforts to convince me otherwise, I couldn't just slip out without waking Alex, so I went first and tiptoed across the still damp rug to where he was quietly dozing on the sofa. He looked exactly as we'd left him, apart from one noticeable addition in his boxers.

'Nice!' Jenny mouthed giving me a double OK sign by the door and stifling giggles. I replied with my middle finger. Plus, I couldn't help but notice it was nothing to laugh at.

'Alex,' I said softly, keeping enough of a distance between us for my dog breath not to be too much of a problem. I'd swilled quickly in the bathroom and tried the old toothpaste on the finger trick, but it hadn't had nearly enough of an effect.

'Huh?' He opened one eye, looking confused. 'Angela?'

'We're going to get off now,' I whispered, my hand lightly on his shoulder, eyes well away from the below the waist area. 'Me and Jenny, we're going to go.'

'OK,' he mumbled, rolling over onto his front.

'That's going to hurt,' Jenny called lightly across the room. Another middle finger for her as we made our way out of the flat.

With only a couple of hours before I was supposed to meet Tyler at the park, I had some serious damage control to deal with. I packed Jenny off to bed with two Advil, a large bottle of water and half the pastry counter of the deli on the corner, then took up residency in the bathroom. For the first time in for ever, I ran a bath and got ready to soak. I needed to get all thoughts of Alex out of my head and all of Jenny's drool out of my hair. If I'd had longer, I'd cancel, I thought, stepping into the tiny tub and relaxing. I didn't think I was the kind of girl who thrived on drama, but then my life had been so boring for so long, maybe a bit of drama would do me good. And at least it made for a more interesting blog entry than my old life would have: got up, wrote a thirty-two-page book about a talking bee, ate some calorie-controlled rice cakes, waited around for my boyfriend to come home from shagging his tennis partner, went to bed in button-up old man's pyjamas.

Eventually, I forced myself out of the bath and smothered myself in body lotion, sure I could still smell post-gig mustiness on me. Hopefully, a nice walk in the park would sort that right out. I picked out a shorts and shirt combo and accessorized with my beautiful Tiffany necklace, which I still hadn't worn yet, and started to look forward to the fresh air, if not trying to talk to Tyler without mentioning any of my adventures with Alex.

As Tyler had predicted, Central Park was busy, but it was also incredible.

'How can this exist in the middle of the city?' I marvelled. As we ventured further and further into the greenery, the city seemed to fade away, leaving a complete oasis, packed with joggers, families, couples, groups of friends. Just about every sort of person you could imagine was in that park.

'Would you like the history lesson or was that a rhetorical question?' Tyler offered. He was carrying a large rucksack that I prayed was packed with food. I'd spent so long getting ready, applying de-puffing eye gel and checking Jenny was still breathing, I hadn't even eaten. 'It's great though. They call it the lungs of the city.'

'I can see that,' I nodded as we veered off the path and over to a sunny, relatively unoccupied spot by a beautiful large lake. 'It's just madness to me that all this is man-made.'

'You don't have parks like this in London?' he asked, spreading a blanket before he let me sit down.

'We have parks,' I nodded, 'loads of parks, but this is so impressive. London is so higgledy-piggledy, which I love, but the idea that someone sat down and said, we've got to have a massive park in the middle of this planned, organized city, that's ace. And even more I love that no one has been allowed to build on it when they started running out of space – not the case in London.'

'I'm really sorry,' Tyler smiled, unzipping the rucksack and producing a bottle of red wine. 'I lost you at "higgledy piggledy".'

'Ha ha!' I accepted a wineglass and let him pour. Please let there be some food in there too? 'You make me feel so English.'

'Is that a bad thing?' He poured himself a glass and pushed the cork back in the bottle. 'I love it when you say things like that.'

'No, of course it's not a bad thing.' Why was there still no food? 'It just reminds me I can't stay here for ever. Which sucks.'

'They won't take you back if you start saying thinks like "sucks",' he scolded lightly.

'Sorry,' I smiled, holding my hand up to shield my eyes from the sun. 'One thinks it's a terrible shame that those dreadful builders should be allowed to build on such marvellous greenery.'

'More like it,' Tyler smiled, planting a tiny kiss on the end of my nose.

I lay back on the blanket and stared up at the cloudless sky. This must be the only place on the whole of Manhattan where I could look upwards and not see skyscrapers. It felt so far away from the real world.

'And besides, you never know what's going to happen.' I felt Tyler lie down next to me, he was so solid and reassuring. 'Who knows where you'll be in six months?'

'Bizarrely, you're not the first person to say exactly that,' I smiled, remembering what Alex had told me, hundreds of feet up in the air. Tyler leaned over and kissed me softly, bringing me back down to earth with a bump.

'I guess you have to go back sometime,' he said, producing a bag of crisps from the rucksack. Really? Crisps? 'Cheeto?'

'Thanks.' Quite frankly, I'd have eaten anything at that second, but I had sort of been expecting something a little bit classier. He was such a smoothie. 'Tyler,' I rolled onto my belly and looked at him happily munching away, 'have you ever had your heart broken?'

'There's nothing I love more than hiding in the park with a bag of Cheetos,' he replied. 'Is that really bad?'

'No, but it is avoiding my question,' I said, throwing a couple of cheesy crisps at him. Impressively he caught them in his mouth. 'Have you?'

'I've had girls break up with me, sure,' he said, thoughtfully sipping his wine, 'but I'm not sure I could honestly say I've had my heart broken.'

'Wow, really?' I tried to drink my wine, but it did not go well with the Cheetos. This slightly tarnished his sheen of sophistication, but it did prove he was human. 'I suppose some people are just lucky.'

'Maybe,' Tyler went back into the bag and produced a beautifully wrapped gold box and handed it to me, 'or maybe I've been unlucky. It's hard to get your heart broken if your heart's never really in it.'

I took the box and unfastened the ribbon. Oh thank God. It was chocolate. Glossy, handmade truffles. And lots of them. Sophistication regained, superhuman status restored.

'You've never been in love?' I asked, taking one of the chocolates and placing it in his mouth. 'I don't believe you.'

'I don't know, maybe,' he said, catching my hand and kissing the tips of my fingers. 'I can't say I've ever fallen apart when a relationship ended. I've never left the country anyway.'

'I'm fairly sure if you don't know whether or not you've been in love then you probably haven't.' I happily accepted the chocolate he held to my lips and nipped at his fingers. 'I just can't believe you haven't had women falling all over themselves to be in love with you.'

'Maybe they have been in love with me,' he shrugged. 'I just haven't met anyone I feel that strongly about.'

'So you're the heartbreaker,' I laughed. It hardly seemed likely, he was so lovely. 'Those poor girls.'

'Maybe I'm just waiting for the right girl?'

'And who would that girl be?' I went back to my wine. It was starting to slip down far better with the chocolate than the Cheetos, so much so, I had almost forgotten how hungry I'd been. I rolled over to lean backwards against Tyler's broad chest.

'I don't know yet,' he replied, stroking my hair. 'I suppose she would be smart and interesting, so we would have a lot to talk about. I don't want to come across as shallow, but she would have to be pretty. And she should make me smile all the time.'

I tilted my head back and smiled at him. 'She sounds

nice.' I hadn't even realized I'd got to the bottom of my glass already. Tyler topped me up.

'And I should want to kiss her every time I see her,' he said, stretching across for another kiss. 'Like that.'

'I think you've got good criteria,' I said, rolling back onto the blanket and avoiding too many kisses.

After the frenzy of last night's gig, of dealing with Jenny, of getting so near and yet so far with Alex, this was so serene. Glorious weather, the smell of fresh grass and an attentive, sweet man hand-feeding me chocolates and soft warm kisses. I loved the way Tyler made me feel, as if I were something to be treated delicately and protected. It made me almost believe it myself. We lay together, talking about our weeks, drinking the wine, me eating chocolates and Tyler munching away on his disgusting Cheetos until we ran dry.

'I knew I should have bought two bottles,' Tyler said, shaking the last drops into my glass. 'What with you being such an old lush.'

'I hardly ever drink,' I defended myself without much credibility. 'Honestly, I normally go months without a drop, let alone knock back the best part of two bottles before three in the afternoon. I think that's why I'm such a lightweight.'

And is was true, my head was pleasantly fuzzy and full of the cotton wool that Tyler seemed intent on wrapping me in.

'You're just making up for lost time then,' he grinned, putting the empty bottle, glasses and empty packets back in the rucksack. No littering here, what a lovely, lovely man.

'I'm just tired,' I yawned for effect. 'I had a bit of a late night.'

'Anything fun?' he asked.

'Alex's gig in Brooklyn,' I said, without thinking.

'Alex?' It wasn't accusatory, but it was definitely inquisitive.

'Oh, one of Jenny's boyfriend's friends,' I said quickly. It wasn't strictly a lie. 'And you know, it took for ever to get home.'

'I just don't get the whole Brooklyn thing,' Tyler shook his head, not pursuing the Alex thing. Phew. 'Sure, Park Slope is nice, Peter Luger is great, but why everyone thinks it's so hip to travel all the way over to Williamsburg for a beer? No thanks.'

'It was nice over there,' I felt as though I ought at least to try and defend it, but too much red wine was starting to weaken my thought process. 'Everyone was really cool.'

'Exactly,' Tyler screwed up his face. 'Someone needs to remind those rich kid hipsters that college was a long time ago. It's time to get over your ironic T-shirts and stop getting stoned. And how tight are those guys' jeans? Do they realize they will never have children?'

I thought of Alex in his skinny jeans and his little T-shirts and had to smile. Or possibly, the half-bottle of red wine had to smile, I wasn't entirely sure. I was however, entirely drunk.

'Are you a secret hipster? I don't remember seeing any piercings.'

'I'm more of a tattoo girl,' I laughed as he tried to pull up my T-shirt. 'Stop it, everyone can see!'

'I've got to find these tattoos,' he said, holding my wrists above my head with one hand and searching with the other. 'I can't believe I didn't see them the other night.'

'I don't really have tattoos,' I said breathlessly, half from the laughing, half from the way he was pinning me down. A familiar feeling started to build up in my stomach, surging through my body.

'I think you do,' he said, staring me into submission. 'Maybe I just didn't see them because it was so dark.'

'Maybe,' I whispered, willing him to scoop me up and take me home. I reckoned he had approximately ten seconds to suggest it before I made a public spectacle of myself. And potentially got us both arrested.

'Shall we just go?' he asked, his eyes glowing and his voice gruff. I nodded and let him pull me roughly to my feet. His hand burned into the small of my back as we wandered out across the park. I didn't want to drag him, but it almost felt as though he was walking extra slowly, dragging it out, making me wait. But I couldn't wait. I squeezed his hand gently, but he just squeezed back and gave me a promising smile.

'You're in a rush?' Tyler held me back as I made for the gate at something between a canter and a gallop.

I didn't have a response that didn't make me sound like a massive slag, so I went with the truth 'Aren't you?' I asked.

'Good point,' he replied, pulling my chin upwards and kissing me hard. I felt my legs completely melt away, there was nothing else in the world apart from me and Tyler and, fingers bloody crossed, his apartment in less than ten minutes.

My second visit to Tyler's was just as educational as the first. More than anything else, as I lay in his huge, soft bed, watching him doze, it was a complete wake-up call as to how long mine and Mark's relationship had been dead. I couldn't actually remember the last time we'd had sex in the daytime, but it really was like riding a bike. Not that I ride a bike. And it was remarkable just how bendy you can really be if you put your mind to it. I slipped silently out of the bedroom and recovered my knickers and top for a trip to the bathroom. After some quick reparatory work to my mascara and a cold flannel pressed to my stubble-grazed chin, I did the obligatory 'check out the bathroom cabinet' thing.

The first thing I noticed was that, for a man, he had a lot of stuff. It had taken me months of hint dropping and several advertorials in *GQ* for Mark to even start using Nivea for Men aftershave balm, but Tyler had more products than I did. Shampoo, conditioner, hair mask, gel, mousse, wax, eye cream, scrub, face wash, moisturizer with sunscreen, night cream with retinol. I wasn't sure whether to be intimidated and impressed, but then I remembered how great he always looked, and settled on accepting. Maybe I should look into some of this stuff. Beyond the creams, gels, lotions and potions were several bottles of painkillers, some off the shelf, some prescription. Anyone can have painkillers, I told myself, I still had tonnes of Co-codamol from when I had my wisdom teeth out. Right at the back, on the top shelf, was a black travel wash bag. With a quick look at the door, I whipped it down. I couldn't help myself. If he had cute little travel-sized toiletries, I was moving in. But it wasn't full of men's toiletries. It was a morning-after kit. For a woman. Deodorant, a new toothbrush, eye make-up remover and Jesus, even Tampax.

I replaced the bag and sat back down on the edge of the bath. So, he really did date around a lot. Reality check. I had absolutely no room for complaint here, I was dating someone else and hadn't really told him about it, maybe he was dating other girls too, but something about the whole thing just felt off with me. The idea of dating two people and sleeping with two people seemed mutually exclusive. Perhaps if I'd slept with Alex I'd feel differently, one way or another.

I ran my hands under the cold water tap to cool down. There was just one problem with that theory. I hadn't slept with Alex, and for the longest time, I'd had virtually no sex life at all. But with Tyler, it was like, God, I didn't even have anything to compare it with. Even when it had been good with Mark it had never, ever left me shaking from head to toe, unable to breathe but unable to stop. As soon as I was with Tyler, the rest of the world just melted away. It was utterly intoxicating, but somewhere inside it didn't feel real, didn't feel permanent. I tried to think of what Jenny would tell me, that I was sabotaging my own happiness, trying to find a reason not just to enjoy a fun relationship for what it was.

'Angela?' Tyler knocked gently on the bathroom door. 'You OK?'

'Yep,' I looked around for inspiration, finding nothing, 'I think I got a bit sunburned, I was just cooling down.'

'I have some lotion in there somewhere,' he said, peering around the door. 'Want me to find it out?'

'Yes, please,' I nodded. He was so wonderful. So what if he was seeing other girls? When he was with me, he was only with me.

'Let me see.' he took a large bottle of aftersun from a cabinet and squeezed some out into his hands. 'Where's the sunburn? You don't look red.'

'Oh, it's my back,' I said, pulling the shoulder of my top down an inch. It wasn't red because it wasn't burned, but it was the best lie I had at the time. 'It's just really sore. I don't think the red has come out yet.'

'I don't want to get this on your clothes,' he held up cream-covered hands and nodded at my top. 'You'd better take that off.'

'I suppose I had,' I smiled, trying not to think about what I had found in his cabinet. Not thinking was all the easier as he slid his cool hands onto my warm skin, massaging in the aftersun.

'Better?' he asked, rubbing gently up and down my back.

'Better,' I said softly, feeling his hands slide all the way down to the waistline of my knickers. His thumbs hooked under the elastic as he pulled them down gently.

'I was thinking,' he whispered into my ear, his bare chest sticking to the lotion on my back. 'If your back is burned, you'd better go on top.'

He was a very, very thoughtful man.

The afternoon turned into the evening and the evening turned into night with nothing to do but each other. After we'd finished with the bathroom floor, we headed back into the bedroom for more lazy fumbling and dozing and eventually, surfaced in the kitchen after christening his new granite work surface. Some hours later, I found myself curled up on his sofa, wearing a vintage Yankees shirt and eating Chinese takeaway. Apparently it was cute that I called it takeaway. I loved that it was cute. Patronizing, but very sweet. If everything I did naturally was cute to him, this was going to be really easy for me.

'How long have you lived here?' I asked, looking around at his impeccably designed penthouse. Everything was stainless steel and shiny and new. Apart from where I'd been, obviously.

'Ah, what, two years?' he mused, wandering over to

the kitchen and rifling through an invisible drawer. 'Why? You don't like it?'

'I love it,' I replied, willing him not to pull out a bottle opener. 'Did you design it yourself?'

'Like I have the time,' he shook his head and pulled out a bottle opener. 'It pretty much came this way.'

'Oh,' I frowned, resting my chin on the arm of the square sofa. The apartment was gorgeous, totally luxe, but now it felt sort of impersonal. I wondered if every apartment in the block had the same art on the walls.

'You want to stay over?' Tyler asked, wandering over from the kitchen with the open bottle of wine. 'I don't have to be anywhere in the morning.'

'It is sort of late,' I said, waving the wine away. I'd had quite enough for one day. For one week actually. 'Oh, but I don't have any stuff.'

The words were out of my mouth before I could take them back. I waited for him to offer me his secret sleep-over stash.

'Don't laugh at me,' he said, settling back onto the sofa and taking custody of his remote control. Didn't matter to me, I couldn't work the damn thing. 'But I have some girl stuff. I'm not sure what though, my mom left it last time she stayed over.'

'Your mum?' I smiled at his blushes. 'Now who's cute?'

'She lives in Florida,' he said, pointing towards a small family picture hidden up high on a shelf. The whole brood. Wow. 'But since my dad died she comes to visit a lot.'

'That's really lovely,' I said, snuggling down against him. 'I think it's great when people are close to their parents.'

'You close to yours?' he asked, flicking through the channels.

'Not massively to be honest, but you know, they're my parents. I love them. Even my mother.'

'I guess it's harder for girls and their moms,' he leaned his cheek against my head. 'And I bet you were a total wild child.'

'Oh my God, so the opposite,' I laughed at the very thought. 'In by nine, no boyfriends until I was sixteen, top marks at school. I think my mum was worried I might end up a spinster librarian or something.'

'Want me to call her and let her know that's not a problem?' he asked, settling on a sports channel. If this had been Mark with the football, I would have complained, but then, if Mark had spent all afternoon giving me multiple orgasms, perhaps I would have been more compassionate about the plight of Nottingham Forest.

'I don't think she needs all the details,' I kissed him quickly and hopped up. 'But I should call Jenny and let her know I'm not coming back.'

I padded back into the bedroom in search of my handbag and found it safely at the end of the bed, underneath my shorts.

'Hi Jenny,' I said as the machine picked up. 'It's just me, I'm going to stay here tonight so don't—'

'Hey, hey!' Jenny picked up, out of breath. 'I got it, I'm here.'

'Hi,' I said. 'You're going to be so proud, I'm staying at Tyler's. See, I can totally do this multiple dating thing.'

'Oh. OK.'

'Did you want me to come home?' I asked, hoping she wasn't feeling abandoned. I was still new at this roommate thing.

'No, no,' her voice lowered slightly. 'Jeff is here, I just thought, he might mention to Alex that you weren't home or something. I didn't know if he knew that you and Tyler were . . .'

'Shit!' I absolutely hadn't thought about that at all. 'I don't think he does, not really. And I don't want him to. Please don't say anything.'

'Of course I won't,' she said more easily. 'I'll just tell him you're at Erin's or something, that you wanted us to have alone time. Oh, but he did invite us over for dinner tomorrow, to apologize for Friday night.'

'To apologize for you throwing up all over Alex's apartment?' I asked, reflecting on the fact that Jeff knowing Alex could really make things difficult.

'Yes, Mom,' Jenny replied. 'I've got to go, the pizza's here. Alex already told Jeff he could make it, so it's tomorrow at seven, OK? Try and get your pants on for then. Love you.'

I turned off my phone and resumed my position in the living room.

'Everything OK?' Tyler asked, pulling me in close to him.

'Yep,' I said, wriggling into place back under his arm. 'Just tired.'

'You want to go to bed?' He stroked my hair absently.

'I'm OK,' I replied, resting my eyes just long enough to fall fast asleep on the sofa, the sounds of the baseball match echoing in my ears.

CHAPTER EIGHTEEN

The Adventures of Angela: CPDA –
Central Park Display of Affection

As a newcomer to New York, I have no idea what level of indecency is considered, well, decent in your fair city's fairest park. I'm just back from another great date with Wall Street, a very romantic picnic with wine, Godiva truffles and Cheetos (no one said he was perfect) and I'm wondering whether or not to expect a policeman (mmm, hot cop!) to turn up at my door. Obviously there was nothing removed during the outdoor sesh, but what's worse – the hot and heavy petting or the unbearable levels of smugness we forced those around us to endure. Vom-worthy, really. Pre-New York dating extravaganza, I would have happily put Wall Street's corkscrew through his temple if I'd seen a couple so terribly pleased with themselves as we were (Cheetos aside) but I really don't want to kill him just yet. And I don't want to stop getting touched up in the park either.

Hmm. This is going to be a tricky one.

After arguing with myself over the content of my post for twenty minutes, I just couldn't do it. And in a radical bid to distract myself, I did something drastic.

'Hello?'

'Mum? It's Angela.'

'Darling, how are you?' she asked, sounding fairly relieved, as though she thought it might have been the Avon lady from number fifty-four. 'Are you coming home?'

'No, not yet,' I said, pacing the apartment. 'I'm fine though, I'm staying with my friend still and I'm working for this magazine. Things are really good.'

'But you're coming home soon, dear?' she asked again. I could just see her frowning in the mirror above the phone, probably fiddling with her hair, looking out of the window into her impeccably kept garden, watching next door's cat shit all over her flowerbed.

'I don't know, Mum,' I said, eventually coming to a standstill by the window. 'I'm having a really good time. The writing thing is really exciting, I'm doing an online diary for the magazine's website.'

'That's lovely, I'm very proud.' The same dismissive tone that she had used for my GCSE, A level and degree results. Grrr. 'But darling, you know, I would really like you to let me know when you're coming back. You must have a date for your flight? And the hotel must be costing you a fortune.'

'Mum, I've just told you, I'm staying with a friend. I don't know when I'm – do you know what? It doesn't matter. Why was Mark at your house when I called last week?'

'I just don't know why you can't tell me when your flight is,' she chuntered on. I was starting to regret the phone call all together.

'I don't have a flight booked so I don't know when it will be,' I repeated, thinking about how different the views were out of our windows. I could see yellow taxi cabs, the Chrysler Building and thousands of New Yorkers hustling and bustling around the city. From my mum's window, she would be lucky to be able to see her Clio in the drive, the post office, and Mr Tucker from next door, possibly thrilling the neighbourhood by gardening shirtless. He was fifty-two. 'Why was Mark answering your phone?'

'He was dropping off some of your things, Angela.' I could tell she was starting to get just as pissed off with me as I was with her. 'I know he's done a terrible thing to you, but I have known him for a lot of years. I can't just pretend he doesn't exist.'

'Yes you can.' Was she serious? 'You can very easily pretend he doesn't exist. He doesn't as far as our family is concerned.'

'Just because you have chosen to run away instead of confronting your problems, doesn't mean I can,' Mum tutted down the line. 'I see Mark's mother every week at Tescos.'

'I haven't run away,' I said. This was not the supportive mother-daughter talk I'd been envisioning. 'I'm doing something with my life.'

'And maybe if you had stayed and talked to Mark, you would have realized how terrible he feels about things,' she carried on, completely ignoring everything I was saying. 'Maybe you would have been able to sort things out. Not that I'm saying you should, he did cheat on you, I know.'

'He wants to sort things out?' I asked. The idea hadn't even crossed my mind.

'Well, maybe he would have if you hadn't run away, I don't know,' she said, sounding distracted. 'But now he's moved in that Katie girl, I don't suppose the two of you will ever get back on track. I suppose if you called him . . .'

'He's moved in with – he's moved her with in?' I stopped her in the middle of her sentence. 'Into our house?'

'Well, you disappeared, dear,' she seemed to be listening again. 'What was he supposed to do? Not that I'm making excuses for him. He should never have done what he did, but, he did explain—'

'Mum, I've got to get off, I'm going out,' I needed to be off the phone right away. 'I'll call you when I know more about coming home.'

'All right, darling, speak to you soon,' and she hung up before I could.

Knowing for a fact that Mark had moved that girl into my house was all too much for my brain to process, but it did put the blog problem into perspective. I sat down in front of the laptop, blocked out the images of the filthy mare wearing my Cath Kidston apron and cooking with my beloved lime green Le Creuset casserole dish and emailed the blog to Mary. Mark who?

Once Jenny had returned from her Sunday spa appointment at Rapture and checked that everything had been exfoliated, waxed and moisturized to her own high and Jeff-ready standards, we headed out to Brooklyn. I was justifiably nervous, not having spoken to Alex about our 'double date' and not having spent more than fifteen minutes forcing my hair into some sort of shape, slapping on some of my miraculous MAC mascara and lipgloss. But my (still amazing) Marc Jacobs bag made everything better. I wondered if I could feasibly go out in my pyjamas and still feel like a grown-up if I were carrying this. Jenny practically skipped all the way to the L train, barely a sentence tripping over her tongue that wasn't directly related to Jeff.

'So it's totally on with Alex tonight?' she asked, holding my hand and skipping lightly as we crossed the road over to the subway.

'I don't know,' I confessed. 'I was with Tyler this morning, don't you think it might be a bit tacky to sleep with Alex tonight?' But just saying the words sent shivers all the way down my spine.

'I knew this would happen,' Jenny shook her head, swiping her Metrocard. 'You weren't even OK dating two guys, you were never going to be able to sleep with two guys. Not at once.'

'Christ, it's not a threesome, Jenny.' I followed her down the stairs, shaking my head. 'And you didn't want to share that information with me? Really, I'm OK seeing them both, I like them both in different ways, but I don't know. Tyler is so much fun, and Alex is, well, it's different.'

'But you like him more than Tyler?' she asked.

'It's different with Alex, harder to explain. I like the way he makes me feel about myself. With Tyler it's kind of more about how he literally makes me feel,' I tried to explain without blushing. 'Did you ever do that experiment at school where you get three white flowers and you put one in an empty vase, one in a vase with water and one in a vase with food colouring?'

'Yeah,' Jenny nodded, 'but I really don't know what that's got to do with you getting your kicks with some hot banker.'

'Shut up,' I smiled wryly and hopped on the train as the doors slid open. 'OK, don't laugh but the flower without any water just wilts and dies, right? And the flower with the water blossoms and it's just really ordinary but beautiful, then when you add the food colouring it—'

'It takes the colour into the flower,' she finished for me. 'Oh my God, you're so meta! Doll, your first analogy. I'm so proud of you.'

'Thanks. I feel validated,' I said, patting her thigh. 'I know it's cheesy, but it's the best I can come up with. Before I was just suffocating, with Tyler, it's like classic and romantic, he has a structure to his life that I recognize. But with Alex, it's fun and exciting and different. I don't know where it's going, everything is so new.'

'New and exciting is good,' Jenny said, nodding thoughtfully. 'But when you're in a delicate emotional state, that's you doll, or when you just need to go out and have lots of great sex because you've only slept with one guy your whole life, again like you, maybe classic and romantic is the best.'

'Maybe. I just don't know. And I don't know how long I can keep seeing them both. It does feel weird, whether it should or not. But seeing Tyler almost takes the pressure off whatever's happening with Alex. Not that anything bloody has.'

'Well, how about you give Alex his shot in the bedroom tonight and make your decision tomorrow?' She grinned as the train slowed down, approaching our stop. 'God knows, I'm going to need you to get the hell out of Jeff's, oh, I don't know, as soon as we get there.'

'Things are going well then?' I smiled. 'I'm really pleased. I'm not going to say anything other than, I'm glad things are working out.'

'Like I said,' she said, hopping out of the carriage, 'it's fate. Sometimes you have to put all the psychobabble stuff on one side and go with your heart.'

'Wow!' I linked arms with her as we strutted up the stairs. 'I just lost all respect for you.'

'I know,' she smiled, happily. 'Isn't it amazing?'

The first thing I would have liked to have known, before I agreed to dinner at Jeff's, was that he was a terrible cook. Which he was. The second thing that would have been helpful to know, was that, in Jenny and Jeff world, 'dinner' was apparently a euphemistic term for practising oral sex skills on each other's forks and fingers. I tried not to watch while I nibbled a polite amount of the spaghetti and mush that had been presented to us the second we walked through the door. We had only been in the apartment for approximately fifteen minutes and already, it was quite clear that Alex and I were in the way. Alex openly stared, occasionally nudging me with his knee. I couldn't even look at him. Apart from the awkward hello and half-kiss we'd shared before being rushed to our seats, we hadn't really spoken. Jenny and Jeff's red-light show was making the atmosphere so tense, I didn't know where to put myself. I felt like a maiden aunt at an orgy.

'So, how was your weekend?' Alex asked me and Jenny, breaking the strained silence and twirling limp spaghetti around his fork. I noticed no one's plates matched. The apartment was super swank on a Tyler scale, but it seemed as if it was just possible that Jeff hadn't been too worried about his housekeeping recently. I figured he had something else on his mind. And possibly other parts of his anatomy.

Jenny response to Alex was a low moan as Jeff's hand vanished under the table, so I took it upon myself to answer-slash-try to distract Alex from the incredibly inappropriate behaviour on the opposite side of the table.

'It was OK, I wrote.' It wasn't a lie, I had written. 'What did you get up to?'

'I wrote too,' he nodded, looking dead ahead. 'It was good actually, I think I got some good stuff out.'

I smiled and nodded politely, trying to think of something to say that wasn't 'For Christ's sake, get your hands back on the table, it's unsanitary' but our hosts beat me to it, dropping their cutlery and more or less giving up any pretense of eating, before moving on to the main course, each other. I could have killed Jenny.

'So, Jeff,' Alex started. So brave, to try to attract his attention. 'Your food tastes like complete shit. What is it supposed to be again?'

'Pasta,' Jeff said, distracted by Jenny, massaging his shoulders. I couldn't think what strenuous activity he might have undertaken that would necessitate a massage, it certainly wasn't the cooking. 'It's just pasta.'

'It's delightful.' Jenny tried some sort of erotic manoeuvre with a forkful of soggy pasta, but it did not come off well. Unlike the pasta, which dropped directly into her lap.

'OK, then,' Alex gave me a sideways smile, 'nice. This totally makes up for your girlfriend throwing up all over my place.'

'I want to know what's for dessert,' Jenny asked, actually getting out of her seat and putting herself in Jeff's lap. Jesus, she was shameless.

'I have ice cream,' Jeff breathed heavily. 'I got your favourite.'

'I don't really feel much in the mood for ice cream,' Alex said, pushing his chair back and standing to leave. 'But I do have some excellent day-old-pizza that's crying out to be eaten. Angela, can I interest you in a slice of pepperoni?'

'Yes. Yes, you can,' I said, following him away from the table. 'Thanks Jeff, Jenny.'

'You're going?' Jenny started to make some noises about staying for coffee, but whatever Jeff whispered in her ear sent them off into squeals of delight and a short sharp 'bye'.

'Jesus, what was that all about?' Alex laughed, slamming his apartment door behind him. 'Does your friend like an audience or something?'

'I want to say "no", but the best I can give you is, I really hope not,' I said, hovering by the sofa. There didn't seem to be any puke stains on there, so I sat down cautiously.

'Beer?' He opened his huge fridge, balancing a pizza box and a six-pack on one arm.

'Thanks.' I took the bottle and sat in silence, not sure about what my next move was supposed to be. His apartment was the opposite of Tyler's, every inch of it breathed him. There were CDs lying around on every available surface, notebooks littered the coffee table, and I was never more than three feet away from a chewed-on pen or pencil.

'I don't know, I guess it's cool that they're so in to each other.' He settled down and opened the pizza box. No really, it was at least one-day-old pepperoni pizza. 'I just figured when Jeff invited me round for dinner, it would actually be dinner.'

'Me too,' I nodded, accepting the pizza against my better judgment. It was actually really good. 'If nothing else, it reassured me of my hostess skills in case I ever have to repay the favour. Compared to Jeff, I'm a shit-hot cook.'

'Really?' He leaned back and looked at me. 'Yeah, I bet you are.'

'What's that supposed to mean?' I asked. Was this another sly New Yorker way of telling me I was a porker?

'Nothing,' he defended himself by waving a piece of pizza around. 'I just think you can tell a lot about a person by the way they cook. Not that Jeff was playing his cards close to his chest, but you could tell by his shitty food he's not too worried about the preparation. He's all about getting straight to it.'

'I suppose so,' I smiled. I really should drop the porker thing. 'Jenny can't cook for anything. It's all takeaways and Starbucks. Made for each other.'

'What's your favourite thing to cook?' he asked, resting his head in his hand, his elbow on the arm of the sofa.

'Hmm,' I thought. I didn't have a particularly wide repertoire, but I did have a feeling a good answer was needed here. 'I have this Balinese chicken thing that I do. You make this paste with lemongrass and dried chillies and then you rub it into the chicken and cook it really slowly wrapped in a banana leaf. It's gorgeous.'

'See what I mean?' he said, closing his eyes and smiling a deep, delicious smile. 'Spicy, adventurous, long and slow. Tells you a lot about a person.'

'What about you?' I knew I was blushing from head to toe. It was my most impressive dish, but I really hoped I wasn't going to have to cook it without the book. It was a complete bitch of a recipe.

'Honestly, I'm a pretty shitty cook,' he admitted, taking my beer out of my hands and leaning across towards me. 'But I'm kind of good at other stuff.'

'Doesn't that ruin your metaphor?' I whispered as he crept across the sofa and placed his arms on either side of my head.

'I just wanted to see you blush.'

His lips were soft and firm, but his kisses were hard and unrelenting. Within seconds, we were putting on a show to shame even Jenny and Jeff. The rough fabric of his jeans chafed against my thighs as I brought my legs up around his waist, pulling him in towards me. The nervous tickle that had been growing in my stomach migrated south as I lost my hands in his hair, my lips on his throat, my mind . . . just gone. Alex pulled me up and half carried me towards his room. No time for candles, for low music, just the twinkling cityscape behind us lighting his silhouette as he pulled off his T-shirt and tossed it aside. We stood in front of the window, kissing desperately, tussling with belts, zips and buttons until there was nothing left between us but our underwear. I silently thanked Jenny for my matching set pep talk as Alex sighed his approval at my black balconette and French knickers.

'Why does it feel like this has been such a long time coming?' he asked, sliding one of the straps off my shoulder and replacing it with a long line of kisses.

'I know what you mean,' I whispered. I placed one arm around his neck, obsessed with losing my fingers in that thick, black hair, the other hand somehow finding its way down his chest, his stomach, the waistband of his tight jersey boxers. My legs were beginning to shake, and all I could think about was getting onto that bed. So *this* was what they meant when they talked about knee trembling.

'Hey,' he said softly, replacing my bra strap and holding my face in his hands. 'I just want to take it slow, OK?'

'You don't want to . . .' I was confused. 'I thought?' He had waited until I was in my underwear with one hand down his shorts to tell me he wanted to take it slow?

'No,' he shook his head, smiling. 'I mean this, now. I want to be able to remember every second of it.'

'Oh, OK,' I smiled back, biting my bottom lip. Was I in that much of a rush I'd forgotten about actual romance? 'Sorry, I thought you meant . . .'

'Don't be sorry.' Alex pulled my hair back from my face and kissed me tenderly. His skin glowed against the light of the window as his eyes met mine. 'And stop thinking so much.'

He took my hand and led me over to the bed, laying me down and peppering my face, my throat, my shoulders with kisses. I wanted him so badly, every second he wasn't inside me I thought I would explode. His kisses trailed down my collarbone, over my bra and down my stomach.

'I thought you wanted to go slowly?' I asked, the words catching in my throat as his lips reached the top of my thighs.

'I should have been clearer,' he said, pulling the silk of my underwear aside. 'I meant slow for me. But I think that's going to work out kind of well for you.'

'Glad to clear things up,' I whispered, closing my eyes and letting go.

If Tyler had been an education, Alex was an awakening. From the moment we rolled back on to the bed, through the long sweaty hours until dawn, he put my entire body through its paces, taking me right to the edge and then snatching me back again. When I woke, in a tussle of tangled sheets and tangled limbs, I was upside down at the foot of the bed, and so exhausted I didn't know if I was coming or going. But I was absolutely certain, that at least three times in the past few hours, I'd been coming like never before. I stretched a leg, feeling out the floor with my toes, trying to work out how to extricate myself from Alex's vice-like grip without waking him. Not going to happen. Feeling me stir, he half opened one eye. Without words, without any sort of verbal communication, he drew me back to him and we picked up exactly where we had left off.

CHAPTER NINETEEN

It was Monday morning, but blissfully, Alex didn't have anywhere to be except in bed with me. He didn't need to let his housekeeper in, he didn't have errands to run, he sure as shit didn't have to go to the office. We dozed on and off all morning, only waking up to reach out and check the other was still there, still waiting. Eventually, I was forced to seek out the bathroom, slipping away from Alex and padding across the flat. Sitting on the toilet, I was well aware I had a completely stupid grin on my face. I just didn't know what to do with myself. Compared to the only sex I had ever known, Tyler had been amazing in bed. He was, technically speaking, a god. He knew which buttons to press, in which order and, most importantly, he knew exactly when to press them. But Alex . . . It had just been so intense. I felt raw and exposed, as if he had stripped me down completely and then put me back together, new and improved. It was incredible. After a sly mouthwash, face splash and mascara removal combo, I tiptoed back through the living room, checking my mobile on the way. A message from Jenny asking if I was OK, a message from Erin to say she'd seen the blog (the blog! I'd forgotten it was out there already) and a message from Tyler, asking if I wanted to go to dinner tomorrow night. I paused in the living room for a moment, perching on the arm of the sofa. Looking back towards Alex's bedroom door, I thought for a moment. Did I want to go to dinner tomorrow night? I liked Tyler, he was a great guy, but Alex was something else altogether. I quickly replied, a short acceptance. Either way, I had to see Tyler, whether it was a date or I was ending it. And I did have the blog to think about. It would be fine. I tapped out replies to Jenny and Erin, then hurried back into the bedroom, to Alex's arms.

A couple of indulgent hours later and I reluctantly hit the shower so I could go home and blog. I could hear Alex singing in the kitchen, while I lathered up and smiled. It was such a different world to everything I was used to, and I liked it. Without a walk of shame kit, I did my best, tying my wet hair up, dabbing on some lip gloss and mascara, really not needing any blusher. Slipping back into my dress seemed to put a full stop at the end of the sentence. I really did have to go outside now, it had to be done. I didn't have another pair of knickers, home was the only option.

Alex was making coffee, real coffee, in a T-shirt and shorts when I emerged. It was so wrong that I had just spent twenty minutes putting myself back together and he looked as cute, as sexy as ever, pillow creases, bedhead and all.

'So you do know how to use your kitchen,' I said, accepting a steaming mug of black coffee and dropping back onto the sofa. I knew I had to leave, but my legs were determined to make it difficult by refusing to work.

'I live on my coffee when we're recording.' He sat down next to me. 'Sorry if it's a little strong. Coffee I'm good with, but I never seem to have milk.'

'Don't worry, it's nice,' I lied. It was like tar. 'What are you up to today?'

He shrugged. 'I might try and write some more. I got some good stuff yesterday.'

'Do you just write here?' I asked, swirling my cup. The 'coffee' barely moved.

'Yeah, well, the music,' he nodded towards an acoustic guitar leaning against the wall. 'I usually write the music with that, then take it in to the guys and we work it up. The lyrics I write all over the place. Wherever they come to me.'

'It must be so cool to be able to do that,' I shook my head in awe. 'I can't imagine sitting down with a guitar and just pulling something out of the air like that.'

'It's only what you do when you write.' He smiled lazily and pushed a stray strand of damp hair behind my ear. It was well past midday and so warm that my hair was almost dry. 'It's just writing what you're thinking.'

'I suppose so,' I said, letting my cheek rest against his hand. It would have been so easy just to stay there with him.

'You sure you've got to go?' he whispered, his eyes glowing, his voice deepening.

No no no no no no no.

'Yes,' I sighed. I leaned in for a soft, promising kiss and then pulled myself back. 'I really can't get behind, and I have to file my blog by four.'

'I can't imagine what you're going to write about,' he grinned. 'What if my mom reads it?'

'Don't!' I flushed and stood up. 'I'm not writing porn,

it's a diary about my experiences. And it runs four days behind anyway.'

'Don't tell me that wasn't an experience.' He flicked at my hem with his foot. 'And how come it's so behind, so they can edit out all the good stuff?'

'No, it's just what they do, in case I get ill or something.' I picked up my bag. I wanted to sink back onto that sofa by the side of him more than anything. 'So you'll have to wait until next week to see what I'm going to post.'

'I'm not too worried,' he said, dragging himself up and walking over to the door. 'I don't think anyone has any cause for complaint.'

He pulled me in close for a deep goodbye kiss, making me drop my beautiful, beautiful bag. Bad man.

'I'll call you later?' He opened the door while I slowly backed out.

'OK.' I nodded, crossing the threshold into the hall. Wow, this was hard. 'Talk to you later then?'

'Yeah.' He leaned out for one more kiss before I turned and headed to the lift.

Get in the lift. Get in the lift.

I sneaked a quick look back, Alex just leaning against his doorway. I shook my head and pushed myself through the lift doors as they slid open, and pressed the G button. I definitely deserved an award for leaving, first time and everything.

I was so wrapped up in Alex, it didn't even occur to me to be proud as I headed towards the L, hopped straight on the subway and changed at Union Square, heading north to Grand Central. My first non-pre-planned subway journey and I'd only looked at a map once.

Jenny was already home when I dashed through the

door, drinkable coffee in one hand, keys in the other.

'Hey,' she said, rising from the sofa as I flashed through the room. 'What's up?'

'Got to email my blog,' I called from my room. And despite how well the evening had gone, I was still a little bit pissed off with her and her one-woman show. 'Give me half an hour?'

'OK, but then I want all the details,' she yelled from the living room.

I looked at the screen of my laptop. It glowed impatiently, demanding me to spill every last little fact like an iJenny. But I couldn't do it. It had been so easy, practically cathartic, to write about things with Tyler, but this was different. I wanted to protect it. Instead of hashing out every new position, every new sensation, I found myself bashing out 200 words on *The Adventures of Angela: When is it OK to break The Rules?* I wrote about Jenny and Jeff getting back together, I wrote about accepting dates less than two days in advance, and I wrote about just how bloody hard it was to stick to the stupid bloody things. Who came up with them in the first place? They hadn't seemed to work for anyone I'd met yet. Erin was rocketing through husbands like last season's Manolos, and Jenny cheated on her ex, but got him back. That wasn't in The Rules.

I stopped tapping away and paused. There was so much I could say about Alex, but it just didn't seem to want to put itself into words. It wasn't as if I was denying Alex's existence, I just didn't want to go into details yet. Or mention I'd stayed over. Or that I'd had the most incredible sex ever. I wanted to keep that to myself for a little while longer.

Well, I was open to sharing with Jenny. And Erin. And the manager of Scottie's Diner.

* * *

'What happened to Jenny's life plan? I thought she was making all your big decisions for you?' Erin asked, sipping on some iced water. 'Like she does for everyone else whether they like it or not.'

'She's not been so helpful since she got back together with Jeff,' I said, shaking my head at the goofy grin on Jenny's face. 'She's not actually been very much of anything apart from gagging for it as far as I can tell.'

'So what?' Jenny grinned, munching away. 'My head is kind of somewhere else. But, and you know I like Alex, realistically, I think you're going too fast too soon and you should be out there having fun. You've been single for what, two weeks?'

'Is it really only two weeks?' I suppose it had to be. I felt as if I'd been in New York my whole life. 'Feels like for ever.'

'All the more reason to keep seeing this Tyler guy,' Erin said, gingerly trying a chip. 'If you're going to fall head-over-heels for Alex, who we already know has more or less fucked his way around the whole of lower Manhattan, you need to keep a part of yourself detached. Seeing Tyler might help take the pressure off.'

'Well, clearly Jenny has filled you in,' I said, giving Jenny the look. 'But he didn't have to tell me about his past already. He could have just, you know . . .'

'Used you? Playing devil's advocate,' Jenny held up her hands, 'and that's all I'm doing, but how do you know he's not? Both Alex and Tyler know you've got to go back home sooner or later, how do you know this isn't just a totally harmless fling for both of them, and they're not seeing seventeen other women on the side? I just think you should pull back a little before you start getting attached.'

'She's right, and you know I hate saying that,' Erin

gave me a half-smile, 'but what's going to happen if you let yourself get totally wrapped up in Alex, then go back to England and you never hear from him again?'

'I know all that, I'm just having fun,' I lied badly. I didn't want to think about Alex using me, and I certainly didn't want to think about going home. 'And you know, they could say the same thing. They could say I'm using them.'

'Well, honey. You kind of are.'

I shook my head. 'No, I'm . . . Well, I'm just not.'

Cue awkward silence.

'OK, maybe Tyler.'

'So,' Erin wiped her hands on a napkin, 'you've got two and a half months left unless you start applying for a work visa right now. You came here to get away from your ex and sort your head out, work out what you want to do. Have you done that?'

'I don't know,' I confessed. 'Is that really bad?'

'No,' Erin smiled. 'But you shouldn't be worrying about any relationship stuff with either of these guys until you can answer those questions.'

'I know. It's just loads more difficult than I thought it was going to be. When I'm with you two, it's easy to be OK, and I think yeah, this might be me, even if I'm a bit of a whiny cow. Tyler makes everything easy in a different way, like, I don't even need to think because he's already thought of everything. I don't have to stress about anything, so I'm just kind of the same person I've always been, but with better sex and presents.'

'And with Alex?' Jenny asked, signalling the waitress and ordering more or less the whole dessert menu.

'I really, really like how I feel when I'm with him, but realistically, I don't know if I could keep it up all the time. It's bloody hard work being on all the time,'

I said, surprising myself with my answer. 'But maybe I'm just being lazy. It's hard work, but it's amazing. He makes me feel amazing. Bloody hell, you two must be so bored of me.'

They were quick to refute it, but even I was sick of hearing myself whine on. 'Do you know what? Forget it, I just want to hear about Jeff and Jenny.'

Jenny was quick to pick up the baton. Unfortunately, it was a highly detailed and descriptive account of Jeff's baton, which made eating a little bit difficult.

'Did you have to give her an in?' Erin grinned, ditching her diet and getting stuck into the cheesecake that had joined the ice cream on the table. 'Honestly, I can't listen to you two talk about your amazing sex lives any more. I'm over The Rules from right now.'

'Man, I hadn't even got started,' Jenny laughed and pointed at me with her spoon. 'And you should remember that Jeff and Alex's bedrooms are only separated by about a foot of interior wall before you start calling me on my performance.'

I blushed, horrified. 'Really? God, that's so embarrassing.'

'Pretty inspirational, actually,' Jenny grinned, clearly enjoying watching me squirm. 'I don't know exactly what's going to happen to you doll, but I do know you need a good night's sleep tonight.'

She wasn't wrong. Once we'd finished up, all three of us headed back to the apartment for a *Friends* marathon in the hopes of getting some sage advice from the thirty-five-year-old twenty-somethings, and before I knew it, I was out for the count.

Having passed out in a cheesecake coma so early the night before, I woke up at the crack of dawn on Tuesday determined to work out some answers. Erin and Jenny were right, I'd come to New York looking for something, and it hadn't been men. I headed out early, passing Erin on the sofa bed, Jenny still snoring in her room, so pleased to have found some fellow anti-nine-to-fivers. I'd promised myself I would keep walking until something hit me, so I took the subway as far as I could go and still be in Manhattan and walked back to Battery Park. Seemed like a good place to start. Leaning back over the railing that Jenny had first brought me to, more than a fortnight ago, I reflected on how much life had changed, leaving out the boys. Yes, I had new hair, new clothes (and a fabulous handbag) but (almost) more importantly, I had my confidence. I was doing this, actually living. It didn't matter that there was a legally imposed schedule, helpfully enforced by US immigration, I had lived more in the last two weeks than I had in the last two years. I gave the Statue of Liberty a thankful smile and headed back north, thinking about all the other things I had to be grateful for. Jenny, despite her mildly schizophrenic Jeff-related issues, was clearly a good person. Erin was a complete sweetheart. And I was actually writing. I was writing my own words for a massive international magazine's website, not ghostwriting movie novels about mutant hero turtles or style advice for billionaire tweenagers.

Looking up I realized I was heading towards Ground Zero. As I passed through, I could hardly believe that so much life was going on all around this site of utter devastation. Shops, hotels, restaurants, offices, everything. It seemed like such a short time ago that I had watched this place literally collapse on TV, but the entire city had picked up and moved on, healing rapidly around this ugly scar. I almost slapped myself in the street. If everyone here could pick themselves up and dust themselves down, what did I have to be so mopy and introspective about? It was just like Jenny had said, New York wasn't somewhere you came to find yourself again, it was somewhere you came to become something, someone, new.

In a Starbucks with wireless internet I logged on. My blog was short and to the point. *The Adventures of Angela: Moving On From Moving On.* Yes, I had a lot of crap to wallow in, and I could feel sorry for myself for the next five years if I wanted, but I also had a lot to be glad about and from here on in, that was what this diary was going to be about. I emailed it to Mary and sat staring out of the window, occasionally catching my reflection when a car parked up or someone paused to look inside. I didn't look different any more, I just looked like me. One battle won.

'Hey, excuse me,' a tall, skinny girl stood at my shoulder, clutching a takeaway coffee cup. 'Are you that girl from *The Look* website?'

'Oh,' I said, flustered. 'Yes, I suppose I am.'

She sat down at my table and beamed, pushing curly red hair away from her lip gloss. 'I knew it was you, I saw the Marc Jacobs bag. I was just reading your last entry. My friend is like, obsessed with blogs, she forwarded me yours. I'm Rebecca'

'Oh,' I repeated. It hadn't occurred to me that people might recognize me. Eeep. 'Sorry, I'm Angela. Did you like it? The blog?'

'Shit, it was hilarious!' She grinned. 'It's like, you're totally living my life. My boyfriend cheated on me too, he was a complete shit. But your life is way funnier. And I didn't hook up with two really hot guys, like, days later.'

'Oh,' I really didn't know what else to say. I hadn't

looked at the website since it went live, I just couldn't bear to see that before picture of myself again. 'It's not totally like that, I mean, I'm not, you know.'

'So it's not real?' She frowned. 'You make it up?'

'No,' I said quickly. 'It is real, it's just a bit weird talking about it. You're the first person I've met who has read it.' I managed a smile. 'Sorry.'

'No worries,' she smiled again. 'You're just a total hero to me. I wish I had got up and done something amazing when I found out about my ex, instead of throwing up for three days and then burning all his stuff.'

'I wouldn't have been against burning his stuff. Between you and me, I might have peed in my ex's toiletry bag. I know, it's disgusting.'

'Oh my God,' she squealed. 'That's awesome. I didn't think British people did shit like that. Are you going to be in the magazine?'

'I don't think so.' This was fun, I was a minor celebrity! 'It's just a little online thing. I can't believe you've even seen it.'

'Are you kidding me?' She shook her head in disbelief. 'Haven't you seen how many hits your page has had? It's like, thousands.'

'Really?' I asked, looking at my laptop. Was she serious?

'Yeah, like, so many more than the other *Look* blogs. Yours is so the best thing on that site.' She stood up, leaving her coffee cup half empty, behind. 'I've got to run back to the office, but it was so cool to meet you. I hope they print the diary, I'm totally going to email them.'

'Bye, nice to meet you!' I called after her. The second she was out of the coffee shop, I was back online. There it was, TheLook.com, *The Adventures of Angela*. And according to the counter, there had indeed been thousands of visitors to the site. Hundreds of thousands. Thousands of people reading about me. It felt out and out weird. And then, when I thought about what I'd written, it felt scary. Forget Alex's mum, what if my mum read it? And Mark. He had no right to know what I was doing. Who I was doing . . . The post about my night with Tyler, oh my God. Not good.

While I sat scanning my previous posts, wondering if Mary would let me go back and edit, an email popped up in my inbox from her *Look* email address.

> *Angela,*
> *Got today's entry, really interesting. So did you see the blog is a big success?*
> *Can you make a meeting on Friday? 4.00 p.m. my office.*
> *Thanks,*
> *Mary*

I pulled out my mobile and hit Alex's number. It clicked through for a moment giving me just enough time to think and hang up.

He hadn't called.

Why hadn't he called?

It had been more than a whole day since I had left his apartment. Instead, I dialled Jenny at work, hoping she had made it to the concierge desk on time.

'The Union,' she answered in a sleepy monotone. Still playing sleep catch-up from the night before, clearly.

'Jenny, it's me,' I said quickly, rambling the whole story about the blog and the hits and the redhead fan and Mary's email, leaving out the part where I faux-called Alex. I had promised not to go into the boy stuff until I'd sorted out the Angela stuff after all.

‘Wow, that’s so cool,’ she yawned. ‘You want to come over here? I’ve got a break in half an hour.’

‘I’m supposed to meet Tyler for dinner,’ I said cautiously. ‘I should probably go and get changed or something.’

‘You should go and buy something fabulous,’ she said, giving me permission to abuse my credit card without even knowing it. ‘Seriously, I’d totally celebrate. And you need more stuff if you’re going to be a celeb.’

‘I really don’t need more stuff!’ I shut down my laptop and placed it back in my (sigh) bag. ‘I think my credit card is about to snap. See you tonight.’

‘You’re not going to stay at Tyler’s?’ she asked. I wasn’t sure if this was a test or not.

‘Don’t think so,’ I said, as offhanded as I could manage. ‘I’ve got stuff to do tomorrow and I’m sort of thinking about breaking it off.’

‘Cool,’ she yawned again. Clearly too tired to be testing me. ‘Well, I’ll be home around midnight. Provided that Disney bee-otch staying in the penthouse doesn’t decide to throw another orgy I have to cover up. See you then?’

‘I love that this is your everyday life. Have you thought about counselling her?’

‘I told her she was worth more when I found her butt naked on the balcony with three of the *Gossip Girl* cast this morning,’ Jenny sighed. It was a beautiful image. ‘And she told me she was worth exactly seventeen point six million at the last count and could I bring up some clean towels. She’s eighteen. I’ve started to worry about my future as the next Oprah. Oprah wouldn’t want to knock her ass over the balcony.’

‘Try and refrain from manslaughter and remember it’s all material,’ I said, hanging up.

I checked my missed calls list.

Nothing.

I was so annoyed with myself. I really thought I'd got somewhere today and now, here I was, obsessing over why Alex hadn't called me.

'Why don't you just call him?' asked the little voice in my head. It seemed like a good idea, why didn't I? Before I had the chance to second guess myself, I dialled and let it ring. And ring. And eventually, go to answer phone.

'Hi, Alex, it's Angela, uhhhhh,' I started. One day I'm going to have the perfect answer phone message. Just not today apparently. 'I just wondered if you wanted to do something tomorrow, but don't worry if you're busy or something. Talk to you later. Bye.' I hung up and frowned.

Maybe I did need a little bit more stuff.

CHAPTER TWENTY

When Tyler rang my buzzer at seven, Alex still hadn't called. I refused to think about what that did or didn't mean and instead, took one last look in the mirror and checked out my make-up. It looked fairly good, better than I would have managed two weeks ago. And my new Nanette Lepore dress was gorgeous. Seriously though, why hadn't Alex called? I checked my phone once more, then threw it into my (wonderful) bag and walked out of the door.

From the moment I ducked into the cab, I knew I should have cancelled. Tyler was his usual lovely self, asking me questions about my week, which I evaded by bouncing them right back.

'Same old, same old,' he smiled easily, directing the taxi driver downtown. 'Been running a lot, work's been a pain in the ass the last couple of days. I actually could really use a break. Just a couple of days away somewhere.'

'Yeah,' I said, staring out of the window, watching the Washington Square Arch zoom by. 'It's good to get away.'

'You want to do it next weekend?' he asked, squeezing

my hand. He looked immaculate as usual. Yes, he was a city boy like Mark, but the similarities really did start and end there. His hair was ruffled from product, not a slightly off-putting nervous hair-tugging habit and his suit was immaculately cut, and I was fairly certain it wasn't M&S crease-resistant. It certainly wasn't machine-washable. 'My friend has a house in the Hamptons, and he's going to be away on business. You would love the Hamptons, parties to go to, it's way cooler than in the city, and there's the beach. Did you bring a swimsuit?'

'Oh, uh, swimsuit?' I asked, caught off guard. I'd been staring at his forearms for just a second too long. Was it wrong to have a fetish for forearms? They were more tanned than Alex's, but maybe not as nice. Not that I was thinking about Alex. At all. 'Where are we going tonight?'

'Oh, Balthazar, it's great. The *moules frites* are perfection, and it's probably just cool enough for you,' he teased. 'Been to any gigs lately?'

'Not since I saw you last.' I didn't want to think about gigs.

'Are you OK?' Tyler asked as the cab pulled up. 'You seem a little out of it.'

'No, I'm fine.' It hardly seemed fair, mooning over Alex's forearms when he hadn't even called, and Tyler was here, taking me out to dinner, offering to take me away for the weekend. 'I'm sorry, I've just been thinking about the website and stuff. My editor asked me to come in again, but I don't really know what for. I suppose I'm a bit worried.'

'It's all good though, right?' he asked, directing me inside. The restaurant was stunning, a packed-out little French bistro, crammed with beautiful people. More Brownie points for another amazing venue. 'The website thing?'

'You haven't looked?' I was half surprised and entirely relieved. 'Apparently, it's doing well.'

'I did mean to take a look,' he confessed, smiling comfortably at the maître d' and sailing past the waiting couples. We were seated at a quiet corner table for two and quickly presented with iced water, bread, and champagne that Tyler had apparently preordered. I'd got so hot and bothered about a certain non-existent phone call, I'd forgotten how much fun it was to be with Tyler. 'I've just been so busy at work and I hardly ever go online at home. Sorry, I'm glad it's going so well though.'

'Don't be, I'd rather you didn't look,' I smiled, trying to invest myself in the date. 'It's completely embarrassing. This girl came up to me in a café this morning because she recognized me. I nearly died.'

'If I'd known I was dating a celebrity, I'd have dressed up,' he said, ordering appetizers for both of us. I could feel my brain turning to mush and a silly smile taking over my face. Sod the non-phoner.

'I am not a celebrity!' I wondered what he classed as dressing up. Relieved of his suit jacket, his shirt crisp and smart, and as usual, he smelled delicious. 'And you know you look great.'

'You don't look too bad yourself. That's a great dress,' he grinned, tapping me under the table with his foot. 'I can't help but think you'd look better out of it though.'

'Really,' I laughed, colouring slightly as the waiter hovered at Tyler's elbow with the champagne. I was starting to be glad I hadn't cancelled, and also starting to worry as to whether or not I'd be able to keep my gorgeous new dress on at the end of the night. What a slut!

Dinner was divine. Tyler really knew his food, and for the most part, I managed to put Alex out of my mind. During the appetizers, we planned our dream holidays – me taking in a cross America road trip in a turquoise Cadillac, Tyler touring Europe in a private plane – and by the time the waiters cleared away our entrées, we'd covered favourite films, TV shows and books. At last I was really starting to think I knew something about Tyler.

'And I already know you're into your hipster music, right?' Tyler smiled, accepting the dessert menu. 'I bet you love all those skinny boys with greasy girls' hair and band names that start with "The".'

I smiled and shook my head, trying not to remember soft, smoky-smelling hair brushing against my lips. 'What about you?'

'I like everything, I guess,' he shrugged. 'I like all music.'

Biting my lip, I thought back to what Alex had said in the coffee shop. Saying you liked all music meant you didn't love any. God, he was so arrogant. And why hadn't he called me?

'I just have to go to the bathroom,' I excused myself, rifling through my (beautiful) bag before I'd even made it down the stairs. Shit, three missed calls. All from Alex. I ran my wrists under cold water in the bathroom, then towelled off before I dialled my voicemail, promising myself I'd only listen to his message once.

'Hey, it's Alex,' he began, 'you still want to meet tomorrow? Give me a call.' That was it. I looked at my watch, it was only 9.30. I still had time to call for tomorrow, but not while I was out with Tyler, that was too weird.

'I wondered if you were coming back,' Tyler said as I took my seat. 'Something exciting happening in there?'

'Oh, it was really busy,' I said, hoping he didn't

know how many toilets there were. 'Too many women, not enough loos.'

'Loos,' he shook his head smiling. He really was incredibly good-looking, I thought, trying to concentrate. The wavy hair, mussed up from a day in the office, his crinkly, smiley eyes, his light tan. But when he took my hands in his, all I could think about was his manicured nails and Alex's calloused fingertips, and they just didn't compare.

'You want to get dessert?' he asked, leaning across the table and lowering his voice. 'Or do you want to head back to mine and get something really good?'

'I, uh, I have to meet my editor at nine,' I mumbled, trying to ignore the heat rising in my cheeks, the tingle in my belly. 'I think I really ought to be in my bed tonight.'

'I have to be up early too,' he shrugged, waving the waiter over to bring the bill. 'Unless you just really want me to see your room.'

'Oh, I sort of meant, maybe not tonight.' I was so red, I was practically glowing. 'To be honest, I've had a headache all day. I'm sorry.'

'Don't be. If you're not well . . .' he trailed off, looking around the room, tapping his fingers on the table.

'Do you want to do something later in the week?' I blurted out. God, what was wrong with me? I was going to end up married to him out of politeness if I wasn't careful. 'I could cook dinner, Friday night?'

'Yeah, sure,' he nodded, still not looking at me. 'Sounds great.'

We headed out on to the street in an awkward silence, luckily flagging a cab down right away. I tried to think of something to say, but there was nothing there at all.

'Great restaurant,' I tried. Tragic.

'Yeah, it's always good.'

'Great.'

'Yeah.'

Clearly this wasn't going to be made easy. I tried placing my hand on his knee and giving him a sweet smile, but he just covered it with his own without looking at me. I stared out of my window, racking my brain for something to say that wouldn't end in me asking him up for a coffee. Before I'd had time to muster up another pathetic attempt at conversation, we were cornering onto Lexington Avenue and pulling up outside my flat.

'Friday, then?' I asked, as he let me out. Pissed off he might be, but Tyler was always the gentleman.

'Yeah,' he said, softening slightly for a goodnight kiss. 'You take care of yourself. No headaches allowed on the weekends.'

I smiled and waved him off, before opening my bag, taking out my phone and calling Alex. It felt slightly shitty waving one man off and then calling another, but I couldn't help it.

'Hi, Alex?' I tried to sound casual when he picked up on the third ring. 'It's Angela.'

'Hey,' he yawned. Yawning at ten p.m.? Not very rock and roll. 'Sorry I missed your calls, I've been in the studio the whole time since you left. I'm so fucking tired.'

'The studio?' I asked. Another fabulous question from the world's greatest conversationalist.

'Yeah, I wanted to demo some of those new songs,' he said. 'I just completely lost track of time, and, well, what day it was. Where are you?'

'I've just been at dinner with a friend,' I said, leaning against the wall. The evening was still pleasantly warm, but Alex's sleepy voice was giving me goosebumps. 'So, what about tomorrow?'

'Yeah, I'm not doing anything.' I could hear music on low in the background. It sounded like Alex singing. 'I could give you the tour of Williamsburg if you're free?' he suggested.

'Sounds good.' I smiled to a passing stranger who looked at me oddly. 'Where should I meet you?'

'Uh, at the Bedford Avenue station? About eleven?' he yawned again. He really was too cute.

'I'll see you there.' I yawned a little myself. It was even contagious on the phone. 'Hope you sleep well.'

'I will, I'll be saving my energy for tomorrow,' he said. 'Sleep tight.'

I smiled as I hung up, date with Tyler forgotten, date with Alex buzzing around my mind.

It was still so early, I'd beaten Jenny home from work. I grabbed my laptop and lay on the sofa, thinking about what to write. If I stored a blog entry now, I could just email it from Alex's without interrupting our day tomorrow. I quickly bashed out the details of my date with Tyler and made some vague references to my day out in Brooklyn with Alex, *Balthazar or Brooklyn?* before logging off and dozing on the sofa. Mary had said her readers would go crazy for a Wall Street type, so after all, I was just giving the people what they wanted.

CHAPTER TWENTY-ONE

The thirty-minute journey to Brooklyn felt like an eternity. What if Alex hadn't rushed to call because it wasn't as incredible for him as it had been for me? After all, he wasn't the one who had tripled the number of people he had ever slept with inside the last fortnight. Just before the train stopped, I pulled my compact out of my handbag, quickly swiped at my shiny nose with powder and ran my fingers through my hair. Thank God it was supposed to look messy.

I skipped up the steps of the subway station, pulling Jenny's sunglasses down off my head and over my eyes, searching for Alex. Despite the oddly high numbers of hipster types littering the streets at a time they really ought to be at work, I spotted him almost immediately. He was leaning against a lamppost, arms folded, bobbing his head gently to whatever was on his iPod. His black hair shone almost blue in the sun, and his daily uniform of jeans and T-shirt clung to him like a second skin. I lifted up my sunglasses and watched him, bleached out by the sun for a moment. The whole scene was almost too perfect to disturb.

'Hey,' Alex shaded his eyes with his hands, when I

finally burst the bubble and went over. 'I didn't see you sneaking up on me.'

'Well, that's the point in sneaking up on you,' I smiled, kissing him hello. Hopefully, there would be lots more kissing. 'You OK?'

'Yeah, a little tired, but really good,' he took my hand and we started down the street, passing cute little boutiques, dark vintage clothes emporiums and poky record shop after poky record shop after poky record shop. 'You want to get something to eat?'

'Sounds like a plan,' I said. For the first time in the last couple of days, nothing felt complicated. I was in the sunshine, I was holding hands with a beautiful boy and I was happy. Yay!

We ducked into a tiny diner for coffee and bagels while Alex gave me a brief history lesson on his neighbourhood. Williamsburg had been home to hundreds of artists and musicians, he told me, generally all kinds of creative types that had been driven out of Manhattan due to the crazy spiralling rents. It had been his home for almost ten years, and he loved it. He loved going to bars where he knew everyone, he loved feeling like he had a neighbourhood, and he loved that in less than fifteen minutes, he could lose himself in the city. Unfortunately, he hated the fact that property prices were starting to go crazy around him, that the musicians and artists were being replaced by rich hipsters with nothing to do but buy up real estate and make it harder for people to live there. And most of all, he hated that a lot of his friends had started moving away again, either further into Brooklyn or back to Manhattan.

As the sun slipped over the Manhattan skyline, we stopped in a dark little bar back on Bedford Avenue. The walls were lined with tankards and beer mugs, the dim lighting was only boosted by a TV screen showing sport, and someone, somewhere was cooking chips. It felt scarily like a real pub.

'Beer?' Alex asked as I slid into a chair. Wandering around, blissfully happy, was exhausting. Sitting in a chair, staring at Alex's rear bent over the bar in his sexy low-slung jeans, was much easier. He returned with two pints, actual pints, while I tried to pretend I hadn't been totally ogling him. 'So, you like it here?'

'I do,' I said, gratefully sipping the cold lager. 'I would never have thought to have come here. It's so different to the city.'

'You can still get this stuff in Manhattan.' Alex sipped his beer thoughtfully. 'It's just a little harder to find, a little harder to afford.'

'Well, I'm glad I got to see it,' I said, squeezing his hand. 'I'm glad you offered.'

'Me too,' he smiled, squeezing back and holding my gaze for a moment too long. 'How long are you going to stick around for, Angela?'

'You know, I've managed to go a really long time today without thinking about that.' I nursed my beer and tried a wry smile that wouldn't stick.

'Sorry.' He looked down into his drink. 'What can I say, I'm a planner?'

'That's not very rock and roll, is it?' I asked, pushing my hair behind my ears, really wanting to comb my fingers through his. 'What happened to living for the moment?'

'Living for the moment doesn't really work if what's making this moment so great might disappear to another continent in a couple of weeks,' he smiled, taking my hand back and shrugging. 'I really like being with you.'

'Yeah.' I looked at him, not knowing what else to say.

'Too much?' He half smiled, half frowned. 'Sorry. I forget the real world isn't ready for my over-emoting sometimes. Fuck, that even sounded pretentious to me. Sorry.'

'Over-Emoting is OK,' I said, biting my lip. 'It's just all so weird. I keep getting these flashes where this starts to feel like real life, like this is something I could have, and then, bang, I come back down and remember this is actually just a glorified holiday.'

'Doesn't have to be,' Alex said. 'There's nothing stopping you from getting a visa, getting a job. There are always options if you're prepared to work for them. If living here, having a life here, is what you want.'

'Apparently, my problem is not knowing what I want,' I sighed. 'Just the idea of having to go back there . . .' The thought of home was instinctively tied to thoughts of Mark and my stomach seized.

'So don't go,' Alex shrugged. 'Seriously, you could at least look into it. If you could do absolutely anything, nothing at all stopping you, what would it be?'

'I asked someone else that question once,' I smiled, shaking my head. 'And they said they'd follow the Yankees for a year.'

'Then they had no imagination.' Alex squeezed my hand. 'And that's why you're here with me. What would you do?'

'Right now? If I could do anything?' I asked. He nodded. 'If I could do anything, I would magic myself a work permit, start getting paid real money for writing at *The Look*, and stay here as long as I wanted. Not running away, not being on holiday, just living. Going to the supermarket, paying bills, doing the washing, just having a life.'

'Then do it. You're young, you've got work here, just apply for the visa. Stay.'

'Everyone likes to make things sound so easy,' I said, leaning back and staring up at the ceiling. 'I wish they were.'

'You know what would be easy?' he said, reaching a hand across to my cheek, guiding my eyes back into his. 'Just going back to mine. Just not thinking about any of this right now.'

I put my drink down, not even half finished and stood up. 'I'm so sick of thinking,' I nodded, holding out my hand.

That evening, that night, the early dawn hours, everything was just as intense as the first time. By Thursday morning, I was emotionally and physically knackered, but in so deep, I didn't know how I was supposed to find a way back out. It was hard enough finding a way out of the bedroom. After several attempts, we finally managed to install ourselves on his sofa in T-shirts and underwear, to listen to his new demos. They were totally stripped back, just Alex and his guitar, nothing like the songs I was used to hearing from his band.

'Is this how all your songs start out?' I asked, my head resting in his lap.

'Yeah,' he nodded, gently tapping out the rhythm on my collarbone. 'They all start this way. Sometimes they get built up, sometimes they get thrown away. These are still really new though.'

'I think they're beautiful,' I said, nodding along. 'They're so soft.'

'Glad you think so,' he said. 'They're kind of about you.'

'Really?' I craned my neck up and looked at him. 'They are?'

'Uh-huh,' he said, pushing me up gently and curling his body around mine. I could feel his heartbeat speeding up against my shoulder blade. 'About you, me, about this. Meeting you has really helped me clear my head up. I think I've figured out what I want again.'

'That's funny,' I felt my heartbeat find its rhythm against his, 'you've managed to have the completely opposite effect on my life. I don't have a clue what I want.'

'I think you do,' Alex said, 'you're just not ready to deal with it yet. That's OK. I'm just ready, that's all.'

'You're not going to split up the band, then?' I asked, resting my head against his chest just underneath his chin.

'I'll give it another shot,' he said. 'It was me that was messed up, not the band. I wasn't being fair.'

'Well that's good news. You're really feeling better?'

'Really, really,' he nodded, stroking my hair. 'What about you, how you doing working your stuff out?'

'I don't know,' I said, rolling over and looked at him, all sharp cheekbones and dark eyes. 'I'm getting a fairly certain feeling about some stuff.' I stretched up and kissed him gently. 'And I can't stop thinking about what you said, about staying here. Maybe it is possible.'

My hair dropped down into my eyes as I turned, just as Alex's long, messy fringe flopped into his. Before I could reach out to comb it back, his long fingers were brushing the hair out of my eyes.

'Well, why don't we just work more on the stuff you're certain about?' He kissed my forehead gently. His hand stroked my hair, then moved back down my cheekbone, tracing the line of my face all the way down my chin, my throat, my collarbone. I pushed against him, wedging my body underneath his, forcing him on top of me. 'And once you're absolutely positive about that,' Alex whispered, 'we can start thinking about everything else.'

* * *

Afterwards, when Alex had dozed off, I slid off the sofa, pulled my underwear out from its hiding place under the coffee table, and logged on to my Gmail. I sat, gazing at him sleeping and really didn't know what to write. I didn't want to pretend this wasn't happening any more, even on the blog. I absolutely had to end it with Tyler and find out where this was going. I looked at the empty screen and decided to be honest. With Tyler, with Alex, with Mary and with myself.

The Adventures of Angela: Last Exit to Brooklyn

So, I've been writing to you for about two weeks now. Does it feel loads longer to you? I feel like I've been here for ever.

Since I left London, it's been the craziest two weeks of my life. I'd forgotten that there were lots of cool and interesting people out there who can make your life incredibly exciting if you let them. I've had the most amazing opportunities and well, between me and you, I've met a couple of people I think might change my life for ever. Even as someone who loved London with a fiery passion when I moved there, I can't get over what an unbelievable place New York City really is.

When I found out about my ex and his extracurricular tennis lessons, all I could think about was what a horrible, awful thing he had done to me. And I'm not making excuses for him, he still is a great big giant scumbag, but, and this didn't even occur to me until today, if he hadn't done what he did, if I hadn't caught them at it in my car, if I hadn't completely destroyed my best friend's wedding (that actually feels worse every time I mention it) I wouldn't be here today. I wouldn't be writing to you at all. I wouldn't be in Brooklyn, blogging in the living room of a wonderful man who is asleep on his settee with a smile on his face. A man I would never even have met if it weren't for that turd and his two-timing.

So, and I really mean this, thank you, Mr Ex, you hateful little scumbag, I hope you're having fun back in England.

I'm learning how to have fun again and it feels nice.

I emailed the entry to Mary. It felt good to get that out, but it hurt to admit it. At least some stuff was finally starting to make sense, I had to let go of the past before I could move on to the future.

CHAPTER TWENTY-TWO

For someone who had flat out refused to go to Brooklyn for one evening only one week ago, I returned to the apartment on Friday morning to find a note from Jenny saying she was staying at Jeff's for the weekend. As far as I could tell, she hadn't been in our apartment since we'd had dinner at Scottie's on Monday, but it was weird how the place already felt like home to me, whether she was there or not. Jenny had been quick to add some photos of us from Gina's leaving party to her clip-frame montages, and since we had terrifyingly similar taste in films and TV (read hot actors), heaps of my favourite DVDs were lying around the place. I'd even picked up some copies of books by my favourite authors at The Strand second-hand bookshop. I couldn't think of a single thing I needed from the flat in London. Not one single thing.

Necking what was left of my iced coffee, I logged on to check my email. I had precisely two hours before my meeting with Mary and in that time I needed to shower, choose an outfit that said 'please don't fire me', and come up with my very first 'it's not you, it's me' speech for dinner with Tyler that night. Flicking through the acres of spam in my Gmail account, I played the scenario over and over in my head. I was sure he would be fine, we could just be friends, it would be great. Absolutely fine. And I definitely wasn't going to be terribly terribly English if he wasn't OK with it, and accidentally sleep with him. Nope. Wasn't going to happen. I was just reassuring myself that one single polite goodbye kiss would probably be OK, when I spotted an email from *The Look*. But it wasn't from Mary or Cissy, it was from someone called Sara Stevens.

Dear Angela,
I hope you don't mind me emailing, this was the only contact information on The Look *server.*

Firstly, I just want to say I absolutely love your blog – so much fun! I really feel like Im in New York with you.

So here comes the exciting bit. We're currently setting up the UK version of The Look, *launching in January and I would absolutely love to talk to you about you working with us as senior staff writer. Everyone here thinks your style is perfect for our magazine, and we've been tracking the popularity of the blog here in the UK as well as in the US, you're a hit!*

Obviously I'm not sure how long you're planning to be in New York, but we'd need you back in the UK by the end of August to prepare for the launch issue.

Give me a call, my numbers are at the bottom of the email and we can talk over any questions you might have, salary, benefits, etc.

It was almost one-thirty here, so six-thirty in London. Only one way to find out if she was a late worker.

'Sara Stevens.'

Yes, yes, she was.

'Hi, Sara? It's Angela Clark here.' This was officially the last time I was going to dial a phone number without having a blind clue what I was going to say if someone answered. 'I just got your email.'

'Angela, I'm so excited that you called me! We absolutely *love* you here in the UK office. Are you excited? It's exciting isn't it?'

So far, so different from Mary.

'Erm, yes? It is?' I plopped down on the back of the sofa.

'Oh my God, it SO is!'

I wasn't sure I was OK with Sara showing such an early propensity for screeching.

'So, when are you back, hun? I love that you nicked off to New York for a jolly instead of sitting around being a lil miss victim. Very fun. But we need you back here! When's your flight booked?' she yelled.

'I haven't actually booked a flight back.' Sara might only need to stop for breath every seven minutes, I was struggling. 'I don't know if I'm actually coming back.'

'What? You haven't married that Wall Street banker have you? Not that I would blame you! No, really, it's better. We will absolutely pay for your flight back, Virgin Upper Class all the way, baby! So the senior writer position is really exciting. You'd be writing about just about anything you think would be interesting to *The Look* readers, so there's lots of scope for getting around. I was reading your blog and it just hit, pow! This girl can write fashion, dating, travel, food, sex—'

'What did Mary say?' I interrupted. Yes I know it's rude, but she wasn't going to shut up if I didn't.

'Mary?'

'Mary Stein? My editor here.'

'Oh,' Sara actually paused, 'I haven't exactly spoken to her. It's not really poaching is it? You're British, you're coming back to London, we need a writer. Really, we're just keeping it in the family. I'm sure she'll be pleased as. And I don't want to be vulgar, but Angela, the money on this position is going to shit all over whatever pennies the web team are paying you.'

'But you will speak to her?'

'Oh yeah, right now, I'll call her right now. I just need you to say you're coming to work for me, you ridiculously talented woman!'

'OK, well, this is really interesting,' I just wanted to get off the phone as soon as humanly possible, 'but I actually have to dash off to a meeting, and—'

'I need to know by the end of the day, your time, on Monday,' Sara said bluntly. All the giggles and enthusiasm gone out of her voice. 'Unfortunately I don't have time for you to think too long and hard about this – I didn't think you'd need to actually – I have a writer to recruit in a very short space of time. I'll email the job spec and salary and you can reply. Right?'

I suddenly realized she couldn't see me nodding down the phone. 'Yes.'

'Right. I'll speak to you Monday. Bye hun, have a great weekend in the Big Apple!'

'Bye. You too. In London, I mean.' But she had already hung up. I looked around the apartment, still holding the phone to my ear and softly bit my lip. 'Bugger me.'

As if Sara's phone call wasn't enough to mess with my tiny mind, the tourists on their way to Times Square really didn't want me to get to my meeting with Mary on time. I'd spent far too long scrubbing at my hair in the shower and troughing Goldfish crackers, watching The View instead of doing any of the things I was supposed to do, and now I was late. I could understand why Alex loved Williamsburg, it was so chilled out, but I was still in love with Manhattan, despite the maddening crowds. The noise, the people, the feeling that anything could happen at any given second. That was what inflated my blood pressure, that was what sent adrenaline surging through me as the streets got narrower, more congested. I loved the neon billboards, the giant Target ads, the garish Hershey store, Bubba Gump's Shrimp Co, Virgin, Sephora, ToysЯus. They were just adverts, stores, restaurants, but it was the clicking cameras and the pushing people with the happiest faces you'd ever seen that made the place what it was. And it was amazing to me.

Also amazing, was the hit of the air conditioning when I walked into the Spencer Media building. Bliss. I was late, but sent straight up to Mary's office and without a lecture and shockingly, given coffee and iced water and, Jesus, a smile, by Cissy, as soon as I stepped over the threshold.

'Angela Clark, get in here!' Mary yelled from behind her desk.

'I'm in,' I said nervously, balancing the drinks, trying not to spill anything on my bag. 'Hi, Mary.'

'So yesterday's post? Oh my God?' She was actually grinning. Not a wry smile, not a disappointed frown. A big fat grin. 'Great writing, Angela, I can't wait to post it.'

'So the blog is still going?' I sighed with relief.

'Of course it's still fucking going!' Mary stood up and gave me a hug that was much bigger than she was. 'You're my little success story. Do you know how many emails we've had about your column? More than about anything else on the website. Hell, more than most things in the magazine. Everyone at *The Look* loves your column.'

'Everyone,' I said cautiously. I couldn't tell whether Sara had called yet. 'I mean, that's good. Isn't it?'

'It's really fucking good. People love you, Angela, and they love to live vicariously through someone else. They don't want to run away to another continent and leave everything they've ever known, but they love that you're doing it for them,' Mary nodded, perching on the edge of her huge desk and pushing me backwards into a seat. I managed to keep the coffee in the cup, but the water went everywhere. Except on my bag. Phew. 'It's good for me and it's really good for you. So I need to put you on a contract.'

'What?'

'A. Contract,' Mary said slowly. 'We want to keep the blog going long-term, Angela. I won't make you sign it in blood, but I will make you sign it.'

Shitshitshitshitshitshitshitshitshitshitshit.

'A Sara Stevens hasn't called you from the UK office has she?' I asked, gulping down the coffee in case Mary felt like taking it away shortly.

'The UK *Look*? How do you know about that?' Mary asked, hopping back behind her desk at lightning speed. 'That hasn't even been announced internally yet.'

Fuckfuckfuckfuckfuckfuckfuckfuckfuck.

'Well, they called me today and asked if I would go and work for them. As senior staff writer.'

'Are you shitting me?' Mary's face went from red to white to purple in what seemed like a heartbeat. 'They tried to poach my fucking writer?'

'She said it wouldn't be like poaching . . .'

'What else is it exactly? When was this? Why didn't you tell me?' Angry Mary was very, very scary.

'It was just now, literally, like an hour ago,' I explained hurriedly. 'Right before this meeting. I didn't think I should call to talk about it when we were meeting now.'

'Right. I suppose I should appreciate your coming to tell me face to face, even if those sly London bitches couldn't be respectful enough to tell me,' she shook her head. 'Congratulations Angela, it's a great opportunity for you and I think you'll be very good at it. I'm just fucking furious to have found you and then to lose you.'

'But I haven't accepted yet, I have until Monday,' I bleated, jumping up off the leather chair and leaving half my thighs behind. Ouch. 'I'm not sure I really want to go back to London, or work for Sara.'

Especially work for Sara, I added silently, she's clearly nuts.

Mary stared over her desk, not speaking. I didn't know whether or not that was a good thing.

'Are you serious?' she said eventually.

'About?'

'About not going home and taking up this huge opportunity to risk it all to write a blog in a city that you've lived in for three weeks?'

'Well, when you put it like that, I know it sounds a bit silly.' I sat back down, trying to pull my Velvet T-shirt dress underneath me.

'Don't you want to go back home to London?' Mary asked.

'Does it matter what I want?' I bit my lip hard. 'I've got to go, haven't I? Everyone keeps telling me.' Everyone but Alex, I reminded myself unhelpfully.

'Well, you're not a US national, so it wouldn't necessarily be easy,' Mary stood up and walked back around her desk. She bent down in front of me, forcing me to look at her. I was so embarrassed. 'But if you wanted to stay, you would always have a job with me.'

'Really?' I blinked back a tiny tear before it could make a real break for it.

'Angela, I've been reading your diary for three weeks now, and it's quite clear that you really don't know what you want,' Mary knelt on the floor, one hand on my knee. 'That's why people are relating to your blog, they want to be there when you work it out. I don't know if that's going to be here in New York, or back in London, but I do know you don't have for ever to work it out any more.'

'I know,' I said, taking a deep breath and wiping my eyes. I really had to pull myself together.

'You know I'm pissed about the UK team,' she said, 'but if you're planning on going home, you should go now. This really is an amazing opportunity. If you stay here, who knows? The blog isn't going to pay as much as a staff job, but it will pay. We can help you apply for a visa, but I can't tell you what will happen after that.'

I stared at the pavement all the way back to the apartment, only just aware of people and cars and any other potential obstructions. Fumbling my keys into the lock, I rolled straight over the back of the sofa and stared at the ceiling. I had just worked out I was happy, I had just worked out it was definitely Alex, not Tyler, and now this. Jenny would say it was life testing my decisions. My mum would tell me it was fate bringing me home. I would say, enough, have we got any more Ring Dings. And since I was the only person in the room, I went with my option.

* * *

Tyler arrived on the dot of seven to find me on my doorstep, juggling brown paper grocery bags, my handbag and my keys. I'd completely forgotten he was coming over in my wallowing, and by the time it hit me, during the Thanksgiving episode of *Friends*, I had just enough time to run to the food halls in Grand Central station and pick up pasta, sauce and an enormous chocolate cheesecake. I had been planning to pass it all off as my own work, but I'd spent so long internally debating the merits of cheesecake over tarte tartin, I had run out of time.

'So this is my romantic dinner?' he smiled, taking the bags from me.

'I'm so sorry,' I grimaced, tussling with the door. 'I had that meeting with my editor, and it was all a bit, eurgh, just a bit much. I was going to cook properly, honest.'

'Another meeting?' Tyler followed me through the door and up the stairs. 'You must have almost as many meetings as me.'

'Yeah, it's a long story,' I said, turning up the next staircase. 'I dare say you'll get the pleasure of it over dinner.'

Walking into the apartment together made me realize what a state it was compared to Tyler's luxury pad. I desperately tried to kick some of the piles of crap under the settee and distract Tyler with the wine he had brought, but I couldn't find a bottle opener in the kitchen. Naturally, in the apartment of two singlish girls, it was in the living room. I was relieved that Tyler was in a much better mood than when I had bailed on him earlier in the week, but I couldn't help but feel that wouldn't last long once I broached the 'dumping him' portion of the evening.

We cooked together (I boiled the pasta, he microwaved the sauce) then we sat down at the coffee table, cross-legged on the floor. For a while, we chatted about nothing, Tyler wolfing down his dinner, me pushing it around my plate. I wasn't really in the mood for the pasta or the conversation, but I was hoping he would leave before we hit the cheesecake. It had me, Jenny and a weepy bottle of wine written all over it.

'So what was so bad about this meeting today?' Tyler asked, topping up my drink.

'I can't hand on heart say it was bad,' I said, grinding more black pepper on my uneaten pasta. 'I've been offered a full-time job.'

'Really?' he asked, emptying his plate and starting work on mine.

'Really,' I nodded. 'Staff writer on the magazine. On *The Look*. Only thing is, it's in London.'

'But that's fantastic,' he said, leaning over for a quick one-armed hug. 'It's a real writing job like you wanted. I told you this blog thing would be your big break.'

'But it's in London,' I repeated, watching him pick up his fork and start eating again. 'I'd have to leave almost right away.'

'You were always going to have to leave, weren't you?' Tyler helped himself to my untouched food. 'Isn't it amazing that you have this to go back to?'

'Well, the web editor said if I stayed then she would always have work for me.' I couldn't stop staring at him. He hadn't even flinched at the idea of me leaving. 'So I *could* stay.'

'But surely you're not going to,' he looked up, mid-mouthful. 'I mean, the webby thing is one thing, but staff writer on a magazine, that's a real job isn't it? It's being a journalist, not just playing at it.'

'You think the blog is just "playing at" writing?' I asked. He was making my worries about breaking things off easier every time he opened his mouth.

'Angela, honey, why are you getting all stressed?' Tyler asked. Having finished my food and his, he crawled around to my side of the table and held my face in his hands. 'I think you're a very talented writer and I think this job is a fantastic opportunity for you. Now, why don't we go and celebrate?'

For the want of an answer, I let him kiss me, but it was strange. I didn't feel anything.

'Tyler, would you still want to see me if I stayed in New York?' I asked, breaking away.

'Of course,' he murmured into my hair, nuzzling my ear.

'What if I went back to London?' I asked, pulling away. 'What if I went back to London but I wanted to keep seeing you. Do the long distance thing. Would you do that?'

'I don't know where all this is coming from,' Tyler said, tensing slightly. 'We're having fun, aren't we?'

'Apparently you are,' I said, pushing up off the floor and grabbing the plates off the table. I placed them on the kitchen counter. Maybe it was slightly more of a slam than a place. 'So if I went back to England this would be over?'

'Angela,' Tyler stood up, 'I don't know what's going on here. Aren't we just supposed to be having a nice dinner?'

'Yes, supposed to be. I suppose I just didn't realize this wasn't important to you at all.'

'What the . . .' he threw his hands in the air. 'Like you're serious about me? For fuck's sake, you've been screwing some guy in Brooklyn while you've been screwing me, so don't come over all "is this going anywhere?" with me.'

'I've been . . .' I trailed off. He'd been reading the blog. 'Why didn't you say anything if it was a problem?'

'Because it wasn't a problem.' Tyler shook his head. 'You've been seeing other people, so what? So have I. I see lots of other girls. Isn't this what you were looking for when you ran away in the first place?'

'I don't know.' He wasn't actually wrong. 'But it's not what I'm looking for now.'

'I don't think you know what you're looking for,' he laughed, making for the door. 'This is why I don't do relationships, especially psycho rebound girls.'

'Psycho rebound . . .' I repeated. My God I was not going to miss him after all. Such a charmer.

'You totally got what you were looking for out of this, Angela. You just wanted to fuck some hot guy to make you feel better about getting cheated on. It's not my fault that you're too scared to go back to Britain. I do not have time for this emotional "will I won't I" bullshit.'

'Emotional bullshit? You think this is emotional bullshit?' I asked. Before he could escape, I positioned myself squarely between him and the door. 'All right then, you may as well have all of it. You know what? Yes, I've been seeing someone else, but do you know why I kept seeing you?'

He looked away. The ceiling was apparently very interesting.

'I kept seeing you because I thought you were nice. No, really! How stupid was I? And just so you know, it certainly wasn't because you're *so good* in bed that I couldn't help myself, because it turns out there are a few things you could learn there.'

That got his attention.

'Yeah, cause you were faking *that*,' he sniffed.

'One of the benefits of being a "psycho rebound girl",' I smirked right back. He didn't need to know I was lying my arse off. 'When you've been faking it for ten years, you get really fucking good at it.'

He shook his head, his lips set in a thin line. The last time all my frustrations had built up inside me like this, I'd practically ripped his clothes off in the street. Tonight I would settle for just ripping into him.

'I thought you were charming, a bit cheesy, but basically a nice guy. God, I even felt bad about seeing you and Alex at the same time. Obviously, I didn't realize you were seeing so very many "other people". And even though I was going to dump you tonight, yes, I was, I was hoping you would want to be friends. But if my emotional bullshit is too much, you'd better just leave.'

He looked at me, shaking his head. 'I don't have to put up with this just to get laid,' he said, pushing past me, out of the door.

'And neither do I!' I yelled after him, slamming the door right behind him.

For a long time after Tyler had gone, I stood completely still, absolutely furious. But I didn't know who I was more angry at, Tyler or myself. He was right, I had been using him, so why was I so pissed off that he had been doing the same? If I did go back to London, it wouldn't be Tyler I'd be lying awake at night thinking about. Finally freeing my feet, I picked up my mobile and dialled Alex. I just needed to talk to him.

But he wasn't there. I couldn't call Jenny, she was having her big romantic evening with Jeff. I thought about ringing Erin or Vanessa, but I didn't really feel close enough to them. Instead I did what any confused, angry girl would do when the shops were closed. I opened another bottle of wine, I took the entire chocolate cheesecake out of the fridge, and I sat down in front of the TV. Sod the diet and pray that this season will favour the smock, I thought as I chowed down.

By the time I couldn't force another thing into my mouth, I'd eaten more than half of the cheesecake and drunk the entire bottle of wine. It wasn't going to feel good in the morning, but the sugar-wine coma I was slipping into felt great at that moment.

CHAPTER TWENTY-THREE

I was expecting to be woken by an overwhelming desire to vomit, but instead, it was a loud slam of the door on Saturday morning. I pushed myself up, peering over the back of the settee and praying it wasn't burglars. Or murderers. Maybe burglars wouldn't be so bad actually, I thought, cautiously peeping. It was neither. Instead of huge threatening men dressed in black, I saw a tiny, harassed-looking Jenny, dressed in her underwear and a man's T-shirt. It was an interesting look for her, and one, and this was just a hunch, that was not attached to a happy story.

'Jenny?' I started cautiously. 'You OK?'

'We broke up,' she said, shaking her head in disbelief. Her eyes were fixed on something in the middle distance only she could see. 'He dumped me. Again.'

'What?' I tried to stretch and move over as she stumbled around the room and collapsed onto the settee. If her fashion forward ensemble wasn't weird enough, she absolutely reeked of booze. 'You and Jeff broke up?'

'He said he loves me but he can't be with me.' She screwed her face up, still staring straight ahead. 'He said every time I leave he's worried I might cheat again, and he doesn't think he can live like that.'

'But he loves you,' I said, pulling her in for a hug, 'and you love him.'

'He says it's not enough.' Her voice was getting quieter and quieter. 'He says he doesn't trust me.'

'God, Jenny, I'm sorry,' I said, pulling her feet up underneath her. She was just like a ragdoll.

'I thought he was going to ask me to move back in with him.' She tried a smile. 'I was so worried about how I was going to tell you I was moving out. But he doesn't even want to see me, let alone live with me.'

'But he loves you, it's obvious to anyone,' I said, trying to break through to her. I was getting scared by the glassy stare. 'Maybe he just needs time to realize it.'

Jenny shook her head. 'He's had the time. He's had all the fucking time in the world. I'm the one who's been sitting here for the last year, my entire life on hold waiting for him to realize how much he needs me.' A deep, loud sob escaped. 'I can't do it any more. I love him so much.'

'Did you tell him that?' I asked, relaxing my grip as she began to shake.

'What do you think?' she asked, covering her face with her hands. 'He doesn't fucking care. It's all shit! He loves me too much? Fuck, he doesn't even know what love is. If he did, he wouldn't do this. He couldn't do this.'

'I'm starting to think most blokes don't get it at all,' I sighed in agreement.

Jenny stared at me. Apparently not the right thing to say.

'Are you serious?' She shook her head. 'I can't sit here and listen to you cry about who you like, who you love, why your ex didn't love you, again. It's not all about you sometimes.'

'That's not what I was going to say,' I tried to defend myself, to remember that she didn't mean it when she got like this. 'I was just going to say, even when you think they're good guys, sometimes they're not. Maybe that's Jeff too. You're too good for this Jenny.'

'Fuck!' she shouted. 'There you go! It's just not true, Angela. We go around talking all this shit about how men are all assholes and we're poor little women, used and abused, but it's just not true. Jeff doesn't love me because I cheated on him. Your ex doesn't love you because, fuck, I don't even know, how could he? How can he love someone who doesn't even like herself?'

'This wasn't about Mark,' I said, standing up to leave. I had to get out of there before I said something I regretted. Before I couldn't forgive her. 'I was talking about Tyler actually. He turned out not to be such a nice guy after all.'

'Who gives a fuck? You were only screwing him because he reminded you of your ex. Oh and yeah, he was really fucking rich,' she carried on. I turned to watch her empty the remains of my wine into a mug and down it. 'At least now you can get on with your little "I'm with the band" fantasy.'

'I'm just not going to listen to this,' I said, grabbing my bag from by the door. 'I don't have to. I don't know how you dare put yourself across as this great person who really cares, who really wants to help people, when you can't even help yourself.'

'Why don't you just run back home?' Jenny waved me away. 'And leave me and Alex and everyone else to our real lives. It's been fun, but maybe, just maybe, when you get home, you'll stop trying to be something you're not. Had you thought about that, Angela? Maybe the reason you couldn't work out who you wanted to be is because you're already her. This dumbass indecisive fuck-up of a person *is* who you are. It's who we all are, and the sooner you realize that, the better. I'm sick of holding your hand and waiting for you to work it out for yourself.'

I walked out and slammed the door for the second time. Not knowing what else to do, I grabbed my phone and dialled.

'Hello?'

'Louisa?'

'Angela?'

I was confused. I'd dialled my mum's house, not Louisa's.

'Where's my mum?' I asked. I wasn't sure I could cope with this.

'She's making tea, I just brought the wedding photos around on the way to tennis. I got them yesterday,' Louisa said.

Just hearing her voice brought it all back. Not the wedding or Mark's cheating, but my actual life. My twenty-seven years of life. She was having tea with my mum on a Saturday morning, looking at the wedding photos, at me in the wedding photos, as though none of the last three weeks had happened. And I guessed to them, most of it hadn't.

'Where are you, Angela?' Louisa asked. She wasn't shouting and she didn't sound angry. 'Your mum said you're still in America.'

'I'm in New York,' I sat down on the bottom step of the staircase, 'I've been here since . . .'

'Gosh, doesn't it seem like a long time ago,' Louisa sighed. 'I wish the honeymoon could have lasted longer . . .'

'Louisa,' I said slowly, 'aren't you pissed off with me?'

'Pissed off with you?' she asked, sounding shocked. 'Aren't you pissed off with me?'

I bit my lip and stared at the doorway, my eyes welling up fast. 'But I ruined your wedding,' I gasped, trying not to let the tears go all at once. 'I am so sorry.'

'Oh, Angela,' Louisa sobbed, tears catching in her voice across the line. 'Is that really what you've been thinking for three weeks? I thought you'd be angry with me. I'm the one in the wrong, I should have told you about Mark and that slag Katie as soon as I found out.'

'Mum said he's moved in with her,' I whispered, pulling my knees up. 'Have you seen him?'

'I've seen them at the tennis club,' Louisa said reluctantly. 'But he knows what me and Tim think of him, we're not exactly sharing a post-match drink. Oh, Angela, please don't tell me you've been out there all on your own thinking I don't care?'

'I haven't been on my own,' I managed. 'I've been staying with a friend, this girl I met, but I think I'm going to have to come back soon.'

'Of course you're coming home,' Louisa said. Her voice was so familiar, yet it sounded foreign, I'd been immersed in American accents for such a long time now. 'You can stay with us. We'll look after you.'

'I've been offered a job, on this new magazine,' I said, trying to find some strong ground to stand on. 'I've been doing some stuff for the website here, and they've offered me a staff writer job.'

'There you go. It's not all bad then is it? Why don't you go and pack your bag and come back. Come back today, I could meet you at the airport tomorrow! I can't stand thinking of you there, being upset on your own.

Please Angela, I just want to know you're all right. I just want to see you.'

'I haven't been on my own,' I said again, looking out of the door, watching New York buzz by. 'And I love it here. Honestly, I've actually been sort of OK.'

'You don't sound it, Angela,' Louisa sighed. 'Why don't you call me when you've booked your flight. You know what we need, we need Ben & Jerry's and *Dirty Dancing*.'

'I've already done all that, Louisa.' I shook my head, remembering why I had left in the first place. 'Things aren't perfect here, but just coming home won't make everything better either.

'Angela, you need your friends, listen to yourself!' she replied. 'What Mark did was bloody awful, and we'll never forgive him for it, but you have to come home sooner or later. You can't run away for ever.'

'I don't think you understand,' I said, standing up and walking out into the almost fresh air. 'I'm not running away. I was, when I left, I was, but now I've got some real opportunities here. Some really exciting things have happened.'

'It always seems that way when you're on holiday,' Louisa was starting to talk to me as if I were drunk. Or five years old. It was frustrating. 'But be real Angela, you've got to get on with life.'

'Yes, you're right,' I nodded, rounding the corner and looking up at the Chrysler Building. It still broke my heart, it was so beautiful. 'But coming home wouldn't be getting on with life, it would be going back to something I was unhappy with.'

'Angela,' Louisa was starting to get impatient. 'I get it, you think you've put the Mark-cheating-on-you-thing behind you.'

'Don't tell me what I think,' I said, my voice growing

stronger. 'And yes, Mark is a shit. If I ever see him again, I'm likely to try to castrate him, but what he did to me wasn't nearly as bad as what I did to myself . . .' I could almost hear Alex's words coming out of my mouth. Fancy that. 'I hadn't been happy with him for years. He wouldn't have looked at someone else if things were good between us. I should have left him, Louisa, but I was too scared. I wasted years of both our lives. Just pissed them away.'

'But—' Louisa tried to interrupt, but I wasn't ready to stop.

'And in the last three weeks, I feel like I've actually been living. Making good decisions, doing good things. If I came back now, what would happen?'

'You'd be with people who love you and care about you,' Louisa said. Her voice certainly didn't sound like that of someone who loved and cared about me. I took a deep breath before I said anything else. Before I could, I heard the call waiting beeping quietly on the line.

'I have to go, Louisa,' I said, shielding my eyes and looking back up towards the apartment. I could see Jenny pressed up against the window, looking for me, her phone in her hand. 'I don't know exactly what I'm going to do, but can you tell Mum I'm OK, and I'll call on Monday?'

'Angela, for God's sake,' Louisa sounded incredibly cross, 'you're living in a dream world. Wake up and come home'

'I don't know about that,' I said, shrugging. 'But I'll know by Monday. Love you, Louisa, I'm glad you're OK.'

Before she could start trying to talk me home again I hung up. Jenny had already rung off, and when I looked up at the window, she had vanished. I wasn't ready to go back in there just yet, but I wasn't ready to belly up and go back to London either. I needed somewhere to think.

For an hour I wandered the streets. Down, across, across, up, back down again. I didn't even realize I'd arrived at the Empire State Building until I walked straight into the queue of people.

'Watch where you're bloody going,' an unnecessarily fat British man tutted and sighed as I backed away with incoherent apologies. 'Bloody Americans,' he nodded to his companion, 'they're so bloody rude.'

Finding a tiny space outside a pharmacy on the corner of the street, I stared up at the building, but it didn't offer any easy answers. Just memories forged from countless hours of TV and movie watching, spliced with scenes from my visit with Alex. Feeling choked by the crowd, I shook off the fug and turned on my ballet pump. Uptown. Up and out. For the first fifteen blocks, I thought I was heading to the park, but as I crossed over Fifth and onto Sixth, a different refuge came to mind. Hopefully one where I could fill my head with something other than the hamster wheel of questions that were tracking over and over.

Although it was still fairly quiet, it was a museum after all, MoMA was busier than it had been the last time I'd been there. I paid my $20 and hopped straight on to the escalator, travelling up to the fifth floor. I was surprised at the number of kids running around. Very cool parents, I thought to myself, although secretly wishing the very cool parents would scoop all of them up and take them across the road to FAO Schwarz. Even though there were dozens of people loitering, not one of them uttered a word to me as I sank down against the wall opposite *Christina's World* and stared.

I didn't even cry. I just stared, losing myself in every last blade of grass. I ignored the curious whispers, although I did pull a bit of a face when one tit in a cagoule suggested to his girlfriend that I was a performance artist. Was I wearing a bear suit? I just shut it all out, every word of everyone. The people who were there, the people who weren't. I shut out all of the advice, requested or otherwise, not one of them had told me anything I wanted to hear, but they were all right. Jenny was right, I *was* a big fuck-up, Louisa was right, I *had* run away, and Tyler was right, I really didn't know what I wanted. But it was time to work it out.

An hour or a whole day could have passed before I eventually pushed myself up off the floor, it really didn't matter. As I wiped away a few sneaky tears that had slipped out unnoticed and pulled my messy hair back into a ponytail, I spotted someone else having a good stare. There, leaning against the escalator, was Alex. He smiled sadly and raised a hand. I froze for a second, and then waved back, not knowing what else to do. He gave me a cool single nod and came over.

'Hey,' he said softly.

'Hey,' I replied. My voice sounded strange after being silent for so long. 'What are you doing here?'

'Jenny called Jeff, Jeff called me, I called you, you didn't answer,' he said. 'It's a big long chain of people calling people until I figured out you might be here.'

'Oh,' I nodded. 'Wait, Jenny called Jeff?'

'She didn't have my number, and I guess she thought you might have come over to mine,' he explained. I couldn't even begin to think how awful I must look. 'She was worried about you.'

'They broke up,' I said quietly, thinking about how

furious Jenny had been. I wished I could go back and try that conversation again. 'Jenny and Jeff. She's so upset.'

'Him too,' Alex looked at me. 'I hope they work it out, but it's hard when you can't trust the other person.'

'It's all anyone seems to be doing, working stuff out. Gets tiring after a while.'

'It does, but what else are you supposed to do?' Alex put one hand gently on my shoulder. 'You want to talk?'

'Not in here though,' I said, letting him guide me towards the escalators and outside.

'So, what's going on?' he asked after watching me scratch at a small mark on my jeans for three solid minutes.

'I've been offered a job back in London,' I said, looking up at him. Seemed like as good a place to start as any. 'I had a huge row with Jenny and then I called home and had a huge row with my friend there and now, just when I thought I had some idea of what I wanted, I'm sort of back to square one.'

'Wow, I only saw you yesterday, right?' he asked. 'So what do you want to do?'

'What would you do if you were me?' I asked, head tipped to one side, trying to read him. He was playing everything pretty close to his chest. 'If you could go back to your friends and family, have no visa worries and a great job, or you could stay here, where you're not quite sure of anything.'

'I can't make that decision for you,' Alex said, taking my hands and holding them lightly. 'It wouldn't be fair.'

'It would if I asked you to.' I gave him a half-smile, but he didn't return it.

'It wouldn't be fair because I don't know what you

should do,' he said, squeezing my hand. 'You know how I feel, but I won't ask you to stay for me. Besides, it's not just me, is it? What about this other guy?'

Tell me this isn't happening, I thought, watching Alex turn away.

'There is no other guy,' I said quickly. 'It's just you.'

'I read your blog, Ange, and I just kinda know. Please don't lie,' Alex shook his head and slackened his grip on my hands. 'And Jenny said you'd had this huge row with him? I don't know Angela, I really like you, but I only just got my head back together, I can't be in another relationship where I can't trust the other person. Where I don't know what's going to happen.'

'How can you ever know what's going to happen?' I asked, pulling his hands back. 'But I can honestly tell you there is no other guy. Whatever Jenny might have said, she was so mad at me. Honestly, there was only ever another guy in the tiniest way. And it wasn't a huge row, I was telling him I didn't want to see him again. I want to see you. Just you. What did she tell you?'

'Doesn't matter. Would you have told me that you had been seeing someone else if I hadn't fronted you on it?' he asked. He was smiling now, but it was so, so sad I couldn't bear it. 'If I hadn't had to read about it on your blog?'

'Oh, God, I wish I'd never even started that thing,' I groaned. 'Please, Alex, honestly, it's just you. I met him before I met you and I just, I was only seeing him because, well, I don't even know why. The bloody blog, Jenny, Erin . . . none of it matters. It's just you. Really and honestly and completely.'

'OK then,' he said. His voice was so thick I couldn't even look at him. 'What would you do if there was no me, no Jenny, no "other guy", and you still had the same choice to make entirely on your own? Because that's what it's going to have to come down to.'

'I'm not sure, but I don't want to be on my own, Alex.'

'You're not,' he said, cupping my cheek with one hand, as the tears starting to track down my face. 'You're so not. Do you think Jenny would have put herself through calling Jeff if she didn't care about you?'

'No,' I whispered. 'But I don't mean Jenny, do I?'

'That's just going to have to have some time,' he said, after a moment's pause. 'I need a little bit more time, and I think you do too. Whatever we might have, I'm pretty sure we shouldn't be sitting crying about it after only three weeks.'

'Don't,' I stumbled over my words, noticing Jenny loitering. She was still wearing Jeff's T-shirt, but she had managed to find some jeans before coming out. Thank God. 'Don't make it out to be bad.'

'It's not bad,' Alex smiled. 'It's good. Really good, you know? Maybe it's just not right. Not the right time.'

'Do you think I should go home?' I asked, willing him not to answer.

'Maybe,' he nodded, wiping my tears away with his thumb and leaning in to kiss me. His tears left new slippery tracks down my cheeks. 'I think you should do what you want to do, what you really want to do. Look, I'm going to go, but I'll call you. Or you call me when you've talked to Jenny?'

I nodded, not wanting to let go of his hand. He wasn't going to call me. I watched him walk across the courtyard, following him down the street until he was gone.

'Angela?' Jenny was the quietest I'd ever known her. She had smudged mascara all around her eyes and her hair was a complete bird's nest. She looked exactly how I felt. Probably exactly how I looked, actually. 'Angie?'

'I'm so sorry,' I whispered as she sat down on the step next to me. 'I shouldn't have even mentioned Tyler or anything. I know how much you love Jeff.'

'Shut up!' Jenny smiled through a new set of tears. 'If you don't stop being so goddamned polite we're never going to work out as roommates. I absolutely needed to hear what you had to say. Jeff can't forgive me because I can't forgive myself, that's hardly your fault. I should never ever have said any of the things I said to you. And I never meant to say anything to Alex about Tyler, it just all came out at once. I told him he was the one. I would totally understand if you couldn't forgive me.'

'Don't, please just don't even,' I said, resting my head on her shoulder. 'But I think you're the one that's been too polite. If you'd just given me a verbal thrashing the first time we'd met, I might never have been in this mess.'

'So you're coming home?' Jenny asked, taking my hand and standing up. Her hands were smaller and softer than Alex's, but they were just as strong.

'I've been offered a job back in London, Jenny,' I said soberly. 'I should just take it, Jenny.'

'Seriously?' She sat back down. 'You would just leave?'

'It's the sensible thing to do,' I nodded. 'It seems like the logical thing. It's a great job.'

'You know whatever you want to do, you're stuck with me now, right?' Jenny said. 'You don't survive two Hurricane Jenny attacks and then get rid of me.'

'I wouldn't know what to do without you now,' I smiled. It was true, I couldn't imagine her not being in my life. In just three weeks, she was as much a part of me as Louisa.

'What did Alex say about you leaving?' she asked.

I tried to smile, to talk, but all I could do was shake my head and let some more tears loose.

Jenny pulled me in close for a tight, long hug. It helped. 'I don't think I ate every last crumb of that cheesecake you left in the living room,' she whispered after a while. 'Want to go see what's left?'

I nodded numbly and let her pull me to my feet. Although I managed to stand up, my stomach was still stuck on the step and my heart was so heavy, I thought it might drop out of my chest at any second. Funny how I hadn't felt this way about Mark, I thought. So this is what it felt like to lose someone.

'Whatever you decide to do,' Jenny said, brushing my hair back behind my ears and speaking clearly, as though I might have trouble understanding, 'it'll be the right decision, you know that? I didn't phrase myself too well this morning, but if this confused messy ball of shit is you, then doll, I still think you're freaking amazing.'

I took her hand and we exited out onto the street. No one stared at us, no one even gave us a second glance. Two weepy girls in last night's clothes, holding on to each other as if our lives depended on it. If only it was the strangest thing they'd seen on the street that day.

The city was so hot, I started to think New York had frozen the clock until I decided what I was going to do. It was almost nine, and still so light and so unbearably humid, it could have been the middle of the afternoon. But it wasn't. In the middle of the afternoon I had been sobbing on the steps of MoMA watching Alex walk away from me, and now I was sitting in my windowsill watching Jenny wave up at me on her way to work. It had taken all of my persuasive powers (not something I was renowned for) to convince her I wasn't going to up and vamoose before she got back, or just throw myself out of the window. At least not without calling her first and giving her a fifteen-minute warning. She'd already skipped out on one shift to come and find me, I didn't want her to get in any more trouble, but a *Ghostbusters/Ghostbusters 2* marathon supplemented with about three pints of Ben & Jerry's really wouldn't have gone amiss.

The people below me were literally walking down the street pouring bottles of water over their heads and watching the drops sizzle on the pavement. Even the spire of the Chrysler Building was fuzzed out of focus way up in the heat haze. I was not made for this heat. Or for getting dumped. Or for making many major life-changing decisions in a very short space of time. Next month I was definitely going to try to keep it down to one. Maybe two tops. I really didn't know what to do. The last few weeks had been amazing, but what was the point in being in New York if it was even harder than being in London?

And how fantastic would it be to go back, to be all super *Sex and the City*'d up with my fab new wardrobe, my gorgeous handbag and my amazing dream job? I knew in my heart I'd moved on from Mark, I wasn't afraid of seeing him. Mum and Dad would be, well, they'd like to know where they could find me in case they needed a cat sitter when they went on holiday. And Louisa and I would work everything out. Things would have to be different now. I was different.

'I'd be completely mad,' I whispered to myself. 'If I don't do this, I'm completely mad.'

I peeled my thighs off the windowsill, leaving several layers of sunburned skin behind, and began the search for my passport. It wasn't in my (fabulous) handbag and it wasn't at the back of my bedside drawer. There was only one other place I could think of. Kneeling down, I pulled my travel bag out from under the bed. All that was in there was my passport, my old handbag and a screwed-up hunk of coffee-coloured taffeta.

My bridesmaid's dress.

I dragged it out into the light and held it up in front of me. Having done nothing but eat for the last three weeks, it looked tiny. For the first time in months, I had no idea what I weighed. Jenny didn't believe in scales, they had a 'negative impact on her self-esteem', and all my new clothes were so fabulously smocky. Couldn't hurt to try it? Even if going back to London feeling like a porker would take the shine off my triumphant return.

The fabric was cold against my sticky skin and the bodice felt uncomfortable, as if it had been rinsed out with wallpaper paste, but it wasn't as tight as I had expected. In fact, it wasn't tight at all. Apparently you can do all the eating as long as you're doing all the walking around New York and all the shagging of the hot boys. After stumbling over the hem twice and actually going the full length of the room once, I slipped on my Louboutins and teetered over to the mirror, pulled my hair back from my face and held it up into a tight chignon. My eyes were still red and swollen, the dress all scrunched up. It wasn't a good look, but it was a familiar one. All that was missing was my engagement ring, and I really wouldn't want to put that on again, given where I had left it.

Jenny had stuck photographs from the last couple of weeks all around my mirror to 'help me live in the now'. My after photos from Rapture, when Gina had transformed my hair. Me, Jenny and Erin at karaoke.

The photo Jenny had snapped of me and Alex at his gig. But the girl in those pictures wasn't the same girl looking back at me right now. The girl looking back at me was Angela Clark from a month ago. It was the Angela Clark who had slept in this dress and woken up sobbing every twenty minutes. It was the Angela Clark who ran as far away as possible when things got hard. But that was all that I remembered about her. Did I really, honestly want to go back?

The Angela in the photos looked happy. Yes, she was a little bit drunk, but she was happy and healthy and she had pretty good eye make-up. And in the post-haircut photo, she looked positively ecstatic. I pulled down the photo of me and Alex and tossed it onto the floor. No point making myself more miserable by leaving it up there. Nope, even without the hot boy pictures, this girl was much happier.

I wriggled out of the bridesmaid dress and shuffled it across the room and into the bin with my gorgeously shod feet. It felt good to be out of that dress. It felt weird to be in my underwear and Louboutins. Pulling on a T-shirt so as not to scare passing pedestrians, I tottered back to the window. The glass was cool against my fingertips even if the weather was scorching. Everything should still be so exciting and new, the steamy sidewalks, the psychic who hovered outside Scottie's Diner, the twenty-four-hour deli below us, but all I could think was that we were out of milk. Completely random thought, but completely comforting. Before I knew it, I realized my face wasn't wet from the lack of air con in the apartment, but because I'd started crying. Crying at the thought of never going to get milk from the twenty-four-hour deli again. Well Angela, I thought to myself, wiping the tears away, well done, you've reached a new and pathetic low. You're crying over milk, and it's not even spilt. It's not even bought yet.

I bent down to slip off my shoes, and spotted the picture of me and Alex peeking out from under the bed. Looking at it now, even I was surprised by the expression in my eyes. Looked a lot like love. Alex was beautiful, even in a guerilla shot taken precisely two minutes after he had come off stage. Couldn't help but notice he looked pretty happy too.

I was already finding it hard to picture Mark clearly. I might have been living with him just three weeks ago, but I hadn't looked at him for months. I could close my eyes right now and see every strand of Alex's hair. Taste that insanely strong coffee on his breath. Hear him singing to himself in another room. Feel the callouses on his fingers against my skin. But he was gone. And maybe so was the Angela in the other photos.

So I wouldn't be Mark's Angela if I went back to London, and I couldn't be Alex's Angela if I stayed in New York. But I could be someone new. Someone I didn't know yet. And I could go and get the milk. It was a start.

'I am completely mad,' I whispered out of the window. 'Completely, bloody mad.'

EPILOGUE

It had been snowing solidly for three days, and New York was tucked in under a beautiful sheet of thick white snow. Each day, the city turned out and turned the snow into slush. And each evening, a new blanket was laid out. Criss-crossing the streets and avenues, drifting up the park, icing the skyscrapers. To a new New Yorker, it was breathtaking. But as pretty as the snow might be, it was a shock. After a mild Christmas full of strappy dresses and parties, January was terrifying. And they said it was cold up north.

I sat at my desk tapping away, in jeans, a hoodie, fingerless gloves and Ugg boots.

Inside.

With the heating on full.

It hardly made it easy to write an article about feeling frisky in spring time. Luckily, the DHL man was in cahoots with my procrastination and rang the doorbell as I apple-A, apple-Z'd the whole thing.

'Wouldn't fit in the box,' he said, handing over a wide flat package in a yellow plastic bag, 'but it says urgent on it.'

'Thank you,' I smiled, snatching up the package and

ripping it open. There it was, the first ever UK edition of *The Look*. I gazed at the front cover for a moment. With shaky (and not just from the cold) hands, I turned to the staff page.

There I was.

My name, my picture and my title.

Angela Clark, editor-at-large, New York

'Is it here?' Jenny wailed from the bathroom. She came running out, toothbrush in her hand, wearing only a towel. 'Is that the magazine?'

'It is,' I held it back at a safe distance, 'and you're not touching it until you're dry.'

'What, you've got like twenty copies,' she gestured to the other three magazines in the plastic bag. 'Shit, look at you! You're so my hero, doll.'

'Come on,' I said, taking the spare copies and stashing them on a shelf next to the US edition of *The Look* in which my columns had already featured. 'You're going to be late for work.'

'And you're never going to get that spring fling piece to that psycho Brit bitch if you don't do it today,' she reminded me needlessly. 'Did your mom see it yet?'

'They're still on the Christmas cruise.' I closed up my laptop and slipped it into my (slightly battered but still amazing) Marc Jacobs bag. 'They won't be back for a couple of weeks.'

'She's gonna freak when she sees you in a magazine!' Jenny danced around the living room in her towel. 'Last time we talked, she was so excited for you.'

'I can't even begin to tell you how uncomfortable I am with the fact that you two have weekly chats,' I smiled, taking off my hoodie, layering up several

T-shirts and finishing up with my coat. 'How is the life coaching going?'

'She's my best client since you. Seriously, if you would talk to your parents without my having to start the call every week, I wouldn't have to know about Avon's special offers and Anne-next-door's curry night, would I?'

'We talk.' I sighed, throwing underwear at Jenny. Our weekly Sunday evening phone calls home had become a ritual for Jenny and I, whether I liked it or not. 'I just don't think I need to talk to my mother every time you speak to yours. It's not a requirement of my visa. Now get your knickers on, Lopez. We're leaving.'

We walked arm-in-arm, trying not to slip in the snow, all the way down to The Union, where I hugged Jenny goodbye and left her at the door. Union Square Park looked picture perfect in the snow, but it was too cold to go and sit right now. Every time I went outside at the moment I remembered Alex's promise to take me back up the Empire State Building to see the city in the snow.

No, bad Angela, I wasn't supposed to be thinking about him. I turned left and tiptoed down to the music shop on the corner, hoping some new CDs might inspire me to go home and get it on with my laptop. God knows I hadn't got it on with anyone else in months. As I passed through the security gates, I beeped loudly, attracting the attention of the guard, but I smiled, holding up my mobile phone.

'Just a text message,' I said. He smiled back, but he also followed me into the store.

Just got my copy of The Look. *I'm so proud of you! Louisa x x x*

I re-read the message a few times until I had burned it onto my retinas, then I stashed my phone back in my pocket overly dramatically for the security guard's benefit.

I browsed contentedly for a few moments. I'd been sort of out of the music loop since the summer, all part of my Alex Reid cold turkey programme prescribed by Dr Jenny Lopez. I hadn't called Alex and he hadn't called me. As much as I knew he was right, that it was all too much too soon, I really didn't think I could face bumping into him at a gig, with some skinny hipster girl on his arm and I knew that I wouldn't be able to do the 'let's just be friends' nonsense. What I hadn't reckoned on was bumping into him right there and then. I froze, my heart lodged in my throat. There he was, staring back at me, slight smile on his face, hair perfectly dishevelled, his green, green eyes staring right into mine. It was a great photo. I picked up the magazine and flicked to the interview without thinking. Quickly, I paid at the counter and abandoned my CD mission, heading for Starbucks. Before I could cross the road, thinking I would go and say hello to Johnny, I realized I was opposite Max Brenner's. I looked down at the picture of Alex on the magazine and across to the hot chocolate Mecca.

Running across the road and dashing into the wonderfully warm restaurant, I flipped through the pages. For half a second, I looked around, wondering if he would be there. Of course he wasn't, why would he be? It was eleven-thirty on a Monday morning in

January. He would still be in bed or in the studio or . . . I shook my head and smiled at the hostess, yes, table for one. Thinking about Alex wasn't getting me anywhere. Not thinking about him had been getting me along quite nicely, and it had taken a good month of cold turkey (Jenny had confiscated my iPod and CDs and deleted my Stills albums from my iTunes) before I could even get through a day without wondering what he might be up to. Once my hot chocolate arrived, I grasped my mug gratefully and sipped the thick chocolaty soup, opening up the interview. I skipped through their art school beginnings, the first two albums achieving critical acclaim. Like every other underappreciated New York band, they had a huge UK following. Slight exaggeration, I thought, but I'll let it go. But now they were releasing their third album. I put down my drink and read on. It was a more deconstructed sound, the sound of a band that had stripped themselves apart and put themselves back together again.

'"If it sounds that way, it's because that's what it's about," says lead singer, Alex Reid.' I whispered out loud to myself. '"The album was written really quickly and recorded in a couple of weeks. It's just what we were going through as a band, some stuff I was going through personally. It's about what happens when you have your whole life pulled out from underneath you and how you go about working out your place in the world again. I think pretty much everyone can relate to that."'

I pushed the magazine across the table, closing it and turning it over. He hadn't called me and I hadn't called him. I'd thought about it, a million times. I even thought I'd seen him at a welcome back party we threw for Gina at some hip club on the Lower East Side before she upped and left for Paris permanently. I tucked the magazine into my bag, knowing I should just throw it away. But I was so proud of him. His face peered out of my bag, next to my copy of *The Look UK*. He would be so proud of me.

I took a deep breath and rustled my phone out of my pocket. Before I had a chance to talk myself out of five months of aversion therapy, I dialled.

'Hello?' he answered on the first ring.

'Hey,' I said softly, thrown by his voice. 'Alex?'

'Angela?' he asked. He sounded sleepy.

'Yep,' I smiled. When was I going to learn to think about what I was going to say on the phone before I called people? 'I was just thinking about what you said? About seeing the city when it snowed. And I saw the interview. About the new album.'

'Interview? Snow?' he yawned. 'Angela, are you in New York?'

'Yes,' I said, hopefully. 'Actually, I'm in Max Brenner's. I was thinking about – about, well, you.'

'You were?' he asked. I hoped I could hear a smile in his voice.

'I wondered if you fancied a hot chocolate?' I asked, crossing as many of my fingers as gripping my phone would allow.

'Uhh,' he paused for half a moment. 'Angela?'

'Yes?' I said. Please don't hang up, I prayed silently.

'You took a really long time to call me,' he said. 'But I'm really glad you did.'

'Me too,' I said happily. 'Now get your arse out of bed and come meet me.'

I hung up and put my phone in my bag, taking out *The Look*. I opened it on my page and looked at the intro.

The Adventures of Angela. Twenty-something ex-Londoner, Angela Clark, guides us through life and love, finding friends and finding her way in the Big Apple.

It wasn't a very complete description, I thought, but at least it was somewhere to start.

Angela's Guide to NYC

ARRIVING

JFK is a huge airport but it's not too tricky. Just follow all the signs, smile and nod, answer the nice man with the gun's questions and then get your bags. Whatever you do, don't take a gypsy cab into the city. There's a taxi rank right outside the terminal and an official medallion cab is $45 to anywhere in Manhattan plus tolls and tips. Shouldn't come out at more than $60 all-in to get to your hotel safe and quick.

FINDING YOUR WAY AROUND

Always know the cross street of where you're going if you get in a cab. Rolling in and saying 1350 Avenue of the Americas will get you nowhere. You want Sixth Avenue and 55th Street – get a map from your hotel, it will save you so much hassle. Almost all cabbies know where the big attractions are though so don't panic too much.

Hailing a cab is super easy as long as you know what to look for. It's not like London, where cabs are either lit or not – if the centre light is on, the taxi is free and you can hail him down. If there are lights on either side of the main light, then the cab is off-duty, he won't stop for you and you'll look a wee bit silly standing in the road with your arm out in the air. If there are no lights on top of the cab at all, then there's already someone inside. Bah.

Helpful hint, the avenues run up and down town, the streets east to west. If you're headed uptown, don't hail a cab going downtown, you'll just piss off the taxi driver (who has to take you once you're in the cab). Instead, walk the short block across and get a cab going in the same direction as you. Unless you're wearing really high heels or it's raining, in which case, claim tourist ignorance.

Taxis are really cheap and always really easy to get hold of (unless it's shift change, inconveniently around knock-off time between 4.30–5.30) but the subway's pretty easy too and so incredibly cheap. If you can read the map, give it a go, it's the quickest way to get around by far.

HOTELS

There are bazillions in New York, and if you book through a reputable agent, you should be fine. I don't totally advocate just rocking up like I did… try Expedia for deals and then check out the hotel on Tripadvisor.co.uk for candid pics and reviews from other travellers.

Super swank

The Gramercy Park
www.gramercyparkhotel.com
Tel: (+1) 212 920 3300
LEXINGTON AVE BTW 21ST AND 22ND STREETS, MIDTOWN, EASTSIDE
Ian Schrager (Hotel God) has created a vision of luxury boho beauty. It's sexy, it's cool and it's packed with beautiful art and beautiful people. The hotel is quite near my apartment, so you can occasionally see me pretending I belong at the bar, well, maybe on payday. You're far more likely to see an Olsen twin or Lindsay Lohan. Who I'm sure you'd rather see anyway…

Soho Grand
www.sohogrand.com
Tel: (+1) 212 965 3000
W BROADWAY BTW GRAND AND CANAL STREETS
I've never stayed at the Soho Grand, but I have had some adventures in the Grand Bar…It's a gorgeous space, all wrought iron and airy balconies – in the lobby at least. The bedrooms aren't huge, but then, you are in New York, space is at a premium everywhere. What they lack in size, they make up for in swank. Don't be put off by the red-brick façade, it's super sexy inside and right in the heart of the action.

60 Thompson
www.60thompson.com
Tel: (+1) 877 431 0400
THOMPSON AND BROOME STREETS
Another hotel in the heart of Soho, just as hip, but maybe a little younger than the Soho Grand. A real boutique gem of a hotel with a very cool clientele. Along with a hip hip room full of top-notch amenities, residents also get a key to the roof bar, which isn't open to mere mortals. And if a roof terrace packed with the young and the beautiful doesn't swing it for you, the view over Manhattan just might. Amazing. And that's without mentioning the cocktail menu…

Cheaper but still chicer

W Union Square
Whotels.com/UnionSquare
Tel: (+1) 212 253 9119
UNION SQUARE – PARK AVENUE AND 17TH STREET

Ahh, Union Square. For me, this is where New York started. It's also a great base for any holiday. The subway is right on your doorstep, taxis are always running up and down Park and you're within walking distance of a whole lot of sights. And shops. And restaurants. Sigh. A chain hotel this might be, but a W hotel is hardly a Holiday Inn. The hotel itself is a perfect example of New York's beaux arts architecture, which makes it a bit of a landmark in itself. The rooms are packed with Bliss toiletries, giant comfy beds and with a 'Whatever, Whenever' guest policy, two bars and an award-winning restaurant, you really can't go wrong here.

The Hudson
www.hudsonhotel.com
Tel: (+1) 212 247 0769
58TH STREET BTW EIGHTH AND NINTH AVES

Heading a little further uptown, The Hudson is a great choice if you're shopping tastes are more Barneys and Bergdorf, not to mention it's mere blocks from Tiffany. The Hudson prides itself on being 'cheap chic', but that's cheap by New York standards, i.e. not very. It is however, beautiful and totally worth the money. The rooms are on the small side, but you're getting a really swanky payoff if you can stand it – besides, how much time are you planning to spend in your room? There's a rooftop garden, a business centre, gym, bars and cafeteria – pause for breath – you could do a lot worse than making The Hudson your home away from home.

Budget beauties

The Pod Hotel
www.thepodhotel.com
Tel: (+1) 212 355 0300
E 51ST STREET BTW SECOND AND THIRD AVES

Looking for something unique and a little bit funky? At The Pod Hotel you can stay in a single, queen, double or even bunkbed room, complete with your very own iPod dock. Some of the rooms have shared bathrooms, which keeps the prices way down, and while that might sound a little bit more YMCA than NYC, the in-room alert lets you know whether the bathroom is free before you even set a slipper out of your bedroom. Or you could just bag a room with an en-suite shower room. Wuss. There are also larger, bargainous rooms available for groups and families, and a cool bar for pre-dinner/post-dinner drinks.

Solita SOHO Hotel
www.clarionhotel.com
Tel: (+1) 212 925 3600
GRAND STREET BTW CENTRE AND LAYFAYETTE STREETS

Back down to Soho for this hidden gem. The rooms might be wee, but the location is to die for, and the lack of a minibar is made up for by the fact that Soho, Chinatown and Little Italy are all literally on your doorstep. One word of caution, there is a club next door, so try and pitch for a room as high up as you can if you're sensitive to noise. The hotel is super clean, the staff are super helpful and, yeah, there's no minibar, but that means you're not going to get a nasty surprise on your bill. There is complimentary tea, coffee and bottled water, as well as free internet access in your room. And if you get peckish and can't be bothered to put your shoes on? There are two well-stocked vending machines in the basement. Looks much swankier than it costs…

SHOPPING

You already know New York is a total shopping Mecca, right? It would take a whole book to tell you about my fave shops, but here are some that you can't afford to miss.

Bloomingdale's

www.bloomingdales.com

Tel: (+1) 866 593 2540

LEXINGTON AVENUE AT 59TH STREET

You've got to go, right? Bloomies is an institution and with a great exchange rate, more or less doubles as a Selfridges sale shop. Go, bag your bargains, come home smug.

Tiffany

www.tiffany.com

Tel: 0800 2000 1122

FIFTH AVENUE AND 57TH ST

Sigh…Go and have your Audrey Hepburn moment with a coffee and croissant, and then hope some hapless Wall Street banker will fall head over heels with you while you look winsomely into the window. Sparkly. Pretty. Busy. Try to avoid peak shopping times.

Anthropologie

www.anthropologie.com

Tel: (+1) 212 343 7070

VARIOUS – I LIKE THE WEST BROADWAY ONE IN SOHO

This is a grown-up girlie wonderland, just try popping in and coming out again without a candle. Or a lip gloss. And a sweater. Or maybe some lovely underwear. And a gorgeous gift book you've never seen anywhere else. And that really cute dress! Warning, make some time, you could be a while.

Marc by Marc Jacobs

www.marcjacobs.com

Tel: (+1) 212 924 0026

382 Bleecker Street at W 11th Street

Bleecker is home to one of New York's most famous designers, Marc Jacobs. Happily, it is also home to many many bargains for those frittering away their enviably strong British pound. You can pick up MJ here for more or less half what it would cost at home, so feel free to go a little crazy. As well as Marc by Marc Jacobs women, where you can buy EVERYTHING including Bark by Marc Jacobs dog outfits, and kiddy clothes, there's also now a men's store, accessories store, and super cool special items store, where you can pick up Ts and bags for under twenty bucks. Happiness, thy name is Marc. Home, thy name is Bleecker.

Bond No. 9

www.bondno9.com

Tel: (+1) 877 273 3369

399 Bleecker Street

Looking for a new perfume? How about one inspired by your new favourite city? Bond No. 9 creates scents based on New York neighbourhoods, and presents them in beautiful, beautiful bottles, I heart Chinatown. And Bryant Park. Delish. But if you're not inspired by any of the landmark scents, Bond will mix you a personal perfume. It really is one of those 'only in New York' places (except I think you can buy it in Selfridges now, only at an incredibly inflated price). There are a couple of locations, but head for the Bleecker Street store and tie up with your visit to Marc Jacobs.

Sephora

www.sephora.com

EVERYWHERE!

Beauty fanatics, prick up your ears. All your favourite brands. US dollar prices. BeneFit, Stila, Urban Decay, i.d. bareMinerals, Fekkai, Bliss, Anthony, philosophy, NARS, Ojon, Vincent Longo and alllll the perfumes. Go crazy my sisters.

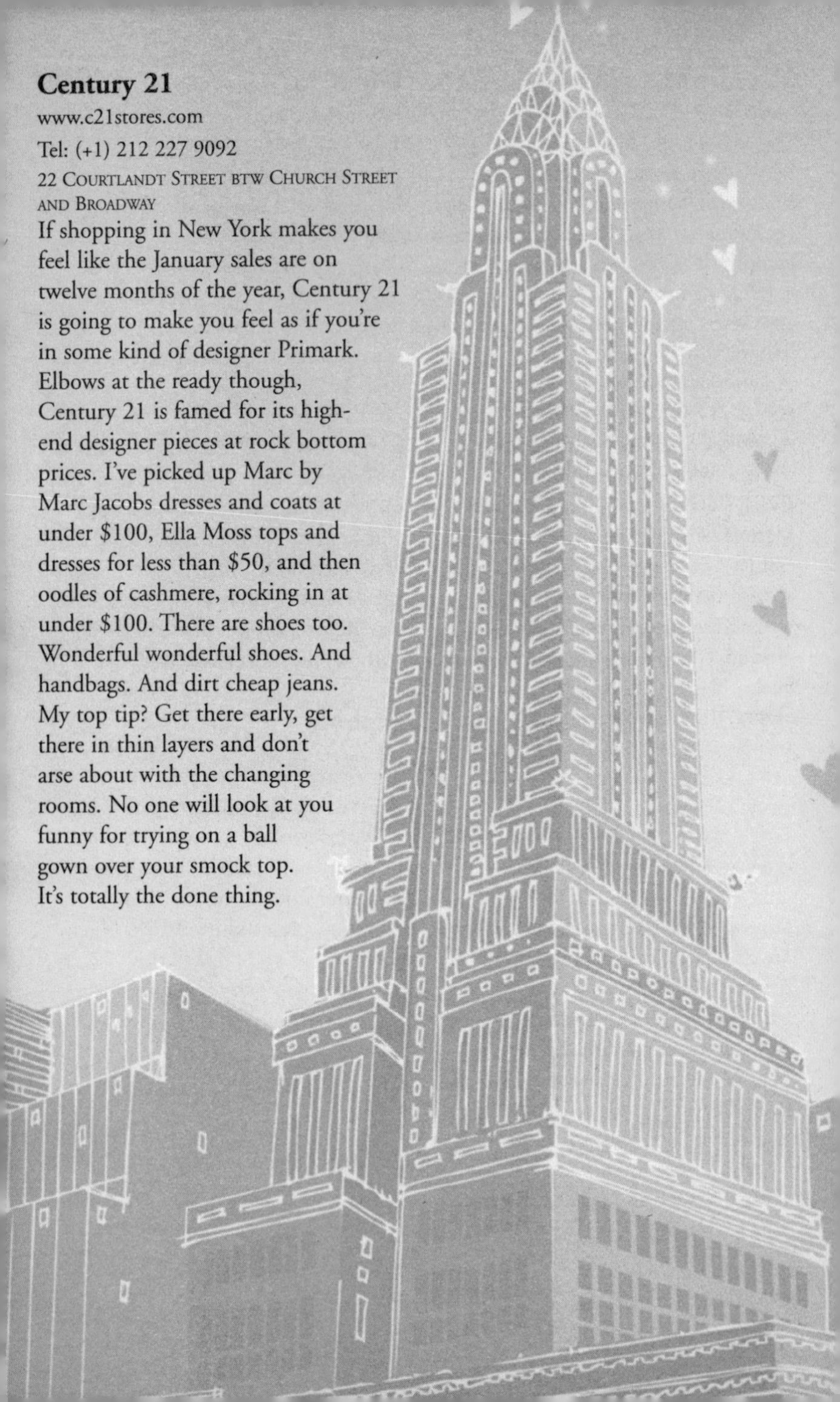

Century 21

www.c21stores.com

Tel: (+1) 212 227 9092

22 Courtlandt Street btw Church Street and Broadway

If shopping in New York makes you feel like the January sales are on twelve months of the year, Century 21 is going to make you feel as if you're in some kind of designer Primark. Elbows at the ready though, Century 21 is famed for its high-end designer pieces at rock bottom prices. I've picked up Marc by Marc Jacobs dresses and coats at under $100, Ella Moss tops and dresses for less than $50, and then oodles of cashmere, rocking in at under $100. There are shoes too. Wonderful wonderful shoes. And handbags. And dirt cheap jeans. My top tip? Get there early, get there in thin layers and don't arse about with the changing rooms. No one will look at you funny for trying on a ball gown over your smock top. It's totally the done thing.

EATING OUT

I heart eating almost as much as I heart New York, so this was the hardest list to whittle down for you. Here are my top five failsafe picks:

Alta

www.altarestaurant.com

Tel: (+1) 212 505 7777

W 10TH STREET AT SIXTH AVENUE

Someone told me they saw Justin Timberlake there and I was sold. Then I ate the food and I was hooked. Alta is a really cool modern tapas place where everything sounds random but is actually delicious. Perfect for a date, the little plates make great sharing food – don't leave without trying the chocolate fondue!

Mercer Kitchen

www.mercerhotel.com

Tel: (+1) 212 966 5454

PRINCE STREET AT MERCER STREET

Go for the cool atmosphere and casual celeb spotting, stay for the roast chicken. Yum! Food is good, atmosphere is great, and the cocktails are strong. I'd ease off them until dessert. Which I would definitely be having. The Mercer Kitchen is famous as a seafood restaurant, but as I've said, gotta love that chicken. And the burgers. And the pizza actually. Oh and the calamari is some of the best I've had – yummy mayo.

SEA Thai

Tel: (+1) 718 384 8850

WILLIAMSBURG, N 6TH STREET BTW BERRY AND WYTHE STREETS

(take the L train from Union Square to Bedford Avenue)

I really, really recommend that you brave it over to Brooklyn for one day, or just one afternoon. If nothing else, the food is yummy, and if possible, even cheaper than in Manhattan. Not only is SEA a wonderful restaurant (with a super swanky koi carp pond and golden Buddha presiding over the diners), but, for all the Sex and the City fans, it's the restaurant where Samantha met Smith! Eat loads, but leave room for the cocktails. They're strong but delicious. Hmm, I'm sensing a theme.

Balthazar

www.balthazarny.com

Tel: (+1) 212 965 1414

SPRING STREET BTW BROADWAY AND CROSBY STREET

If you're going for broke, go for Balthazar. A gorgeous French brasserie that packs many a celeb into its chic dining room. At the first chance of a breakfast meeting (where they're paying) I'll suggest Balthazar for their wonderful, wonderful brekkies. French toast with home-made brioche. Mmm. And as soon as I've been paid, I'm rocking up for the steak frites. My boyfriend likes the moules marinières, but basically, it's all good. Bring someone here for a special treat, perfect for the last night of your holiday.

Manatus

Tel: (+1) 212 989 7042

BLEECKER STREET BTW W 10TH STREET AND CHRISTOPHER STREET

This is a lovely diner, and my recommended first port of call on any shopping day. Manatus proudly boasts my top toast and bacon awards (the eggs, tomatoes and hash browns that go with them aren't bad either) and, get ready, they do a lovely cup of tea. If that isn't enough, Manatus is just a stone's throw from Marc Jacobs, Bond No. 9, and many of my other favourite Bleecker Street shops.

SNACKING OUT

All right, I'm sort of cheating on the eating thing.

Magnolia Bakery

www.magnoliacupcakes.com

Tel: (+1) 212 462 2572

401 Bleecker Street and 11th Street

You will have burned off your massive Manatus breakfast shopping up a storm on Bleecker, so treat yourself to something sweet from Magnolia Bakery. Famous for its cupcakes (as seen on SATC), I actually prefer the brownies. They're fudgy, gooey and oh so delicious.

Dean & Delucca

www.deandeluca.com

Tel: (+1) 212 577 2153

Broadway at Spring Street

You might have noticed I have a sweet tooth…Dean & Delucca is a New York institution, and with good reason. The food at this super deli is amazing, and I'm always getting caught with my hand in the cookie jar. They're only a dollar!

Republic

Tel: (+1) 212 627 7172

37 Union Sq. West, New York, NY 10003, nr 16th St

Right across from where I was staying at The Union. Great, cheap noodles and amazing cocktails. Please try not to get drunk at lunch. Like me.

DRINKING

My experience of this area is ever growing, but places here change so often it's hard to keep up. Here are a couple of my favourite bars:

The Dove

Tel: (+1) 212 254 1435

THOMPSON STREET ABOVE BLEECKER STREET

The Dove rocks. It's a really fab little hideaway in the Village, with a great wine list, some delish cocktails, and some delightful pink flocked wallpaper. What's not to love?

Thom Bar at 60 Thompson

www.60thompson.com

Tel: (+1) 877 431 0400

THOMPSON AND BROOME STREETS

Thom Bar is the marginally less exclusive bar inside 60 Thompson. A lovely little lounge with lots of nooks and crannies to get lost in. Preferably with a hot man and a cold drink. To get up to the celebtastic roof terrace, you either need to be staying at the hotel, know the name of the doorman, or be wearing something teeny tiny. But trust me, it's totally worth disregarding half a century of feminism for the rooftop view, the cool, cool air in summer and the killer cocktails. Mine's a chili lemonade please!

Little Branch

Tel: (+1) 212 929 4360

SEVENTH AVENUE AT LEROY STREET

This former speakeasy makes the best place for a date in the whole of New York. A tiny bar fronts a long, narrow passageway filled with intimate booths where the young and the hot drink cool cocktails. Be brave and go for the bartender's choice, it's always amazing. Get there early, or ring ahead if you want a booth – this place gets so busy after 10.00 p.m., you might not get a table.

CLUBS

I'm not that well versed in traditional clubs, as with bars and restaurants, New Yorkers are a fickle bunch, and the It Club changes on almost a weekly basis. Here are a couple of surefire hits I can vouch for, depending on your tastes.

Bungalow 8

Tel: (+1) 212 629 3333
27TH STREET BTW TENTH AND ELEVENTH AVENUES
You've all heard of Bungalow 8, right? Well, if you're up for it, strap on your best heels and brave that velvet rope. The best times to chance your luck are midweek, when it's a little quieter – Monday or Tuesday aren't too busy. If you make it past the doorman, be prepared to flex your credit card and be prepared to party hard, the celebs won't rock up before midnight. It's not cheap, but it's certainly an experience…

The Beatrice Inn

Tel: (+1) 212 243 4626
Another hip hip club popular with celebs, and another way to wither your credit card. Expect to see lots of super hipsters like Chloë Sevigny hanging out here.

Music Hall of Williamsburg

www.musichallofwilliamsburg.com
Tel: (+1) 866 353 5167
66 N 6TH ST, BROOKLYN, NY 11211, USA
Again, I'm asking you to cross over the river and check out Brooklyn, but if you're into bands and live music, it's so worth it. You're likely to catch The Next Big Thing, as well as touring British bands here, who you would usually see in much bigger venues in London. Check out Ohmyrockness.com for listings before you arrive, and book ahead – it's so cheap!

Bowery Ballroom

www.boweryballroom.com
DELANCEY STREET BTW BOWERY AND CHRYSTIE STREET
Another fun live venue, this time in Manhattan. It's a gorgeous old theatre with a great vibe and intimate crowd. The Bowery has hosted most of rock's big names at one time or another, and it's a total indie Mecca. There's bound to be someone good on whenever you visit.

Log onto
www.iheartnewyork.co.uk
to find out more about
the *I heart* series and read
an exclusive extract from

I heart Hollywood

You'll also have a chance to win exclusive products, keep up-to-date with Angela's adventures abroad through her blog, read Angela's top tips for where to drink, eat, shop and sleep in New York and much much more!

I heart Hollywood

January 2010

Angela Clark can't believe her luck...

She's living in New York, the most FABULOUS city on earth. And, she's bagged the perfect job at hip magazine *The Look* along with a sexy boyfriend – singer Alex Reid.

When Angela's editor sends her off to Hollywood to interview hot actor and fellow Brit James Jacobs, she doesn't exactly jump at the chance.The trip is going to test her new relationship with Alex to the max.

Angela doesn't fall for Hollywood right away. It's not as glossy and shiny as she had imagined and she doesn't feel like she fits in. Despite his lady-killer reputation, the only person who seems genuine is James Jacobs and Angela is suprised to discover they have lots in common.

But then a paparazzi snaps Angela and James in a very compromising position. Will the people Angela trusts come through – or will they believe everything they read?

I heart Paris

July 2010

Angela Clark is a British girl living the life dreams are made of in fabulous New York. But she's never been to the romantic capital of the world: Paris. So when boyfriend Alex suggests a romantic trip there, tying in with his band's tour and Angela writing an insider's guide to the hip city for a glossy fashion mag, Belle, she jumps at the chance.

Soon Angela finds herself meandering along charming streets lined with designer shops, sipping creamy hot chocolate and eating croissants. It's a world away from New York but she could get used to the joie de vivre of Paris.

But when Louisa, Angela's best friend shows up from London, it's not quite the happy, girly catch up she'd hoped for and everything in Paris seems to be going from bad to worse. Louisa reminds Angela that her old life is only a train journey away. With Alex spending so much time partying with the band and meeting up with his ex, for the first time in ages, Angela is homesick.

Suddenly Angela is questioning her new life in New York and wondering – is it make or break for her and Alex?